CHARMING MARJANI

A FADA NOVEL

REBECCA RIVARD

WILD HEARTS PRESS

THE FADA SHAPESHIFTER SERIES

BEST SHIFTER SERIES OF 2018 ~ PARANORMAL ROMANCE
GUILD REVIEWER'S CHOICE AWARDS

The fada.

Shapeshifters created during Dionysus's infamous bacchanals from a mix of fae, human and animal genes.

They're ruthless, untamed—and when they love, it's forever.

Stealing Ula: A Fada Shapeshifter Prequel (Nisio & Ula, set in Ireland)

The Rock Run River Fada

Seducing the Sun Fae (Dion & Cleia)

Claiming Valeria (Rui & Valeria)

Tempting the Dryad (Tiago & Alesia)

Sea Dragon's Hunger (Cassidy & Nic)

The Baltimore Earth Fada (a clan of land-based shifters)

The Darktime Trilogy
Saving Jace (Jace & Evie)
Charming Marjani (Marjani & Fane)
Adric's Heart (Adric & Rosana)

~

Fada Shapeshifter Short Reads

Lir's Lady (#3.5—Lir & Isleen, set in Ireland)
Shifter's Valentine (#3.6—Jenny & Chico)

~

To stay informed and be eligible for giveaways and sneak peeks of upcoming novels, go to rebeccarivard.com or sign up for my newsletter (http://www.subscribepage.com/i6x3j1).

PROLOGUE

Marjani jolted awake, hand on the dagger beneath her pillow.

Someone was hammering on the door at the surface. She waited for Adric to answer it, but her brother must not have come home yet.

The hammering came again.

Damn. It might be important. Adric was clan alpha.

Snatching up the dagger, she threw off the sheet and jogged through the underground den the two of them shared. The amber quartz in the wall sconces glowed on, lighting her way. She took the stairs to the surface two at a time, halting at the thick steel door at the top.

"Who is it?" When no one answered, she tried again, louder. "Hey! Anyone there?"

Shifters had excellent hearing. If a fada waited on the other side, they'd hear her, steel door or not.

She pressed her ear to the cool metal.

Silence.

Her neck tightened. She had a feeling that whoever had

knocked on the door was bad news. Dagger ready, she disengaged the lock and eased the door open.

Other than weeds and a scraggly hawthorn tree, the only living thing in the backyard was an oversized rat rooting through a garbage can. She couldn't even pick up a scent. But a folded slip of paper that had been stuck in the doorjamb fluttered to the ground. Snatching it up, she slammed the door shut and threw the bolt.

The note was addressed to Adric in their cousin Corban's distinctive black scrawl. She frowned. Corban wasn't in Baltimore—was he?

She waited until she was back downstairs before unfolding the paper. The message was short, cryptic.

See you in Reykjavik.—CS

Her heart thumped—hard, uneasy beats. She crumpled the paper in her hand.

Corban Savonett. Her oldest cousin...and the man who wanted her brother dead.

For a long time she just stood there, staring into the glowing amber quartz in the living room fireplace. Then she smoothed and refolded the paper, decision made.

Her internal clock told her it was five a.m. Adric would be home soon, and he'd be hungry. Might as well make breakfast.

The food was almost ready when she heard him run lightly down the steps. He poked his head into the kitchen. "You're making breakfast?" He said it as if she'd grown an extra tail.

"Scrambled eggs and fried ham." She flipped a thick slice of sizzling meat. "And good morning to you, too."

"My favorite." He wrapped his arms around her from behind. "Thanks, Jani."

She leaned her cheek against his. She hadn't been much of a sister lately. Adric wasn't this happy because she'd cooked breakfast; it was because she'd done anything at all. This past year, she'd spent whole days as her cougar, curled up on the living room rug and staring into the fireplace.

She swallowed a pang of guilt. "Make the coffee, okay?"

"Sure." While he fixed two large cups with lots of cream, she filled their plates and set them on the battered kitchen table. The den they shared was furnished in early thrift shop. She frowned at her chipped plate. When had that happened?

Adric dug into the food like he was starving...which he probably was. The man was always forgetting to eat. Like her, he was a cougar fada. Hard, edgy, with black hair bleached blond at the tips, and too handsome for his own good.

But lately, he'd lost weight. Their clan, the Baltimore Earth Fada, had had a rough summer, and as alpha, too much rested on his shoulders. His normally lean body looked downright thin.

Not that she should talk. The other day, she'd actually flinched at the sight of herself in the mirror. Was that skinny, big-eyed stranger with the shaved head *her*?

No more. She needed her strength.

She forked up some eggs and gamely chewed.

In her back pocket, the message seemed strangely heavy, as if it were a rock instead of a slip of paper. She waited until Adric had finished his breakfast before handing it over.

"This came for you. About an hour ago."

"What the fuck?" Adric scowled at the note. "The SOB's in Iceland?"

A wolf fada, Corban had tried for years to overthrow Adric and take over as alpha. But he'd crossed a line when he'd shared the secret of the earth fada's quartz crystals with a night fae. Their cousin was a marked man, sentenced to death by a tribunal of earth fada alphas. But he'd disappeared over six weeks ago, and no one knew where he was.

"Looks like it."

Her brother's dark brows beetled. "Where did you get this?"

"Someone banged on the door at the surface. When I went up top, whoever had left it was gone—I couldn't even pick up their scent."

"He wouldn't come himself. He knows it's too dangerous."

"It's a dare," she burst out. "You can't go. He wants to get you out of Baltimore."

Adric fingered the note. "You really think Corban's stronger than me?"

She blew out a breath. "Of course not. But he's not working alone. We know he's formed alliances with both the night fae and the ice fae."

"So he's in Iceland," Adric said. "That explains why the trackers haven't been able to trace him. The ice fae don't allow any fada clans that close to home."

She nodded. The ice fae and their king, Sindre, were almost as reclusive and territorial as the fada. Marjani had seen one, maybe two, in her entire life.

She and Adric went back and forth a little more on why Corban had summoned Adric to Reykjavik. But in the end, they just didn't have enough information.

"Whoever's working with him," Adric said, "I have to go. Corban's my responsibility. I claimed right of execution before the other alphas."

Marjani's heart clenched. They'd lost their mom and dad during the Darktime, when bloody feuds had split the clan into vicious factions. She'd be damned if she'd lose her brother now, when things were finally getting better.

Yeah, Adric was stronger, but Corban would fight dirty. What did he have to lose? There was no way in Hades she'd let that prick anywhere near her brother.

"No," she said. "I'll go. The clan needs you here right now."

Adric speared his fingers through his spiked-up hair.

"I'm right," she said. "You know I am."

"Jani..." He trailed off and shook his head.

"I'll go," she repeated. "I'm your second. It's my job to have your back."

He growled. "Absolutely not. You're too—"

"Weak," she finished. He couldn't have hurt her more if he'd slammed a fist into her stomach. She set down her fork and concentrated on breathing.

"Fuck. I'm sorry, Jani. I don't really think you're weak. But—"

She lifted her chin. "Maybe you're right. But I need to know, and that's never going to happen if I stay here in Baltimore. Everyone treats me like I'm made of fucking eggshells."

And as Adric knew, she had her own reasons for hating Corban.

He forked up a last piece of ham. "What about Luc?"

"What about him?" she asked in a cool voice.

"I thought maybe you two—"

"No. We're friends, and that's all we'll ever be. I've told him that, straight out, but he thinks he can change my mind." She gave a hard swallow and stared down at the eggs congealing on her plate. "I'll probably never mate."

"Jani. You don't mean that."

"No?" She shrugged and turned the subject. "You're the alpha. You're the one who should find a mate—and not Rosana do Rio."

His bronze eyes went flat. "Shut it."

But hurt made her keep going. "You think I don't know you slip off to Grace Harbor hoping you'll run into her? She's the Rock Run alpha's baby sister, asshat. A river fada. You want to start a fucking war?"

"Shut it, I said."

They glared at each other.

Marjani's chin jutted. "Only if you shut up about me and Luc."

"Deal. But you're not going to Iceland, got it?" He picked up his coffee cup, realized it was empty, and set it back down.

"Yeah." It wasn't a lie, because she *did* get that Adric didn't want her to go.

That didn't mean she wasn't.

She got up and poured them both more coffee.

1
———

There's no such thing as bad weather, just bad clothing.
~Icelandic saying

*L*ike hell. Iceland was freaking cold.

Marjani wrapped her hoodie tightly around her as she slipped out of Keflavik Airport. It was the end of July, for Goddess's sake. She hadn't expected the bite in the wind.

Her cougar did *not* approve. Back home in Baltimore, the weather had been sunny and humid, and the cat liked the heat.

Oh, well, she wasn't here on a pleasure trip.

Beneath the hoodie, her quartz hummed against her heart. A sheath in her right boot held an iron dagger, and she had an iron switchblade in her front pocket, an iron blade being the most efficient way to kill a fada or a fae. Her left boot held a steel stiletto, and her fishing knife was in a pocket on the leg of her pants. To get through TSA, she'd had to stash her blades in her backpack and check it as luggage, but she didn't go anywhere without them.

Reykjavik was thirty miles away. As she got in the bus line, a burly man smelling of alcohol jostled her. Her cat, edgy at being confined for six hours in a plane full of humans, bristled. Her head whipped around, fangs lengthening, eyes flashing a cougar-blue.

The man squawked and stumbled backward.

She hurriedly reined in the cat. This was ice fae territory. If they found her sniffing around, she was fucked.

Worse, Corban might find her before she found him.

She sent a quick glance around, but all she saw were humans. The nearest ones edged away.

Marjani hunched deeper into the hoodie. She would *not* lose control of her animal. Too much depended on this trip.

The bus for Reykjavik pulled up. She took a seat at the back next to the emergency exit and scanned each face as the bus filled up. Nobody but humans boarded, their salty, iron scent pressing in on her like on the jet.

The seat beside her remained empty. Word must have been passed that she was an earth fada. No one wanted to sit next to the predator in a woman's body.

It was almost noon, local time. The weak sun shone on moss-covered black rocks and scrubby tundra grasses. Houses appeared, colorful concrete boxes topped with corrugated steel roofs. To the north, a white-capped mountain range towered over the rapidly approaching city.

The bus let her off near the city center. She leaned against the bright blue wall of a coffee shop for a few minutes, making sure no one had followed her from the airport. When she deemed it safe, she grabbed a coffee and an egg sandwich and ate standing at the counter, one eye on the door.

After that, she walked the streets for several hours, getting the lay of the land and searching for Corban. But if he knew she was in Reykjavik, he wasn't making himself known.

Sleep dragged on her eyelids. Except for a short nap on the flight from Baltimore, she'd been up for more than twenty-four hours. She checked into a hostel and curled up on the pristine white sheets, the switchblade beneath her pillow, her right hand on the iron dagger's smooth ivory handle. She slept lightly in the way of her cat, one ear cocked for danger. But all was quiet.

When she awoke, it was late afternoon. This time, she donned a wool sweater beneath the hoodie. The iron dagger went into her right boot, the stiletto the left, and the switchblade back into her front pocket.

Five minutes after she left the hostel, she scented silver. Her breath sucked in, but she forced herself to look casually around. A couple of tall, glittering ice fae males strode toward her, pointy ears poking through their long, white-blond hair. She turned and stared into a shop window, heart pounding, watching their reflections as they passed by. Against her side, she held the switchblade, open and ready.

But the men only gave her a quick, uninterested glance before continuing into a nearby pub. She released her breath and continued walking.

Where in Hades was Corban? His animal was a wolf. If he was in Reykjavik, he should have scented her by now.

Her stomach grumbled. Dinnertime. She fingered the meager amount of krona in her pocket and chose a pub that didn't look too expensive.

The décor was cozy, with dark wood and warm lighting. A long bar ran the length of the room, and in the back, a small fire was burning in a stone fireplace. A slim, dark-haired waitress greeted Marjani with a cheerful *hallò* and showed her to a small corner table.

Removing her hoodie, Marjani sat with her back to the wall and surveyed the crowd. It was mostly locals, the Nordic rhythms of Icelandic mixing with English, and everyone dressed casually—jeans, T-shirts, cotton sweaters, even a flannel shirt or two.

The waitress recommended a local ale and something called a lamb boat sandwich.

"Sounds good." Marjani shut her menu.

She touched her quartz, which also served as a smartphone, through her sweater. She'd turned the phone off when she boarded the jet and never turned it back on.

She should probably call Adric, but she'd left him a note. If she contacted him, they'd just argue. And then he'd order her back to Baltimore, because he thought she was too broken to be out on her own.

She didn't want to be forced to disobey a direct order from her alpha. Even if he was her brother.

The lamb boat sandwich turned out to be an upscale sub sandwich—a bun stuffed with slices of fried lamb topped with onions, red cabbage and pickles. She ate slowly, sipping the ale between bites.

Her skin prickled. She sipped her ale and glanced around.

A tall, rangy man with shoulder-length blond hair slouched at a nearby table, drinking a beer. He met her eyes, not bothering to hide that he was checking her out.

Her breath snagged.

Holy singing crystals, he was beautiful, with slanted cheekbones and sky-blue eyes framed by dark eyelashes. His straight nose had a small bump on the bridge, a tiny imperfection that only heightened his appeal, and his black ribbed sweater stretched across a hard chest.

His cheek creased in a smile—and fear wrapped icy fingers around her lungs.

She jerked her gaze back to her sandwich, her stomach tight, heart thudding in her ears.

Fuck, she hated this. A couple of years ago, she might have smiled back, seen where this led. But not anymore. No one touched her. She didn't even let members of the clan get too close.

A shadow fell across the table.

She snarled, her cougar rising to meet the threat. She forced it down. Shifting in the middle of a human pub could be fatal. The fada and humans had treaties about those things. A fada shifting in a pub for no reason would be automatically targeted by the authorities as feral.

She could be shot on sight—or slapped into a cage.

And she'd have to admit Adric was right after all—she was too broken, too close to going feral, to be out on her own.

The tall blond smiled down at her. Spoke.

Still fighting the cougar, she had to concentrate to make sense of his words.

"I said, mind if I join you?" A surprisingly deep voice, gravel wrapped in silk.

She gave a shake of her head. "Yes."

He lifted a single dark brow. "No, you don't mind, or yes, you do?"

"Yeah, I mind. I don't want company."

His gaze went to the slight lump her quartz made beneath her sweater. "Your accent is American, which means you're from one of two clans."

Fine hairs rose all over her body. He was correct; the only earth fada clans in North America were her own clan in Baltimore and the Navajo clan in Arizona.

But how the hell had he made her as an earth fada so fast?

Her nostrils flared, subtly testing the air. Human—he smelled of salt and iron—but with a trace of silver. The man had fae blood, although it might be so faint he didn't know it himself. Overlaying it was a pleasant grassy scent, as if he spent a lot of time outdoors.

Her cat liked his smell, but the human part of her didn't like that hint of fae. Not on top of the fact that he knew a little too much about earth fada.

Easing the switchblade from her pocket, she released the catch.

"You don't want to use that." He set his plate and glass on her table and took the chair across from her.

"No?"

He leaned back in his chair and rested an arm on the back as if she were an old friend instead of a pissed-off shifter with a sharp blade aimed at his privates. "Too messy. I'm guessing you don't want to draw attention."

"How did you know I'm an earth fada?" she asked, soft and dangerous. "Did Corban send you?"

"Who?" His surprise seemed genuine—and besides, her cousin would never ally himself with a human.

She shook her head. "Never mind."

"Don't worry." His voice dropped as well. "No one else in here noticed—or if they did, they didn't care. Icelanders are used to magical creatures."

She narrowed her eyes. "That's not an answer."

"What was the question?"

Her breath hissed between her teeth. The man was maddening. "How," she repeated, "did you know what I am?"

He grinned, a flash of white against tanned skin. "It's your walk."

"My *walk*?"

"You didn't walk in here, you flowed—like a dancer...or a cat. Every earth fada I've ever met walks like that."

She made a mental note to clomp out of the pub like a freaking Clydesdale horse. "And that interests you—why?"

Another shrug. "It doesn't. I just liked the look of you. If you want me to leave, I will."

She relaxed fractionally. He was right, she didn't want to draw attention. And his scent had the pureness of truth. He didn't mean her harm.

In fact, all she scented was...interest, of the sexual kind. Was he *flirting* with her?

She scowled, sick of being on edge all the time. Hating that she couldn't have a simple conversation with a stranger without going into fight-or-flight mode. Yeah, she was jumpy because of Corban, but this wasn't just about her cousin.

This was about her.

The blond arched a brow. "Well? Would you like some company?"

She reminded herself that she wanted to blend in and slid the blade back into her pocket. "Sure. Why not?"

He smiled and extended his hand. "Fane."

"Jani." Shaking his hand, she gave him part of her name.

"Jani," he repeated it in that gravelly voice. "I like it. So what brings you to Iceland?"

"I've always wanted to see the Northern Lights." That was the truth...just not the whole truth.

He sipped his beer. "Not much chance of that in July. The peak time is November to February, although I've seen them as early as September first. They're a sight worth seeing."

"Maybe I'll get lucky."

"Maybe you will." His mouth curved, and for a second, the air was charged with something that made her blink—and then hunch her shoulders. He saw that and continued, "So you're heading north? You have to rent a 4x4 to get up there, though—or take a flight."

"Mm." She ate another bite of her sandwich.

The ice fae court was in the north, near the wild Strandir coast, but Corban had told Adric to meet him here in Reykjavik.

But was Corban actually in the city? What if he was at the ice fae court—or even holed up somewhere else in the country? Iceland was an island the size of Virginia.

Topaz blue eyes regarded her, clear as the sky on a cloudless day. "I'm driving north tomorrow. Want a ride?"

She drew a slow breath. He was being too helpful. Her hand went to her switchblade again.

"Look. I don't know you. If you want to share a table, fine. But why I'm here and how I get around is none of your fucking business."

"You're right."

Those clear blue eyes seemed to see straight into her soul, to understand what she wasn't saying: Why she was so wary of strangers, even though she was a cougar and a trained soldier. Why a knot of rage had lodged in her chest, so big and black and tight it threatened to choke her.

What he couldn't know was why she was in Iceland—and what she planned to do when she found her cousin.

2

———

$\mathcal{S}$ometimes Fane hated himself.

He'd recognized the young earth fada immediately. Hell, he'd just seen her a couple of weeks ago at his daughter's mate-bond ritual.

Evie had mated with a Baltimore fada named Jace, and Marjani Savonett had attended with her alpha brother. But Fane had used his Gift to blend into the crowd, so no one but Evie and Jace had known he was present.

His focus had been on Evie, his heart full. How had this daughter he barely knew grown up so strong and smart and pretty?

But he'd spared a glance or two for the slim, dark-eyed shifter.

He'd followed Marjani from the minute she'd arrived in Iceland.

His orders had come from the ice fae king himself, a terse message scrawled on magical paper that dissolved as Fane read it: *An earth fada female will arrive today from Baltimore. Watch her, and inform me of her movements.*

No name, but as he'd told Marjani, it was easy to pick an earth fada out of a crowd.

Sindre had *not* suggested Fane meet Marjani. In fact, the king would be displeased to find his envoy had taken his own initiative. And Fane had had enough of Sindre's displeasure to last a lifetime.

But he hadn't been able to resist approaching the sexy little earth fada. Something about her drew him, despite the fact she was almost feral, her cougar close to the surface.

Her shaved head showed off her fine features and catlike eyes. Her skin was a smooth honey-brown—Evie had mentioned that the Savonetts' mom had been from Jamaica—and her lean body vibrated with suppressed energy.

His mind filled with erotic pictures. Marjani beneath him, or maybe astride so he could run his hands over that smooth, beautiful skin...absorb her warmth...take some of that vital energy into himself. Kiss those lush lips that seemed made for a man's mouth.

He saw her hand slide beneath the table, heard the quiet snick as she released the blade. So she had a weapon—probably more than one.

He almost grinned. He was a wayfarer. She might have a shifter's fast reflexes, but he'd bet he was quicker.

When he promised that he meant her no harm, it was the truth. He was a quarter fae, enough that he couldn't lie without making himself miserably ill. But that didn't mean he wouldn't carry news of her to someone who *did* mean her harm.

Sometimes Fane hated himself.

He gave her a crooked smile and set about coaxing information from her.

"Jani." He repeated her name, rolling it on his tongue. The short, sassy nickname suited her. "I like it. So what brings you to Iceland?" He expected evasion, and he wasn't disappointed.

"I've always wanted to see the Northern Lights."

Summer was the wrong time of year for viewing them, which she had to know. But he played along. "Not much chance of that in July. The peak time is November to February, although I've seen them as early as September first. They're a sight worth seeing."

"Maybe I'll get lucky."

"Maybe you will." His mouth edged up. Was she flirting with him? But no, she fastened her gaze on her sandwich and took a bite without looking at him.

"So you're heading north?" he asked, but she didn't take the bait. Then he took a chance and offered her a ride in his SUV.

He realized his mistake as soon as the words left his mouth.

"Look." She settled back in her chair, mirroring him, but with her muscles tight, battle ready. "I don't know you. If you want to share a table with me, fine. But why I'm here and how I get around is none of your fucking business."

"You're right. I'm just making conversation."

When she scowled, he waved an encouraging hand at her. "Now suppose you ask why I'm here. It's called small talk—give it a try."

The corner of her mouth twitched. "Because you live here?"

"Me? No. I visit from time to time, that's all. I love the hot springs. Did you stop at the Blue Lagoon on your way in from the airport?"

"No." She sipped her ale. "Maybe when I leave."

"You have to try the hot springs while you're here. Best part of visiting Iceland."

"So I've heard."

He took a bite of fish. "Iceland has the best fish and chips. Even better than the UK."

"I'll have to try them."

The conversation continued in that same impersonal vein. They finished dinner without him learning much more than he already knew.

But he was pretty sure Marjani wasn't here for Sindre. No, she had another reason.

And he'd bet a handful of diamonds it had something to do with the wolf fada currently being held at the ice fae court in an iron cage.

Marjani paid for her meal and stood up. She jerked her chin at the ladies' room. "Excuse me."

Her walk was free and easy, and he got distracted by her round ass as she headed toward the bathrooms at the back of the pub. But something about the set of her shoulders made him throw some bills on the table and slip out the front door.

He strolled around the back and leaned against a building a few doors down so she wouldn't scent him. A minute later, she came out the back door.

His mouth stretched in a grin. *Got you.*

He had the fae Gift of wayfaring, with two abilities: he could move fast as a striking snake, and he could blend into his surroundings. If he didn't want you to see him, you didn't.

Marjani hitched up her backpack and strode down the alley in his direction. He activated the charm that Sindre had crafted to disguise his scent and stilled, becoming just another shadow against the concrete wall.

Her nose twitched as she passed him. He tensed and held his breath, afraid her shifter senses would pick up the sound.

She glanced around and then continued walking.

He waited until she rounded the corner before heading after her.

3
____

This far north, the summer sun set late. Marjani did a circuit of the blocks around the pub, but there was still no sign of Corban. By then, it was after eleven and she was dead-tired. With a yawn, she headed back to the hostel.

She slept lightly, waking twice when nightmares insinuated their chilly tendrils into her dreams. She was used to that. She stared at the ceiling, listening to the quiet sounds of the sleeping humans around her through the hostel's thin walls. Waiting for morning.

Breakfast was croissants and yogurt. She washed it down with a cup of coffee and set out to find her cousin.

It was a shame she wasn't really a tourist, because she would've enjoyed exploring the small, quirky city. She loved that the stolid concrete buildings were painted in crayon-box colors—red, green, blue, yellow. Even some of the corrugated steel roofs were brightly colored, and the streets were dotted with sculptures and murals. She passed tiny boutiques, funky coffee shops, and cafés that just invited you to come in and sit for a while.

But she didn't catch even a whiff of her cousin.

And yet, the back of her neck itched. She could've sworn someone was following her.

She leaned against the wall of a combination book-store/record store and looked casually around her. All she saw were locals going about their business. She rubbed her nape and told herself not to be so edgy.

Lunchtime came and went. When her growling stomach became impossible to ignore, she bought bread and cheese and sat on a bench in the Old Harbor to eat. The ocean was a deep, still blue with small boats bustling to and fro. Across the harbor, she could see Mount Esja, its snow-capped flanks covered in plush green moss.

She'd covered most of the center city. Could Corban be in one of the suburbs that spread out to the east and south? If so, she might spend days looking for him.

She was a strategist, a Gift common in cats. Her strat talent had been humming along in the background, fitting facts together along with a heavy dose of intuition—and now she just *knew*.

Corban wasn't in Reykjavik.

She knew her cousin, knew how he thought. After the death of their parents, she and Adric had been taken in by their uncle Leron, Corban's father. It hadn't been a kindness. The man had been one mean SOB.

No one had mourned when Adric had stuck a knife in Leron Savonett one dark night.

His three sons had taken the worst of his abuse, with the eldest, Corban, coming in for more than his share. At times, the five of them had formed an alliance against Leron, covering for each other, helping each other with chores.

But Corban had enjoyed exerting power over his younger cousins. It was as if he had to prove he wasn't the weakling his father said he was.

Adric had protected Marjani as much as he could, but

survival had meant predicting what Corban would do next. She could write a whole book on her eldest cousin—his moods, his likes and dislikes, when to approach him and when to stay far, far away...

If Corban was in Reykjavik, she'd know it. Maybe he wouldn't approach her straight on—more likely, he'd jump her in a dark alley—but he *would* approach her. If nothing else, he'd want to know why Marjani had come and not Adric.

Just before sunset, a chilly rain began to fall. Cold and hungry, she pulled up the hood of her jacket. The rain seemed to find its way between the cracks. She walked down to the Elliðaá River, found a quiet corner to shift to her cougar, and caught herself a fat salmon for dinner.

Corban had to be at the ice fae court. She and Adric had suspected for a while now that he was working with the fae— the night fae, for sure, and possibly the ice fae as well. Adric had managed to get the ice fae court's coordinates, just as he had the coordinates of most of the other fae courts and fada clans around the world. Her brother was scary-good at things like that.

That night, she got another few hours of sleep before checking out of the hostel. Her only luggage was her backpack. It was a simple matter to shower and shrug on the pack. By four a.m., she was on a bus to the outskirts of Reykjavik.

At the last stop, she got out to walk until she reached a deserted stretch of road. The rain had stopped, but above, more heavy gray clouds had moved in.

She set her backpack on the side of the road and stilled, her nape itching again.

Hell.

She raised a hand to the back of her neck and cast a suspicious look around. Her cat relied more on sight than smell, but she inhaled deeply as well. Nothing stirred in the scrubby tundra except for a few intrepid rats.

That didn't mean no one was out there. Iceland was a land of magical creatures, its sparse human population meaning the supernatural world had settled here in large numbers. The ice fae were at the top of the food chain, but the island was also home to goblins and elves.

Skin crawling, she shoved her clothes and shoes into her backpack, cinched the pack around her shoulders and waist with special straps designed to stretch with her, and shifted to her cougar.

Her quartz heated, lending its energy. Colorful sparks of gold, silver and blue danced over her skin. Warmth filled her chest, spreading throughout her body, and then she *disappeared*, for a time neither woman nor cougar, until the change was complete.

Her cougar snarled and scraped its claws in the hard-packed earth next to the pavement, pissed off at being forced to remain a human for most of the last twenty-four hours.

The cat was increasingly bold. Demanding.

Adric feared she was going feral. She'd overheard him discussing it with Suha, Marjani's best friend and the clan's head healer.

They all knew what that meant—as alpha, Adric would have to kill her. You couldn't have a cougar with a human's cunning and an animal's bloodlust roaming around Baltimore.

Just let me do this one last job. For Adric and the clan.

At least if she died, she'd go out with honor.

She loped north toward the ice fae court, using her quartz as a compass so that she could run through the tundra, avoiding the road. The sun rose, a weak, pale thing, and the sense of being watched eased.

By noon, she'd covered twenty miles, passing like a shadow by tiny fishing villages and farms with shaggy Icelandic sheep and the smallest horses she'd ever seen. She swerved west, coming out on a deserted cliff above the North Atlantic, and made her way down to the beach, where she shifted back to human. Shedding her backpack, she found her fishing knife and strode naked into the icy surf. Within minutes, she had two fish, which she filleted and roasted on a tiny camp stove.

The taste was fresh and wild. Perfect.

She was licking her fingers when a movement on the cliff above made her bolt to her feet.

It was Fane, looking like a freaking model for *Iceland Magazine* in a silver shirt and worn jeans, long legs braced apart and his golden hair secured with a leather tie. His gaze traveled down her naked body, and his sexy mouth curved.

She ignored the smile to zero in on his ears. A diamond stud glittered in one earlobe, but what made her growl were the pointed tops, obvious now his hair was pulled back. He had more fae in him than she'd guessed.

Without taking her gaze from him, she picked up the fishing knife, flipping it from hand to hand with the ease of long practice. "What the fuck are you doing here?"

"Easy." He raised a hand, palm out, in a placating gesture she didn't trust for a second. "I can explain."

"Yeah, right."

She closed the still-warm camp stove and shoved it into her backpack along with the knife. She strapped the pack on, aware of him watching the entire time. Let him look his fill. One false move and she'd slit his throat.

But he remained on the cliff.

She shifted to cougar and bounded up the cliff, where she snarled right in his pretty face, making sure to show plenty of teeth.

The man was either stupid—or brave. He stood his ground, hands loose at his sides. Not aggressive, but not giving an inch.

She stalked around him, growling lowly.

"I mean you no harm," he said, which earned him another snarl.

She reached his front and paused, tail twitching in confusion. Her cougar didn't know what to make of him, but it didn't scent a threat. In fact, to her cat, Fane smelled somehow *right*, just as he had last night to the human Marjani.

A smile curled over his lips. "By the gods," he said in his smoky voice, "you're beautiful. And you'd rip out my throat in a heartbeat, wouldn't you?"

Her response was a snarl, but inside, the cougar preened itself at the compliment.

He lifted a brow. "Are you ready to listen?"

She gave one last growl and sat on her haunches.

"Good." He expelled a breath. "I don't have much time—I'm supposed to be somewhere else right now."

She stared back unblinkingly.

"Right," he muttered. "You know, I'm risking my bloody neck to help you. And you couldn't give a fuck, could you?"

Another twitch of her tail. Because he was right, she didn't give a fuck.

His hands curled into fists, a crack in his calm façade.

"I can't tell you much, or they'll—" He set his jaw. "It's not important. But the ice fae king knows you're here. Get out of Iceland, Jani. Today. While you still can."

4

———

Fane stared into Marjani-the-cougar's turquoise eyes. It hadn't been easy to follow her, but it didn't take a genius to deduce she'd head north toward Strandir and the ice fae court.

He'd shadowed her in Reykjavik as she searched the city. Hovered nearby as she ate lunch alone on a bench, an island of solitude in a sea of tourists. She'd stared out at the water, face bleak, dark eyes haunted.

And damn if he hadn't wanted to sit beside her and try to tease her into a better mood.

He knew a little about what had put that bleak expression on her face. Something bad had happened involving the local river fada. According to his source, the men concerned were all dead. So whatever had happened—and you didn't have to be a genius to guess what a group of men might do to a woman— the SOBs had gotten what was coming to them.

She's an animal, Fane. A mixed bag of genes breathed into life by Dionysus and his wild fae followers.

But she fascinated him, and he had time to burn. He had a day, maybe two, before King Sindre would expect a report.

That night, instead of returning to his own room at a fae-owned inn, he'd waited outside the hostel where she'd taken a room. His patience had been rewarded when she slipped out early the next morning. He'd followed in his SUV, using his Gift to conceal the vehicle, as the bus took her to the edge of town. When she'd taken off as her cougar, he'd driven north, taking his time so he wouldn't pass her.

But he'd lost her when she headed away from the road and into the tundra, only to catch sight of her again on the cliff. He'd parked and slipped closer—and damn near lost all the air in his lungs at seeing her lithe, honey-smooth body.

Now he squeezed his nape, wondering why he was sticking his neck out for a woman he'd never met. An earth fada, at that.

The cougar twitched her black-tipped tail. She had small, rounded ears and a white patch above each of those startling blue-green eyes. A plume of dark fur started at the inside corner of each eye and continued up her forehead as if drawn by a sooty finger.

In this form, she probably outweighed him, but he'd meant what he said. She was magnificent, all long bones and sleek muscles.

And trouble with a capital T.

"Do you understand?" He placed a hand on her shoulder, and for some reason she allowed it. Her fur was soft, like plush velvet. "You have to leave—today. The king has spies every-where. You can't trust anyone."

She cocked her head in question, and he gave a mirthless chuckle. "That's right. Me included."

She rubbed her head over his chest—a quick thanks-but-no-thanks—and then gathered those lean muscles and loped off. North.

Bloody-minded female.

Well, he'd done what he could. If she wanted to run straight into a trap, that was her funeral.

He scowled and returned to his SUV. After taking his place behind the wheel, his hand went to his chest. Had Marjani been thanking him—or marking him?

He gripped the wheel and watched as her graceful body grew smaller until it was a dot on the horizon. The thought of that stunning, independent creature caged and at the mercy of the fae court's whims made his stomach turn.

With a low growl, he started the engine and continued north. He'd return to the court a day early. As a mixed-blood, he wasn't privy to the pureblood fae's plans, but maybe he could learn something.

He'd become very good at keeping his head down, doing his job as Sindre's envoy and ignoring everything else. It was the only way to survive as a mixed-blood at the heart of a fae court.

But he had a bad feeling that this time, he might not be able to.

5

"Well?" Adric Savonett placed his hands on the war room's round granite table and looked around at his three remaining lieutenants—Zuri, Jace and Luc.

Zuri fingered his soul patch. A wolf shifter, he was the clan pretty-boy, his good looks the genetic inheritance of Mediterranean and African globe-trotters who'd met and mixed in the Caribbean. Tall and brown-skinned, he had a shaved head and narrow black mustache to go with the soul patch. Zuri was so good looking, people tended to underestimate him...until he pinned them with his hard black eyes.

"She took a red-eye out of BWI," the lieutenant reported. "She lands in Iceland at 10:50 a.m., their time. That's 6:50 a.m., our time—which would be right about now."

Adric muttered a curse. Marjani had left a note saying she was on her way to Iceland, but he'd wanted to confirm it. Because he couldn't believe she'd take off like that.

She'd known damn well he didn't want her to leave.

He was the fucking alpha—what he said should count. His claws sprouted against the granite table. Like being alpha mattered when it was your sister.

"You want us to go after her?" That was Jace, a jaguar shifter and one of Adric's oldest friends. "We can grab her, bring her back."

Adric's jaw clenched. Gods, he wanted to say yes. He literally shook with the need to follow her.

But Marjani was right. The clan needed him here.

The clan was still reeling from the events earlier this summer when his cousin Corban had brought night fae assassins to Baltimore. By the time the dust had settled, Tyrus, the night fae prince's son and heir, was dead.

Worse, Adric had killed Corban's middle brother Kane. It had been a fair fight. Nash, the youngest brother, had sworn to it, saying Adric had only been defending himself.

But everyone knew Adric had killed his uncle Leron before taking over as alpha. Now they whispered that he intended to take out his three cousins as well.

The clan was seething, afraid Adric was out of control.

Too many unexplained deaths had happened under his watch. Just like when Leron was alpha. Mistrust. Fear. Anger. Everything Adric had worked so hard to put behind him.

All because of his thrice-damned older cousin.

Pushing away from the table, he got up to pace the length of the small underground room. They were beneath the Factory, the combination test lab and manufacturing plant for the clan's quartz smartphones. Adric had carved the space himself out of the bedrock, along with a couple of trusted stoneworkers.

"She's on the edge," Jace added bluntly. "If you're not careful, you're going to lose her."

Jace was one of the few clan members who'd dare say it aloud. But then, he'd been with Adric and Marjani since the beginning, when they'd first plotted to overthrow their bastard of an uncle.

Adric closed his eyes. The other man was being polite. They both knew Marjani was the next thing to feral. Most days, she spent more time as a cat than as a human. A good portion of the clan thought Adric should do something about her.

"Ric?" Jace's hazel eyes were sympathetic. He'd lost his own sister in the Darktime. "You can't let the fact that she's your sister—"

"She's not feral," he gritted. "Not yet."

Because the clan was wrong. Marjani was still rational.

"You haven't seen her like I do," he said. "She made breakfast for me yesterday, and we discussed what to do about Corban. And she was fine at Jace and Evie's mating ritual. You all saw her as her human."

"True," Jace said. "Doesn't mean she should be in Iceland on her own. It's not just that she could go feral—it's that Corban wants her dead. And she might be a hard-ass, but he outweighs her by fifty or sixty pounds. Plus, the motherfucker has nothing to lose."

Luc moved in his seat. The wolves in the clan tended to be taller than the cats, and Luc was no exception. A wild, fierce fighter, he was over six feet of solid muscle, with dark skin and wiry black hair.

"Why the fuck didn't you stop her? You must have known she'd go after the prick." His gold eyes accused Adric.

Adric slapped his hands on the hand-worked granite. He didn't normally explain his decisions, but Luc was in love with Marjani. Had been for years.

"You try and stop her when she's got an idea in her head."

"Don't give me that. You could've done something."

"What? Lock her in her fucking room?"

"At least then she'd be alive!" Luc snarled back.

They glared at each other. Adric's claws pricked out.

"Are you questioning how I handle my own sister?"

Luc's jaw worked. Then he dropped his gaze. "No," he muttered.

Jace spoke into the taut silence. "The question is, what do we do now?"

Adric retracted his claws and retook his seat. "Ideas?"

"We send a man to watch over her," Jace said. "But only one. More than that, and we'll just piss off the ice fae."

Zuri shook his head. "I say we risk sending four or five men. She's not just Adric's sister, she's the clan second, and a damn good one. We can't afford to lose her. And if and when she finds Corban, she'll need help."

Luc growled. "Corban can go fuck himself. I vote we send five men to bring her home, ASAP."

Adric blew out a breath. "Dragging her home isn't an option." She was on edge as it was. When she did spend time in her human form, she'd become a one-woman arsenal, with two or three knives on her at all times. "She needs to do this. Otherwise, we're going to lose her."

Luc set his teeth but nodded curtly.

Adric touched the quartz around his neck, pinging her one last time. But she didn't answer. His claws pricked out again. The cougar was about to explode out of his skin, insistent on going after Marjani. But the cougar also knew that the clan came first.

He made up his mind. "We'll send one man to serve as backup."

Luc rose to his feet. "I'll go."

Adric considered him. The wolf fada looked back, big hands fisted. If Adric refused, he'd have another AWOL lieutenant, because Luc was determined to go, alpha or no alpha. At least if he had Adric's permission, he'd report in regularly.

"All right." Adric jerked his chin in assent. "But you're only there as backup. Unless things go south, you're not to interfere —and that's an order. I don't even want her to know you're there. Pretend you're a fucking ghost."

"Understood." The lieutenant's shoulders released. "I'll catch the next flight."

"The next flight isn't until seven o'clock tonight," Zuri told him. "You won't get there until five a.m. tomorrow, their time."

Adric grimaced. That meant Marjani would be in Iceland for almost a day without back up. But it couldn't be helped.

"Contact me when you're on the ground," he told Luc. "I can use my link to her quartz to give you her general direction."

"Will do." The wolf disappeared up the ladder to the Factory's main floor.

Adric turned to Zuri, his chief of security. "While I have you here, any word about the night fae prince?"

In the past six weeks Prince Langdon of the night fae had been seen twice in Baltimore, when he normally only visited the city once every few years. They all knew why—he was searching for his son, Lord Tyrus.

Baltimore was located between two powerful fae clans—the Rising Sun Fae in northern Maryland, and Langdon's clan, the New Moon Night Fae in Virginia. Adric had kept his dealings with the local fae to a minimum until Corban had teamed up with Tyrus to try and pick off Adric's lieutenants.

Which was why Lord Tyrus was buried deep underground in Druid Hill Park.

"Nothing," Zuri replied. "I have my people on high alert, but the prince hasn't been seen in the city in over a week. Word is he's searching cities up and down the East Coast, not just Baltimore."

Relief washed over Adric. "Then he's not sure where his son died."

"No."

"Good. For now, keep your people on high alert. If the prince shows his face anywhere in the city, I want to know, stat. That goes for any night fae."

"Of course," Zuri replied.

The meeting over, the three of them headed up the ladder.

Up in the Factory, the techies were hard at work on the latest smartphone design. Right now, the Factory was just a small test lab in a former grocery in West Baltimore, but someday, it would be a cash cow for the clan. He hoped.

Jace was the engineer in charge of the quartz smartphone project. Adric listened as the lieutenant brought him up to date, and then told everyone to keep up the good work before leaving with Zuri.

Outside, the two of them squinted against the morning sun. Zuri settled a pair of dark sunglasses on his broad nose.

"Luc will find her. You know he's one of the clan's best trackers. And it's Jani, so..."

Adric nodded. They both knew the wolf would die for Marjani in a heartbeat. "But will she let him catch her?"

Zuri moved a big shoulder. "It's in the gods' hands now."

Adric put on his own sunglasses and they set off, Zuri to meet with his security team, Adric to crisscross Baltimore, checking in with the dens scattered across the city to try and calm the gossip.

All he wanted was for the clan to put the Darktime behind them. For the cubs to be safe and well-fed, and the adults able to afford a treat now and then. A stretch of forest for everyone —young and old—to run and play in.

And his sister back to how she'd been before those river fada bastards had gotten hold of her.

Was that too fucking much to ask?

6

———

The journey north took Marjani a week. She remained in her cougar form, traveling mainly at night. At first she followed the Ring Road, staying out of sight of the spotty traffic. The terrain changed from flat plains to arctic highlands, the days slipping by almost unnoticed as they did when she was her cat.

An earth fada alpha was connected to his clan through their quartzes—a magical bond like a mate bond, but weaker. An alpha like Adric could track a clan member through his or her quartz. If Corban were still a member of the Baltimore clan, Adric could've used his quartz to find him, but Corban had smashed his quartz and found another, renouncing Adric as his alpha.

Marjani wasn't alpha, but her quartz hummed a quiet song whenever she turned north, and fell silent if she tried a different direction. That was good enough for her. When the Ring Road veered west, she continued due north.

A steady drizzle alternated with periods of heavy rain. By the third night, she was chilled to the bone, her stomach hollow with hunger. When dawn came, she found a cave and slept huddled near a thermal pool for warmth.

When she awoke, she washed her face and paws in the steaming water. A meal of a few mice barely took the edge off, but she ignored the hunger pangs to set off again.

She only turned on her smartphone once. Adric had tried repeatedly to get in touch with her. She hesitated, and then tapped the off button. He could track her by her quartz, and he'd know if she were seriously injured, or dead.

So he wouldn't worry. Much.

It still hurt, that last conversation. He'd only just stopped himself from saying she was weak—possibly feral. She'd thought Adric still believed in her, even if no one else did. To learn he didn't had been a hard blow.

Maybe you are *too weak to hold off the cougar.*

She shook her head, dislodging the sly voice. But it returned, again and again.

Another night passed. Sometime after midnight, the cat came alert. A plump white sheep had escaped its fence. She swerved toward it, her mouth watering. Already tasting the sheep's sweet flesh.

No.

Marjani-the-human fought a silent battle with the cat. It wasn't worth it. She didn't want to attract attention. She was hungry, yes, but not starving.

The cat pulled up short, snarling at being thwarted. The sheep let out a terrified bleat and galloped off as fast as its sturdy legs could carry it.

Marjani halted, lungs pumping hard and fast. Was this the night she went feral?

Because each time it was harder to say no.

The cougar was a badass with sharp claws and two-inch fangs. No one messed with Marjani when she was in that form.

Yes, the cat whispered. *Let me win. I'm strong. Fierce. No one will ever hurt you again.*

She clenched her jaw and resisted.

Because she was *not* an animal. She was a fada, with the blood of three species in her veins: human, cougar and fae. And she loved her woman form as much as her cougar, even if it *was* weaker.

Another few days passed. Her hunger had forced her to draw heavily on her quartz, depleting the energy in the tiny crystals. She needed food and rest, and the quartz needed time to replenish itself.

The rain had finally stopped when she came upon a river. By then, she was shaky with hunger. She waded in up to her chest and drank deeply before scanning the water for something to eat—fish, shellfish, a water bird...anything. At a flash of silver, she pounced and emerged victorious with a large fish. She settled on the sandy bank and tore into it, devouring everything but the tail and fins.

Replete, she had another drink and then sat on the bank to groom herself. Above her, the clouds had finally cleared to reveal the Milky Way, a glittering band of light flung against the black sky. Her breath snagged. She sank onto her haunches, awed, the crystals in her quartz humming.

As the sun rose, she crept into a hiding place beneath two large boulders and fell into a deep, healing sleep. When she opened her eyes again, the sun was on the opposite side of the sky—although this far north, sunset wouldn't be for hours—and her quartz's energy level was back to a hundred percent.

She was in a bleak highland dotted with steaming volcanic vents and large black boulders. Other than moss, the only green things were the scrubby trees and bushes dotting the riverbank. To the west, stony mountains rose like rugged giants from the ocean, white-capped and harsh.

She caught another fish for breakfast before setting out

again, her belly full for the first time since Reykjavik. An hour later, she stumbled upon a dirt track heading northeast in the same direction she was being led by her quartz. She followed the track, hiding whenever a vehicle passed, but for most of the afternoon and evening she was alone in the deserted highland.

Dusk was approaching when her skin tingled. She was surrounded by magic. Powerful magic. She froze, heart slapping against her rib cage.

She'd reached the ice fae court. But where was it?

Dense steam rose from slashes in the ground, wafting over bedraggled clumps of grass and lush moss. The stench of sulfur was everywhere, overlaid by the telltale odor of silver. But the court itself had to be concealed by *look-away* spells, because she couldn't see a trace of it. And probably protected by wards, as well.

She hunkered down in a hollow between two boulders to wait. Sooner or later, a fae would enter or leave, allowing her to get a fix on a portal.

The sun had sunk behind the mountains before her patience was rewarded. A leather-clad fae rode up on a motorbike. Tall and sharp-faced, his cropped silver hair formed a striking contrast to his ebony skin. He halted and muttered a few words in an ancient fae language before flicking his fingers.

A portal opened, a shimmering circle cut out of the very air. He drove through and headed down the dirt track on the other side.

Marjani crept closer. The circle contracted, preparing to close behind him.

No. She leapt through the rapidly closing opening, landing on silent paws next to the track. The silver-haired fae was already thirty yards away, aiming for a black castle rising in the distance out of the otherworldly fog.

Her hackles rose. She didn't like this. It had been way too easy to get in.

But behind her, the portal had closed, the opening erased as if it had never existed.

She was trapped on the ice fae side.

Chill fingers tripped up her spine. She instinctively bared her fangs. But there was nothing to fight, and panicking would only make things worse.

Taking a deep breath, she slipped off the track into the dense white mist and examined the black castle. It appeared to have been carved out of a dead volcano, with a craggy spire at each of the four compass points. A high, crenellated wall surrounded the center, its toothy protrusions like a bear trap waiting to snap shut on an unwary intruder.

Staying concealed in the fog next to the track, she started toward the castle. The ground was uneven, with bogs and boiling hot vents to avoid, so she had to step with care. The stench of sulfur stung her nostrils. By the time she reached the castle, the silver-haired fae had disappeared.

But a round steel door had been left temptingly ajar.

Fuck that. Slipping back into the fog, she slunk west around the rough black wall, picking her way through the tundra, ears pricked and eyes straining.

High-pitched voices came from behind and to the left. She dropped to her belly, hidden by the eerie vapor. The sour stink of unwashed bodies reached her first, then two brown-skinned beings dressed in fur hats and animal skins raced by. They were about four feet high with large, pointy ears and sharp white teeth.

Goblins.

The female seemed to be scolding the male in an odd, chittering language.

This close to the castle, they'd work for the court. She waited, heart pounding, until she could no longer hear them, and then continued creeping along the wall.

She'd gone too far to turn back, even if she wanted to. She'd known when she'd left Baltimore that she might not ever see home again.

It was worth it. Corban had to die. Adric would never be safe while he was alive.

And she had her own reasons for wanting her cousin dead.

Corban was inside the ice fae castle. The weird tingle in her gut told her, the tingle that signaled her strategist's Gift—half intuition, half data-crunching. Her quartz murmured agreement, sensing the closeness of another earth fada, maybe two.

She inched along the wall. A half hour passed. The chilly mist deepened until she couldn't see more than a few feet ahead.

She stumbled into a bog and got mired in the cold black muck. It sucked at her paws, dragging her deeper until she sank up to her chest. She set her jaw and grimly fought her way back to stable ground.

She hung her head, chest heaving, her triumph at getting this far gone. She was moving in circles through the foggy night. King Sindre was an old, powerful fae with the Gift of chicanery. People said he could create illusions as real as a nightmare and use them to manipulate emotions.

If this were a trap, he might keep her creeping along the wall for days until she starved—or gave up.

She growled and set out again. She'd go through Hades itself to stick a knife in Corban's black heart.

The goblins rushed by again, this time in a pack of six. She dove to the left and froze as they passed like an evil wind, chittering to themselves.

When she dared lift her head, she couldn't see the wall— just thick fog in every direction. Dread lumped in her stomach. Digging her claws into the cold dirt, she swung her head back and forth, desperately trying to make out the black castle.

A hint of silver and iron in the air made her lip curl in a

silent snarl. Her muscles coiled in preparation. The fog coalesced, moved—and a tall blond man stood beside her.

"Follow me," he muttered without looking at her, his lips barely moving.

Fane? She did a double take and hissed angrily.

His strong dark brows snapped together. "God's balls, woman—don't argue. The *huldufólk* are looking for you." When she gave him a blank look, he said, "The goblins and a few of the king's tame elves. They'll be on you any second. Now come." He strode off.

She hesitated, afraid it was a trap, but Fane was clearly pissed off—at her. If it were a trick, wouldn't he at least try to exert some charm?

And she needed to get inside. Corban was here. She was sure of that.

She loped after him. Fane waited until she caught up, then stooped to whisper, "Shift. Most of them can't tell a fada from a human."

She nodded and obeyed—and then almost didn't make it when the cat blindsided her, fighting to remain in control.

No. I am strong. A picture of claws and fangs flashed in her mind. *I will fight these goblins.*

For several heart-stopping seconds, she wavered halfway between cougar and human. That was bad. If you got caught between shifts, you died, a twisted half-animal, half-human monster.

If she hadn't taken the time to replenish her quartz, she might not have made it. She drew hard on the crystals' energy, determined to complete the shift.

And then she was a woman, crouched at Fane's feet, chest heaving.

He glanced around uneasily. "Bloody hell, can you hurry it up?"

She dragged in a breath. Holy mother, that had been close.

But there was no time to think about it. Quickly, she pulled on cargo pants and a long-sleeved T-shirt, not bothering with underwear or shoes.

"Ready." She tucked her quartz into her shirt's neck.

Fane wrapped a wiry arm around her shoulders. She stiffened, but he muttered, "I'm a wayfarer."

"So it was you following me."

A curt nod. "Keep touching me at all times, and they won't see either of us."

He waited until she jerked her chin in assent and then set his palm to a crack in the weathered volcanic rock. The rock melted away to reveal an arched doorway. Together, they stepped through into a large tunnel.

Marjani's eyes widened. Instead of the black she'd expected, the curved walls were a smooth and bluish-white, like the inside of an ice cave. Silver fae lights floated near the glossy ceiling, and bright blue tiles paved the tunnel floor. The temperature was comfortable, like a warm spring day, and the air crisp and clean-smelling.

Fane took her hand and crept forward, following the wall to the west. They passed a double door opening into a huge room at the center of the maze.

"That's the great hall," he murmured.

It was a huge, intricately-shaped hexagon that reminded her of a giant snowflake. At the center, several hundred chic, glittering fae dined at linen-covered tables. Ethereal silver chandeliers floated overhead, and ice sculptures of magical creatures were scattered here and there. From hidden speakers emanated dreamy music, intermingling with the murmur of voices and the clink of fine crystal. Through the tables moved slim, pointy-eared elves, filling glasses and ensuring no one's plate was empty.

Marjani's feet slowed. Other than the few times she'd been to the sun fae court, she'd never seen so many fae in one place.

Like sun fae, the ice fae's skin came in every shade from translucent white to deep brown, but their hair was a variation on snow and ice: white, silver, blond, with the occasional shimmering gold or red. And every single one of them was model-beautiful, like Fane.

The clothes were incredible—stylish, fae-tailored creations that would cost a year's pay in the human world—but it was the jewels that made her stare. Ice-cube-sized diamonds. Fiery opals. Blue and purple sapphires, and chunky green emeralds.

With his single diamond stud, Fane was a model of restraint.

"Keep moving," he hissed, and with a start, she realized she'd slowed down to stare.

She sped up, moving silent as a wraith alongside him. To her amazement, no one even glanced their way. It was as if the two of them were invisible.

They traveled another few hundred yards before reaching a short hall with several doors. Fane stopped at the end of the hall in front of a green door and ushered her inside.

"We can talk," he said in a normal tone as he locked the door and dropped his jacket on a chair. "The rooms are soundproof and warded. The fae don't trust each other worth a damn."

He was wearing skinny black jeans and a baby blue shirt that matched his eyes. He raised his arms in a bone-cracking stretch that strained the soft material across his chest. Marjani couldn't help taking in his body, lean and powerful in the form-fitting clothes.

He brought his arms down. "That was too damn close."

"Yeah," Marjani said, still staring at his chest.

His lips edged up and their eyes met.

She looked away first. "This is your room?"

"When I'm at court."

"It's...nice." It was—a small, cozy space.

A walnut sleigh bed with a moss-green comforter hugged one wall, and three sparkling gold fae lights floated overhead, warming the creamy walls. In addition to the plain wood chair that held his jacket, there was an easy chair with a small round table between them. Through a partially open door, she saw a bathroom with a shower and huge oval tub.

He moved a shoulder in a half-shrug. "It suits me well enough."

"You don't live here in Iceland?"

"Gods, no. I spend as little time here as possible. I'm a quarter-fae." His handsome mouth twisted. "They don't treat me much better than they treat the fada. Which is why you'd better talk. Now."

Suddenly he loomed over her. She stared back, not betraying by a flicker of an eyelash that her heart had sped up. The friendly, easy-going man of the pub was gone, replaced by a steely-eyed fae. But she'd been threatened—and worse—by men a hell of a lot more dangerous.

She held her ground and palmed the switchblade.

He blew out a breath. "I'm not your enemy, Jani."

"No?"

"No. In fact, I fucking stuck my neck out for you. Do you know what the goblins would have done if they caught you? They swarm over you like a pack of rats." A muscle flexed in his jaw. "You might kill a few of them, but they just keep coming, clawing and biting until you're half-conscious and bleeding in a dozen places, and then they bind you and put you in an iron cage."

She swallowed. "I guess I owe you one."

He nodded, and she was reminded that it was never a good thing to owe a fae. But somehow, she kept forgetting that Fane had fae blood. He seemed too warm...too *human*. The only fae she'd known had been cold-hearted pricks, with the possible exception of Cleia, the sun fae queen.

"You can start by telling me why you're here."

He was so close she could see all the gradations of blue in his eyes—the navy rim, the silver that streaked his sky-colored irises.

She drew a ragged breath, and his face softened.

"Jani?" He touched her cheek.

She jerked away and he took a step back. She released the switchblade and held it loose and ready at her side.

"I'm not here for that," she said evenly. But inside she was trembling. She edged toward the doorway.

"Fair enough."

But his arm came up, and she dropped into a fighting crouch. "Back off. Or I'll take my chances out there."

"Easy, love. I was just going to invite you to sit down." He pointed to the easy chair. "Let's have a conversation without all this snapping and snarling."

She growled but retracted the switchblade, although she didn't put it back in her pocket. "Okay. Fine."

She needed to know more, and Fane seemed willing to help her. Shrugging out of the backpack, she sat down, the pack at her feet, the switchblade in her hand.

Fane hung his jacket in a small walk-in closet and indicated her backpack. "Want me to put that in the closet for you?"

"No." She pulled it closer. If she had to leave in a hurry, the pack was coming with her.

His mouth curved. "You're a prickly little hedgehog, aren't you?"

"Yeah. You have a problem with that?"

He shrugged. "And yet I found you creeping along the outer wall with a horde of goblins after you."

"They didn't find me, did they?"

He shook his head. "By Hades, I can't tell if you're naïve or foolish."

"Not naïve." Her flat voice made him raise a brow.

"No, you're not, are you?" Sympathy shaded his voice.

What did he know? Shame twisted in her belly. She scowled.

If this model-pretty man dared to pity her, she just might have to prick him with one of her blades. Not to hurt him—at least, not much—but to teach him that Marjani Savonett didn't need anyone's pity.

But all he said was, "This isn't your world, Jani. You might not be naïve, but you don't know how the ice fae court works."

"Then tell me."

He took two bottles of pale ale from a cooling unit and handed her one. "How about I start by telling you why you're here?"

"I'm all ears." Shoving the switchblade back into her pocket, she twisted off the cap and took a sip.

He sat on the wood chair—or rather, sprawled, his long legs stretched out, his bottle of ale in one long-fingered hand. "To spring the big black wolf fada from his cage."

She jolted. "His *cage*?"

7

*F*ane could practically see the gears whirring in Marjani's intelligent brain.

Gods, she fascinated him from the top of her shaved head to the tips of her cute little toes. She was so serious, so determined. He wanted to tease her, see her unbend a bit. Make her smile. So far all he'd seen was that twitch of her lips in the pub when she'd tried not to be amused.

Someday, he vowed, he'd coax a true smile out of her...but today was not that day. He was genuinely worried about her. The woman had no idea what she'd walked into.

She recovered quickly. "What's this wolf's name?"

"No idea. There was an earth fada hanging around the court last year. Corban. But I don't know if it's the same guy—I never saw him as his animal. All I know is the wolf in the cage wears an earth fada's quartz."

She worried the bottle label with her thumbnail. "He's black? What color are his eyes?"

"Hell, I don't know. I only got a quick look at him. He's in a tower that belongs to one of the king's top advisors."

Her fine brows drew together. "It must be him. Corban."

"You know him?"

"Yeah," she said flatly. "He's my cousin. But in a cage?" She shook her head. "We thought he was working with the ice fae."

"He was," Fane confirmed. "But things have changed. The only fada in the court are caged or under a *geas*."

A *geas* was an obligation or prohibition, binding to the person who accepted it. Breaking a *geas* was almost impossible, and if you did manage it, you'd lose what mattered to you most —wealth, your magic, even your life. But observe a *geas*, and you gained power, or money, or whatever you most wanted... but especially power.

And power was everything in the ice fae court—especially since Lady Blaer had come of age.

"I see." Marjani rubbed her forehead. He saw with a pang that she had bruised shadows under her eyes, and he could swear she'd lost weight in the week since he'd last seen her. "This...changes things."

"Leave." He leveled a hard look at her. "I'm telling you again —get the hell out of Iceland. You can't save your friend."

"Friend?" The corner of her mouth quirked. "You think I'm here to save that asshole?"

"Then why are you here?"

Her gaze slid from his.

"Tell me." He set his bottle on the small table between them with a snap. "I stuck my bloody neck out for you. You owe me the truth."

"Fine." She leaned forward, cougar-blue mixing with the brown in her irises. "I'm here to slit his throat."

"Ah." He fingered his chin, his mind rearranging things. Part of him was fiercely glad that the wolf wasn't her lover—or worse, her mate. The other part considered why she'd come so far to kill the other fada, risking her own life in the process— and he didn't like what he came up with. He had the bad feeling the black wolf had been one of the men who'd attacked her.

Rage curled through him. He ruthlessly suppressed it. *Not your fight, Fane.*

"Then you'll leave," he said. "The wolf will be dead soon, anyway. For a while he fought to get out, battering himself against the cage until he was bloody. But now he just sits on the floor, staring at nothing."

"I don't know." Marjani watched as the fae lights changed from gold to green, the colors swirling lazily around each other before the gold faded away. "I guess if he's almost dead, there's no reason for me to stay. You're sure?"

"Yeah. But you can't leave now—the goblins' blood is up tonight. No one but the most powerful fae will go outside until morning. You can stay here, and I'll sneak you out at dusk tomorrow."

Her catlike eyes narrowed. "Why are you helping me?"

He gave her a truth. "In the human world, I'm known as Fane Morningstar."

Her jaw dropped. "You're Evie's dad?"

"I am."

"So you knew who I was all along?"

He nodded. "Lord Adric's sister. I was at Evie and Jace's mating ritual."

"The hell you were. We would've seen you."

He spread his hands. "I'm a wayfarer, remember? No one sees me if I don't want them to. Only Evie and her mate knew I was there."

"But we would've smelled you. That silver in your scent—it marks you as fae."

"The king gave me a charm that disguises my scent for short periods of time."

She scowled. "So you can come and go in Baltimore as often as you please without us knowing?"

He moved a shoulder. "Don't worry. The king has better uses for me than to spy on the fada."

Except he *had* been spying on Marjani since she'd landed in Iceland. But that was different—Sindre's envoys watched any fada or fae who entered his territory. And as far as Sindre was concerned, the entire island of Iceland was his territory. In fact, he claimed most of the land north of the Arctic Circle.

She stared back steadily. He had a feeling she knew damn well he wasn't telling her everything.

"Now that you mention it," she said, "I can see the resemblance to Evie. But you're even prettier than she is."

A chuckle rustled in his throat. "I'll take that as a compliment."

"It's not." But a smile tugged at her mouth.

Warmth blossomed in his chest as if she'd given him a gift. He gave himself a shake—because allowing himself to like this woman was a damn fool thing to do—and rose from the chair. "Would you like food? A bath? The hot water is piped in from a geothermal well."

"Both." She made a wry face. "I've been traveling as my cougar for a week, although I did wash in a stream a few times. But you already knew that, didn't you? I *thought* someone was watching me."

He gave a noncommittal shrug. He actually hadn't followed her the whole time because after she'd found the dirt track, he'd known she'd end up at the court.

"Take a bath," he suggested, "and I'll get you something to eat from the great hall."

"Thank you."

The huge, hexagon-shaped hall was large enough to hold a thousand dancing fae, but tonight it held only a few hundred diners. Fane had been a member of the court for sixty turns of the sun, but the ice fae still acted like he was one step up from a servant. For once, he was happy to be ignored. He strolled toward the serving table against one wall, hands in his pockets, just a mixed-blood minding his own business.

"Fane." A large man with a beard and mane of copper hair rose from a nearby table. He was dressed all in black, and unlike the other fae, he wore no jewelry except for a heavy gold bracelet.

Fane muttered a curse. There went his plan to slip in and out of the great hall unobserved.

A pureblood fae, Roald was one of Sindre's top warriors—and Fane's grandfather, although the older man preferred to ignore the connection. Heads turned as everyone looked from him to Roald and back again like a bloody tennis match.

Fane pasted a smile on his face. "Roald. Peace to you and yours." He refused to address his own grandfather as "my lord," although Sindre had elevated him to a lord of the court after Roald had won a particularly important battle.

"Peace," his grandfather returned in his gruff voice. "Come. I wish to speak to you." He strode out the door, not bothering to see if Fane followed.

What now? And why did Roald have to choose tonight of all nights to speak to him, when Fane had a fada hiding in his apartment?

But you didn't ignore a summons from Roald-the-mighty-warrior-Morningstar. Fane headed after him. Once he would have been thrilled by this public acknowledgment from his grandfather. Roald Morningstar was renowned in the fae world —in the six centuries he'd been alive, the man had never lost a battle.

During Fane's first year at court, he'd tried to get to know Roald, but the older man had made it clear he wanted nothing to do with his mixed-blood grandson. So Fane had said the hell with it. As far as Fane knew, Roald didn't even know he had a great-granddaughter, Evie.

But recently, the burly redhead had unbent enough to nod

to Fane in the hall. He'd even stopped a couple of times to ask how Fane was doing. Fane had been coolly polite, and that was how they'd left things.

Roald headed for his spacious apartment near the north tower. Fane had to extend his stride to keep up. His grandfather was one of the largest men at court, with long legs and shoulders as wide as a door. He made Fane feel puny, although compared to other ice fae, Fane was heavily muscled.

The door to Roald's apartment swung open as they reached it, a throwaway bit of magic that only the most powerful fae indulged in. Fane had never been past the living room, furnished with severe Scandinavian furniture in white oak. The only touch of comfort was the blue velvet cushions, and Fane suspected those had been introduced by his human grandmother.

He glanced at her portrait, centered over a huge stone fireplace. His grandfather had mated with a human from Norway, a stunning blonde with a wide smile whom Roald had clearly adored. Saga had passed to the other side more than three centuries ago, but his grandfather had never taken another lover. In the portrait, Saga wore an emerald silk dress, her throat and wrists adorned with a fortune in jewels.

An elf couple—two mate-bonded men who'd served Roald as long as Fane had known him—offered them drinks. When they both refused, the slim, black-haired elves bowed themselves out of the room.

Roald folded his arms across his impressive chest and frowned down his beaky nose at Fane. His eyes were a fierce gold—hawk's eyes, a perfect match for his aquiline features.

Fane crossed his arms and stared right back. His grandfather had requested this meeting. Let him speak first.

Roald gave a short nod, as if confirming something. "It's been too long since you were at court."

"The king keeps me busy."

The older man allowed himself a faint smile. "You've done well as his envoy."

Fane had to force his face to remain expressionless. Was his grandfather *proud* of him? "Thank you."

"No thanks are due me. I've done little enough to help you."

That was certainly true. Fane shrugged. "I prefer to make my own way."

"As is right for a man."

Fane shifted his weight, impatient to get back to Marjani. The gods save him from fae etiquette. At this rate, he'd be here half the night before his grandfather got to the point.

"Look, Roald, what do you want?"

His grandfather's dark brows lowered. "Your father should have schooled you in fae ways."

Fane shrugged. Arne had come and gone as he pleased, leaving Fane's raising to his mom. Fane hadn't even known he was part fae until he was an adult.

"So I'm a primitive bastard who doesn't know his arse from his elbow. You think I haven't heard that a hundred times?"

Roald glowered at him. Then he sighed. "You remind me of your grandmother."

"Saga?"

They both glanced at the painting above the fireplace.

Roald's gaze turned inward. "She was a lot like you and your father. A cheerful, easygoing woman—but she had pluck. Push her too far, and she pushed right back. But even that was done so tactfully I barely noticed I hadn't gotten my own way."

Fane uncrossed his arms. "I wish I could've met her."

"She would have loved you—her only grandson. I'm sorry she didn't live long enough to see you born." Roald's strong throat worked. "I think of her...more and more, as I age. I wonder if I'll see her when I pass to the other side."

"I—"

"But that's an old man talking." Roald's fierce eyes fastened on Fane again. "I hear you sired a daughter on a human. Is it true?"

Fane went rigid. Evie was his secret. Only Arne knew about her, and he'd agreed that Fane should hide her from the fae world. You never knew when someone would take it into his or her head to use Evie against him.

How in Hades had his grandfather heard? But now that he had, Fane had to tell the truth. He couldn't lie, and evading the question would be as good as admitting it.

"Yes. I do."

Roald sighed. "What is it with this family and humans? I suppose she has no Gift."

Fane moved a shoulder. "She's mostly human."

It was an evasion. Evie might be only one-eighth fae, but she'd turned out to be a Gifted amplifier who could boost another fae or fada's Gift. It was a rare and very valuable talent, one the fae would prize as much as her mate's clan did. Evie was now training with Baltimore's healers to amplify their healing Gifts.

"They tell me she mated with a fada." Roald's voice was heavy with disapproval.

"She did. A jaguar shifter."

"A jaguar." Roald pursed his lips. "What can you expect from a woman? The fada have a certain animal appeal."

Fane stiffened. "She's happy with her mate, and he treats her like a princess."

Roald shook his head, but changed the subject. "I have good news. Your father will be arriving in a few hours. I'd like you both to join me later for dinner."

Harsh words rose in Fane's throat. It was too little, too late. But this was his grandfather—and he hadn't seen his father in years. They never seemed to be at the court at the same time.

"I can't," he said. "Not tonight. I'm sorry."

And damn it, he *was* sorry. He'd thought he was done trying to win Roald's approval, but apparently he wasn't. Still, a formal fae dinner lasted for hours. No way was he leaving Marjani alone for that long.

"The king's business?" murmured Roald.

Fane stared back expressionlessly. An envoy didn't speak of what he did for Sindre.

"Tomorrow evening then," his grandfather said. "I'll speak to Arne when he arrives."

"I'll look forward to it." Tomorrow night Fane would be sneaking Marjani out of the castle, but he'd fit in the drink somehow. It would be the perfect cover if Sindre got suspicious.

"And thank you for the invitation," he added. "Please tell Arne I'm sorry I can't be there tonight. Now if you'll excuse me—"

The other man inclined his copper head. "Until tomorrow."

Fane turned to leave and then halted. "My lord?"

His grandfather had already turned to gaze at Saga's portrait. "Mm?"

"I'd appreciate it if you didn't mention my daughter to the king."

Roald turned his head and their eyes met. "No," he agreed. "It would be best if he didn't know."

"Thank you." Fane nodded to the two elves, who were holding open the door for him.

Back in the hall, he expelled a breath. For six decades, his grandfather had pretty much ignored his existence. So what had changed? Unless he suddenly felt a belated duty to his deceased mate, who after all, had been one hundred percent human.

With a shrug, Fane set the puzzle aside. He had a bigger problem waiting in his room. One he needed to get back to before she took it into her head to come looking for him.

Returning to the great hall, he heaped a large plate with food—cheese, herb-encrusted roast chicken, salad, whole-grain rolls fresh from the ovens. He popped a silver cover over the whole thing, pocketed a couple of apples, and wended his way back through the bluish-white maze to his room.

Stars, he was sick of all the unending white and silver and blue. He yearned for green grass and lush trees and flowers that bloomed longer than a few short weeks.

Back in the room, Marjani was fully dressed down to her boots, but she was slumped in the easy chair, eyes half-closed. One hand cupped the quartz on her chest, a pretty conglomeration of amethyst crystals in a soft gray and purple. The center glowed weakly.

His breath snagged. She looked so exhausted, her beautiful oval face drawn.

The earth fada didn't share the secrets of their quartz with anyone, but he knew it was a symbiotic relationship. A quartz didn't come to "life" until chosen by an earth fada, and the earth fada in turn drew life energy from the quartz's crystals.

But both Marjani and her quartz looked depleted. He grimaced, helpless and not liking it.

He eased the door shut as quietly as possible, but her eyes opened. She straightened, her gaze on the plate. He passed it over and set the apples on the table.

"Sorry I took so long. I ran into my grandfather."

"Your grandfather?" She paused in the act of lifting her fork and frowned. "He's at the court?"

"Yeah, but don't worry. He won't be stopping by. We're not exactly friendly."

He tried to keep the bitterness out of his tone, but the way Marjani tilted her head told him he hadn't succeeded.

"No?"

"He's a pureblood."

"Ah," she said, a world of understand in that single syllable. Everyone knew how purebloods were about tainting their bloodlines.

Fane dropped onto the wood chair and picked up his ale. But he didn't take a drink, just turned the brown bottle in his hands, unsettled by the encounter with Roald.

Marjani began eating with a delicate greed that reminded him of a stray cat that had adopted his family when he was a kid in Newfoundland. A sleek gray female, the cat hadn't been able to look awkward if it tried—just like Marjani.

She was halfway through when she gave a rueful grin and offered him the plate. "I'm starved—sorry. Would you like some?"

He helped himself to some bread and cheese and then handed back the plate, telling her to finish it. "You need it more than me."

"Thanks. I've burned a lot of energy this past week." She touched the quartz, and then flicked him a look and hurriedly dropped her hand as if afraid to draw his attention to it.

Irritation spiked through him. What did she think he was going to do, rip the goddamn quartz from her neck? Then he remembered that she'd been attacked. Maybe some man *had* ripped it from her neck.

He took a gulp of ale.

She ate more slowly now. Her tongue flicked a crumb from the corner of her mouth, and he was reminded again of the graceful gray cat. He half expected her to swipe a tongue over her palm and use it to wash her face.

And why the hell was that arousing? But it was. He pictured her strong dancer's body under his while he licked and nipped at her lush rose lips. Or maybe straddling him, slim fingers wrapped around his cock as she closed those soft lips around the head...

She licked a dab of goat cheese off her finger and he shifted on the chair, so hard it hurt.

He dragged his gaze from her and finished his ale. When he spoke, his voice was hoarse. "Marjani."

She paused in the act of lifting her bottle to her mouth. Whatever she saw on his face made her set it on the small table between them. A steel stiletto jumped into her hand.

At least that was an improvement on the iron switchblade. She could cut him with steel, but with his fae blood, he'd heal fast. Iron, on the other hand, could do some serious damage.

He blew out a breath. "Put that damn thing away. You have nothing to fear from me."

"No?" She cast a pointed look at the tent in his jeans.

He lifted a shoulder. "I'm a man—and a fae. I like sex and I find you attractive. Doesn't mean I'm going to act on it."

She set the tip of the blade on her index finger. A flick of her hand, and the stiletto began spinning. She let it spin for a few seconds and then sent it flipping over the back of her hand. She caught it with her other hand and threaded it through her fingers in a dazzling display.

His mouth quirked. If she thought her little demonstration frightened him off, she was mistaken. But he was sorry if he'd made her uncomfortable.

"I get the point, love." He leaned back in his chair, left foot hooked over his right thigh. "Literally. And if it helps, I already knew you were lethal."

She slipped the stiletto back into her boot. "And you know this how?"

"It's my business to know things. You're Adric's second— one of his top people. No one knows much about you, except that you were at his side as he fought his way to alpha. But I've heard those knives aren't just for show. "

In fact, she was the Baltimore clan's top assassin, but he was too canny to say it aloud. Let her guess how much he knew.

Her smile was full of teeth. "Just for the record, you might want me—but there's no way in Hades you're going to have me."

"As you say." He waved a negligent hand. "Now, how about I

tell you a story about a little girl who grew up at court? A beautiful and Gifted girl with more natural power than the court had seen in a generation. She would've been a court favorite except for one thing. She was born of an ice fae father and a night fae mother."

"Go on." Marjani drew up her legs and wrapped her arms around them, resting her chin on her knees.

He stared at a softly glowing fae light, formulating his words. He wasn't telling the story to be clever. He was forbidden to speak of Lady Blaer directly to an outsider.

"Maybe she was born twisted, or maybe it was because she was shunned from a young age. I don't know. Her mother kept her for the first decade or so and then dumped her in Reykjavik and told her to make her way to the ice fae court. The king took her in and kept her close—she was too powerful to do otherwise—but she spent most of her time in the east tower with only goblins for company."

"Holy mother. That's inhuman." Marjani shook her head against her knees. "And you people call us animals."

"They're not my people," he growled. Once, he'd hoped… But not now—they'd made it clear he was an outsider, one of the lesser races. "And yes, they *are* inhuman. They're fae."

She blinked. "Gotcha. So who is this lady and why do I care?"

"I can't tell you her name. But if you listen, you might learn something."

"Can't—or won't?"

"Can't." He waited until understanding dawned on her face before continuing, "A couple of decades passed. In the human world, it was more like fifty turns of the sun. One winter solstice, the young lady broke out of the east tower and appeared at the court—and proceeded to become one of the king's advisors."

"And?"

"She's one of the most powerful fae in the court now. The king is old and she amuses him. He lets her have her way, more than he should. She's so beautiful it hurts your eyes to look at her. Men—including fada—fall at her feet. She binds them to her with sex, and then if they're lucky, she sends them away... even if they don't want to go."

"And the unlucky ones?"

He gave her a stark look. "She keeps them."

"In a cage." Marjani tightened her grip on her legs.

"She's half night fae. She feeds on their pain."

"We go crazy if we're caged. The animal has to be free."

"I'm afraid the black wolf is already halfway there. It's been weeks since I saw him as a man."

She lifted her head from her knees. "But he sent my brother a message. That's why I came."

Fane straightened up. "The hell he did. When?"

"Last week—about ten days ago. He told Adric to meet him in Reykjavik. Dared him to meet him."

"That's impossible." Fane's heart started to pound in slow, hard strokes. "He's not in any condition to send a message. Not without help."

8

———

*L*uc crouched on his haunches, watching the boulders near the dirt track where Marjani had concealed herself.

Finally, he'd caught a damn break. He'd been just missing her all week. His flight had been delayed because of a fucking tropical storm. He'd spent twenty-four hours at the Baltimore airport, then another six in that metal tube that passed for transportation.

By the time he'd landed in Iceland, she must've already headed north, but he'd lost another day in Reykjavik, following her scent all over the city.

He stayed in contact with Adric, but the alpha couldn't get a read on her other than to say she was definitely in Iceland. Finally Marjani had turned on her phone, but only long enough for Adric to confirm she'd headed north. So Luc had followed, increasingly anxious.

He'd thought his luck had turned when he caught her scent near the beach. But it was mixed with the silver of a male fae, which made his wolf want to chew nails. Who was this man who kept crossing her path?

Then a huge storm had blown up and he'd lost both their scents in the deluge. Luc had waited out the storm in a barn with a herd of cranky goats who were *not* happy to share their space with a wolf. As soon as the rain slacked off, he'd resumed his trek north.

If Marjani had mated with him, he could've followed the bond. But she'd refused to accept him as her mate—although he'd asked. More than once.

But he'd finally caught up to her.

As a wolf, his sense of smell far surpassed hers, so after sending the alpha a quick text that he'd found her and she was all right, he took up a vigil downwind and out of sight. Just breathing her in like the lovesick ass he was.

He'd loved Marjani Savonett from the moment he'd first set eyes on the skinny teen with the soft voice and flashing knives. He'd known damn well she was scared—of her bastard of an uncle, that she'd lose Adric like she'd lost her mom and dad—but no one would've guessed it.

Until the night Corban's people had kidnapped her and handed her over to that den of feral river fada. When Luc and his men had picked her up the next morning on a Baltimore street, she'd been bruised and hollow-eyed. He just wished her rapists were still alive so he could cut off their fucking balls and then stuff them down their throats.

A cold-eyed fae with silver hair zoomed up on a motorbike.

Luc crept closer. And then his heart damn near stopped as Marjani dove through the portal after the fae.

He pelted after her, narrowly avoiding plunging into a bog concealed by the unnatural fog. The portal closed as he arrived. Luc tried to leap through anyway. He caught a glimpse of a menacing black castle—and then it disappeared. He landed on the sparse grass, still in the human world.

He threw back his head and howled. He *had* to get to Marjani.

Even at the best of times, he was more wolf than human. Knowing she was inside a fae court without any backup made him half-crazed with worry. If something happened to her, he'd never forgive himself.

He took several paces back and forth in front of the portal before forcing himself to halt. This was getting him nowhere. He had to hide before the ice fae wondered what the big, brown, backpack-wearing wolf was up to.

Moving a few yards off the path, he hunkered down next to a pile of boulders. Around him, the fog thickened until he couldn't see more than a few feet in any direction.

He pricked his ears and heightened his sense of smell. The locals had spoken of the vicious goblins that guarded this area. He had no desire to be set upon and torn to pieces.

The sun set and a cold breeze teased his fur. He hunched his shoulders, thankful for his thick coat, because he wasn't moving from this spot.

Sooner or later, another fae would go through the portal, and this time, Luc would be ready.

Fear congealed in his stomach. *Please let her be safe. Please don't let the fae catch her.*

The fae wouldn't harm her. Not at first. They'd be more likely to force her into some one-sided bargain, keeping her as an assassin...or a sex toy.

But in Marjani's current state of mind, just being held captive might be enough to drive her over the edge.

He growled, low and anxious, still pissed off at Adric. Why the fuck had he let her leave Baltimore?

Something in her was broken, even if Adric refused to admit it. People said she should step down as second, although no one was brave enough to say that to the alpha's face.

If Marjani were Luc's, he'd have tied her to the damn bed if necessary. She was too fragile to tangle with the fae.

But she wasn't his, and he was beginning to fear she never

would be. He loved her with all his heart, but the mate bond wasn't there.

He expelled a breath.

Slipping out of the pack without shifting, he worked the clasp open with his teeth and munched through a couple of energy bars and a large chunk of beef jerky.

After that, he settled his head on his paws and dozed, ears pricked. But the night remained quiet save for the occasional squeak and growl of nocturnal creatures.

Just before dawn, he jerked awake as two fae in an SUV drove out of the portal heading south.

The portal remained open. He crept closer. The dirt track wound through the mist to the ominous black castle.

He sniffed, testing the air. He caught a whiff of silver, but that he'd expected. He darted through the shimmering circle.

It closed behind him, but he ignored it as he picked up Marjani's trail. He paced forward, all his senses on high alert.

The high-pitched chatter reached him first. He dropped to his belly and froze.

A sour stench filled his nostrils. Shadows moved. Crept closer.

The fur on his neck stood straight up. He scrambled back up and took off at a run, but it was too late. A manic screech split the air.

He turned to face them, but they were all around him. Ripping at him with razor-like teeth and sharp black claws. Piling on his back until he went down under the sheer weight.

His last thought was a prayer that they hadn't caught Marjani, too.

9

———

Fane watched as Marjani climbed into bed fully dressed except for her shoes. The switchblade went under her pillow. He'd bet she had a knife or two hidden on her body as well.

A corner of his mouth lifted in a self-mocking smile. Guess it was up to him to be a gentleman and leave the bed to her. "I'll take the chair," he said and went into the bathroom to wash up. He exchanged his button-up shirt for a T-shirt but left his pants on.

When he returned, she was on her side facing him, the comforter tucked around her so that all he saw was a nose and cat-shaped eyes. He took a quilt from the closet and padded to the easy chair.

"You don't have to sleep in the chair." A quiet voice came from the bed.

He sent her a look over his shoulder. Did she mean what he thought she did?

"It's a big bed," she said. "You stay on your side, and I'll stay on mine."

No, she didn't. With a philosophical shrug, he sat down and settled the quilt around him. "I'm good."

He flicked his fingers and the fae lights dimmed to a soft amber. Marjani's breath slowed, and he thought she'd fallen asleep until she murmured, "Why are you being so nice?"

"I'm a bloody philanthropist. Now go to sleep already."

"Okay." A drowsy mumble. "But...thank you."

He grunted. When he was sure she was asleep, he muttered, "Because I like you. Too much," and then shut his eyes. As the king's envoy, he'd learned to sleep wherever he could.

He was deep in an enjoyable dream involving him and his sexy guest when a whimper jolted him awake. Heart pounding, he scanned the room. Had Blaer found out he was hiding a fada?

Marjani gave another forlorn mewl.

Hell and damnation. She was having a nightmare.

He threw off the quilt and padded to the bed. Sensing motion, the fae lights brightened enough for him to see his guest curled in a tight ball, tears streaking her cheeks.

He stared down at her helplessly. "Hey." He touched her shoulder. "Wake up. It's just a bad dream."

A guttural growl ripped from her throat. Claws sprouted from her fingertips.

He jerked his hand away. "Calm down. It's me, Fane."

Her breath shuddered in. She raised herself on an elbow. The eyes that met his were an unnerving turquoise, and he knew he was face-to-face with the cougar.

The center of her quartz glowed a similar aqua-blue. She touched it and blinked. Awareness dawned.

"I—sorry," she said gruffly. Her claws detracted.

He sat on the mattress. "Want to tell me about it?"

She shook her head. "Excuse me," she muttered and pushed past him into the bathroom. The water ran. He heard a couple of choked sobs that were immediately cut off.

He looked down at his hands and stayed where he was.

When she returned, her face was freshly scrubbed. He rose to his feet. Her eyes met his, red and swollen, the irises back to brown. Daring him to say something.

Lord, he didn't want to care. For the past six decades, he'd done just fine not caring about much at all, and this woman was nothing to him. But his heart constricted at how tense she held herself—shoulders high, feet apart. Prepared to strike if he offered sympathy.

She spoke first. "You can have the bed now."

"I changed my mind. If it's still all right, I'll share it with you."

Relief flashed across her face, but her voice was cool. "It's your bed."

He reached out a hand. "Come here."

She looked from the hand to his face. "Why?"

"I think you need to be held."

Another challenging look. "And why would I want *you* to hold me?"

He set his jaw. "Because I'm the only one here. Now come." He beckoned with his fingers.

She dragged a hand over her shaved head. "I suppose it's the only way we'll get any sleep."

"That's right. Now come here. You can have the outside." He got under the comforter and scooted toward the wall.

She crept under the comforter and lay facing him, her expression neutral. But he'd seen that relief on her face. She wanted this.

Turning onto his back, he slid an arm under her shoulders. When she didn't resist, he pulled her into the curve of his shoulder. She held herself stiff for a few moments and then her breasts heaved.

"You think I'm weak," she muttered against his T-shirt.

He huffed a laugh. "Like hell. You're probably the strongest woman I know."

"Then you don't know many fada."

"Not true. In my work for the king, I've met my share."

"Yeah? What do you do, anyway?"

"I'm one of his envoys. I'm part messenger, part negotiator. I've been to all the major fae courts—ice fae, sun fae, and night fae—and I've also visited a number of fae and fada clans."

"Sounds interesting." She settled more comfortably into the crook of his shoulder, probably not even realizing she'd relaxed. She had a sweet, earthy scent that reminded him of a baby animal's.

He turned so that his cheek was against Marjani's shaved head. Something about the short bristles against his skin was unbearably erotic. He pulled his head back, putting some space between them, and firmly tamped down his desire.

He was offering comfort, nothing more, even if his cock hadn't gotten the message.

"It can be. But..." He trailed off, because what was the use of complaining? He was in for the duration.

But he was sick and tired of being at Sindre's beck and call. He wanted his own life back. He'd spent six decades trotting about on king's errands. Working his way up in the ice fae court —and for what? He was still on the outer fringes, tolerated, but not respected.

Hell, he'd had to hide at his own daughter's mate ritual because no one at court knew he had a daughter—and that was how he wanted to keep it. Instead, he'd observed the ceremony from the back of the crowd, an odd pressure in his chest.

Evie was his only child, and he'd missed too much of her growing up. It was his biggest regret.

Still, he couldn't help feeling happy that his Evie had found a mate. And damn, she'd sparkled in a pretty dress with a star adorning her short blond hair, her face wreathed in smiles as she'd walked toward Jace. He'd stayed for the first toast and then left. Evie was in good hands with her earth fada mate, and Fane was supposed to be in Canada on a job for Sindre. The king wouldn't be happy to know he'd made an unscheduled visit to Baltimore, and he'd be furious to learn Fane had a daughter he didn't know about.

But it was safer for Evie if the ice fae didn't know she existed.

Besides, time passed differently in the fae world. A month could go by and he'd return to the States to find Evie another year older. And frankly, he wasn't good at the commitment thing, even when it was his own daughter.

He inhaled Marjani's fresh, wild scent. "Your dream. Was it about the cages?"

"No. Just something bad that happened to me once."

He squeezed her shoulders. "I'm sorry."

She shrugged and turned the subject. "I'll tell you one thing —I'd pay good money to know who sent that message to my brother. It was in my cousin's handwriting."

"I told you, he's in no condition to send a message. Someone here helped him."

"That's what I figured. So that fae lady you told me about must've been trying to lure Adric to Iceland. Or maybe it was the king?"

"I didn't say that."

"No," she agreed, "you didn't. I'm just glad I came, not Ric."

"Because you can win against a fae where he can't?"

She shook her head. "He's stronger than me. He wouldn't be alpha if he wasn't."

"Then why?"

"I'm expendable," she said in a flat voice. "He's not. You don't know what it was like before he took over as alpha. We can't lose him."

That's when he realized that Marjani had known what she was getting into. This was a suicide mission.

Bloody hell. He tightened his grip on her. "I'll help any way I can." It was a fucking evasive promise, but it was the best he could do.

She should've called him on it. Instead she murmured a thank you.

"You should never have come here." He sounded like a broken record, but he had the bad feeling it was already too late to sneak her back out of the castle—and the thought of this proud, beautiful woman at the mercy of Lady Blaer made him a little sick.

"I had to."

He mentally shook his head. But he supposed to Marjani, there'd been no other choice. That was the kind of woman she was.

She patted his chest. "Don't worry. I'll be okay."

His mouth twisted. Because all of a sudden, he wasn't sure who was comforting whom.

10

*A*dric Savonett pinged Marjani's smartphone for what had to be the hundredth time.

No answer. Still.

She'd been gone for over a week now. Radio silence on her end, but he'd tracked her through her quartz. From this distance he couldn't pinpoint her exact location, but she was somewhere to the north and east, and Luc had confirmed she was in Iceland.

Safe enough, since her quartz was still alive and humming —until twelve hours ago, when it had gone completely silent.

She's okay. There's more than one reason for her quartz to go silent.

It didn't mean she was dead. The quartz could've been depleted. But most likely she'd reached her goal and passed through a fae portal into the ice fae court.

Then Luc's quartz went silent, too.

Adric's worry ratcheted up. But he was stuck in goddamn Baltimore, holding things together.

He paced barefoot across the living room's stone floor, threading his way through the secondhand couch and battered coffee table that he and Marjani had rescued from a dumpster when they were dirt-poor and never gotten around to replacing. The plush orange shag rug was his only luxury. His cougar liked to stretch out on it and stare into the fireplace.

He stalked down the hall to her room to stare at the neatly made bed. The bedspread, a colorful geometric print, was a painful reminder of the sister he used to have. The one who'd loved bright tunics and leggings.

Until those feral river fada had gotten a hold of her, thanks to Corban and his little band of followers. Now she shaved her head and dressed like a soldier in camo.

He muttered a curse and strode back to the living room where he stared into the glowing amber quartz in his fireplace. Outside, it was a humid night in early August, but his den was carved out of the bedrock two stories below the surface, so he kept the quartz-powered fire burning all year round.

Marjani had loved to sit by the fire.

She's in danger.

All evening, he'd been agitated. At midnight, he'd fallen asleep for a few hours and then got up to pace, his cat clawing at his insides, itching to go to her.

Growing up, he and Marjani had always had each other's backs. Otherwise they'd never have survived the clan war known as the Darktime. But Marjani had been scarred by those terrible years.

She appeared tough, assertive. Only he knew that she still had nightmares about losing their parents and the years they'd spent on the run, hiding from their uncle. She might be a pit bull, but it was protective coating for her soft heart. She wanted to believe that the clan would never again turn on one another like cold-eyed, vicious reptiles.

And because Adric loved her, he did his best not to dispel that belief. His sister might be his most trusted advisor, but she didn't know everything.

Did she really think he'd kill her? No fucking way. He'd lie, cheat and even murder if it meant hiding his sister was a feral.

He squeezed his quartz, willing her to contact him. Damn it, Luc was supposed to have found her by now.

But he'd missed her in Reykjavik—and since then Adric had received only two short communications. In the first, Luc had explained he was heading to the ice fae court's location in northern Iceland. In the second, he'd said he'd found her and was temporarily cutting off communication for safety.

And for the past two days, nothing from either of them.

That made two of his lieutenants lost somewhere in Iceland. The place was a freaking Venus flytrap.

He rubbed his nape and told himself not to worry. Luc and Jani were both strong, capable soldiers.

But she's not herself...

On the surface two stories above, a motorcycle rumbled up to the rowhouse he rented out to a couple of teenage drug dealers as camouflage. Very few people suspected the Baltimore Earth Fada alpha himself lived in the neighborhood.

A minute later, booted footsteps clattered down Adric's stairs.

He stilled.

No one but his lieutenants and a few trusted clanspeople had permission to pass through the ward guarding his den. And they wouldn't come in the middle of the night if it wasn't important.

"It's me," called Jace at the same instant that Adric sensed his quartz on the other side of the door.

Adric ushered him inside and closed the door. "What's up?"

Jace shook his head. Like Adric, his cat genes were evident in his lean, powerful build. He had close-cropped black hair, warm brown skin and his Native American dad's broad face and long cheekbones. He'd dressed in a hurry—his T-shirt was shoved haphazardly into the waistband of his jeans, and he hadn't buckled his short black moto boots.

"Bad news," he said, his mouth a hard line.

Adric's heart sank. He really didn't need any more bad news right now. He gestured for the jaguar shifter to go into the living room. Neither of them sat down.

Jace got right to the point. "Langdon wants to meet with you."

Adric stiffened. Jace had said the night fae prince's name. Clearly, they'd draw his attention.

Hell. This had to be about Tyrus.

"The prince contacted you himself?"

Jace's face sharpened, his cat's fury simmering green in his eyes. "He sent a fucking night fae envoy to our house in Grace Harbor." Jace's mate Evie had kept her house in Grace Harbor, a small city on the Chesapeake Bay, even though she and her teenage brother Kyler lived in Jace's Baltimore den much of the time.

"They're all right?"

Evie was a pretty blond human with a touch of fae, and her brother Kyler, although full human, was smart, scrappy, and— although he'd hate to hear it—loveable. Even though Evie wasn't an earth fada, Adric would've tolerated her for Jace's sake, but the two siblings had earned a special place in his heart when they'd saved Jace from Tyrus's assassins.

"Yeah." His friend growled. "But it scared the shit out of her. The prick wants me to know I'm vulnerable, that he knows where my mate and her brother live."

A cold anger rolled through Adric. "The hell he does." Evie was innocent in all this, and Kyler was a cub—not even out of high school yet.

"His envoy knocked on our front door—at midnight. I scented that he was a night fae, of course, so I told Evie not to open the door. Meanwhile, I changed to my jag and slipped around the house for a better look. Thank the gods her dad gave her that protection charm. At least the bastard didn't pick up that she's a mixed-blood."

Adric nodded.

"But he upset everyone. Even Mrs. Linney. You know how she has her nose in everyone's business." Jace paced across the living room, agitated.

"Hell. I'm sorry." Mrs. Linney was Evie's elderly, chain-smoking, neon-clothes-wearing neighbor. The woman never seemed to sleep—she was better than a watchdog.

"Mrs. Linney came out on her stoop and cussed the envoy out. Called him an ass for waking up the whole neighborhood at midnight."

Adric couldn't help grinning. "The woman has balls."

Jace snorted. "I swear, she's going to give me gray hairs. I don't know what he'd have done to her if I hadn't been there. But as soon as she saw my cat, she went back inside."

"This is why you need to move Evie and Kyler to Baltimore. The three of you are too isolated up there."

"You think I don't know that? But I promised Kyler he could finish high school in Grace Harbor."

Adric scowled, but gave a curt nod. A promise was a promise.

"Anyway, the night fae announced he was the prince's envoy, tossed me the message and disappeared back into whatever slimy hole he crawled out of. Here." Jace handed over an unsealed black envelope. "Read it for yourself."

Adric removed a sheet of paper the same coal black as the envelope. On it was a message inscribed in silver ink.

Prince Langdon requests the pleasure of a meeting with Lord Adric at his earliest convenience. The envoy will return for your response at midnight.

He crumpled the paper and tossed it on the coffee table. "All right. I'll meet with him."

"No fucking way," Jace returned. "You can't. What if he asks you straight out who killed Tyrus?"

Adric speared his fingers through his spiked-up hair. Langdon couldn't find who'd killed his son. The Darktime would look like a warm-up compared to what he'd bring down on the clan.

He met his friend's eyes. "Then I'll have to lie, won't I?"

Jace squeezed his nape. "A lie like that would be like taking a knife to the gut."

"I've survived worse."

"As your lieutenant—and friend—I'd advise against it."

"You got a better idea?"

His friend's dark brows lowered. "No, damn you."

They'd been over this already. They'd known it was only a matter of time before Langdon tracked his son to Baltimore and demanded answers.

"That's what I thought." Adric's smile was thin. "Sending an envoy to your mate's house was just the start. The prince probably knows the location of every single one of our dens. If I ignore this or go into hiding, he'll go after the clan. I knew this was coming, Jace. Ever since Marjani stuck a knife into his fucking psycho of a son."

11

———

Marjani stared into space, listening to Fane's breath.

She hated Corban. She was here to kill him.

The prick deserved to be in a cage, and she knew damn well if their positions were reversed, he wouldn't lose any sleep over it. The man should've been a serpent, not a wolf.

It did something to you, to know your own cousin had been behind the plot to drug and rape you. Oh, Corban had kept his hands clean so that he could swear to Adric he hadn't touched her—but he'd masterminded her kidnapping by a small den of half-insane river fada. The den had also kidnapped Tiago do Rio, the Rock Run alpha's youngest brother, in an attempt to set her clan against his, the local river fada. If things had gone as planned, both alphas would've been dead, leaving Corban as the Baltimore alpha and the Rock Run fada in disarray.

Somehow Tiago had fought back, even though he'd been drugged himself, and saved them both. But not before the men had had her...

It was her cougar who had kept her sane by stepping in and taking control.

Corban deserved to die—a slow, miserable death. So why couldn't she stop thinking about him, locked in that iron cage and gradually going mad?

Uncle Leron had been right. She *was* weak.

You're soft. His harsh voice rang in her ears. *A female, and a scrawny one at that. You'll do whatever I fucking say, understand?*

Leron had been a wolf shifter, tall and powerfully built. She'd stared up at him, defiant but hollow with fear. Leron rarely beat her like he did his three sons and Adric, but the threat was always there.

She couldn't do anything about her size—she had her mom's slim build. But both her parents had been clan soldiers, and they'd trained her and Adric in fighting techniques from the time they were toddlers. But her parents were dead, and Leron's mate was even more afraid of him than Marjani was.

So Marjani had trained even harder until her body was a finely honed machine, and she was a wizard with knives. She knew the best way to cut a man so that he'd bleed out in less than a minute, and she was never without two or three blades concealed around her body.

And none of that had helped that night in Baltimore when Shania had slipped the aphrodisiac into her drink. A woman she'd thought was a friend—a den mate.

You survived.

She had to focus on that or go insane.

But is it survival when your nightmares make you mewl like a cub?

Her hand flexed on Fane's chest. Gods, she was pathetic, snuggled up to a man she barely knew—and a part-fae at that. But she liked that wild meadow scent of his. Her cat wanted to roll around in it, take the scent on its fur.

Even the thump of his heart beneath her hand was comforting.

You're weak. A female, and a scrawny one at that. You should've been drowned at birth.

She ground her teeth.

Maybe Adric was right—she was too broken to be out in the world. But she'd spent the past year hiding in their den. Sinking deeper and deeper into her animal.

Fada healed more quickly as their animals, so no one had questioned it. In fact, Adric had encouraged her to remain as her cougar.

By the time she was stronger, it was too late. The cat often overrode the human part of her. Not even Adric knew how much. She'd let the cougar remain in control for long days as she'd healed.

Because she felt afraid as a woman. The woman was weak, vulnerable—but not the cougar. If those men had attacked her cat, it would've ripped out their fucking throats.

"You're thinking too hard," Fane murmured. "Go to sleep."

She grimaced. "Sorry."

He sighed. "You can't, can you?"

Her cheeks heated. She mutely shook her head.

He set his other arm around her waist, and she stiffened, but he kept the touch nonsexual. His long fingers spread over her stomach, warm and comforting. He hummed, low and hoarse, a rough purr like something out of a ratty old tomcat.

She bit her lower lip, trying not to laugh.

He began to sing, and her jaw slackened. He was *good*, his rough voice perfectly on pitch, but with an edge that made it intriguing...and fucking sexy.

Deep inside, parts of her stirred to life. Parts that hadn't shown any interest in more than a year.

The man could bottle that voice and sell it as a love potion.

She didn't recognize the song, but she guessed it was an old folk song. Dark and mournful, about a woman and her dead lover.

Her breath released. Her eyelids fluttered shut.

"That's it," he murmured. "Sleep." He switched to another sad song.

I can't.

She was out before the end of the second verse.

FANE WOKE BEFORE HER. In the night, they had turned so that his back was to her and she was curled up against his side. Marjani came awake as he slid out of bed. She turned over and watched, slit-eyed, as he moved around the room. Not embarrassed, exactly, but not wanting to talk with him either.

He disappeared into the bathroom and the shower came on.

She fingered the amethyst crystals of her quartz, a gift from Adric after her kidnapping. He'd found her a good match, and she loved how the amethyst ranged in shades from deep purple to smoky gray, but she still mourned her old quartz.

The one the river fada had smashed into pieces and tossed into the filthy waters of the Inner Harbor.

Enough. It wasn't her nature to hide. So she'd embarrassed herself—who gave a shit?

Throwing off the comforter, she got out of bed and pulled a sweater over her T-shirt before lacing on her hiking boots. Her blades went back into their usual places—the dagger and stiletto into the leather sheaths in her boots, the switchblade in her right front pocket. The fishing knife she left in the backpack.

The little round table had an inlaid checkerboard, and she found a box of checkers on a shelf beneath the table. She set up the pieces and idly pushed them around, working on a new strategy.

She'd learned the game from her dad and then kept it up.

She and Adric had often played matches on the little checkerboard she carried around with her as they shivered during a long, cold stakeout ordered by Uncle Leron.

The thought of her smart, serious dad made her squeeze her eyes shut. Will Savonett hadn't even wanted to be a soldier. If he'd had his way, he would've been a crystal engineer like Jace. His death, along with her mom's, had left a hole in her heart that nothing could fill.

No one should die so young and far from home.

Fane emerged from the bathroom, jolting her back to the present. His blue eyes crinkled in a smile. "Morning."

"Morning."

All he wore were the skinny black jeans from last night. She couldn't help a quick perusal of his bare chest, all lean, hard muscle with dark blond hair curling over it.

That spark of interest heated her insides again. She pressed her mouth into a line and looked away.

Going into his closet, he pulled on a clean T-shirt and an oatmeal-colored sweater with a black-and-white band across the chest in a traditional Icelandic pattern.

"Hungry?" he asked. "I can get us some breakfast."

"Thank you." She rose to her feet. She wanted to be standing for this. "But first, I want to see this wolf."

He stilled. "No. It's too dangerous."

"I'm not asking your permission. Take me to him, or I'll go myself."

He studied her, clearly trying to decide how best to manage her. She raised her chin, because she wasn't going to be "managed."

"I should call your bluff," he said. "You wouldn't get within ten yards of him before you found yourself locked in a cage, too."

She swallowed hard—and reined in her pride. Clashing

with him would get her nowhere. In Baltimore, she was a person of power, the alpha's second. Here she was a fada, lower than dirt as far as the ice fae were concerned. But Fane had treated her well. Hell, he'd probably saved her life.

"Please. I have to make sure it's really him. No one has to know. You can conceal me like you did last night, can't you?"

"How do I know you won't try to stick one of those knives into him?"

"I won't. That's a promise." She'd already rejected that as a bad idea. The fae would know a fada was running loose in the castle.

His hand cupped her face. "I have a hard time saying no to you. Why is that, do you think?" His thumb caressed her cheek.

Their gazes snagged. His eyes were very blue.

She moistened her lips. "I don't know," she whispered.

Those sky-colored eyes heated like twin blue flames. "I think you do." He blew out a breath and released her. "I'll probably regret this, but all right. I'll take you to him. We'll go now, while everyone else is at breakfast."

"Thank you." She scraped a hand over her shaved head and then took a step back. "I just need a minute." She dashed into the bathroom to pee and run a brush over her teeth.

Fane was waiting, arms crossed over his broad chest. "I'll have your promise before we leave this room. You're just going to take a look—nothing else. Is that clear?"

"Yes." She instinctively touched her chest over her quartz. "I give you my word."

He looked at her feet. "Better take the boots off—I don't want you clomping around."

"Don't worry." She paced in a soundless circle around him.

His smile was wry. "I keep forgetting you're a cat. Hang on, let me check the hall." He cracked open the door. "It's clear." He beckoned her closer and took her hand. "You know the drill.

Stay close to me and no will see you. Don't talk, and be careful not to brush up against anyone."

"Got it."

Together, they strode into the hall.

———

ane had lost his bloody mind.

That was the only explanation. He'd worked hard to make his way in the ice fae court, even though he was only a quarter fae. Earned some respect.

Was he going to throw it all away on some fada he'd just met?

He looked at the somber assassin striding alongside him. Apparently the answer was yes.

The wolf shifter was in Blaer's tower on the castle's east side. Fane chose to walk back the way they'd come, avoiding Sindre's tower to the north.

The maze had remade itself overnight, forming new paths, but since Fane was at the court with Sindre's permission, it opened a passage for him, somehow sensing where he was headed. Fane was used to it, but Marjani glanced from side to side, clearly trying to recognize landmarks.

"Don't bother," he murmured. "It's always changing."

They passed a small pack of fur-clad goblins. Marjani stiffened. The goblins sniffed the air suspiciously, pig-like noses twitching, but when they couldn't see anything, trotted on.

They took another few turns before coming upon twin fae lords—Sindre's nephews—blocking the passageway as they murmured to each other in Icelandic.

When Fane was in stealth mode, no one could see him, but he'd adjusted the magic so that he was visible to Marjani and vice versa. He watched her eye the twins, gorgeous in flowing white shirts and black leather pants, their pointed ears poking through long, wavy blond hair.

Most women would've been stunned speechless at the twins' unearthly beauty, but she merely nodded at the small space between the two men and the wall, and mouthed, "You first."

He couldn't help grinning. Perplexed, she tilted her head in a very feline way. He winked and slid through the gap, Marjani right behind him.

A few turns and they were at the east tower. There they had a piece of luck—the door was open. They walked inside.

Blaer might be equal parts ice fae and night fae, but the night fae was dominant. The large circular room they entered could've been decorated by a vampire. A brass chandelier brooded over the center with tiny fae lights flickering where the candles should have been, and a mist curled over the black marble floor. The walls were covered in red wallpaper flecked with black velvet, and the furniture dark and ornately carved.

Marjani exchanged a look with him, part amusement, part horror.

Setting his mouth to her ear, he pointed at the spiral staircase to the left. "The room with the fada is at the top of the tower."

Together, they walked noiselessly up the three flights. But at the top, their luck didn't hold. The door—a thick oak with steel handles—was shut tight.

Fane muttered a curse. He and Marjani might be invisible,

but if a door opened, anyone in the tower would guess a wayfarer had just entered.

He placed an ear to the wood. Beside him, Marjani did the same. When he heard nothing, he lifted a brow at her. Maybe her shifter senses had picked up something he hadn't.

She shook her head. "It's quiet," she whispered. "I don't think anyone else is in there."

"Stay behind me," he whispered back. "If I have to, I'll show myself and make up some story. But you can't let anyone see you."

He waited for her nod and then eased open the door.

The top floor was one large room. The skylights had been covered with some kind of magic, so that dim, constantly moving shadows slithered across the floor.

From his position behind the door, Fane could only see the black wolf's cage, but he knew the room held a kitchenette, a couple of plush black couches—and five 10-by-15-foot iron cages. Bright, shiny cages.

In its pure form, iron was a bright white metal, and Blaer's magic kept the cages from rusting. Somehow those gleaming cages seemed even worse, like a cold, sterile laboratory where unspeakable things went on. Blaer didn't even give the imprisoned fada the dignity of a private bathroom, just had a rudimentary toilet and sink in each cage and straw scattered on the floor.

In the nearest cage, the big black wolf lay listlessly on a sheepskin.

He had to be in agony, surrounded by iron like that. To a fae or fada, even cold iron burned like fire. The sheepskin provided some protection, but the surrounding iron would slowly drain the wolf's energy. And each time he touched one of the bars, it would sear his skin, seeping into his veins until his entire body was inflamed.

As the door opened, the wolf lifted his head a few inches,

then let it drop back to the sheepskin. His coat was dull and falling off in patches, his eyes rheumy.

Shame filled Fane. Whatever the wolf may or may not have done, this was just wrong. He didn't even want to tell Marjani that Blaer referred to the room as her "zoo."

The earth fada slid past him into the room. He kept a grip on her arm so that she remained invisible.

An open switchblade appeared in her hand. An iron switchblade.

"Remember your promise," he told her. "You get a look only."

She nodded, her gaze on the sick wolf. A shadow slid over him, creeping across his patchy fur like a ghostly creature from another dimension. Marjani's face was expressionless, but the arm beneath his hand vibrated with suppressed tension.

The black wolf's nostrils twitched. Marjani shook off Fane to move closer.

"Corban," she said. The single word held a world of hate.

The black wolf forced himself up on trembling legs. Mad gold eyes narrowed at her.

"I came here to kill you." Her tone dripped with scorn. "But now I just pity you. Killing you would be a kindness you don't deserve."

Her cousin's lips peeled back in a snarl. Fane couldn't tell if he was warning them off—or laughing at them. A thin stream of saliva dripped from a corner of his jaws.

Marjani stopped a few feet away from the cage.

"You think I don't know why you sent that message to Adric? He"—she jerked her head at Fane—"thinks you couldn't have done it without help, but I bet it didn't take much to convince you. Because you'd love to have Ric here, wouldn't you? But it didn't work. You got me, instead." She compressed her mouth. "Goddess, you're an ass. The clan would never have followed you. They don't want more of Leron. We're making something different. Better."

Corban shuddered. His quartz flickered weakly.

Marjani fingered her own quartz. The purple amethyst shimmered blue, and Fane had the feeling she was sending energy to the other fada. But why?

"You've lost," she said, low and hard. "Die with dignity."

A growl rasped from the wolf's throat. Then he lowered his head in defeat.

She released the quartz. "Damn you," she said in a shaking voice.

"We have to leave." Fane crossed the room and grabbed her arm.

Then they both froze at the sound of voices on the stairs below.

13

Marjani's heart slammed into gear. If they were caught, she didn't know what they'd do to Fane. But she'd be thrown into one of those gleaming iron cages.

Fuck that. She'd die first.

Her cougar surged to life, trying to take over. Claws pricked her fingertips and she knew her eyes had gone a feral blue.

"How many?" Fane whispered, reminding her that she wasn't alone. She had him to think about, too. And he knew the court—if she worked with him, they might both get out of here undetected.

Not now, she hissed at her cougar.

It snarled warningly.

Fane jerked, and she realized she'd snarled aloud.

"Jani?" Their eyes met, and she knew he must see the cougar. And then he did something unexpected. Instead of pulling away like any sensible person would, he wrapped an arm around her. "Shh. I won't let them get you. Now how many?"

She gulped. To her surprise, the cougar subsided, soothed by his scent and calm voice.

Quickly, she sorted the voices and footsteps into separate people—a man and two women. Keeping the switchblade ready in her right hand, she held up her left, showing Fane three fingers.

He nodded and put his finger to his lips. Taking her hand, he made the two of them disappear, and together, they crept toward the door.

Marjani sent a last look at Corban. He panted softly, painfully, head on his paws, eyes half-shut.

Waiting for death.

She gritted her teeth, feeling cheated and angry and deflated, all at the same time. She'd come all this way to kill him, hated him for so long. The man wasn't just her enemy, he was her brother's enemy, too.

And he'd proven he would do anything to be alpha, even tear apart their still-healing clan. Just like his father.

She didn't want to pity Corban. He'd made her and Adric's teenage years a living hell. And later, when he couldn't beat Adric in a fair fight for alpha, he'd tried every dirty trick in the book to undermine him. Marjani and Jace had simply been collateral damage.

Corban needed to die. But not like this, weak and maddened from iron poisoning and as mangy as a third-world dog.

The three fae were on the landing below. "The goblins reported activity in the tower." A man's voice.

Fane eased the door shut and pulled her into a corner opposite the door, keeping her tight against his body. He'd put himself between her and the fae, but she peered around him as the man reached the top of the stairs.

Her jaw loosened. It was the tall, leather-clad fae with cropped silver hair that she'd followed through the portal. So she'd been right to be uneasy; he must've known she was there. But why hadn't he captured her immediately?

Behind him came two women. One rail-thin with ebony skin and silver hair who Marjani would bet was his sister; the other curvy with a night fae's black eyes and an ice fae's blond hair. Both wore short dresses that appeared to have been spun from glitter and cobwebs.

Marjani caught a whiff of the curvy blonde's scent and recoiled. Night fae smelled of graveyards and dank basements, and this woman's odor was strong. She had to be the fae lady in Fane's story.

The silver-haired man shoved the door open and strode inside, followed by the woman who looked like his sister.

"Someone was here," he snapped at Corban. "Who?"

The wolf responded with a feeble growl.

With a curse, the man reappeared in the doorway. "He can't tell me anything as a wolf," he told the curvy blonde. "Can you force him to shift?"

She gave him a level look. "Of course."

He nodded and turned back to Corban.

Marjani gulped soundlessly. Fear sheeted up her spine. Only a fae who knew the secret of their quartz could force an earth fada to shift.

How many fae had Corban told, anyway?

The curvy blonde glanced around, black eyes narrowed. A dark, questing energy whispered over Marjani's skin.

She stilled, afraid to even breathe. Beside her, Fane did the same.

Calm. Cool. Emotionless as a chunk of cheese. A slice of bread.

Night fae fed on negative emotion; the blonde must have sensed Marjani's spike of fear. The only way to hide from a night fae was to remain still—and very, very calm. Another hint of fear, and the woman would be on them.

Marjani's fingers tightened on the switchblade.

A frown creased the blonde's unnaturally perfect face. The seconds ticked by.

One. Two. Three.

More tendrils snaked over Marjani's skin, cold and oily. A scream gathered in her lungs, ready to punch out of her chest.

Four. Five. Six.

"Blaer?" Just when Marjani thought she'd break, the silver-haired man appeared in the doorway. "Is something wrong, love?"

The fae lady shrugged. "I thought I sensed something." She crossed to him, her diamond-studded high heels clicking on the marble floor.

The door closed. Marjani went limp.

She scrubbed her hands over her skin, trying to brush away the slimy feel of the tendrils. And then she went stiff. *Blaer?* She recognized that name. Last year, Sindre had hired Adric to find a Lady Blaer in northern India and bring her home. By then, they'd suspected Corban was behind Marjani's kidnapping, but without proof, Adric couldn't accuse him. Corban had too many allies in the clan. So her brother had sent Corban to India to get him as far away from her—and the clan—as possible.

Beside her, Fane drew a slow inhale through his teeth, and then reached for her hand and glided toward the stairs. She kept her switchblade out as they noiselessly descended the three flights.

As soon as they entered the maze, Fane sped up. She closed the switchblade, shoved it into her pocket and loped alongside him. She couldn't help being impressed. The man moved as swiftly and silently as a shifter.

He didn't slow down until they were a hundred yards from the dark tower and its shiny cages. He continued at a fast walk, long legs eating up the distance as he slipped between the few fae they encountered. She had to trot to keep up.

The maze twisted and turned in unexpected ways, but he always seemed to know which way to go. She tuned into her quartz, trying to use the tiny crystals to orient herself, but it was like being on a spinning merry-go-round with the directions continually changing. If Fane hadn't been with her, she'd have been lost within a minute.

He didn't speak until they were safely back inside his room. "That's the fada who sent you the message?"

"Yeah." She rubbed her upper arms. "It's funny. I thought when I caught up to Corban and finally had my revenge, I'd feel happy—triumphant. The bastard was behind the attack on me, and he's made no secret of the fact that he wants my brother dead."

Fane touched her cheek. "I'm sorry."

She fought the urge to lean into his hand. She was so damned tired. It seemed like forever since she'd had a good night's sleep.

"I thought I'd feel happy. But I just feel hollow." She sank onto the wood chair and stared at her boots. "Guess I could've stayed home in Baltimore. He's going to be dead in a few days anyway."

Fane slouched on the easy chair, face a little pale. "Sometimes I'm glad I'm not a pureblood."

"That blonde with the scent of a night fae—she's the fae lady in your story?"

"She is. Now you see why I wanted you to leave."

"I felt her energy reaching for us." Marjani rubbed her upper arms, recalling the feel of those snake-like tendrils. "Like during the Darktime."

"The Darktime?"

"My clan—we went through a bad time when I was growing up. A civil war. You must've heard about it."

"Yeah." Fane's eyes were sympathetic. "It's just one more story the purebloods tell about the fada so they can justify treating you as animals."

She grimaced. "Sometimes they're not so far off. The bitch

of it was that it was started by the clan elders. The ones who should've known better."

"I didn't know. I'm sorry."

"Yeah," she said flatly. "Killing each other off. Going after whole families. And the night fae were behind it—working with the alpha, my uncle Leron."

"I thought you fada have as little to do with the fae as possible?"

"It's...complicated. It was an alpha challenge that set off the Darktime battles. But it turned ugly, and the night fae helped it along—whipping up people's anger, encouraging revenge killings—so they could feed on the darkness. And my SOB of an uncle let it happen. Hell, he encouraged it. To him, it was all about power."

She heard the tremor in her voice and took a deep breath. Now was not the time for her to dwell on Leron. The man was feeding the trees in the dark Appalachian forest where she and Adric had buried him—and she had more important things to worry about, like the fact that Corban had apparently shared the secret of the earth fada's quartz with more fae than they realized.

"Can this Lady B really force Corban to shift?" she asked Fane.

He lifted a shoulder and let it drop. "I don't know. We're not exactly friends. But you heard her—she seemed sure of herself, like she'd done it before."

"Well, right now, he's too weak to shift. I don't care how strong she is, you can't force a shift on a fada that low in energy. If she tries, she'll kill him."

And it wouldn't be an easy death. A fada caught between shifts died in agony, a monster made up of body parts from both the human and the animal.

"I hope you're right. You don't want him shifting and telling her you're in the castle."

Her mouth twisted. "If she doesn't already know."

He straightened. "What do you mean?"

"That man with her? He's how I got through the portal. He was on a motorbike and I followed him."

"Hell. Why didn't you tell me that last night?"

"I didn't think he saw me, but now I'm not so sure."

"That explains why the goblins were out. That was Jon. He and his twin Krysten are Lady B's right-hand people. They're always with her. We have to assume they know you're in the castle." Fane scraped a hand over his hair. "God's balls. I'm not sure if it would be safe for you to leave even tonight."

"Then maybe I should stay until tomorrow night?" Despite everything, her heart lurched at the chance to spend another day with Fane. "Unless," she added, "I'm a danger to you."

"No. She can't enter this room without my permission. But —" He shook his head.

"What?"

"She's not the only problem here. I'm afraid the king will find out you're in the castle. We can only hide you from him so long."

"Then I'll leave tonight like we agreed."

He blew out a breath. "Let's think on it—maybe I can come up with another plan. Meanwhile, I'll get us some breakfast."

Marjani hesitated, and then nodded. Her stomach was still tight from her encounter with Corban, but when you spend half your life hungry, you learn to eat when you can.

Fane left and she bent forward, elbows on her knees, fingers interlinked.

"Damn you, Corban." She closed her eyes, but all she saw was his too-thin body and mangy fur.

No, damn it. I fucking refuse to feel sorry for him.

He'd tormented her and Adric when they'd been forced to move into Leron's den after the death of their parents. As an adult, he'd supported his father right to the end, even when it became clear that Leron was the worst sort of alpha, tearing the clan apart with his petty feuds and killing any who opposed him. Marjani's own parents had been forced to spend years apart, fighting on separate continents as mercenaries to enrich Leron.

At first Marjani had felt bad for Corban. As the eldest, he took the brunt of Leron's heavy hand. Nothing he did satisfied his dad. But Corban had turned around and beat on his two younger brothers and Adric.

Later, after Adric bested him in the challenge for alpha, Corban had pretended to support him while secretly working against him.

She touched the sharp iron dagger in her boot. It had an ivory handle and a sheath of thick leather to protect her from the iron's poisonous effects. The iron switchblade worked in a pinch, but the dagger was her weapon of choice against a fada or fae.

She was a killer, an assassin. She could slip into that creepy tower and slice Corban's throat in under a minute.

You can't, Jani. You might as well send up a signal announcing there's a fada running loose inside the castle.

What a fucking irony. She'd come to Iceland to kill Corban, and now that he was almost dead, she couldn't just leave it be. Because why the hell would she endanger herself for that prick?

Rising to her feet, she paced across the small room.

An earth fada could kill himself with his quartz. You simply directed all the energy into your heart, speeding it up, making it beat harder and harder until it broke. But Corban's quartz was too weak. Maybe he could've killed himself at the beginning, but he'd waited too long.

She'd tried to send him some energy, but without touching him, very little energy had been transferred. She was a soldier, not a healer.

She fisted her hands and brought them to her forehead, breathing hard. She'd promised Fane just to look—and she had.

If she went back later to do more, that wasn't breaking her promise—was it?

Because if she left without putting her cousin out of his misery, she wasn't any better than him.

14

———

Jane returned with two cups of coffee and a steel box holding fruit, granola, nuts and *skyr*, the Icelandic version of yogurt. Jumping up, she took the coffee from him while he set the box on the little table. One cup was nearly white with cream, the other black.

She eyed the coffee with cream longingly, but her mama had raised her to be polite. "Which one do you want?"

"Your choice."

"You sure?"

His lips twitched. "I prefer my coffee black. The cream's for you. I had a feeling you'd like it."

"You guessed right." She handed him the black coffee and took a sip of her own milky-brown brew. *Perfect.* Her eyes slit with pleasure.

"Have a seat and I'll make you a bowl of granola."

"You don't have to wait on me."

"Jani. Have a seat."

She sat back down and watched as he spooned the *skyr* into two bowls of granola, sprinkling nuts on top. He handed one to her and took the other chair.

"I heard some people talking," he said. "The goblins have been called off. That's something, anyway."

She nodded. "Do you know how long Corban has been in the cage?"

"A week, maybe more. But in your world, that's close to a month."

"What do you mean 'in my world'?"

"Time runs differently here. Sometimes a day is a day, and sometimes a day is ten days. But I was here a month ago when Lady B threw him in the cage. Before that, he was her lover."

"Her *lover*?"

He nodded. "For over a year. I don't know what went wrong. Maybe she just got tired of him."

Marjani shook her head. "I thought Corban was smarter than that."

"She's a beautiful woman, and when she amps up her glamour..." Fane spread his hands. "She can have just about any man she wants."

She slid him a look. She had to ask, even if she didn't like the answer. "What about you?"

"Me?" He snorted. "I prefer my balls attached to my body, thank you very much."

She nodded, her cat quietly satisfied. For some damn reason, it was feeling possessive about this man.

"I wish—" He shook his head.

She ate another mouthful of granola. "Maybe"—she looked down at the cereal, suddenly bashful—"you can look me up the next time you're in Baltimore."

Then she forced herself to meet his eyes. Because her—bashful? Adric would split a gut laughing.

But Fane was unlike any man she'd ever known. He was older, cultured. As polished as that diamond in his earlobe. Hell, the man even dressed better than her.

Still, he'd been sending some very definite signals. Last

night he'd all but said he'd like to fuck her.

"Maybe." He looked back at his granola. "But I don't get there much."

Well, there was her answer. She'd read his signals wrong. But she couldn't leave it alone. "What about Evie? Don't you ever visit her?"

"Every few years or so. She's better off without me."

She frowned. She couldn't understand a father feeling like that. "I bet she doesn't think so."

He finished his coffee and set it on the small table between them. "Trust me, she is," he said in a tone that didn't invite further questions.

She took the hint and fell silent, concentrating on her breakfast. When she finished the granola, she reached for a peach. It was small but perfectly formed. The first bite sent a tart burst of flavor into her mouth.

She gave a hum of pleasure. "That's so good. It tastes like it was just picked."

"We grow them here."

Fane's gaze was on her mouth. Her heart sped up.

"In Iceland?" she managed to ask.

"There's a huge conservatory on the south side of the castle. The king invited a couple of dryads to live here when their trees were young, and they've grown up in the conservatory. They grow things year-round—fruit, vegetables."

She nodded and took another bite of her peach. Dryads were famous for their green thumbs.

Fane was still looking at her mouth. Her lips tingled. She swallowed the bite. "What?"

He leaned forward. "You have peach juice—here." He touched the corner of her mouth, brushing the juice away with his thumb.

"Thanks." His eyes were so beautiful with that dark fringe of eyelashes, like a clear pool surrounded by lush vegetation.

Cool fingers caught her chin.

She stilled. In the past year, no man but her brother had touched her.

The fear was there, but her hunger for touch was stronger. Fane took the half-eaten peach and set it on the table, then stood up, drawing her with him.

She raised her eyes to his. He was a good foot taller than her. He might not be a fada, but the man had muscles. In a bare-handed fight between the two of them, he might just be able to win.

She braced herself for a wave of panic, but her cat gave a happy little rumble. It wanted to rub up against him, roll in his grass-green scent like catnip.

And even the human part of her recalled how he'd held her last night when she'd needed it.

"We have some time to kill." His husky voice vibrated in her body.

"Yes."

He trailed the backs of his fingers over her cheek. "I know something bad happened to you."

She growled, a harsh, feral sound. Knowing her anger was misplaced—she wasn't pissed off at him, she was angry at the men who'd attacked her—but unable to help it.

"What do you know about it?"

"Hey." He stroked her nape. "Fine—we won't talk about that. But I'm going to kiss you, all right?"

"I—" She moistened her lips, and his eyes tracked the movement. "I don't know."

"What do you mean?"

"I don't know," she repeated miserably. "I haven't been kissed for so long. Not in that way."

"Why don't we take it slow? If you don't like it, just tell me to stop and I will. Any time—you just say the word."

All the spit left her mouth. But it was only a kiss. She

trusted that when he said he'd stop at any time, he would.

"All right," she whispered.

"Mm." His hum of approval was almost a purr. He gathered her closer, one arm around her waist, while his other hand kept up those soothing strokes on her nape. "You're so beautiful."

She traced her fingers over his high cheekbones, touched his full lower lip. His jaw was covered with dark, grainy stubble. "So are you."

"You think?" He chuckled—and then his mouth touched hers. She stiffened, but he merely brushed his lips over hers, soft and easy. His breath was coffee-scented.

He traced his tongue over the seam of her lips and she closed her eyes. He touched his mouth to each lid, and then continued to her earlobe where he sucked the small gold hoop into his mouth along with the lobe. He gave it a nip, and when she gave a shiver of delight, licked his way up the rim of her ear before bringing his mouth back to hers.

A glow filled her, a warm, easy sensuousness that she floated on like a summer river, afraid to dive deeper.

Afraid even to think about it for fear it wouldn't last.

His tongue slipped into her mouth, sliding along her still closed teeth. She opened them and swayed closer, and he swept inside. Her tongue rose to meet his, and for the first time in forever, she was kissing a man.

Wonder filled her, mixed with the warmth.

He gave a sexy growl that sent tingles up her spine and raised his head long enough to say, "You taste like peaches."

Then he slanted his head and gave her a deep kiss. The kind a man gives a woman he wants to take to bed.

She rose up on her toes to get closer, fingers digging into his shoulders.

The position put her lower belly against his erection. He pressed against her, hard. Insistent.

She stilled. Not pulling away, but not participating any

longer either.

He loosened his grip on her and lifted his head. "That's enough, I think." He pressed a last kiss to her forehead and set her away.

Her eyelids lifted slowly, reluctantly.

A smile tugged at his mouth. She felt a slash of hurt—he found this amusing?—until she saw how his eyes had darkened to midnight.

"Best not to start anything we can't finish."

She gulped. She longed to tell him she wanted to finish it—but she didn't. Not really. It was enough for now that she'd kissed a man without freaking out and going clawed on him.

Her mouth trembled around the edges.

"Hey, it's okay." He tapped her nose.

Her cheeks heated. She clenched her fists and blew out a breath. Both Adric and Suha, the clan healer, had told her repeatedly that she had nothing to be ashamed of. It wasn't her fault she'd been kidnapped and drugged, then forced to submit to the four men in the den. They'd even smashed her quartz so she couldn't shift or draw on its energy.

There was no way she could've stopped them. Four against one just wasn't fair.

She *knew* this—in her head, and maybe even in her heart.

But sometimes the shame still threatened to swamp her. She was a trained fada soldier and her brother's second. She'd helped Adric win control of the clan against impossible odds. More importantly, she was a Gifted strategist, someone who could plot things out so far in advance it was almost like she could predict the future.

So how in Hades had she got caught in Corban's fucking trap?

Fane turned away. She sent him a sad look, but his attention was on the white mist forming in his palm.

A fae message.

Marjani tensed. She edged closer, trying to read it, but the black words scrolling over the mist were in a language she didn't know.

Fane's jaw hardened. The mist dissolved, and he slammed the side of his fist against the wall. "Bloody hell."

"Something wrong?" Uneasiness prickled her scalp even though she knew there were a hundred reasons why Sindre might send Fane a message, none of them having to do with her.

Until he turned, face set. "King Sindre requests the honor of your presence."

Her stomach lurched. "Me? He found out I'm here?"

A curt nod.

"But how?"

His gaze slid from hers. "I told him."

"You told him?" She desperately searched his face. "But why? I thought—"

"Haven't you figured it out?" A self-mocking smile curled his mouth. "I'm his spy, love. He sent me to watch you."

"His *spy*?" She took a step back. "You'd give me to them? Put me in one of those fucking cages?" Her voice rose. It felt like all the air had been sucked from the room.

She swallowed and tried to take a deep breath.

But it was too late. Her cougar awakened. Her claws slid out and a furious growl ripped from her chest.

Fane stiffened but did nothing to defend himself. "No. Not in a cage. That's Lady B's thing, not the king."

She stalked toward him. "You're dead," she said in a thick, barely human voice.

He spread his hands. "You can tear me to pieces, love, but Sindre still wants to see you."

The cougar didn't want to hear that. It tried to force the change on her, but she maintained control—barely.

But both of them wanted blood. She retracted her claws

and reached for her iron dagger. In the next instant, she had Fane backed up to the wall, the knife at the sweet spot over his carotid.

The iron seared his skin. A blister formed at the point, and the scent of burning flesh filled her nostrils. His throat worked, but he remained silent, gazing back with those fucking sky-colored eyes.

"You didn't have to bring me inside the castle." Her voice was harsh with her cougar's rasp. "You could've opened a portal and let me out."

"Would you have left?"

No, but he couldn't have known that. Not for sure. She glared at him without speaking.

"And besides," he added, "the goblins would've caught you. They were hoping to flush you out. The minute we moved away from the wall, they'd have been on us, and you'd be in a cage right now."

She sneered. "Why should I believe you?"

"Because you can scent a lie."

She scowled. But he was right—his scent had the clean bite of truth.

"This way," he said, "you have a chance. The king is old, and frankly, a little bored. Even a spider eventually gets tired of spinning webs. If you interest him, he won't let Lady B get hold of you."

"What do you mean if I interest him?" She pressed the dagger's point deeper.

Blood welled up, and then the iron seared the tiny wound, sealing it. He had to be in pain, but he didn't blink an eye. The man might be a manipulative, two-faced prick, but he was no coward.

"Talk to him," he urged. "That's all I'm saying."

She bared her teeth. "And if I kill you first?"

"That's your choice, of course. But I'm your only friend in

the court."

"My friend?" She sneered. "I'd like to see how you treat your enemies."

His eyes flickered but he stared back calmly until she cursed and released him. Stepping back, she dragged the back of her hand over her mouth in a deliberate gesture.

Wiping the taste of him away.

He had the grace to look ashamed. "I'm sorry. I shouldn't have kissed you."

"You think?" Her look should've fried him where he stood.

Turning on her heel, she strode into the bathroom to rinse her dagger. She shoved it back into her boot and gripped the stone sink, Fane's words thudding in her mind. *If you interest him, he won't let Lady B get hold of you.*

Boredom was a fae weakness, especially with an old fae like Sindre who'd been everywhere, done everything. She'd slit her own throat before she'd be any fae's whore, but maybe she could use Sindre's boredom against him. Play his games for a short while and watch for a chance to escape.

Think, Jani.

But even the most Gifted strategist needed data to work with, and there was too damn much she didn't know. She could guess why Lady Blaer was capturing fada—she fed on their emotional distress—but why did Sindre allow it? And why have her followed? Was it standard procedure, or had he been watching for her—or maybe Adric—in particular?

But anything was better than a cage. To be enclosed like that, trapped and at that fae bitch's mercy…

Her throat closed up. She gulped several breaths and then splashed cold water on her face.

When she returned to the bedroom, Fane was seated on the wood chair gazing down at his clasped hands. He looked…so alone.

Her growl was for herself. She was *not* going to soften

toward the prick.

As he rose to his feet, his gaze swept over her. She tensed, wondering if he'd try and take her knives from her. She'd beg if she had to—without the iron dagger, she was helpless against Sindre. Teeth and claws would be useless against such a powerful fae.

But instead, he asked something totally unexpected. "Do you have to wear the quartz over your heart, or can you hide it somewhere else on your body?"

She instinctively brought her hand to where it was tucked beneath her sweater. "Why?"

He expelled a breath. "You didn't hear this from me, understand?" When she nodded, he continued, "Because if Lady B captures you, you don't want to be wearing that quartz. I can confirm this much—she's figured out a way to control earth fada with their quartz. You can hide that one on your body, and I'll get you another."

Marjani fingered the switchblade in her front pocket. Could she trust Fane? She was still reeling at the big fat secret he'd hidden from her.

But it was true that the fada could be controlled by their quartz. With the right words, a fae could enslave a fada. And apparently Corban had been stupid enough to give Blaer the secret words.

"All right. But I want your promise that you won't tell anyone I switched."

"I promise," he said immediately. "Unless Sindre asks me directly. I can't lie to him."

Can't, he'd said. And something else he'd said niggled at her.

"What do you mean, you can confirm this much? What aren't you telling me?"

"Haven't you figured it out?" He eyed her sorrowfully. "I'm under a *geas*, love. I made a bargain with the king."

15
———

*A*geas.

Marjani's mouth twisted. Fane was bound to the king…had been working for him all this time.

He'd warned her that Sindre had spies everywhere. Hell, he'd flat out told her not to trust him. But had she listened? No.

She'd willingly come with him inside the castle, slept in the same bed. She'd even allowed the bastard to kiss her.

Holy singing crystals, did she know how to pick men.

His eyes flickered, and she knew he'd seen her contempt. He stared down his straight nose at her. "Do you want another quartz or not?"

"Yes." She swallowed and made herself say, "Thank you."

Because if it kept her out of a cage, she'd be grateful to him even if it choked her.

"We don't have much time. Sindre's an impatient man. But I know where I can get one outside the castle. I'll be right back."

And then he was gone, like the Flash in those human movies. One second, he was there; the next, the room was empty.

She sat down and fiddled with the checkers again. But she couldn't focus.

She gazed unseeingly at the red checker in her hand. *I trusted you.*

She felt again his mouth on hers, his hands on her body. He'd been so gentle with her. Careful.

A black rage filled her head. She slammed the checker down on the board, denting the inlaid wood and scattering the other pieces across the table. A few fell on the floor.

With a growl, she gathered up the checkers and returned them to their box before getting up to pace restlessly to and fro. *Forget him. It's Sindre you have to worry about.*

After what felt like an hour but was really only about ten minutes, Fane slipped back into the room with a quartz about the same size as hers. "Will this do?"

She turned the quartz over in her hand. It was an ordinary milky quartz, not amethyst, but it hummed a weak tune. If necessary, she could probably even make it glow to fool the fae.

"I think so. Yeah."

She undid the knot in the leather cord securing her amethyst and tucked it into her bra before tying a new knot around the substitute quartz. She dropped the cord over her head. "I'm ready."

"Jani?" Fane reached for her. When she just stared at his hand, he let it drop to his side. "I'm sorry."

"Why?" Anger and hurt crammed her throat like sharp gravel. "I'm nothing to you. Just a job for the king."

"That's not true."

She picked up her backpack. "Just take me to him."

He blew out a breath and then opened the door. "Fine."

This time, Fane did nothing to conceal Marjani's presence. She attracted plenty of attention with her shaved head, drab clothes, and hiking boots. The looks ranged from coldly appraising to pity.

She stomped past, deliberately slamming her boot heels onto the bright blue tiles.

A pack of goblins trotted up. They swirled around her, snapping and snarling. She hissed and showed her fangs, and they gave high-pitched laughs like fingernails scraping down a chalkboard before continuing by.

The maze grew increasingly complicated, crisscrossing itself and turning abrupt corners. At times the pearly walls pressed in so the two of them had to walk in single file.

"I thought the king wanted to see me," she muttered.

"He has a peculiar sense of humor."

"Fucking awesome."

Disoriented, she drew on her quartz, and discovered that she could "see" a pattern in the maze: two lefts and a right, three rights and a left, and so on, always heading steadily north. It was kind of like plotting a path to kings row in checkers.

She memorized the sequence. If she somehow escaped Sindre with her fur intact, she didn't want to get lost in his damn maze.

"This way." Fane ducked through an archway. At the end of a long hall was a huge oak door, leading to what her internal GPS told her was the north tower.

Her stomach knotted. She palmed her switchblade.

"Put that away, damn it." He grabbed her arm. "You can't fight your way out of this. You have to bargain with him."

He was right, much as she hated to admit it. She shoved the switchblade back into her pocket.

"There. Now let me go."

His grip tightened. "I'm not your enemy. Remember that."

"So you keep saying," she spat back. "And yet here I am."

Fane released her. "I'm sorry."

The black rage washed over her again. "Go to Hades," she grated, and pushed past him.

Fane easily passed her with those long legs of his and

reached the door first. It swung open on silent hinges, and she stalked into the tower on that wave of anger.

She was in a spacious antechamber. A big bodyguard with long black hair and silver eyes gave her a small bow. No scent, but maybe Sindre had given him one of those charms.

"Welcome, senhorita," he said in a southern European accent. "The king is expecting you. You, also," he said to Fane. "Please, enter."

He indicated an arched doorway. Marjani nodded and continued through the door, Fane on her heels. They were in a huge, high-ceilinged room that took up most of the tower. She blinked.

Because it was snowing.

She shot a look up, but no, a glass-and-steel dome capped the tower. And yet, fat white flakes drifted down to settle on the marbled granite floor and the furniture scattered here and there in intimate groupings.

Silver and blue fae lights floated through the falling snow, augmenting the natural light from the long, narrow windows, and leafless trees around the perimeter stretched gnarled limbs toward the feeble sunlight. The walls held towering bookcases filled with leather-bound books and museum-quality vases and statuettes, and an arched doorway like the one they'd come through marked each of the four compass points.

Presiding over it all was an impossibly beautiful man on an ivory velvet couch, one sinewy arm slung along the back, head tipped to the snowflakes. His white-blond hair spilled over broad shoulders, and he wore pale gray pants and a collarless white linen shirt that hugged his lean torso.

Sindre.

She didn't need Fane's whisper to know who he was. The man reeked of silver and power, the kind only an old, old fae could gather.

Not that he looked his age. She knew the king had seen

more than a thousand turns of the sun, but he could've been Fane's slightly older brother. They had the same sculpted features with slanted cheekbones and a straight, definite nose.

He lowered his chin to look at Marjani. She concealed a shiver, because his eyes gave his age away. They were the cold gray of glacial ice, the eyes of a man who's seen entire civilizations come and go.

"Marjani Savonett." Sindre scrutinized her as if she were a butterfly pinned to a corkboard. "Welcome to my court."

The knot in her belly tightened another notch. It was never a good thing when a fae addressed you by your full name.

Setting her backpack by the door, she squared her shoulders and made herself walk forward. "Your highness. Peace to you and yours." She inclined her head. "I apologize if I'm intruding."

Those frosty eyes bored into hers. She forced herself not to squirm.

"You couldn't have entered the castle without an invitation. Who invited you, I wonder?" He glanced at Fane, who remained a little behind her and to the side, feet apart and hands at his sides like a soldier at attention.

"I followed a man in," she said before Fane could reply. "A dark-skinned man with silver hair," she added, carefully sticking to the truth. "He didn't see me. He was on a motorbike."

"Lord Jon?" Sindre asked Fane.

"I wasn't there, your highness."

"No matter." The king returned his gaze to Marjani. "I wanted to meet you, anyway."

She swallowed. "Oh?"

A snowflake landed on her cheek and instantly melted, leaving an icy droplet behind. She brushed it away as Sindre unfolded his long body from the couch and strolled toward her.

She clenched her toes in her boots and remained where she was.

He paused a few feet away, smelling of silver and snow.

She had to tip back her head to meet his eyes. He was even taller than Fane, with eyebrows and lashes the same white-blond as his hair. The snowflakes caught on them, forming glittering crystals.

Her fingers twitched. She'd never craved the reassurance of one of her knives so much, even though Sindre would probably freeze her in her tracks—literally—before she could stick a blade into him. Ice fae drew life-energy from the movement of molecules. Even young ice fae could suck the energy out of liquid water, turning it to ice, and the most powerful could draw energy from living things.

"You did well, Fane," Sindre said without taking his gaze from her. "Bringing her to me. I like a man who thinks for himself."

Out of the corner of her eye, she saw Fane give a tight nod.

Her lungs constricted. Was that what he'd done? *Brought* her to Sindre?

Fane shot her a miserable look.

Don't think about it. Whatever Fane had or hadn't done wasn't important now. Not with this beautiful, deadly male eyeing her like a hungry lion would a rabbit.

Her chin lifted. "I brought myself. If Fane helped, he was only doing what I wanted."

Sindre quirked a brow. "I beg your pardon." His voice was soft and silky. Mocking.

She shrugged, out of her depth and sinking fast. Gods, she hated playing fae games. But the rage still burned in her, and it was rapidly being transferred to this mocking male.

She set her jaw. "Are you going to put me in one of those iron cages?"

Displeasure flitted across his face. "You know about the

cages?" The falling snow came down harder, and the already cool tower grew even chillier.

"Why? Are they a secret?" She deliberately didn't glance at Fane, but Sindre did.

"A secret? That's a strong word for it." He paced a slow circle around her, his expensive leather shoes kicking up the snow into small white clouds. "But an envoy should know better than to share my private business."

She turned with him. "The man in that cage is *my* business."

"Not anymore. He renounced your brother as his alpha."

Was there anything Sindre didn't know? Fuck trying to talk her way out of this. She might be a strategist, but she had the feeling he was five moves ahead of her.

She slipped her iron dagger from her boot. "Look, just let me leave and—" At a sound behind her, she broke off and whirled around, backing up so she could keep Sindre in sight.

The big, long-haired guard sprinted toward her, an iron dagger in each hand. She gripped her dagger and took a fighting stance.

The king flung up a hand. "Stop. I'll handle this."

The guard halted, and then with a jerk of his chin, sheathed his daggers. But he remained in the tower, standing beneath a twisted gray tree with his arms folded over his broad chest.

She turned back to Sindre. "I swear I'm not here to mess with you or any of your people. That fada you have in the cage? He's my enemy. I'm not here to release him—in fact, I came to kill him."

"And if I'd like you to stay here at the court for a few days? We get so few fada visitors."

"A few days? And then I can leave?"

The king's mouth curved. "It's a deal." He held out his hand for Marjani to shake.

Behind him, Fane gave a tiny shake of his head.

She licked dry lips. Fane had deceived her—and yet, for some damn reason, she trusted him to help her to the extent he could.

"What, exactly," she asked Sindre, "are the terms of this deal?"

The king brought his hand back to his side. "You owe me, Marjani Savonett. You *will* stay for as long as I desire."

Crap, there was her full name again. At least he didn't know her true-name, the one given to her by her parents. But she still felt a pull to obey him.

"I owe you? How?"

"You spent the night in my castle. You ate my food, drank my ale."

Fane made a small movement. "That was my food, willingly shared. She ate and drank nothing of yours. And she stayed in my room."

"But I own you," Sindre returned.

Fane's eyes flickered. But he just replied calmly, "Room and board when I'm at the court are part of the terms."

Marjani's gaze darted between the two men. Was it true? She didn't actually owe Sindre anything?

The king's mouth compressed. He strolled past her, hands clasped behind his back. She stayed in place, gripping the dagger and turning with him in a strange little dance.

He halted. "Name your price. Cash. Land. Precious stones." He flicked his fingers, and a handful of diamonds the size of walnuts showered onto a round marble table.

Marjani's jaw slackened.

"Well?" Sindre demanded.

She wrenched her gaze from the glittering pile. "I'm not for sale."

"No? Then take it and give it to your brother Adric. He's done his best, but it will be a long time before your clan recovers from the Darktime. And meanwhile, you live in your cramped city dens instead of running free as your animals. You have so few young—one or two live births a year at most. If something doesn't happen soon—or if Adric dies—your clan won't survive."

"Damn you," she breathed. Because it was true. Every word of it.

And together, those diamonds were probably worth more than the entire clan made in a year.

She fingered the dagger's ivory handle. "Stay here at the court. What does that mean?"

"You'll be my guest. No cages, I promise."

"And how long is a few days?"

"That's negotiable. A turn of the sun, perhaps more."

"And my duties?"

Suddenly, Sindre was right in front of her. He ran a finger down her cheek. "Take the diamonds. I promise you'll enjoy yourself. And your brother will thank you."

She sent a last look at the diamonds and backed up. Because she couldn't do it, not even for the clan. And Adric wouldn't thank her. In fact, if she sold her freedom for the clan, it just might break him.

"I said, I'm not for sale."

"As you say." Sindre snapped his fingers.

A black-haired female with an Irish woman's creamy skin appeared with two crystal flutes balanced on a silver tray. She crossed the floor with a supple grace that reminded Marjani of a fada, although she didn't smell like a fada.

In fact, like the big guard, she had no scent at all. And why did the guard look so familiar?

Sindre took the crystal flutes from her tray and offered one to Marjani. "Champagne?"

She shook her head. No way was she going to take even a single thing from this man. "No thanks."

With a shrug, he took a sip of champagne, and then set

both glasses back on the tray. The woman set the tray on a side table and then gathered up the diamonds, placing them in a drawer that opened in the trunk of one of the leafless trees before going to stand next to the big, expressionless guard.

Sindre strolled closer, his gray eyes glinting like sun on ice. She stared into them, mesmerized.

Why fight him? She wasn't mated. It might even be fun... And he was so fucking beautiful.

Fane cleared his throat. "Excuse me. Frog in my throat."

But the spell was broken. Sindre scowled, and she realized he'd tried to ensnare her with a glamour.

Inside, the cat angrily swished its tale.

"What about power?" the king asked. "You're strong. Smart. You must've wondered why your brother is alpha instead of you."

Her mouth moved in a soundless no, but she couldn't make herself utter it out loud—because it would be a lie. She *had* wondered. She'd been at Adric's side from the start. They acted almost as co-alphas, making most decisions together. But the final say was his.

Sindre pressed his advantage. "You could be alpha instead. Your power would be such that your brother would willingly follow you. In fact, you could allow him to remain as alpha of your home clan and rule over all the earth fada clans. Think about it." Soft, seductive tones. "All you have to do in exchange is stay with me for a little while. No cage—I promise. And then you'd be free to go home and take your place as the most powerful earth fada in the world."

Her palms were sweating. She tightened her grip on the dagger. Yeah, she was tempted—who wouldn't be?

But deep down, she knew Adric made a better alpha than she ever would. He wasn't just strong, he was a natural leader. She might be the one with the Gift of strategy, but he had both vision and the ability to gain people's cooperation. The clan followed him because they believed in him, trusted that he had their best interests at heart.

And he'd earned her loyalty a hundred times over.

"No," she said in a clear, strong voice. "I have all the power I need. Just let me go."

Sindre stared at her for a moment that stretched on and on until Marjani's nerves screamed with the tension.

"All right," he said at last. "I have one last offer for you."

A hush fell over the room. At some point, the snow had stopped falling.

Her gut tingled uneasily. This was it. The offer he'd been leading up to, the one he expected to clinch the deal.

But what could he offer besides wealth and power?

For some reason she glanced at where the man and woman waited by the tree. Their faces were expressionless, the perfect servants. But she could've sworn they were urging her to say no.

Fane spoke. "Your highness?"

"What?" Sindre growled.

"Pardon the interruption, but as you know, the woman is the Baltimore alpha's only sister. It wouldn't do to make an enemy of him."

The king brushed that away with a wave of his elegant hand. "But does he want to make an enemy of me?"

"Still," Fane said. "Lord Adric won't let this go. He recently did a favor for the sun fae, and the queen might ally herself with him."

Actually, that favor had been done over six years ago, and the sun fae had paid Adric well. But Marjani wasn't stupid enough to point that out.

Sindre seated himself on the couch again, his arms stretched along the back like the wings of a large bird of prey. "But if our guest agrees, then how could he possibly be upset?"

Fane opened his mouth to argue, but Sindre cut him off. "Let her answer." His pale eyes turned on her. "I can gift you with a protection charm that would make you impossible to kill. No one could even *touch* you without your permission. Think about it. No one could hurt you, ever again."

She swallowed sickly. "What do you know about that?"

A shrug. "I hear things. Knowledge, after all, is power. Think about it. You'd never be afraid again."

She stared at him. To never feel afraid again. Never to feel helpless. That would be a gift indeed.

Temptation sucked at her, seductive as Sindre's glamour.

Because those feral river fada had stripped her bare in the worst possible way. They'd tricked her into drinking an aphrodisiac, a powerful magical drug. She'd started out fighting them, but in the end, she'd lost all her pride and begged for more.

Suha had explained it was the fault of the aphrodisiac. The drug made you crave sensation—the pleasure of sex, the bite of pain...

"You survived, honey," the healer had told her, over and over. "That's the important thing. No one could've held out against the dose they gave you."

But Marjani couldn't shake the shame. That she'd lost control, begged her rapists for more...she, a soldier and Adric's second-in-command.

"No." She backed toward the exit, dagger out, hoping no one saw the tremble in her hand. "I can protect myself."

"Can you?"

The click of high heels sounded behind her. Marjani spun around as the bodyguard moved to intercept the newcomer.

"It's Lady Blaer," said Sindre. "Let her in."

The guard inclined his head. "As you wish." He ushered in the fae lady with a flourish just this side of mocking.

"My lord." She crossed to where Sindre sat on the couch and placed an air kiss on each of his cheeks before turning to Marjani. "So you found the other fada."

The *other* fada? Marjani glanced at Fane, but he seemed as puzzled as she was.

"You're trying to strike a bargain with her, aren't you?" Blaer's black gaze moved over Marjani.

An icy sweat trickled down her vertebrae.

"And if I am?" Sindre said.

"Perhaps I can help."

"Be my guest."

Anger flared in Marjani. Typical fae, discussing her as if she weren't there—as if she were somehow less than them. *Well, fuck you, too.*

A growl vibrated her chest. Inside, the cat tried to claw its way out. She was tempted to let it, but first, she needed more information.

Blaer's eyes narrowed. "It was you in my tower earlier, wasn't it? If you're here to free Corban, I might take you in his place."

Marjani stared back stonily.

"Not him, then." The fae woman nodded—and went for the jugular. "But what about the big brown wolf?"

Marjani's heart skipped a beat. "What big brown wolf?"

"I didn't get his name. Yet."

Marjani's stomach hollowed. *Please don't let it be Luc.*

She'd been half-expecting him ever since she landed in Iceland. When she hadn't seen him, she'd figured Adric had held him off, that her brother had trusted she could handle this herself.

She should've known better.

Blaer's pink lips stretched in triumph. Meanwhile, Sindre looked on detached, like they were pawns on a chessboard being pushed around for his amusement.

Marjani's fury spiked. Inside, her cougar spat and snarled. Luc might not be her mate, but he was a friend. A good one.

"Look, bitch." She stepped closer to Blaer, crowding her.

"It's one thing to cage a man who's turned his back on us. But mess with the brown wolf, and you'll be sorry. We'll hunt you down." She touched her dagger to Blaer's stomach where the poison from the iron would do the most damage.

"Is that a threat?" the mixed-blood fae hissed back.

"Yeah." She let the cat blaze into her eyes. "It is."

"But your clan tried that already, remember? When Sindre hired you to find me. Your brother sent Corban after me, and look how that turned out." Ignoring the dagger, Blaer leaned closer. "Do. Your. Worst. *Fada.*"

"Blaer, *min*," Sindre interrupted. "You don't have my permission to bargain with the fada."

"No?" Blaer slanted him a smile. "I'm only trying to help, my lord. She's worried about that brown wolf. He's a friend, maybe more. You could use him as leverage."

"So I gathered." He raised a blond brow at Marjani. "So what do you say? Will you trade your freedom for his?"

Her limbs locked.

The king's mouth curved. He'd won, and he knew it.

She fingered the dagger. Sweet Goddess, she wanted to thrust it into his conniving heart. "I want to see this wolf first."

"Your highness." Fane again. "Let her go. This is beneath you."

Without taking his gaze from her, Sindre flicked his fingers. Magic hummed in the air. She gasped as frost spread up Fane's legs. He sucked in a breath and locked his knees.

Blaer watched with an avid expression, clearly feeding on his pain.

"Accept the bargain," the king told Marjani. "Or Fane dies."

No. Hell, no.

Fane was nothing to her. The man had been lying to her ever since she arrived. Maybe not straight out, but lies of omission were still lies. He'd let her think he was on her side when the whole time he'd been spying on her.

The ice covered Fane's chest and crept toward his throat. He moved his mouth but the only sound he could make was a croak that raised every hair on her body.

His eyes met hers, desperate and yet stoic.

She swung back to Sindre. "Enough," she gritted. "I said I'll bargain with you. But first, I want to see this wolf."

The king cast a pointed look at her dagger. Without taking her gaze from his, she bent and shoved it into its sheath.

"Happy?" she growled as she straightened back up.

"Very," was the silky reply.

16

———

*I*t had been a long time since Fane had been subjected to one of Sindre's punishments. He'd forgotten how much it hurt.

And the king was a master at dragging out the torture.

His feet went cold, and then hot, as if they'd been plunged into an ice bath. Then they went numb. The ice crept up his body as Sindre sucked energy from vital molecules.

It was like being buried alive. His heart and lungs slowed. He couldn't move or speak.

Panic galloped up his spine, and he couldn't even beg for mercy because his fucking vocal cords wouldn't work. He stood there, frozen in place, hoping he wouldn't lose his balance and topple to the floor.

Just when he thought that this time Sindre meant to kill him, the king waved his hand and the ice melted. Now the real agony began as his frozen limbs came back to life. First, his hands and feet pricked like a thousand needles were being driven into them, then the nerve endings lit up like he'd been set on fire.

He put his hands on his thighs and bent over, sucking in oxygen and shaking so hard his teeth clattered like castanets.

"Come." Sindre held out a hand to Marjani.

Fane jerked up his head. "No," he rasped as the king teleported her out of the room, followed immediately by Blaer. "You bloody bastard."

The terms of the *geas* bound him to obey Sindre's direct orders in return for his generous pay—he was a millionaire in the human world—but the king hadn't thought to forbid Fane to follow. Probably figured he wouldn't dare.

What could he do against two fae as powerful as Sindre and Blaer? But he couldn't just return to his room without trying to help Marjani. He felt enough of a coward as it was.

Pushing himself upright, he staggered to the door and leaned against the jamb, lungs heaving.

Gods, he'd never hated himself so much as when he'd confessed to Marjani that he'd been spying on her.

That was the problem with a *geas*. You never knew when it would turn around and bite you in the arse. Back when he'd made the agreement with Sindre, it had seemed like a good idea. He was forty years old and his human mom had just died. He'd been making a living as a fisherman in Newfoundland. His dad had set him up with his own boat, and he had a crew of two, men he'd grown up with. But already his friends had started to comment on how Fane never seemed to age.

And he'd itched to see more of the world.

Then he'd discovered he had this Gift for moving fast...and disappearing. When he'd shown his dad, Arne had invited him to the ice fae court to meet Sindre, saying, "The king can always use another wayfarer."

A fae king's envoy? Fane had jumped at the chance. Hell, it was an opportunity most men would've killed for—and Fane felt a little as if he had.

Only the man he'd slain was himself. As the king's envoy, he'd seen things that had made his blood curdle.

He'd never directly harmed someone, but no one would call him innocent. With each decade, a bit more of him died, until he was becoming as jaded as a pureblood.

But he'd be damned if he'd let Marjani get sucked into this world.

Think. He pressed a hand to his pounding head.

He couldn't ignore a direct command from Sindre, but the king hadn't ordered Fane *not* to help her. So he had to get her away from the king before he could invoke the *geas*.

The black-haired guard opened the door for Fane. A Portuguese river fada, he was under a *geas*, too, along with his Irish mate. The Irishwoman came up on Fane's other side.

"Go after her," she hissed. "Before it's too late."

Fane lurched into the hall and started toward the east tower.

There was no way he could use his Gift to race to Marjani. Even a slow walk was agony, each step spiking pain up his legs. He gritted his teeth and concentrated on putting one foot in front of the other.

The maze was suddenly in a forgiving mood; or more likely, Sindre was too distracted to play his games. Instead of hindering Fane, the path led him straight to Blaer's tower.

By the time he arrived, he was covered in a cold sweat. The three flights loomed before him like a steep mountain. He clutched the banister and started climbing. By the second landing, his heart felt like it was about to explode out of his chest. He halted to catch his breath, and then grimly continued up.

The thick oak door was shut tight. No chance of sneaking in.

The hell with it, then. He shoved it open.

Marjani stood between Sindre and Blaer, staring at the new

fada. Fane's stomach twisted. She looked so small and defenseless between the pair of tall, blond fae.

Blaer flicked him a speculative glance, but Sindre's gaze was locked on Marjani, his lean face hungry. Like she was a special treat, one he intended to savor for long hours.

Nearby, the black wolf lay on its side, eyes closed and tongue hanging out of its mouth, panting softly. But Marjani only had eyes for the rangy earth fada crouched in the cage next to the black wolf's. He was naked save for his quartz. Deep scratches and bites marred his teak skin—the poor bastard must have been caught by the goblins—and his face was bruised, his eyes swollen shut.

Marjani bit her lower lip. "Oh, Luc."

At her voice, the man started. "Jani?"

"Yeah."

He pulled himself up to his full height, glaring at Sindre and Blaer from beneath swollen lids before looking back at her. "You're here."

The king set a hand on Marjani's arm, but she shook him off to move closer to her friend. To Fane's surprise, Sindre allowed it. But then, he was a canny man, and patient when it suited him.

She shook her head sorrowfully. "You had to follow me, didn't you?"

Luc's bloodied mouth turned up in a lopsided grin. "You knew I would."

She blew out a breath. "Yeah. But I hoped I was wrong."

"You're all right?" The fada moved as close to the iron bars as he could without touching them. "Those motherfuckers haven't hurt you?" His fierce look included all three of them: Sindre, Blaer and Fane.

"I'm fine. But you…"

The fada's hard face softened. "Don't worry about me." He

reached for the bars and then stopped himself from grabbing them just in time. His hands fisted.

"Let her go," he growled at Sindre. "You've got me and Corban. I'll agree to anything you say if you just let her go."

Blaer's dark eyes glowed, lapping up his fear and anger.

"No!" exclaimed Marjani. "Don't make any promises. Let me handle this."

"Actually," the king said, "Marjani and I were about to make a deal."

"Like hell," Luc snarled. His claws slid out and his teeth lengthened so he looked barely human. "Let me out of this fucking cage. Fight me like a real man."

"Is that what real men do?" Sindre asked, interested. "Fight?"

"You win." Marjani whirled to face him. "Let him go. I'll stay here in his place."

"Jani, no!" The fada rammed a shoulder against the cage's iron door. It seared his skin with a sickening hiss, but he did it again and again before giving up to stare helplessly at Marjani. Red stripes from the bars marked his shoulder and arm, and the stomach-turning odor of burnt flesh filled the tower.

"*No.*" Fane was across the room before he'd realized he moved. He grabbed Marjani's arm. "Bargain with him. Make him set a time limit or you'll be here the rest of your life."

Sindre's brows pinched together. "You become tedious, Fane. Step away from her."

He clenched his fists—and then obeyed. Because he had to.

"Bargain with him," he muttered one last time.

"Come, your highness." Marjani crossed her arms and tilted her head to one side. "Surely you don't think a fada can best you in a bargain? What are your terms?"

"A year and a day—in my court."

Her eyes narrowed. "How long would that be in my world?"

Good. She was using that intelligent brain of hers.

"About ten turns of the sun," the king replied.

"And what would my duties be?"

A smile curved Sindre's lips. "To entertain me."

"*No.*" Luc's snarl tore through the room. He slammed against the cage over and over, uncaring of his seared and bruised flesh.

Marjani's chin jutted. "I won't be your whore."

The king inclined his head. "If anything happens, it will be with your full cooperation."

For some reason, that made her freeze. Her lips went white around the edges. "You'll swear to that."

"I will."

Suddenly, Fane couldn't bear it. Sindre had dark tastes— and ways of ensuring an unwilling person's cooperation. A year and a day with him would age Marjani in ways she couldn't know.

He dragged in a breath. The hell with it. He'd break the *geas*. He couldn't live with himself if he stood by while Marjani bound herself to Sindre.

Then Blaer stepped forward and grabbed the quartz around Marjani's neck. Marjani's hand shot out, gripping the fae's wrist.

The two women stared at each other. Marjani's lip peeled to show a single sharp canine. "Let. It. Go."

Blaer squeezed the milky chunk of rock and shot Sindre a triumphant grin. "You don't have to bargain with the animal, my lord. She'll do anything I say."

Sindre shook his head, but remained silent as Blaer tightened her grip on the substitute quartz.

"You're in my power now, fada," she said gleefully. "Drop to your knees."

Marjani stared back. Blaer's brow creased.

Marjani exploded into action, tossing Luc a stiletto at the same time she jerked her head back, ripping the quartz from

Blaer's hand. A moment later she was airborne. Her booted feet struck Blaer's chest. The fae staggered backward.

Marjani was right there. She aimed a roundhouse kick at Blaer's solar plexus, dropping her to the floor.

Sindre raised his hand, preparing to freeze Marjani.

Pulling her dagger from her boot, she darted forward and sliced his arm. Blood welled, soaking the white linen. Sindre's breath sucked in. He eyed the slash in disbelief, and then lunged for Marjani.

She danced away in Fane's direction. He grabbed her wrist and somehow managed to summon the energy to conceal them both.

Luc inserted the stiletto's skinny blade in the cage's lock. It released with a click.

"Get Jani out of here," he said in Fane's general direction as he shoved open the door. He leapt at Sindre, shifting in mid-air to a huge brown wolf. He slammed Sindre to the floor just as the king opened his mouth, probably to order Fane to release Marjani.

Fane hustled her toward the door, but she dug in her heels and tried to twist out of his grip. "Let me go, damn it. I'm not leaving without Luc."

A cursing Blaer rose to her feet. Blood trickled from her mouth and her pale skin was bruised from her struggle with Marjani, but a powerful fae like her could heal in minutes from a blow that would've broken the ribs of a human.

Her gaze swung in Marjani and Fane's direction. Dark tendrils slid over his skin. Despair filled him.

Give yourself up—you'll never escape.

They had to leave. Now, while Sindre was occupied with fighting Luc and couldn't order Fane to release Marjani. Because when it came down to it, he wasn't sure he'd have the strength to resist the compulsion the *geas* put on him.

Marjani slashed at him with her dagger. "I said, let me go."

He leapt back just as the blade ripped through his sweater, narrowly missing his stomach. His mouth dropped open. The woman had tried to disembowel him.

Fuck this.

He twisted her right arm behind her back and shoved her into the hall. There, he clamped both arms around her from behind, immobilizing her arms against her body, and raced down the stairs, Marjani fighting him the whole way. Twice, she nearly escaped, but somehow he managed to hang on to her.

He dashed for the nearest exit, and a few seconds later, they were outside the castle by a little-used portal. Still gripping her, he flicked his fingers and muttered the incantation, and then jumped through into the human world.

Unfortunately, to shut the portal required both hands. As soon as he released Marjani, she leapt for the shimmering circle. He rapped out the correct words and made the closing motion with both hands, wayfarer-fast, and then grabbed her by the waist and hung on until it contracted, leaving them on the outside.

Marjani rounded on him. "You asshole." She crouched, her dagger raised. "Let me back in—*now*. I won't leave without Luc."

Jealousy twisted through him. What was the other man to her?

He dragged in a breath. "No."

"No?" She growled and lunged at him with the knife, but this time he was ready and easily evaded her.

"No. The goblins would be on you the second you stepped through. Because you can bet Lady B is sending them after us. You didn't make a bargain with the king, so as far as she's concerned, you're fair game. And she'll have his blessing, because he wants you, too."

She stared at him, both of them panting. High above, the sun peeked out from behind a fluffy white cloud. It was noon—

a point in their favor. Goblins were nocturnal; Blaer would have to wake them, buying him and Marjani a little time—as long as they didn't waste time arguing.

"Please," he said. "Your friend—Luc—doesn't want you there. You heard him. He told me to get you out."

"Fuck that. You want to go, fine. I don't need you. Just let me back in."

He set his jaw. So bloody self-sufficient, she was. But a woman didn't get so self-sufficient unless life had made her that way.

"How about if I promise I'll help you get back in? But not right now. You saw what the goblins did to your friend. Their orders will be to bring you back alive, but Lady B won't care if they beat the shit out of you first. Please. Just come with me until we can figure out a plan." He held out his hand.

Marjani's mouth compressed into a tight line, but she put her hand in his. "If he dies," she ground out, "I'll never forgive you. *Never.*"

Still weak and hurting from Sindre's attack, he glared down at her. He'd just thwarted the ice fae king for her, putting his own life on the line, and all she wanted to do was put herself back in the king's power.

And on top of that, now Blaer was after them, too.

It was a hell of a time to realize he was falling in love with the woman.

"At least you'll be alive," he gritted.

17

———

uc slammed into Sindre's chest. He fell down and the two of them rolled across the floor.

The ice fae king was strong. He had to be hurting as the iron entered his system, but he didn't show it. Luc strained to reach the king's pale neck and the carotid pulsing so temptingly beneath his ear. But Sindre dug his fingers into Luc's fur, holding him off long enough to mutter a few words.

The air around the king shimmered and he 'ported across the tower. Luc loped after him. As he gathered his muscles to leap, Sindre flung up a hand.

Icy fingers reached inside Luc's chest and squeezed his heart. He dropped like a stone to the floor and lay there, writhing with pain.

Blaer hurried over and grabbed Luc's quartz. He groaned, the pain even worse than what Sindre had done to him.

"Freeze," she hissed, and his muscles locked. He lay on the floor, twitching and humiliated as she yanked the pendant off his head.

"No," he rasped. He tried to make his hand move so he could snatch it back from her. But he couldn't.

"I know the secret," she whispered. "Even the king doesn't know what I know. That it's easiest for a night fae to get to the heart of your quartz."

She chanted the secret words, and dark talons closed around the magic at the center of his quartz. The humming crystals stuttered, and then started up a new, unfamiliar music —a tune that somehow connected him to Blaer.

His bowels iced.

Her lips curved. "You have to obey me."

"*No,*" he said, but it was the last, desperate gasp of a drowning man.

Sindre came up beside her, nursing his injured arm. "Blaer, *min.* Do you really need two? Fane has a point. We don't want to get the earth fada all stirred up. I'll have to fight back, and that might bring the sun fae into this. The queen seems to have adopted the local fada."

Blaer moved a smooth shoulder. "I wasn't planning to keep this one. He's simply bait. The female will come back for him."

"You seem so sure."

"I am. Clan is everything to them—she won't leave Iceland without him."

Sindre's mouth curved. "And when she does, I'll be waiting."

"Exactly."

They exchanged a smile. Then Sindre said, "I'll just take care of this one for you." He 'ported Luc back into the cage and slammed the door shut, then glanced at his bloody arm. "I suppose I'd better have a healer look at this."

The fae lady nodded. "And if I may summon the goblins?"

"I thought you were sure she'll return."

"I am. But it wouldn't hurt to offer her a little incentive."

They headed out the door, ignoring Luc's furious growl.

The last thing he heard was Blaer asking, "And you? What are you going to do about the mixed-blood?"

"Don't worry," the king returned. "He can't go far without my permission."

18

———

*T*hrice-damned interfering prick.

Marjani glowered at Fane, moving grim-faced beside her on those long, ground-eating legs. She could've cheerfully slit his throat and walked away smiling.

And why was he helping her, anyway? There was nothing in it for him. In fact, Sindre was going to be out for his blood. And she'd seen how scary a pissed-off Sindre could be.

Her heart clenched—not for Fane, who deserved whatever he got—but for Luc.

Gods, she hated to leave him behind with Sindre and that fae bitch. Luc must know Marjani wouldn't abandon him. Still, that didn't make her feel any less guilty. She'd known Luc would follow her, with or without Adric's say-so.

They covered a mile, then another at a slower pace. Fane wavered, hand to his chest, lips white. He must be running on fumes.

She scowled. "You okay?"

He nodded and pressed on, going slower and slower until he was stumbling forward, feet dragging.

"You have to rest." She grabbed his arm, worried in spite of herself.

He placed his hands on his thighs and dragged in a breath. "My energy. The king...drained me. Almost gone." He nodded at a pile of boulders. "In there...a cavern."

"I'm on it." She wrapped her arm around his waist. "Lean on me."

He tried to pull away. "Too...heavy."

"I'm stronger than I look." She tightened her arm around his waist.

"Stubborn." But he let himself lean on her.

"Yeah, I get that a lot." She headed toward the boulders, half-dragging, half-carrying him.

"There." He indicated a fissure in the boulders. "A cave. Secret."

She snorted. The fissure didn't look big enough for a very skinny elf. "You're kidding, right?"

He grimaced without answering. Okay, now she was definitely worried. In her experience, Fane had a ready response to just about anything. If he wasn't talking, he must really feel shitty.

They had to turn sideways to get through the opening. She pushed him in first, frowning when he stopped to rest his forehead on a boulder.

"Keep going." She nudged him. "You can do it."

He lurched into movement again, eyes half-closed, feeling his way along the boulders. The passageway turned down and tunneled underground. Things went completely dark, and her eyes went night-glow. Not that there was much to see except the rough basalt pressed up against her cheek. Still, it was easier for her; Fane might be lean, but he was still bigger than her.

The tunnel narrowed even more. Fane halted, his cheek against the rock, panting raggedly.

A high-pitched, excited chittering came from far away. The

goblins, still distant but moving in their direction. Goose pimples popped up all over her body.

"Move," she said in a hard voice and nudged him with her hip.

He continued to inch sideways, her following—until his shoulders got caught.

She muttered a curse. "You sure you've done this before?"

"Yeah...my secret...place."

"Well, then, you've gained some weight."

That earned her a weak chuckle.

"Okay. When I give the word, blow out your breath—and say a fucking prayer." She managed to turn enough to shove his nearest shoulder with both hands. "*Now.*"

He exhaled with a grunt. There was a tearing sound as his shirt ripped, and then he was through. She slipped after him.

Shortly after that, the passage widened, and suddenly, they were in a small underground cavern. A crack in the ceiling let in enough light to show walls of rough gray basalt. At the opposite end, a turquoise-blue thermal pool steamed gently.

Fane fell to his hands and knees, chest heaving. Marjani almost knelt down next to him, just to give thanks.

"Hey." She touched his back. "You still with me?"

"Don't feel...so good..." He collapsed the rest of the way and curled up on the cavern floor.

Her breath caught. He looked so still, his face pale under his golden tan, mouth a bluish-pink. But his chest was moving.

She gave him a shake. "Damn it, Fane. You better not die on me."

No response.

Dragging off her sweater, she draped it over his chest before sitting cross-legged on the stone floor to take stock.

The cavern was a rough oval shape about ten feet wide and twenty feet long. They had light and fresh air from that crack in the ceiling. But the best part was the thermal pool. The steaming blue water kept the cavern at a comfortable temperature.

And she still had her knives—and her quartz, thanks to Fane.

That was the good news.

The bad news was she was holed up with an unconscious man and no food. She thought longingly of the backpack she'd left in Sindre's tower and everything inside it, including the fishing knife.

At least they had water. She'd done her research and knew Iceland had some of the cleanest water in the world. She glanced again at the pool. The water might smell of sulfur, but it was drinkable. All in all, her cat approved of their temporary den—it was safely underground, easy to defend, and even had its own water supply.

And she could hunt for food, assuming it was safe to go outside. She glanced at the ceiling crack, straining to hear the goblins. For now, it was quiet.

Fane dragged in a breath and pillowed his head on his arm. At some point, he'd lost the leather tie around his hair and blond strands spilled over his shoulders. Her fingers twitched, recalling how silky it had felt when he'd kissed her.

Then she recalled how he'd played her and balled those fingers into a fist. All that time she'd thought he'd been helping her, and instead, the prick had been spying on her.

You were a job to him, nothing more.

Then why had he held her in bed last night without asking for more?

And this morning, why had he obtained a decoy quartz for her—and then helped her escape?

Gods, even after Sindre's attack, he'd come to Blaer's tower. To help her, Marjani.

The man was a fucking onion, with layers upon layers. She had a feeling she could know him for a decade and still not understand how his mind worked. And the bitch of it was, she wouldn't mind sticking around for that long. Fane intrigued her. Inside, her cat hummed agreement.

She scowled and removed her quartz from her bra. For now, she'd keep the other quartz around her neck as a decoy. She didn't think she could stand losing her real quartz again. Once in a lifetime had been enough.

She bit the inner side of her cheek. A part of her would always mourn her first quartz. The pain as the men ripped it from her had been excruciating, like having her heart torn out, and when they'd smashed it in front of her, the agony had doubled and redoubled.

Only a mate or close relative could touch an earth fada's quartz without it hurting. Bad.

And that had just been the start...

She exhaled and dragged her thoughts back to the present.

Time to report to Adric. She hadn't intended to call him until Corban was dead, but he needed to know what was going on with Blaer and her cages. The other earth fada alphas should be informed, and maybe even the water fada clans. This was bigger than Marjani trying to prove herself.

She tapped a slight depression, accessing the quartz's smartphone. Another tap pinged Adric.

He answered immediately. "Jani? You okay? Where the fuck are you? It's been over a month."

For some damn reason, her eyes stung. Goddess, she missed him. The two of them had never been apart for this long. She could just picture him scrubbing a hand over his spiky hair, his hard face a mixture of anger and worry.

He was as much feared as loved. Very few people saw the big heart concealed behind that ruthless façade. But Marjani did.

Adric was only two years older than her, and the two of them were more like twins than siblings, especially after the death of their mom and dad. You tended to bond with someone when you were fighting for survival.

This past year, her brother had been so damn patient with her, gently coaxing her back to something resembling a normal life again. He'd fed her. Talked to her, even though she spent most days as her cat. Asked her advice when her only response was a twitch of her tail.

When she'd gotten so depressed that all she did was lie on the living room rug staring into the fireplace, he'd changed to his cougar and slept curled next to her, knowing that what she needed most of all was touch. And when nightmares left her whimpering and shaken, he nudged her awake and told her stories from their childhood.

Without him, she'd have gone completely feral.

"Jani?" Adric said. "You still there?"

She gave a hard swallow. "I'm fine." She glanced around the cavern and decided her brother didn't need to know everything. "And don't worry, I'm safe."

Then she realized what he'd said. "What do you mean it's been over a month? What day is it?"

"August thirty-first."

"Holy shit. By my reckoning it's only August eighth."

"So you got inside the ice fae court."

"Yeah," she said, still reeling at how much time she'd lost. "And Ric, Luc did, too, but they caught him. Put him in a fucking iron cage. I got him out, but I'm not sure he got away. The last I saw he was fighting with the ice fae king."

"A cage? The king put him in a cage?" Her brother's voice was chillier than Sindre's tower.

She shook her head. "That's the strange thing. The king definitely knows about it, but the person behind it seems to be a lady in his court—a Lady B, who's also the woman the king hired you to track down in India."

"The fae lady I sent Corban after?"

"Yeah. And Ric, it's bad. She knows the secret of our quartzes. She grabbed mine and tried to use it to compel me, but I'd switched it out for a fake quartz. Corban must've told her."

Adric muttered something dark. Only a few fae knew the secret of controlling the earth fada through their quartz—and those fae had been either bribed or threatened into keeping quiet. "What the hell's going on?"

"It's a long story. I promise I'll explain everything when I get back. For now, you need to get the word out to the other earth fada clans."

"Agreed. I'll contact the other alphas as soon as we're done. And Corban?"

"He's in an iron cage, too, completely under her power. I was told they were lovers, but now he's her prisoner. There's no way he could've sent that message to you on his own."

"But it was his writing. The motherfucker tried to sell me out to save himself."

"Yeah. Or she ordered him to send the message." She rubbed a thumb over the quartz's chunky crystals. "He's sick, Ric. Iron poisoning. It's bad—he's almost gone."

"Saves you the trouble of offing him."

She huffed a laugh with zero humor. "There is that."

"Where are you now?"

"Safe in a cavern about three miles from the court. The court itself is in a castle carved out of a dead volcano." She gave him the castle's precise coordinates, knowing he'd file the information for future use. "You can't see it in the human world. It's completely hidden behind *look-away* spells and warded to keep out intruders. The only way in is through portals that the ice fae have to open."

"So how did you get inside?"

She glanced at Fane, curled into a ball and shivering helplessly. Somehow, she couldn't bring herself to tell Adric that the

SOB had played her. Her brother didn't need another reason to question her judgment—and besides, Fane was Evie's father, and she liked Evie. Jace's mate might be mostly human, but she was good people.

"Evie's father helped me." It was the truth—just not the whole truth.

"He knew who you were?"

"Yeah. Turns out he's a wayfarer. He was at Jace and Evie's mating."

Adric didn't like that. "And none of us scented him?"

"He says the king gave him a charm that disguises his scent."

"Huh." She could almost hear her alpha brother filing that away for future investigation. "You need to come home, Jani."

"What about Luc? I can't leave without him."

"He's a big boy."

Marjani gave the quartz a look of disbelief. Sometimes her brother could be so damn cold.

"I am *not* leaving him to that night fae bitch. She puts fada in those cages so she can feed on their fear and anger. You should see Corban. He's—broken, just this side of feral. I only saw him as his wolf."

Silence. Then a careful question. "And you? You're...all right?"

Her jaw clenched. She knew he meant well, but it hurt, to have her own brother doubting her control. "What d'you think?"

"You sound good," he said immediately. "I'm sorry."

She unclenched her jaw. After all, Adric had a right to doubt her. She *had* almost lost it last winter. And she was still having trouble with control. "Okay. Okay."

"But I still want you home," he added, and made her angry all over again, especially when he added, "I could make it an order."

"Try it," she snarled.

Another taut silence. Then Adric expelled a breath. "Damn it, I'm your alpha. When I give you an order, you obey it."

"I'm your second for a reason," she shot back. "You trust me to tell you when you have your head up your ass."

A low growl—and then she heard him swallow. "I can't lose you, Jani."

Her heart constricted. Because she felt the same way—if she lost her only brother, she really would go feral.

She softened her tone. "We can't leave Luc here to die in a fucking cage. You know if the shoe were on the other foot, he'd do anything he could to rescue me—or you, for that matter."

"Then I'll send someone else. Please, Jani. I'd come myself, but I can't."

"Why not?" Not that she wanted him to come, but she knew her brother. It must be killing him to stay home while she and Luc hunted Corban.

"We have a situation here."

She got that odd tingle in her gut; her Gift at work. "The night fae are looking for me, aren't they?"

He took a long time answering. "Not you in particular—at least, not as far as I know. But a few days after you left, the prince demanded a meeting."

"Hell." She stared at the steam rising from the pool. "What happened?"

"He hinted that he knows who killed his son. But you know the fae. We danced around the question, each of us trying to gauge how much the other knows. But he's going to come back, and when he does, I'd better be here."

"And if he asks straight out who killed his son?"

"I'll tell him to go to Hades. He has no right to ask anything of me. His son died because he was in *my* territory, fucking with *my* lieutenant and his mate."

"We can't afford to make an enemy of him."

Adric gave a mirthless laugh. "Too late."

"You know what?" she said slowly. "Iceland might be the safest place for me right now. The last place anyone would expect to find me is deep in ice fae territory."

A pissed-off snarl. "I can protect my own damn sister. He's not going to find out who killed Tyrus. I want you home."

"Ric." She pinched the bridge of her nose. This was why she'd slipped out of Baltimore without telling him. "You have to trust me. Anyone else will only get caught. The only reason I got inside the ice fae castle was because Fane helped me." Well, that and the fact that Sindre and/or Blaer had apparently wanted her inside anyway.

At the sound of his name, Fane groaned, a deep, animal sound.

"What was that?" Adric demanded.

"Fane." She frowned down at the sick man as he flung himself on his back, a shudder jerking his long limbs. She touched his shoulder and he jolted upright, staring at her with glassy eyes.

"He's hurt? What the fuck, Jani?"

"Look, I gotta go. I'll report as soon as I know anything."

She cut the connection and zipped her quartz back into a side pocket of her cargo pants before laying a hand against Fane's forehead. It was burning hot.

She cursed under her breath as she guided him to lie back down. "You're not going to die on me, got it?"

Stripping off her shirt, she wet it in the pool and used it to bathe his forehead. His breath sighed out.

"That's it." She dabbed his face and neck, wishing she could do more. But she hadn't been blessed with even a speck of a healer's Gift. "Feels better, doesn't it? Now rest. You'll feel better when you wake up."

She hoped.

19
____

*A*dric clenched his quartz.

She's safe, at least for now. That's good.

Although he hated to admit it, maybe Marjani was right, she was safer in Iceland than Baltimore. Because Prince Langdon had requested another meeting.

No, demanded it. Tonight.

The prince was a night fae, so of course he'd set the meeting for midnight, choosing a bar on the top floor of a fancy hotel in midtown Baltimore.

Adric arrived at eleven, Jace at his side. Zuri took a seat on a metal stool at the shiny black bar, and several soldiers grabbed a nearby table. They'd dressed to blend in—dark button-up shirts and jeans or dress pants, their quartz pendants tucked discreetly into their shirts.

The bar had a stripped-down, urban feel: concrete floors, exposed brick walls and galvanized steel lights hanging like pendants from the ceiling. Running down one wall were floor-to-ceiling windows with a view of Baltimore's Washington Monument, and across Mount Vernon Place, the waning moon peeked from behind the spires of a gothic cathedral dating to the late 1800s.

Adric and Jace chose a table in the corner with a view of the entrance. A pretty redhead in a white shirt, cropped black pants and purple suspenders took their order for a couple of the pricey craft beers.

Adric and Jace nursed their beers as the hour until midnight ticked by. At the bar, two women in tight skirts were flirting with Zuri, and he flirted right back while keeping his back to the bar, dark eyes scanning the room.

Adric looked at Jace. "Any more problem with the night fae?"

"Nah. But I invited Horace to stay with us—for back up. You know how Evie loves him. He's with them right now."

Horace was a cheerful, dreadlocked cougar and a member of Jace's den.

"Good," Adric said. "Let me know if you need more men."

"Will do. But I think the prince was just messing with my head. Still, I'll be glad when Kyler graduates. Evie says she'll sell the house and they'll move in with me for good. She's already after me to redecorate the living room of my den. Says it looks like something you'd find in a frat house."

He grinned at Adric, crazy about his mate and not caring who knew it.

Lucky man.

Midnight approached. Adric scented Prince Langdon before he saw him—silver and decay. The night fae made their homes in elaborate crypts, and their scents held a hint of the graveyard.

Adric's hackles raised. He and Jace exchanged a look and scanned the area.

The prince appeared in a corner a few feet away, coalescing out of the shadows. The night fae were creepy like that. He was flanked by two bodyguards, a male and female—sea fada, by the scent.

"Your highness." Adric rose to his feet and murmured the traditional fae greeting. "Peace to you and yours."

Langdon trod noiselessly forward, dressed in black from his fae-tailored shirt to his Italian leather shoes. His eyes and shoulder-length hair were the same midnight color, a striking contrast to his dead-white skin. His narrow, aristocratic face sported winged black brows in which sparkled several tiny diamonds. More diamonds outlined his pointed ears, and his right index finger was decorated with a square-cut diamond as large as Adric's thumbnail.

"Lord Adric. Peace to you and yours," the prince returned. He had a low, rich voice. From what Adric had heard, women loved it. He nodded to Jace. "And to yours."

The lieutenant jerked his head. "Peace."

Adric indicated the chair across from him. "Please have a seat." The polite words tasted acrid in his mouth, but that was a downside of being alpha. You had to make nice with the fae.

The male guard pulled out the chair and Langdon lowered his tall, elegant body into it. The guards took a stance against the wall, the man scanning the room, the woman keeping her gaze firmly on Adric and Jace.

The pretty waitress bustled up, oozing excitement. She might not know exactly who Langdon was, but she'd guessed he was a fae. "May I get you a drink, sir?"

"You can, love." The prince granted her a small smile that brought a flush to her creamy skin. "Wine." He named a merlot that was no doubt rare and expensive.

"Coming right up. And you?" she asked Adric and Jace. When they shook their heads, she glanced at the stony-eyed guards. "What about your...companions?"

"Nothing for us," the woman said.

The waitress gave Langdon another wide smile. "I'll be right back with that wine." She headed for the bar.

The prince contemplated her very fine ass for a moment before turning back to Adric. "Thank you for agreeing to meet with me."

Like I had a choice. But Adric gave a little nod.

"It's a beautiful night." The prince leaned back in his chair, taking in the dark sky outside the plate glass windows. "Summer is almost over. We'll be celebrating the autumn equinox soon—and then Samhain." He used the Celtic term for Halloween. "My favorite time of the year."

"Yeah?" *Get to the point, damn it.*

The redhead returned with Langdon's wine. When he thanked her in that deep, seductive voice, she backed away as starry-eyed as if he were a Hollywood A-lister.

"In our clan, the little ones trick-or-treat," Langdon said. "Do yours?"

"No. That's not one of our traditions. We honor our dead with a special ceremony, but that's all."

"Ah." Langdon contemplated the blood-red wine in his glass. "I had three sons, once. But you know that."

"Mm." Adric's nape tightened. He willed his heartbeat to stay steady.

"And they're all dead. I know what you fada say about the night fae. That we're heartless. That we feed on the darkness in others."

Because you do.

"But we love our children as much as you do. I've seen six hundred turns of the sun, and in that time I've only been blessed with the three sons. And now they've all passed to the other side...before their time." The prince's black eyes burned into Adric's.

He felt an unwilling twinge of sympathy. The man was

genuinely grieving. But that didn't mean his son Tyrus didn't deserve to be dead.

"Look," he said, "I'm sorry for your loss, but I want you out of Baltimore. This is my town now. Whatever deal you had with my uncle is null and void."

Langdon's eyes blazed red. "You think to tell me what to do? A prince with a lineage going back a thousand turns of the sun?"

Adric bared his fangs. He might be young, but the Darktime had been a crash course in eat-or-be-eaten. "I'm not looking for trouble, your highness. But if you bring it to my doorstep, I'll fight back with everything I have. Are we clear on that?"

The prince took a sip of wine—and changed the subject. "One of my sons had a daughter. Merry Jones."

Jace didn't move, but Adric heard his heart speed up. Langdon's son Silver had mated with Jace's only sister, Takira. Their daughter was Jace's thirteen-year-old niece Merry.

The prince's gaze flicked to Jace, no doubt detecting the lieutenant's agitation with his night fae senses.

"We were told she died in a fire." Adric was careful not to lie. He *had* been told that Merry Jones died in a fire. In fact, he and Jace had believed for years that the girl was dead.

"A fire set by night fae assassins." Jace's voice was a harsh scrape.

Those assassins had also killed first Takira and later, Silver. Only Merry had escaped. And it had been Lord Tyrus who'd set the assassins on them, because Silver was Tyrus's half-brother and Tyrus didn't want any competition for Langdon's throne.

The prince leveled a stare at Adric. "We all know that isn't true. Merry Jones is alive and living at Rock Run. I'm also aware that you see her regularly." He glanced at Jace. "Both of you. I'm sure the Rock Run fada told you about the ward I set, a ward of protection keyed to her quartz. If any of my people try to harm her—if they even lay hands on her without her express permission—they die."

He waited until Adric nodded, then added, "That should be proof enough that I wish the girl no harm. I made no exceptions with the ward except for myself. Even my son Tyrus knew he'd die if he tried to touch her again."

"I know this, yes," Adric said, confused now. Where was Langdon going with this?

The prince's jaw worked. "Tyrus went too far."

"He did. But what does this have to do with Mer—?"

Langdon leaned forward, cutting him off. "You killed my son. We both know it."

"No. I didn't."

Langdon waved that aside. "Oh, you didn't do the deed yourself. But someone in your clan did. I've traced him to Baltimore. He hasn't been seen since. And recently, I received some information from one of your former clan members. Corban, his name is."

Adric went rigid. Because it was Marjani they were talking about—and he had the bad feeling that Langdon had picked up his sudden tension with those Spidey-senses of his.

Damn you, Corban. What have you done?

He set his hands on the table. "Get out of my town. You're not welcome here."

Langdon sat back. "What would the other fae think if I informed them your sister had killed my last surviving son?"

Adric narrowed his eyes. "They'd think it was your son's own fucking fault for sending assassins to off my lieutenant."

Jace growled. After all, he was the lieutenant that Tyrus had targeted. "We know who had your other two sons assassinated," he said. "Tyrus didn't want any rivals for your title, did he?"

A bleak look crossed Langdon's face. "I didn't know. Not until it was too late."

Adric tried not to blink. Had the prince almost apologized

for not reining in his psycho son? But Langdon was a night fae and an arrogant SOB to boot. The moment passed.

Cool black eyes scrutinized Adric. "I want access to the girl. Merry. The sun fae queen has set powerful wards around Rock Run. Nobody can break through them. But you"—his gaze shot to Jace—"you meet with her at least once a week."

The lieutenant's hazel eyes sparked a cat-green. Before he could speak, Adric jumped in.

"I'm sorry, but that's not possible."

"Why not?"

"She...passed. Earlier this summer."

"The girl? My granddaughter?"

"Yes." Adric swallowed against the wave of nausea at the big, fat lie he'd just told. "I'm sorry. You should've been informed."

Beside him, Jace went stiff.

Langdon's fingers tightened on his wineglass. "You're lying."

Adric shook his head. "It was in a flash flood. The caverns where she lives with the river fada flooded. They couldn't get her out in time."

From the corner of his eye, Adric saw Jace bow his head sorrowfully. Backing him up without actually lying.

The prince's winged brows snapped together. "Why wasn't I informed?"

Adric spread his hands. "You'll have to ask them. Rock Run doesn't share any more information with me than necessary."

"I'll want to see the body."

"I'm sorry, but that's not possible. We fada don't bury our dead. We cremate them."

Langdon's eyes narrowed on Adric for an endless minute during which he prayed the night fae wouldn't see the cold sweat prickling his upper lip.

At last he murmured, "I see."

He rose to his feet in an abrupt movement and strode out of

the bar, his guards at his heels. The few people who happened to be in their path literally jumped aside.

"He gone?" Adric asked between clenched teeth, the lie he'd told tearing at his gut.

Because Merry was alive and well and living with Valeria and Rui do Mar, the Rock Run couple who'd adopted her after Silver's death.

Jace glanced at where Zuri had followed Langdon and his guards into the hall. "Yeah. Zuri says he's left the building."

"Good." Adric got up, stumbled the few feet to a potted plant, and vomited into the dirt.

20

———

"Fucking maze," Fane mumbled.

How long had he been wandering the spiraling paths? Hours, maybe days. He was exhausted, his tongue thick from thirst.

Sindre was toying with him, the bastard. The man was a Gifted illusionist. He could conjure up nightmares so real you could touch them.

Fane had to keep moving. To stop—to give in any way—might be fatal.

He set his right hand on the wall. Wasn't there something about a right-hand rule? Touch the wall of a maze with your right hand and at every turn, go right, and you'll eventually find your way out. But you had to do it as soon as you entered the maze, so it was probably too late. And it wouldn't work anyhow on a maze that continually remade itself.

He kept his hand on the wall anyway, and trudged on.

Where was Marjani? Had the goblins captured her while he was lost in this endless white world?

If only he hadn't accepted Sindre's *geas*. But he had, and a *geas* was almost impossible to break.

Even if he did manage to break it, he'd lose everything: his job as an envoy, the money he'd earned since accepting the bargain. Worse, he'd be shamed, known throughout the magical world as a vow-breaker.

The shame wouldn't fall on just him, either. It would attach to his dad, Arne, and maybe even Roald.

Back when he'd accepted the *geas*, ninety-nine human years hadn't seemed that long. But now the years inched by...and he still had thirty-nine to go.

"Sleep," a woman murmured. "You're safe."

"No." He shook his head from side to side. "I'll die. And the king will get Marjani."

"Is that what's bothering you? I'm right here. Safe. We're both safe."

He opened his eyes. Marjani's face swam into view, but he didn't trust his eyes. It would be just like Sindre to taunt him with the one woman Fane most wanted.

"Jani?" he croaked. "It's really you? This isn't some trick?"

"I'm here." A warm hand settled on his chest. "See? You can feel me, right?"

"Thank the gods." He gripped her fingers...and the world whirled away.

He'd walked for another endless day when the wall disintegrated into a chilly white mist that slowly engulfed him. He tried to outrun it, but it was all around him.

No. It's a trick.

He lifted his chin. "Mind over matter, Fane." Because if he could somehow *see* through the illusion, it would disappear.

The fog covered his face. Reaching his arms out in front of him, he stumbled blindly forward until his legs gave out.

So much for mind over matter.

"At least," he told Sindre as the blackness came up to meet him, "you don't have Jani."

He could swore he heard the king chuckle.

"I'm here," she said. "I'm here."

He didn't know how long he was out—an hour? A day? But when he came to, the fog was gone and he was curled up on the stone floor, shivering.

He groaned and wrapped his arms around himself.

"Easy, now." Gentle hands lifted him onto a lap, stroked the side of his face. A woman, but it couldn't be Marjani. After what he'd done, she must be far away by now.

His eyelids seemed to have been glued shut. "Mom?"

"No. It's me—Jani."

He pried open his sticky lids and focused on the woman gazing down at him with a furrowed brow. "Jani?" Relief washed through him. "You're...okay. It wasn't a dream."

"Shh—don't talk. Drink." She slid a hand under his head to lift it, and then set a cup to his lips.

He gulped the water greedily, draining the cup. "More."

"Okay." She set the cup down and started to move him off her.

"No!" Panicked, he grabbed her legs. "Don't leave."

"Just for a minute. You have a fever—you need water."

"No." He tightened his grip on her, not giving a fuck that he was being unreasonable. Marjani was the solid boulder around which the rest of the world swirled. If she left him, he'd be engulfed by the maze again.

"Okay." Cool fingers stroked his hair back from his face. "Calm down."

"Thank you," he rasped and dozed off. When she lifted his head off her lap and set it on something soft, he was too weak to protest. Then he passed out. This time, his sleep was dreamless.

When he next opened his eyes, his head ached and he was hot as Hades, his mouth so dry he could barely swallow. He peered blearily around for Marjani, but she was nowhere to be seen.

His heart slapped wildly against his rib cage.

Had she left him? Or worse, been seized by the goblins?

She murmured something against his shoulder and his heart resumed its normal tempo. She was spooned up against his back, her arm around his waist, her breathing the slow, steady rhythm of sleep.

Relieved, he let out a jagged exhale and then stilled, afraid to wake her in case she left for real. But she had the senses of a cat.

She sat up, yawning, and set her fingers to his forehead. "Holy mother. You're burning up."

Rising to her feet, she stripped off her T-shirt and soaked it in the thermal pool. She had on a plain black exercise bra—of course. This woman wouldn't be caught dead in anything lacy.

As she wrung out the T-shirt, he eyed the strong, beautiful muscles in her shoulders and arms. A wry grin tugged on his mouth. He finally had her stripping off her clothes and he was too damn weak to do anything about it.

She returned with the wet T-shirt and set it on his forehead. He closed his eyes as the ache in his head receded.

"Here. Drink something." She lifted his head—so gently it made his heart clench—and held a cup to his lips. Somehow, he hadn't thought she had it in her.

Not that he deserved her kindness. Hell, if he was Marjani, he'd bang his head on the cavern floor. Hard.

He sucked the water down. "More, please."

She nodded and made another trip to the pool—three trips in all before he'd had enough water. By then the T-shirt had warmed from his skin. He turned it over so that the cooler side lay against his forehead.

Marjani took it and wiped his face and neck before rising to wet it again.

He felt under his head. He was laying on soft wool. He turned his head to look at it.

"You…need your sweater." He tugged at it.

"No worries." She returned to drape the wet cloth over his forehead again, covering his eyes. "It's warm in here, and if I get too cold, I can always shift to my cougar."

He pushed up the T-shirt to look at her. "I…thank you."

Tears leaked from the corners of his eyes. He pulled the cloth back down and lay there, humiliated.

She touched his wrist. "You'd have done the same for me."

"If you believe that…" He trailed off.

Because he would've.

In fact, he'd thrown away his whole way of life for her. If he was lucky, Sindre would release him from the *geas*. If not, he was going to spend the next thirty-nine turns of the sun in a private hell of the ice fae king's making.

Arne was going to be disappointed—he'd stuck his neck out for Fane, arguing that his son deserved a chance even if he was only a quarter fae. And his grandfather Roald would sear him with one of those looks that said, *What do you expect from a mixed-blood?*

His chest tightened, and what felt like a chunk of basalt lodged in his gut.

Marjani sat next to him, legs folded lotus-style. "Rest." She set a hand on his heart. "Right now, you need to get better. Everything else can wait."

He moved his chin, a short up-and-down motion.

She turned over the damp cloth. "Close your eyes."

When he obeyed, she smoothed it over his forehead and then placed her hand over his heart again.

Marjani was safe. That made it all worthwhile.

The tightness in his chest eased and he fell into a deep, healing sleep.

21

Between them, Jace and Zuri managed to get Adric back to his den before he threw up again. At least this time, he made it to the toilet first.

After rinsing out his mouth, he staggered back to the living room to collapse on the couch. He lay there shaking, his body exuding a rank odor.

Zuri sat on the couch's other end. "I'm staying here tonight. I can sleep in Jani's room."

His glare dared Adric to object, but Adric just nodded. "Works."

Jace remained standing, his brow creased with worry. "I have to go back to Grace Harbor. I don't trust the night fae not to mess with Evie and Kyler, even with Horace there."

"Go," Adric rasped. "But call Merry. In the morning."

Because Langdon would investigate to see if she was really dead.

Unfortunately, they couldn't call her adopted parents, because water fada couldn't use small electronics—their bodies tended to short them out. Meanwhile, Merry was protected by

Rock Run's wards, and Adric didn't want to scare her—the kid was only thirteen, after all.

Besides, Rui do Mar, her adopted father, was a scary-ass shark fada. If Langdon wanted Merry, he'd have to get past do Mar, and the shark shifter would die before he let that happen.

"Tell her...get a new quartz," he added. "Throw...the old one in the river. The ward of protection—the prince might be able to trace her through it."

She'd lose the protection, but with Tyrus dead, it probably wasn't necessary anymore.

"Will do." Jace shook his head. "Lord, you're a crazy mofo. I can't believe you told a fae prince a lie right to his face. But you're right. Let him think she's dead—at least until she's grown up."

"The sun fae queen will protect her," Zuri interjected.

"Yeah." Adric hadn't thought of that. But Queen Cleia loved Jace's skinny, serious niece. "Do Mar." He clamped his jaw shut against another wave of queasiness.

Jace understood. "I'll tell Merry to have him contact you."

"Make sure...he knows it's important. The Full Moon Saloon." It was a shifter bar in Fells Point. "Tonight, seven o'clock."

Jace studied him doubtfully. "You sure you're up for it?"

"Yeah." Adric rested his head against the couch's worn fabric. "Just need...sleep."

The rest of the night passed in a feverish haze. Jace left for Grace Harbor, and Zuri contacted Suha. He tried to help Adric to bed, but Adric bared his teeth and he backed off.

And he did it, even though it took him a good five minutes to strip to his boxers and ease himself under the sheets.

Suha arrived shortly after, dressed in a bright, tribal-patterned tunic and leggings. The clan's head healer was a deer fada with short black hair, a pretty oval face, and a doe's calm brown eyes. One look at him, and her full mouth tightened.

"Holy shit, Ric. What did you do now?"

Zuri opened his mouth, but Adric stopped him with a look. "I told a lie."

That was all Suha needed to know. The healer might be like family to him and Jani, but secrets had a way of spreading through the clan. And right now, the clan didn't need any more upsets.

Her fine dark brows climbed. "A whopper, from the looks of it."

Zuri got a stool from the living room and put it next to the bed. Taking a seat, Suha removed her quartz and held it over his heart, her other hand on his arm.

Zuri hovered on the other side of the bed, his good-looking face grim.

"For fuck's sake," Adric said. "I'm not going to die."

Zuri backed up a step and folded his big arms over his chest. "From where I'm standing, that's debatable."

Suha touched the wolf fada's leg. "Why don't you go get something to eat, babe? The bar on the corner makes killer quesadillas."

"And then get some sleep," Adric growled. "I don't need you standing guard over me. If I need you, I'll call."

Zuri hesitated and then jerked his chin. "All right."

Suha waited until the front door closed behind him and then murmured, "Breathe. Let the warmth fill you."

She moved the quartz in a slow circuit from his throat—which had spoken the lie—to his still-upset stomach, and then back to his heart.

Adric rarely allowed Suha to use her healing Gift on him. Healing burned a lot of energy, and he preferred she save it for the clan members who really needed it.

But he had to admit, it felt good. He sighed with relief as a pleasant heat spread like warm honey throughout his body. His painfully clenched stomach eased.

"That's it." The healer's eyes were half-closed. "Relax. Let your own energy work with mine."

His own quartz hummed in response, accepting Suha's healing energy and using it to counteract the toxins that the lie had released in his body.

His eyelids shut. The next thing he knew it was five in the afternoon, and Zuri was frowning down at him.

"Ric. You all right?"

"Yeah." Adric sat up and swung his legs over the edge of the bed. "Yeah," he repeated, more firmly. He felt a little dizzy, but his stomach had settled. Suha's healing energy had done the trick. It would be a few days until he was back to a hundred percent, but his head had cleared and he was no longer shaking.

From the kitchen came a mouthwatering fragrance. His stomach growled.

"You made me your mom's soup?" Zuri's spicy chicken soup —a Moroccan recipe passed down through his mom's family— was famous in the clan.

"Yep." The tall, brown-skinned lieutenant broke into a rare smile. "But first, take a fucking shower."

Adric rubbed his nose. "I was hoping that smell wasn't me."

By 6:45 P.M., Adric was at the Full Moon Saloon, having showered, dressed and downed a big bowl of Zuri's chicken soup.

At ten to seven, Rui do Mar roared up on a big black bike. Adric nodded to the bouncer to let him in. They'd cleared the bar of everyone but Zuri and a handful of trusted soldiers. Even the owner had been told to wait in his office.

Do Mar was a large, olive-skinned man with short dark hair, a square jaw and hooded green eyes. He strode inside, took one sniff and headed for the dark corner table where Adric waited.

The shark shifter could scent a few drops of blood in a fast-flowing river. Detecting Adric's scent in an uncrowded bar must be child's play for him.

"Lord Adric," he said in his Portuguese-accented English as he dropped into the seat across from Adric. "Merry says you wish to speak with me."

No preliminary bullshit with this guy—he went straight to the point. But that was fine with Adric.

"We have a situation. The night fae prince."

"And?" Do Mar lifted a black brow.

"You know his son died."

Do Mar nodded. "We do."

Of course they did. Adric would bet Rock Run even knew that a Baltimore fada had killed Tyrus. But most people believed it had been Adric who'd knifed the man—because that was how he wanted it.

"He asked about Merry," he told do Mar. "He wanted me to agree to give him access to her."

"In exchange for what?"

My sister's life. "That's clan business. But I lied—told him Merry was dead."

Adric caught a hint of surprise in the other man's scent, but his face remained impassive. "I see."

"She got rid of her quartz?" Adric asked, even though he knew the answer. He no longer felt the thin bond connecting him to Merry.

"*Sim*, yes. It was hard, but she trusts you."

Adric's cheek flexed. "I'm sorry." He was Merry's alpha. It was only right that she trusted and obeyed him—no matter that Rock Run had claimed her as an honorary river fada—but he'd hated like hell to give the order. It *hurt* an earth fada to remove their quartz. "It's for her own protection."

"She knows."

"Make sure she finds another quartz—soon. She's still growing. She needs the energy more than ever right now."

Do Mar nodded. "She's already looking for another one. We have a few small deposits within the base."

"Good." The Rock Run Base had been carved out of underground caverns near the mouth of the Susquehanna River, an area rich with quartz deposits.

"There's more," Adric added. "Our best guess is that Tyrus was trying to wipe out everyone connected to Merry. That's why he targeted Jace." He blew out a breath. "And when I met with the prince, he made a point of telling me that all three of his sons are dead."

Adric didn't have to connect the dots. Do Mar bit out something dark in Portuguese. "He wants Merry."

"He didn't say it straight out, but she's his only living heir."

"So he has changed his mind." Do Mar rubbed a hand over his face. "Before, he didn't want his people to know he had a half-blood son with a human. He was happy for us to keep Merry at Rock Run."

"She may be only a quarter night fae, but she's his blood. His only granddaughter."

Their eyes met. Do Mar's shark shone in his eyes, and Adric knew the other man could see cougar-blue streaking his.

"No fucking way," Adric ground out, "am I going to let Merry be raised by the night fae. I wouldn't wish that on my worst enemy, let alone a sweet kid like her."

"Agreed. We will keep a close watch on her. We have one advantage—Dion's mate, Queen Cleia. She loves Merry."

"I'm counting on it." Adric had never thought he'd be grateful the Rock Run alpha had mated with the sun fae queen; it gave Rock Run too much power in their little corner of Maryland. But now he thanked the gods that Merry had Cleia to protect her.

"She's already volunteered one of her best spellcasters to

cast a *look-away* spell for Merry's new quartz," do Mar said. "The prince may look for her, but he won't find her."

"Thank you."

"I have no need of thanks," the other man said as they rose to their feet. "You still don't comprehend, do you? Merry is my daughter, here." He touched a fist to his heart. "I would do anything to keep her safe and happy. And my mate—Valeria—feels the same."

Adric nodded—and then stuck out his hand.

Do Mar's hooded eyes flickered with surprise. In all the years they'd known each other, they'd never touched. Touch was reserved for clan members, or at least people you didn't see as an enemy. But Adric could no longer see the shark fada as an enemy, even if he was the Rock Run second.

The other man gripped his hand firmly. "Peace to you and yours."

Adric met his eyes. "And to you and yours."

22

When Fane awoke that evening, his fever had broken and he felt much better, although weak as an infant.

Night had fallen. The cavern was dark except for a small fire with Marjani crouched beside it, grilling some kind of white fish on a small metal grate. She'd put her T-shirt back on, but her feet were bare. The pool shimmered beside her, the water black in the dim light.

He fingered the thin wool blanket covering him. Where had that come from? He pushed the blanket down to his waist and propped himself up on his forearms.

Marjani immediately crossed to him. "How do you feel?"

"Better, thanks." His voice came out as a croak. He moistened his dry, cracked lips. "But thirsty."

"Hang on and I'll get you some water." Picking up a ceramic cup, she filled it in the pool and brought it to him.

He drained the cup in a few gulps and then turned it in his hand. It was ceramic, the kind the locals kept for everyday use, with no handle and a speckled gray glaze. "Where in Hades did you get this—and the blanket?"

"I made a quick trip outside while you were sleeping. I found a stream to fish in and a little hut with bunk beds and some basic supplies."

He nodded. "The locals rent them to hikers."

"I wish I could've left them something in return, but my backpack is back at the court."

He set the cup on the floor and sat cross-legged, the blanket on his legs. "You're fucking amazing."

"It was either that or go hungry," she said with a shrug. "And I've been in worse situations."

"Yeah, I imagine you have. You're a soldier, aren't you?"

"I was." A shadow crossed her face. "I mean, I *am*."

He'd upset her, the last thing he wanted to do. He pushed the blanket off his lap. "I need—"

"Of course." She helped him to his feet and pointed to a small tunnel behind the pool, where he found the hole she'd dug for wastes. When he was done, he tossed some dirt into it and washed up in the pool.

She was crouched by the grill again. His stomach rumbled at the fish's mouthwatering scent. As he lowered himself onto the cavern floor beside her, she divided the fish into two portions and handed him a plate.

His hands were shaking with hunger. He gripped the plate and gave her a grateful smile. "Thank you."

"You have to eat with your fingers."

"No problem." The fish tasted as good as it smelled. He quickly downed the first couple of pieces, then forced himself to slow down. It wasn't much, but it filled him. His stomach seemed to have shrunk.

He set down his plate. "How long was I out, anyway?"

"Two days. It's around midnight right now."

He gave a low whistle. "No one came looking for us?"

"I heard the goblins the first night, but I haven't seen or heard anything since."

He contemplated the glowing charcoal embers. "The king wants you, then. He wouldn't have sent the goblins after me."

"Why not?"

"He knows I can't go far without his consent. It would break the *geas*."

"Why did you? Accept the *geas*, I mean."

He moved a shoulder. "It seemed like a good idea at the time. My mom had just died, and I didn't fit into the human world anymore. I was a fisherman in Newfoundland—had my own boat with a crew of two. But people were starting to notice how I never seemed to age. Then I found out I had a fae Gift. My dad's an envoy, too. You'd like him—everyone does. Give the man a bottle of wine and a box of crackers and he can make a party. He wasn't home much, but when he was, life was so damn fun."

Marjani rested her chin on her knees, the light from the fire burnishing her profile a rich gold. "Sounds a lot like you."

"I'm afraid so."

Arne had flitted in and out of Fane's life just as Fane had Evie's. Try and talk about anything deep, and Arne shrugged it off with a laugh. His motto was, "Life's too short and time goes by."

Fane blew out a breath. "Anyway, I'd always looked up to my dad...would've done anything to be like him. I was late to come into my Gift, but as soon as Dad found out I was a wayfarer, he brought me to Iceland and talked the king into giving me a chance. Turned out I was good at it. Hell, how many people would turn down an offer to be part of a fae court?"

She shrugged.

He shot her a look. Because Marjani had turned Sindre down—multiple times.

"The king did his damnedest to tempt you, didn't he? And

you just kept telling him no. You know how much I admire you for that?"

"Don't." She made a sharp movement with her hand. "I'm— I've made some bad choices myself."

"Yeah? Well, this was the mother of all bad choices." He gave a humorless laugh. "Hell, I was like a fucking kid with my nose pressed to the window of a candy store. The fae are—the fae. Rich, glamorous, sexy as hell—and they wanted me. Fane Morningstar, a fisherman from Canada. The women, well... " He swallowed against the bitter taste in his mouth. "But to them, I was just a shiny new plaything. No pureblood would mate with a mixed-blood like me."

She touched his leg. "I'm sorry."

"Hey, it's not all bad. It's a good job—interesting, and the pay is fucking awesome." His mouth twisted. "Most of the time I don't even have to hurt someone else to do it. And when I do, I tell myself that if I don't do it, someone else will. The king has a half-dozen other envoys."

She took her hand from his leg and straightened up. "That's an excuse. Your actions shouldn't depend on anyone else."

"It's not so black and white."

"For me, it is."

"Well, that's the difference between you and me, isn't it?" He picked up a piece of gravel and tossed it into the pool. It landed with a plunk and sank below the dark, steaming surface. "I can tell you one thing, all the excuses in the world didn't make me feel better about spying on you. A woman I'd come to like. A lot."

She took his empty plate and set it on top of hers. "But you did it anyway."

"Yeah." He briefly closed his eyes. "I owe you an apology for that."

"Would you do it again?" A quiet question in the shadowy cavern.

He took a deep, pained breath. "Probably. Under the terms of the *geas*, I can't disobey a direct order from the king."

"Then don't bother saying you're sorry. Because then I have to respond that it's all right. And it's not. You tricked me, Fane."

He nodded, accepting that. "I'm sor—" He halted and then tried again. "At least let me thank you for taking care of me these past two days. No one would've blamed you if you'd left me outside for the goblins."

"I didn't do it for you," she returned. "I did it for Evie. She's clan now, and you're her dad."

"Ah." He fingered another piece of gravel. "Well, thanks anyway."

"Okay," she added grudgingly, as if he'd argued with her. "Maybe I did do it a little bit for you. That doesn't mean I didn't think about leaving you—because you're right, no one would've blamed me. But you were so sick, and I knew it was because of me."

"You should have left. You need to get the hell out of Iceland. The king is all powerful here. Even the humans obey him."

"How? They're probably watching the airport, and I don't have enough money to hire a boat."

He shook his head. "And you won't leave until you find out what happened to your friend Luc, will you? No, don't answer that. That way if the king asks, I can honestly say I don't know. But the goblins are nocturnal. They hunt at night."

"So you're saying I should wait until morning before I leave."

"Yeah."

She nodded—and then slanted him a look that made him instantly hard.

He swallowed. "Jani?"

"I shouldn't want you," she said, almost to herself. "I was so fucking angry at you when I found out you'd been playing me all this time."

"I'm sorry. So bloody sorry."

"But these past couple of days, I had a lot of time to think." She stared into the fire. "You did try to warn me. Told me I should leave Iceland, more than once. And you wouldn't have been so sick if you hadn't tried to interfere between me and the king."

His fingers tightened around the gravel. "I couldn't just stand by and do nothing. And your friend Luc agreed. He wanted you out of there."

That earned him a growl. "If Luc had his way, I'd be safe in his den, having his cubs."

"You?" He made small, disbelieving sound. "He doesn't know you very well, does he?"

"No. I mean, he *does* know me. But he can't help himself. He's a fada male—he wants to protect his mate—even if it drives me insane."

"All men want to protect their mate. Just like women want to protect theirs."

She looked at him, arrested. "See, that's what Luc doesn't get. That it goes both ways—for me, anyway."

"So what now?"

"I don't know." She looked down at her hands, loose in her lap. "I came to Iceland to kill Corban. After that..." She shrugged and trailed off.

His chest constricted. He'd guessed right; this was a suicide mission.

"I care." He tossed the gravel aside and dared to reach out. When she didn't pull away, he traced a finger over the fine bones of her jaw.

She stilled. "You—what?"

"I care what happens to you. Very much."

She drew a slow breath. "It would just be for tonight. After that, we have to split up—go our separate ways. The *geas* means I can't trust you."

"Okay. Sure." He would've agreed to anything about then. Hell, if she'd asked him for the moon, he'd have grabbed a ladder and started climbing.

"There's something you should know." Her throat worked. "It's...been a while."

He held his breath, afraid to say anything. This woman wouldn't be pressured. She'd have to come to it her own way —or not.

She rose to her feet, cat-supple, and washed the plates before setting them aside to dry. When she turned back, her irises were slivered with turquoise.

And then she flashed him a smile, the first true smile he'd seen from her.

His heart kicked. Her smile was broad and warm and even more beautiful than he'd pictured.

"The water is a perfect temperature," she murmured.

He opened his mouth to reply. But the words died unsaid as she raised her arms, pulled off the T-shirt and black bra, and let them drop to the ground.

23

*M*arjani drew a deep breath, naked from the waist up except for the fake quartz around her neck. Nervous, but wanting this, her skin buzzing and her heart racing.

Fane stared up at her, a sexy dark scruff covering his cheeks and jaw. Even after being sick for two days and to be honest, kind of smelly, the man was fucking hot.

She'd had two days to think things over. She hadn't exactly forgiven him for spying on her, but she no longer blamed him. Within the limits of the *geas*, he'd done what he could. In fact, he'd tried to get her to leave—more than once—but she'd been laser-focused on getting to Corban.

She could even admit he'd been right to drag her out of the tower. If he hadn't, she'd probably be in a cage right now.

So yeah, she didn't blame Fane, but that didn't mean she trusted him. When she left the cavern, she was going alone.

But for the first time in a long time, she wanted a man—and she'd decided to go for it.

Maybe it was a bad idea. There was no way this thing between them could go anywhere. When she chose a mate, she wanted another earth fada, not a human-fae mix. Someone strong, steady—not this sexy, smooth-talking charmer.

So yeah, this would be a one-time thing—but maybe that was exactly why she should go for it. For once, she was completely free, unhampered with all the expectations that went with being Adric's second. No one but her and Fane would know what happened in this cavern—not her clan, not her friends, and certainly not her brother.

Fane rose to his feet and cupped her face. Clear topaz eyes searched hers. "You sure?"

Desire curled through her belly. "Yes."

His breath sucked in. "Gods, I want you." His mouth ghosted across hers.

A fada craved touch, more than other species. Her cat stretched and gave a happy little yowl. She curled her fingers against her thighs, wanting to touch him back, and yet cemented in place, need warring with fear.

His lips outlined the curve of her cheek. He nibbled her earlobe, tugged at the gold hoop with his teeth. Pleasure trilled up and down her spine, vibrated in her core.

His clever mouth continued moving, pressing kisses behind her ear and up her skull to the coarse black stubble.

"I should shave," she muttered. "It's too rough." Usually she ran a razor over it every few days, but she'd been running as her cougar for over a week.

"I like it." He brushed a palm over the back of her head. "Makes you look like a badass. Goes with those knives you love so much."

She pursed her lips, trying not to laugh—and that was the most wonderful, amazing thing. That she even wanted to laugh right now.

"And that's good?" she managed to ask.

"Oh, yeah." He turned her head to the side—and nipped her nape.

Her breath sped up. It was a dominant, very masculine move. She might be a soldier, but she was also a fada female. She liked a man who wasn't afraid to bite.

He nipped again, harder. "It makes me want to do bad things to you."

A moan escaped her lips. He kissed the small pain away and trailed a finger down the sensitive slope of her neck and across one shoulder.

Her throat worked.

He smiled. "You like that."

"Yes," she rasped.

He traced the arc of her collarbones before continuing to her breasts. He rubbed his thumbs over her aching nipples. "So beautiful," he breathed, his gaze on the dusky buds.

She was flat-chested and she knew it. But Fane's heated look made her feel like the sexiest woman alive.

"Mm." He bent and gave each nipple a hard suck before stepping back and dragging off his sweater. "Why don't we get into the pool? I could use a bath, frankly."

She blinked up at him, dazed with desire. Then her face split in a grin. "I sponged you down yesterday. But yeah, you could."

He stilled in the act of removing his T-shirt. "You should smile more often."

"Yeah?" She rubbed her stubbled head a little shyly.

"Yeah. You look good as a badass, but when you smile, you're beautiful."

He dropped the T-shirt on top of his sweater and reached for the button of his black jeans. He was all hard muscles and tanned skin, his chest sprinkled with dark blond hairs.

Her mouth literally watered. She swallowed noisily, following the trail of those wiry, gold-tipped hairs down to where they disappeared into his waistband.

His lips curved in a wicked smile. She'd removed his shoes

the first day to make him more comfortable. Now he slowly and deliberately undid the button of his jeans.

She drew a sluggish breath. The air in the cavern felt heavy, thick.

His smile disappeared. They stared at each other as he slid down his zipper and stepped out of his jeans. His socks followed, and then he stood before her in dark knit boxers tented with an impressive erection.

"Now you." He stepped closer to undo her cargo pants. Dropping to one knee, he helped her out of each leg in turn, leaving her naked except for her black briefs. He caught her hips and nuzzled her belly, rubbing his night beard over the tender skin.

She inhaled in pleasure, taking in his arousal, a hot, salty spice overlaying the grassy green. He pressed a kiss to her mound—and then blew warm, moist air against the material over her clit.

Heat licked up her spine. She grabbed his shoulders and made a low sound, half cat, half human. He nipped and sucked at her sex through the cotton, stoking the heat, getting her good and wet for him.

He gave her a last kiss and lifted his head. "Bath first."

She blinked down at him. "No..."

"Yes. Believe me, you don't want me close to you right now."

And despite her grumbling that she'd been "close" to him for two days, he helped her out of the briefs and rose to his feet.

His gaze tracked down her body in one searing look, and then he dragged her into his arms. "If you knew how fucking much I want you..."

"Same," she managed to say before his mouth covered hers.

It was a deep kiss, involving tongues and teeth. A kiss that demanded she meet him halfway. He'd stopped being careful with her, and she loved it.

She twined her arms around his neck and rubbed her breasts against his bare chest, reveling in the feel of his wiry hair against her nipples. His erection pressed against her belly through the knit boxers. He palmed her bottom and squeezed, muttering hot, sexy things about how he'd wanted to see her naked since the very first day in the pub, how he'd fantasized about her ass.

This time, it was Marjani who broke the kiss.

She walked the few steps to the pool. "Coming?"

His gaze swept over her body again. She had time to see his eyes darken and then she did a shallow dive into the pool, coming up at the opposite end. She swiped the water out of her eyes and watched as he shucked his knit boxers.

His cock was long and hard. He wrapped his hand around himself and looked down at her as he stroked himself.

She moistened her lips, enjoying the view—and then gulped.

Something about the way he stood above her, legs apart, playing with himself...and the bad memories coated the back of her throat, sending fear skittering like a spider up her spine. She set a hand over her jumping heart.

"Jani." He released himself. "Don't."

"Don't what?"

"Don't think." He stepped into the pool and gave her a lopsided grin. "Thinking is way overrated. Ah...that feels good." He sank down on a ledge, the steamy water up to his chest, and stretched his long arms out along the edge of the pool.

She swallowed hard. Gradually, her heart slowed as she realized he was waiting for her to come to him. No coercion here, just a beautiful man who wanted her as much as she wanted him. She let out a breath and removed her hand from over her heart.

You got this, Jani.

If she stopped now, no one would judge her, not even Fane.

She'd survived a gang rape. Fane might not know the details, but she knew he had a pretty good idea of what had happened.

But she didn't want to live the rest of her life celibate. Sex was good, a pleasure she refused to let Corban and those warped, feral river fada steal from her.

Fane rested his head against the ledge. His eyes drifted shut.

She frowned. How the fuck could he be so relaxed? Then she shook her head at how ridiculous she was being, and somehow she was moving, crossing the pool in a few strokes to take a seat on the ledge beside him.

She tipped her head back and let the hot water do its magic on her muscles. Fane touched the back of her head, and when she murmured in pleasure, began stroking it. Her tension eased. She moved her head against his palm, seeking more.

He massaged her nape, his fingers gentle, knowing. Something pinched in her chest.

It had been so long...

She turned her head to look at Fane. His eyelashes were a dark crescent on his lean cheeks, and his corn silk hair floated around his face.

"You may be right," she told him.

"About what?"

"That thinking is overrated."

His smile had a self-mocking edge. "Some would say I live my life by that principle."

"I don't believe that."

"You don't know me very well."

"I know you well enough. If you couldn't think several steps ahead, you wouldn't have lasted long in a fae court. Especially this one."

"Are you saying I'm as devious as they are?"

"Yeah." Her mouth quirked. "I think I am."

He threw back his head and laughed aloud. Then he

sobered. "Gods. It's been so long since I talked to someone like you."

"Like me?"

"Someone who tells me exactly what she thinks of me. I'm so bloody tired of all the doublespeak. If only I'd met you before I—" He shook his head.

She moistened her lips, equal parts flattered and sad for him. "I wasn't even alive when you signed the contract with the king."

"No." He let his eyes drift shut again. "You weren't, were you?"

She studied his sculpted features, the pointed ear peeking through his wet blond hair. How in Hades had she ended up here, naked in a pool with this man?

She had a fada's prejudice against rich, entitled fae. They used fada—as servants, assassins, bodyguards, or for sex—and then looked down their glittering noses at the "animals."

But she was beginning to see that Fane was almost as much an outsider among the purebloods as she was.

Without opening his eyes, he rubbed a lazy hand over his chest. The water beaded on the curly blond hairs.

She drew a breath, her fingers literally tingling with the need to touch him.

"You didn't find any soap in that hut, did you?" he asked.

"No. And I looked, too."

He slid the rest of the way underwater, surfacing in the center where he scrubbed himself off with handfuls of grit before swimming back to her. He stood up in the pool, his waist level with her eyes. The tip of his cock bobbed above the water.

"Come here." He reached out a hand.

She swallowed—and not in a good way. No, this was an *I'm-not-sure-I-can-do-this* swallow. She instinctively crossed her arms over her breasts.

Fane's eyes flickered and she grimaced.

"Sorry." Cat's balls, she was a mess. But she couldn't make herself uncover her breasts.

His mouth thinned. "Don't."

"What?"

"Don't apologize."

She opened her mouth again and he raised a hand, palm out. "I mean it. You have nothing to be sorry for."

She sank deeper in the pool. "I wasn't always like this," she muttered. "So weak."

"You're not weak."

"How the fuck could you know?" she snapped, and then felt ashamed at how bitchy she was being. She was pushing him away, but she couldn't seem to stop herself.

"I just do." Sitting on the ledge, he curled an arm around her shoulders. When she didn't resist, he eased her onto his lap, cuddling her against his chest. "You're a badass to the core, and I'm happy just to hold you."

She sat there stiffly as strong fingers massaged her nape, stroked down her vertebrae. His erection was there against her hip, but he didn't draw attention to it, just kept petting her.

Her shoulders relaxed. How did he always seem to know exactly what she needed? She set a tentative hand over where his heart thumped slow and even beneath her cheek.

He kissed the top of her head. "Nothing's going to happen unless you want it to. You know that, don't you?"

"But I do want this. I *do*."

"Then we'll take it slow, okay?"

She nodded against his chest. "Thanks," she whispered. "For being patient."

He gave an odd little chuckle. "For you, Jani, I have all the patience in the world."

He nudged her chin with the back of his hand, bringing her mouth up so he could kiss her. She caressed his face, letting herself float on his kiss, a warm, weightless feeling. They explored each other's mouths, tasting all the hot, dark corners, sucking on each other's tongues.

By the time he rose to his feet with her in his arms, she thought she just might be able to do this after all. She wrapped an arm around his neck and let him set her on a nest made of their two sweaters.

Even then, he was in no hurry. He knelt beside her, his fingers whispering over her body: her breasts, her thighs, the sensitive skin behind her knees... A slow, easy seduction.

"You're so beautiful." A murmur in the dim light cast by the flickering fire. His wet hair fell around them, the diamond stud glinting in his left earlobe like a star.

Heat slid through her. Her breasts felt full, sensitized. Then his hot mouth closed over her nipple and she heard herself moan.

He gave a hard suck to that nipple, and then moved to the other, flicking the tip with his tongue, and then drawing it into the wet cave of his mouth. Stoking her arousal with teasing touches and sexy murmurs.

Wonder filled her.

That she wasn't afraid.

That she only wanted more.

Because this, what Fane was doing, was nothing like what those men had done to her. That had been an assault. They'd done their best to break her, and damn near succeeded.

But this, this was beautiful. How a woman and a man were meant to come together, in mutual pleasure.

Fane cupped her face and nuzzled her neck. His hairy thighs were between hers, his erection rubbing against her center.

And it felt *good*. Right.

She drew a breath, and then to her dismay, tears stung her eyes. She *never* cried.

Fane lifted his head. "What's wrong, love? Do you want me to—"

"No!" She dashed the tears away. "Nothing's wrong. It's just so good…"

Their eyes met, and she could've sworn he saw right to the heart of her. "It is for me, too."

He touched his lips to each of her eyelids in turn and then continued his exploration of her body, kissing his way down her breastbone to her belly. He trailed his lips over her mound, and she bent her knees to give him more space.

"Mm." He licked her, long and slow. "You taste so good."

Another lick, and then another.

And the good feelings got even better. Desire fizzed in her veins like champagne. She stroked his hair where it lay wet against her thigh.

Without warning, he sucked her clit into his mouth, and she let out a high, surprised mewl. He sucked harder, strong tugs that sent heat sparking through her. He moved lower for more of those delicious licks before returning to her clit again, learning what made her gasp and buck her hips.

Meanwhile, his long, knowing fingers played over her body —her nipples, her bottom, her inner thighs.

She reached for his head, trying to hold him against her sex, and he pulled back, his breath warm against the heated flesh.

She moaned. "Fane."

"I just want a look at you. You're like a flower." He teased her opening with his fingers. "A hot, wet, gorgeous flower that opens only for me."

She bit her lower lip. Desire climbed in her, but somehow she couldn't let go.

Then he husked, "Open for me, love. I want to see you come." He set his mouth to her clit and with a few self-assured licks, broke the tight hold she had on herself.

"Yes," she said. "*Yes.*"

He inserted two long fingers in her, and that was even better. Her sex clamped around him. Stars burst behind her eyes, shooting down to her toes and to the top of her head. Warming her to her very soul.

Fane stroked her inside with his fingers and outside with his tongue until she shuddered back to awareness with a sigh.

He raised his head. "Enough?"

"Oh, yeah. Too much."

"Never too much." With a sexy chuckle, he crawled back up her body to fit his mouth to hers. She tasted herself on his lips, mixed with his own male flavor.

She felt happy, even triumphant.

Because it felt like a victory.

She wrapped her arms around Fane and kissed him back as hard as she could.

24

———

ane lifted his head from Marjani and rolled to one side. Propping his head on his hand, he traced a finger down her nose and over her plush lips, swollen from his kisses. Her delicate features had a faint flush, her cat-shaped eyes heavy with satisfaction.

His heart swelled, because he'd been the one who put that look on her face.

He toyed with one of her small, pretty breasts. He loved her lean, streamlined body. He ached to bury himself in her, but he'd promised he'd move slowly, and he meant to keep that promise.

That this hurting, complicated woman had trusted him with herself as far as she had was an incredible gift.

He'd hated to see those flickers of fear. The gods knew he wasn't a violent man. A wayfarer didn't have to be. When things got rough, Fane simply...disappeared. But at the thought of anyone hurting Marjani, something dark and ugly balled in his chest.

She turned on her side and set her hand on his chest. "Now you." She tiptoed her fingers lower and encircled his erection.

He sucked in a breath, practically jumping out of his skin with pleasure. But he made himself say, "Only if you want."

"I want." The seriousness on her face made his lungs constrict.

"Then have at it, love." He rolled onto his back, pulling her on top.

"Mm," she purred. She straddled his hips, her eyes sparking blue-green.

He filled his hands with her taut, round ass. "I love it when I see your cougar."

She leaned forward to rub the tips of her nipples over his chest. "The cat wants to eat you up." The movement brought her mound against his cock. She gave another sexy purr and wriggled against him.

Heat sizzled up his spine. He flung out his arms. "I'm all yours."

She straightened up, her gaze on where his erection curved between their bellies. His fingers curled into his palms, but he kept still.

"Your move," he murmured.

She smiled—and did exactly what he'd hoped, wrapping those slim, competent fingers around him.

"That's it," he rasped. "Harder."

She slid her hand up and down his hard length, stroking and squeezing. The pads of her fingers were calloused, the slight roughness oddly arousing. The slit wept liquid and she smoothed it over the flushed cap.

His breath quickened. Remaining still became an impossibility.

With a low, inarticulate sound, he thrust into her fist. She worked him with one hand while with the other she played with his balls. Then she curved over his abdomen and swiped her hot little tongue over the cap.

His entire body clenched. "Holy fuck."

And then it got even better, because she lapped at the sensitive underside, licked her way up and down. It was so good, it hurt—and he wanted it to go on forever.

But of course, it couldn't. His balls drew up tight, and pleasure gathered at the base of his spine. He was close to exploding when she came higher onto her knees and placed his tip at her entrance.

He stilled, recalling they had no protection. Teeth clenched, he gripped her hips and lifted her a little away. "I don't want to give you a baby."

Thank the gods she was fada. No STDs, hardly any risk of pregnancy without the mate bond. But even so, he was careful these days. He'd gotten Evie's mom pregnant, after all.

Her brow furrowed. "But we're not mates."

"I wasn't mated to Evie's mom, either. I'll pull out."

She nodded and eased down on his dick. His mind went blank as wet, silky heat enclosed him.

When he was fully inside her, she stroked her hands down his abdomen with an appreciative hum. "You're all muscle."

"One advantage of being a wayfarer."

"You grow hot muscles?" She trailed a fingertip down the ridges of his abdomen.

He chuckled. "We burn a lot of energy, and we're natural athletes." He moved his hips, enjoying how her pupils dilated.

"Ah." She leaned forward, set her hands on his chest and began to move. The milky quartz banged against his chest, and without breaking her rhythm, she dragged it off and dropped it on the cavern floor.

He caressed the smooth, golden-brown skin of her hips and ass. "That's it, love."

He moved his hands to her breasts, playing with her firm little nipples. He gave them a pinch and her breath hissed out.

He smiled. "You like that."

At her murmur of assent, he pinched them harder. She

twisted his nipples in playful retaliation, and his balls drew tight.

He began to move, meeting her thrusts with his own. She ground her pelvis on his, and contracted around him.

"More," she husked. "I need it harder."

Oh, yeah.

Happy to oblige, he rolled over so she lay on her back on the sweaters. Bracing himself on his forearms, he gave her a deep, leisurely kiss and, when she wrapped her arms and legs around him, began thrusting again. Slow at first, and then, when she dug her fingernails into his ass and urged him on with broken cries, hard and fast.

Heated inner walls squeezed him. She breathed out his name and came, the pulsing of her sex almost sending him over the edge with her.

He gritted his teeth and slowed down, riding out her orgasm, and then pulled out. A few strokes against her abdomen, and a goddamned fireball exploded through him. He groaned and buried his face in her neck, breathing her in as he rode the searing wave.

In its aftermath, he curled over her body, breath sawing in and out of his lungs, careful not to put his full weight on her. When he could talk again, he pressed a kiss to each of her eyelids. "Thank you."

Her low chuckle did funny things to his heart. "No thanks necessary."

He heaved himself off her and then lay down beside her on the hard stone, half-off the sweaters. Somehow she found the energy to rearrange the sweaters so they made a small bed. He scooted over so he was fully on them while she rose to clean herself in the pool.

When she returned, she curled up next to him, head on his shoulder. He tucked her close to his side. He hadn't figured her for a cuddler, but he liked it. He looked down at where her eyes were closed, her face relaxed. She looked so damn young. Too young to be a clan second.

His heart filled. *I love you*, he thought, but knew he couldn't say it. She'd probably laugh in his face. Instead, he brushed his lips over her forehead.

Her eyes opened. "You didn't have to pull out. If I did get pregnant, the clan would welcome the baby. We have so few cubs."

"Even so. Since Evie, I've been careful."

She glanced away. "I guess I'm not mom-material anyway. I...I'll probably never mate."

He made a low sound of disagreement. "You'd make a great mother."

"How would you know?"

"Because you love with all your heart—your brother, your friends, your clan. And you've seen enough to know that life's precious. Any kid would be lucky to have you as a mother."

"Yeah?" She gave him a wistful smile. "Well, thanks."

She was silent for a time, and then she pressed a kiss to the underside of his jaw. She smelled of sex and her own earthy spice. "You're not what I expected."

"Neither are you."

"Mm. When I heard how Evie's dad was never around when she was growing up, I figured you for a selfish ass. But then she told me about how you always seemed to show up when they really needed you, and I wondered why."

"Don't kid yourself." He stared bleakly at the ceiling. "I *am* a selfish ass."

"Maybe. But you love Evie, don't you? I think you stayed away to protect her."

He moved a shoulder. "I couldn't be sure the king wouldn't use her against me. Or worse, someone like Lady B. And as long as I'm under the *geas*, my life's not my own."

"Oh, Fane." Her voice was sad. "You're in deep, aren't you?"

His stomach constricted. He hadn't allowed himself to want for a long time. Not another person, anyway. But he wanted Marjani, bad.

He could guess what her life had been like up until now. The Baltimore Earth Fada were a small, poor clan. Most of their elders had died in those bloody feuds she called the Dark-time. She'd probably had to fight for every last scrap she owned.

He yearned to pamper her. Drape her in pearls and diamonds, buy her flowers and chocolate. Indulge her with expensive clothes and trips to exotic, sunny places.

Evie's mom had been a mistake, but he'd been good to her in his own way. When she'd found another man—one who loved her back and was willing to take on Evie—Fane had been happy for her. And he was older now, smarter.

But Marjani was her brother's second, and intensely loyal. She'd never leave Adric and Baltimore.

And even though Fane was allowed his own women, there was no fucking way Sindre would allow him *this* woman. Besides, he was under a *geas*. Even if Sindre allowed it, it would just give the king power over them both.

The words spilled out anyway. "You asked if I ever come to Baltimore. I've been thinking—this doesn't have to be a one-night thing. The king will forgive me." He hoped. "I'll wait a couple of months, and then send you a message. I have a condo on the Mediterranean—in Spain, near Barcelona. We can meet there. No one has to know."

"Yeah?"

Encouraged, he said, "Say yes, Jani. I'll buy you anything you want. Clothes. Jewels…"

She stiffened and he trailed off.

"Fane." That was all she said. But it was all she needed to say.

He took her mouth, pouring everything he knew about seduction into the kiss. "Think about it. That's all I ask."

She turned her head away. "If we do meet, it won't be because you fucking pay me."

He swore under his breath. "I'm sorry." He nudged her chin until she was looking at him again. "I didn't mean it that way. It's just that I want to buy you pretty things."

Because I love you, damn it.

"But you don't have to. I don't need them."

"Got that. Loud and clear."

The hell with talking. He had the sinking feeling that nothing he could say would change her mind. And she'd made it clear this was a one-time thing. He might as well enjoy it while he could.

He inserted his thigh between hers, wrapped his hand around her nape and gave her a deep kiss.

Their lovemaking this time was urgent, frenzied. The bittersweet coming together of two people who knew something was ending almost before it had begun.

25

———

$\mathcal{M}$arjani let out a sigh and rested her head on Fane's chest. The second time had been even better than the first. She'd been able to enjoy it without worrying she was going to freak out on him and go clawed.

Now dawn was speeding toward them way too fast. If she could just stop time, have another day with him. But they had only a few hours.

She stroked a hand down the hard planes of his abdomen to where his cock lay nestled on a patch of wiry dark hair.

"Hold that thought, love." He pressed a drowsy kiss to her temple. "You wore me out."

She grinned. "I guess you *are* just getting over a fever." She wrapped an arm around his waist and drifted off, sure that tonight, there'd be no nightmares.

She was wrong.

Men. Stinking of alcohol and lust.

Grabbing her, so hard they bruised her. Throwing her down on the floor. Thrusting into her.

Hurting her.

Shame filled every corner of her...spilled onto the floor along with her cries.

Weak. She was so damn weak.

The aphrodisiac burned like fire in her belly...and lower. And after a while, she'd stopped fighting—and begged, instead.

They'd made her beg. That was the one thing she couldn't forget...or forgive. She'd held out for as long as she could—fighting them, and then when she couldn't fight anymore, closed her eyes and pretended it wasn't happening to her.

The drug racing through her veins...making her weak and needy. That was what an aphrodisiac did to you—made you crave sensation. Sex. Pain. Drugs. Alcohol.

And when they ordered her to beg for more, she did.

They just laughed and passed her from man to man, until she curled into a tiny ball in her mind and tried not to go mad.

From far away she heard whimpering and knew it was her. But her eyelids stayed glued shut.

Without Tiago do Rio, she didn't know what would've happened.

He'd killed one man and scattered the others. Then he'd passed out and she'd spent the night beside his unconscious body, trembling from the effects of the drug...wondering if he'd wake up and rape her too, because they'd both been given the same powerful aphrodisiac.

And the worst thing was, she might not have fought him off. The drug had made her crave sex like a cat in heat.

No. No. No.

She moved her head restlessly from side to side.

"Jani. Jani." Fane stroked a hand down her back. "Wake up, love."

His gravelly voice, his scent—she knew it was him, and yet she didn't. The arms cuddling her became a cage. Terror swamped her.

Never again.

She fought free of his grip and crouched on the stone floor, breath scraping in and out of her lungs.

"Hey," he said. "Calm down. It's only me."

She unpeeled her eyelids. Her fingers were claws. She laid her ears back on her head, hissing in warning.

She realized she'd shifted partially to her cougar.

They stared at each other. She knew what Fane saw: a monster—a woman half-covered in fur with a cougar's paws and ears and teeth.

A corner of his mouth lifted in a sympathetic smile. "Bad dream, huh?"

She hissed again. But the spell was broken. Because she scented absolutely no fear—just concern.

He patted the nest of sweaters. "Come here."

She ignored him to creep to her cargo pants and her quartz, still in a side pocket. She set her paw on it, drew a deep breath —and shifted back to woman. Taking out her quartz, she sat on the cold stone floor facing the pool, the quartz tight in her hand.

Breathe in, breathe out.

The water steamed around her. She'd almost gotten used to the stench of sulfur.

Behind her, she heard movement—Fane curling up on the sweaters. "I'm here," he said. Just that and nothing else.

She moistened her lips. "I'm sorry."

"Jani. You have nothing to be sorry for."

"Yeah? I nearly ripped your throat out."

"But you didn't."

"No." She chuckled darkly. "Give the woman a freaking gold star."

"I'm not afraid of you."

"You should be."

Rising to her feet, she splashed some water on her face and then went around the back to pee. While Fane took his turn, she washed up and pulled on her briefs and a T-shirt. When he came back, she was seated at the pool's edge again, feet dangling in the hot water, the quartz still in her hand.

Fane donned his boxers and sat down beside her. Not touching her, but close enough to feel his body heat. His scent wrapped around her. Familiar...reassuring.

"I've seen a hundred turns of the sun," he said. "Did you know that?"

She shook her head. "You don't look much older than me. Although if you're Evie's dad, I guess you must be."

He nodded. "For sixty of those years, I've been the king's envoy. In that time I've done a lot of things I'm not proud of. But the worst was giving you to him."

"No!" She whipped her head around. "I gave *myself* to him. I might as well have wrapped myself up in shiny paper and mailed myself to the ice fae court."

"I should've stopped you. Way back in Reykjavik."

"You really think you could've stopped me? Even my brother couldn't, and he's my alpha." She looked back at the shimmering black water. "I knew what I was getting into. And I didn't care, as long as I took Corban with me."

"I thought it might be something like that." He inched closer so his shoulder touched hers. "What happened, Jani? What did they do to you?"

"You don't want to know."

"Maybe. But I think you need to tell someone. An outsider."

She pulled her legs out of the water and wrapped her arms around her legs. Maybe he was right. The first month, she shared parts of her story with Suha and Adric, but for the past year, she hadn't talked about it all.

"They gave me an aphrodisiac," she told her toes, the images unspooling in her mind.

He sucked in a breath.

"These were old fada. Going feral. You know what that means?"

"Not exactly."

"When we get old or damaged somehow, the animal takes over. You fae call us animals, but we're not. Trust me, there's a difference."

He touched her back. "I have *never* called you an animal. Even in my thoughts."

She nodded against her legs. "The alpha was from Greece. He mixed the aphrodisiac himself from an old recipe. It was... incredibly strong. It drove me a little crazy. They slapped me. Hurt me. And I wanted it." She sipped a breath. "I even wanted the sex."

"It was the drug, Jani. Not you."

"That's what I tell myself. Sometimes I even believe it."

He started to put an arm around her.

"Don't." She hunched her shoulders. "Let me finish."

"All right." He brought his arm back to his side.

"I begged them, Fane." She forced the words past her lips. "Instead of fighting them, I begged them for more."

His swallow was loud in the quiet cavern. "I'm so sorry. If I could only go back and change things for you, I would. But I can't. All I can say is that you're strong. A warrior who should never have had to fight that kind of battle. But you survived, and I'm so grateful for that."

Sharp glass filled her throat.

"I'm broken," she managed to say. "I spent most of the last year as my cougar. Because it's safer that way. Now I'm afraid to shift. Afraid the cougar will take over once and for all."

"*No.* Not broken. A survivor." He reached for her again, and this time she went into his arms.

He pulled her onto his lap and pressed a kiss to the top of her head. She stared, dry-eyed, at the pool. She was so fucking tired. Most nights, she only slept in snatches.

Fane stroked her back. Slow, soothing caresses. He crooned a wordless tune in his rough, sexy voice. Gradually she relaxed.

He massaged her nape until her head drooped, then murmured, "Let's lie down."

When she nodded, he rose to his feet and carried her the few steps to their sweater-nest, where he lay on his back, her draped over him like a blanket.

Keeping the quartz loosely in her hand, she laid her head on his chest, grateful for the sound of his heartbeat. It made her feel less alone.

"I'm here," he murmured one more time. And for now, that was enough.

26

Fane woke to find the thin light of dawn spilling through a crack in the cavern ceiling. But what had awakened him was the tug of the *geas*.

His heart sank. Guess Sindre knew he'd recovered.

A chilly white mist formed in his palm. Blue writing unfurled against it and then faded away: *Return to court. If the fada is with you, bring her, too.*

He drew a long breath. Such a long-distance command didn't have the same power as when Sindre addressed him directly, but he couldn't ignore it.

He turned to Marjani—but he was alone on the cavern floor.

He lifted up a little and saw her creeping fully dressed toward the exit, her boots in her hands. He felt a sharp hurt that after the night they'd shared, she'd sneak out without even saying goodbye. But how could he blame her?

The *geas* tugged harder. He dropped back on the floor and clenched his jaw, resisting. Let her go. That way, he could truthfully say he didn't know where she was.

Gods, it had nearly broken him to hear her story last night.

The things the woman had survived. It was amazing she was still walking around.

Just before they'd fallen asleep, she'd curled into a ball on her side, wound tight as a watch spring. He'd followed, wrapping his body around her.

Somehow, he'd vowed as his eyes drifted shut, he'd save her from Sindre and Blaer.

Now he glanced at her again. Maybe he could use Sindre's order to help her? Because he *knew* she was going back to the court to save that damn friend of hers—and the king would be waiting. That maze of his would snap shut on her like a wolf's jaws.

He sat up. "Wait."

She whipped around as he snatched up his clothes.

Her eyes blazed cougar-blue. "Let me go, Fane."

"You're going back, aren't you?" He zipped up his jeans and sat down to put on his shoes. "To save your friend."

"I'm not going to answer that. You're under a *geas*, remember?" She stepped into her boots and leaned over to tie them.

He winced but persisted. "He might have escaped."

"Then where is he? He's a wolf. If he got away from them, he would've followed our scent."

He blew out a breath and tried another tack. "You need me. You can't get through the portals without me."

"I did it once."

"And the goblins almost captured you."

She finished tying her boots and straightened up, arms crossed over the pert breasts he'd kissed just a few short hours ago. "Goodbye, Fane," she said in a hard voice. Then she scraped a hand over her shaved head. "Have...a good life, okay?"

She slanted him a crooked smile that arrowed straight to his heart—and slipped into the tunnel.

"Damn it, Jani." He strode across the cavern and inched his way after her.

She bared her teeth at him. "Stay the fuck away from me. Or is this a way to get back on the king's good side?"

His jaw set. "Look, you want back in, and I have to return—so why don't we work together? I'll escort you into the castle, and then you can give me the slip. That should give you a chance to do whatever you need to do."

"No fucking way." She kept going.

"Bloody-minded woman." He followed her as she made her way back to the surface. When the passage narrowed, this time he bent his knees so his shoulders wouldn't get stuck, and squeezed his way through.

When they emerged from the boulders, the rising sun washed the sky a pale pink and gold. To the north, Sindre's magic hid the castle from the human world, but as a member of the court, Fane could see it hunched on the tundra, dark and brooding.

He grabbed Marjani's arm. "Please don't go back there." He desperately tried to come up with an argument that would keep her safe, but he had nothing.

And the *geas* had sunk its talons deep now. If he walked in any direction but toward the castle, it would get stronger until he literally couldn't take another step except in the way Sindre wished him to go.

Marjani's eyes changed to blue frost. She bared her teeth. "Let. Me. Go," she said in a guttural, barely human voice.

Wariness slid up his spine. He loosened his grip, uncomfortably aware he was dealing with a woman who could change into a large, predatory cat. But some stubborn part of him refused to believe she'd attack him.

"At least promise you won't take the king's bargain."

Some of the brown seeped back into her irises. She set a

hand on his cheek. "I can't promise that. Luc is clan, one of my brother's lieutenants. But more than that—we grew up together. I won't leave without him. Not when it's my fault he's here."

"The hell it's your fault. He's an adult; he makes his own choices. And I'd bet if he was here right now, he'd tell you to save yourself."

"Maybe. But..." She moved a shoulder. "He's in love with me. I knew he'd follow me, but I just had to prove I could do this."

Something dark made his fingers tighten on her arm. "Is he your mate?"

"No." Her gaze flew to him, startled. "I...don't feel the same."

That was something, at least. He blew out a breath. "Look, I have to go back anyway. At least let me get you safely inside. But we have to hurry. The best time to slip through the portals undetected is at dawn or dusk when the guard changes."

"No. Now let me go." She looked pointedly at his hand.

He hesitated, knowing he should let her go and yet unable to. And the awful thing was, he wasn't sure how much was him and how much was the *geas*.

"Goodbye, Fane." She wrenched herself from his grip and took a step back, her eyes sad but determined.

He opened his mouth and then shut it again as the truth struck him like a boot to the gut. She didn't trust him. And she was right, because he wasn't sure how far he could go before the *geas* made him betray her.

Sorrow stabbed through him. His throat felt too thick to breathe.

In accepting the *geas*, he'd lost her before he'd ever even had her.

He curled his fingers into his palms to keep himself from reaching for her. "Go, then," he said through numb lips.

She set off for the castle at a jog. He watched her go with

the hungry eyes of a man who'd lost everything, including his self-respect.

Suddenly, she stilled, slim body taut, her eyes trained on a slight rise a hundred yards away. She'd never appeared so catlike.

His scalp lifted. "Jani? What is it?"

She slashed her hand downward. "*Quiet.*"

A high-pitched, excited shrieking came on the wind. *Goblins.*

What the fuck? Why would the king order Fane to return and then allow Blaer to send her little fiends after them? But there was no time to ponder that.

He raced across the grass, scooped up Marjani and turned to run back to the cavern. But they were surrounded, the small, fur-clad beings hurtling at them from every direction.

"We have to fight." She twisted out of his arms. "Here." She shoved the dagger into his hand and stood back to back with him, her switchblade ready.

"Hell." He looked from the dagger to the goblins racing across the tundra. "You think I know how to use this thing?"

"It's iron. Aim for the eyes. The poison will slow them down."

"I have a better idea." Gripping the dagger, point out, he reached back with his other hand, looped his fingers through Marjani's belt loops and made the two of them invisible, a shadow on the tundra. "They can't see us now," he whispered.

"Works." She kept her eyes on the goblins, who had slowed to a creep, chittering in puzzlement to each other.

Marjani lashed out, stabbing the closest ones in the throat. Unable to see her, they fell at her feet, dead. Even Fane managed to take out a goblin that had practically run straight into his dagger.

The rest fell back, muttering to each other. Fane and Marjani stilled, scarcely daring to breathe. But they were surrounded by the dead goblins' bodies. Even goblins—who weren't the brightest creatures on the planet—could deduce where they must be. With a gleeful roar, the remaining goblins piled on.

Razor-sharp teeth sank into Fane's arm. Black claws raked over his face. Behind him, he heard grunts as Marjani's blade found a few more of their attackers.

But ten more goblins took their place, dragging Fane to the ground. Marjani was torn from his grip. He lost his focus, and they both became visible again.

He glanced up to see Blaer had 'ported onto the boulders. The blond hair whipping around her face didn't hide her smug smile.

Then a rock smashed into his temple and everything went black.

ane was down, his head bloody. Marjani's breath hitched.

Please let him be okay. Don't let me lose him, too.

Because walking away from him had been right up there with one of the hardest things she'd ever done in her life. But how could she trust a man under Sindre's *geas*?

The goblins kept coming, so she couldn't even check if he was still breathing. Snatching up the dagger, she grimly fought on, a blade in each hand.

But the vicious little creatures seemed to multiply like rabbits. For every goblin she killed, two more sprang forward to take its place. Biting and gouging her, until she was bleeding from multiple wounds and their sour stench filled her nostrils.

They climbed each other to leap at her until a blow knocked her to her knees beside Fane's prone body. Her knives went flying. She scrabbled for them, but the dagger was too far away, and she didn't know where the switchblade was.

A stir in the air made her lift her head. Blaer had 'ported in, although she chose to perch on the rocks above the fray.

Marjani snarled and inched her way toward the dagger. It wasn't a throwing knife, but she thought she could still hit her mark.

There. She had it.

A shadow near Blaer's leg moved and became a wolf—a wolf with Luc's eyes and a quartz hanging from its neck.

The fae lady set a hand on his head—and smiled.

"*No.*" Marjani wasn't sure if she'd whispered or shouted. She leapt to her feet and aimed the dagger at Blaer's throat.

A small body slammed into her legs at the same time another landed on her back. Wiry arms wrapped around her wrist, pulling her arm down so that the dagger hit a boulder instead of Blaer. Long nails raked down Marjani's body, ripping through her clothes to dig into her skin.

Marjani spun in circles, trying to knock them off, but they kept piling on until she fell flat on her stomach. Maddened with pain and the goblins' high-pitched shrieks, the cat forced its way to the surface. Bloodlust filled her, hot and red. She shifted partway, teeth elongating and claws sprouting from her fingertips, and fought as her animal. Sinking her teeth into the goblins' squat necks. Ripping open their soft bellies with her claws.

Someone moved behind her. She tried to twist away, but there was nowhere to go—she was surrounded. Something hard crashed into the back of her skull and a white light exploded behind her eyes.

The next thing she knew, she lay curled on her side, looking through bars.

Shiny iron bars.

MARJANI SWALLOWED, her mouth still filled with the bitter taste of the goblins' blood. She scrubbed a hand over her lips and tried not to wretch.

She was fully human again and lying on a sheepskin. Not touching the iron directly, but she still felt like crap from the poisonous metal already seeping into her. Not to mention that her body was bruised and bloodied from the fight with the goblins.

From its place against her thigh, her quartz hummed a healing song, valiantly doing what it could, but with the iron surrounding her, the best she could hope for was to maintain.

And the decoy quartz around her neck was gone.

She lifted her head. Pain lanced her brain. The room swooped around the cage, leaving her shaking and nauseated.

"Jani." In the next cage, Fane crouched on his haunches, his clothing in shreds, his face a mass of bruises and an egg-sized lump on his temple. "You all right?"

She closed her eyes and concentrated on not throwing up. Even talking was difficult through her swollen mouth.

"Yeah," she managed to say. "And you?"

"I've been better." Even with her eyes closed, she somehow knew his mouth had kicked up in his trademark wry grin.

"Blaer?" She spoke the fae lady's name, because what did it matter if she drew her attention?

"We're alone for now, except for the black wolf. I'm not sure if he's still alive, though. He hasn't moved once in the last half hour."

Corban could go fuck himself. It was Luc she was worried about. She made herself ask. "Luc?"

"No. It's only us three."

"No. She has...him. I saw."

"Fuck. I'm sorry."

Her chest constricted. Luc had been there for her through thick and thin, patiently waiting for her to grow up and choose him as her mate. For a while, she'd thought maybe... But no. It had been some time since she'd known she just didn't think of him in that way.

But even though she'd told him that, he'd stubbornly insisted on waiting. Hoping.

Tears seeped from her eyes. She cried not because she loved Luc, but because she didn't—at least, not in the way a woman loves her mate. And now he was under Blaer's control. If only she hadn't been so hellbent on proving she still had what it took to be Adric's second, he might still be back in Baltimore.

"It's okay, sweetheart," murmured Fane. "There's a canteen next to you. Drink. It's just water."

Without opening her eyes, she felt for it. The first thing she did was rinse her mouth and spit out the water through the bars of the cage. Then she took a few small sips, needing the fluid but afraid her stomach would rebel. The water soothed her swollen mouth, and she managed to keep it down.

She capped the canteen and set it back down before lifting her hand to explore the bump on the back of her skull. It was caked with dried blood, but at least it was no longer bleeding.

Next, her hand went to her front pocket. Her stomach lurched as she confirmed that she'd lost both the switchblade and the dagger. Even her stiletto would've been something, but she'd tossed it to Luc. She was defenseless.

Panic clawed her nape. Behind her eyelids, black spots danced.

"Hey." Fane's voice. "You still with me?"

She dropped her hand back to the sheepskin. *Answer him.*

But she couldn't seem to summon up the energy.

He muttered something harsh. "Shift, damn it. You'll heal faster."

True. But there was a reason she shouldn't. She feared letting the cat out, weak and exhausted as she was.

She lifted heavy eyelids. This time, the room remained steady.

And at least her quartz was still safe in her cargo pants. The pocket's flap had ripped, but by some miracle, the zipper had held. She set a hand over the material covering it and concentrated on not throwing up.

Fane had dropped onto his hands and knees. His whole body spoke of his worry for her. "Jani. You need to shift."

"Can't," she said between swollen lips.

"Why the fuck not?"

"Not...in control."

His forehead creased. "What do you mean?"

"Cougar...wants to take over."

"So? You won't let it."

She gave a mirthless chuckle. "Not...that simple."

"Screw that." Blue eyes blazed into hers. "You *can*. I know you can."

For some damn reason, she believed him. She wriggled out of the tattered sweater first. Someone had removed her boots. She eased her briefs and pants down her legs at the same time, taking care with the deep slash on her right thigh, and then pulled off her socks.

Next came her T-shirt. Just pulling it over her head made her go blind with pain. A moan escaped her lips. She curled into a panting, agonized ball, and then gritted her teeth and dragged off her bra, too.

"That's my girl," Fane said.

She growled, low and mean, but he just winked back.

Sitting cross-legged on the sheepskin, she dug her quartz out of the pocket. Holding it to her heart, she opened herself to the shift.

Another wave of nausea rolled through her. She clenched her jaw and kept trying. Her quartz warmed against her chest, but the energy level was dangerously low. That was bad—she'd counted on drawing on the tiny crystals to help her through the shift. She estimated she had a fifty-fifty chance of succeeding.

She swallowed dryly. Should she risk it?

But for once, her cat's independence served her. It surged up, determined to be out. For a few frightening seconds she wavered between human and cat—and then she was crouched on the sheepskin as her cougar.

"Excellent," said Fane.

She twitched her tail, pleased with both herself and him.

Already she felt better. The shift had healed the minor cuts and bruises, including her swollen mouth. Even her head ached less.

Her sharp hearing detected a faint heartbeat to her right. Corban—alive, but close to death.

She gave her injured thigh a few soothing licks and then settled onto the rug, positioning her center over her quartz. The healing energy hummed through her, sinking into her very bones. If she could just get out of this fucking cage, she could go looking for Luc. But the iron continued to sap her energy.

Fane lay down on his rug with a sigh. She eyed him anxiously. He was hurt bad—worse than her. His heartbeat was slow and uneven, and blood seeped from cuts and gashes all over his body, its sharp iron-and-silver scent filling her nostrils.

The cat yowled and flexed its claws, frantic to go to him. It couldn't understand why it couldn't batter itself against the cage door until it broke.

Bad. Too much blood. The man needs help.

Marjani mentally stroked its head. *Iron,* she told it. *Bad magic.*

"Love you," Fane rasped.

The cat purred, liking the sound of that. Beneath Marjani's abdomen, the quartz hummed joyfully against her heart.

Love? She didn't know about that, but Fane was hers in some way she didn't want to examine too deeply.

Ours, the cat agreed.

But it was bad that the man was in an iron cage. He needed to get out, to heal.

And then the thing Marjani most feared happened. The cougar wrenched control from her.

28

——————

The cat whined and pushed itself up on all fours.

The human was too cautious. Maybe battering itself against the cage wouldn't help, but it couldn't just lie there and do nothing. And it might bring that fae bitch running, and then the cat could sink its teeth into her.

"Jani?" The blond man with the good smell lifted his head. "What are you doing?"

The cougar flung itself against the door. The iron bars seared its fur. It fell back on the sheepskin, wheezing.

"No!" He pushed himself up on his forearms. "It's okay—honest. I know you can smell the blood, but don't forget, I'm a quarter fae. The cuts are already closing up."

Rising back onto all fours, the cat swung its head in the man's direction. A deep inhale confirmed he spoke the truth. The terror eased.

"Rest, now." A soft command. "If you want to help me, you have to heal first."

Calmer, but still agitated, the cat snarled at the locked door. It still wanted to go to him. It *needed* to go to him.

"Please, Jani." His gaze snagged the cat's. "Calm down. I can't stand for you to get hurt any worse."

Jani? The name belonged to the human part. The woman.

The cat turned it over in its mind. A cougar had no name—or need of one.

It shook its head. The cage pressed in on it from every direction. Something wild and primitive screamed for it to beat itself bloody against the bars. But the man was right—it needed to heal first. Then when the woman who had dared put the cat and its man in a cage returned, it would be ready.

The cat settled back onto the rug.

"That's it," the man said. "Rest."

The cat *was* tired. So tired... Its eyes shut and it dozed.

Time passed. An hour, maybe two. The cat had little use for the way humans marked time.

"Jani. Jani? Wake up, damn it. Someone's coming."

The cat jerked awake just as the heavy oak door banged open. The cat snapped up its quartz, hiding it in the pocket of its cheek. No way was that bitch getting her hands on its real quartz.

But it wasn't Blaer, it was a big, bearded redhead with the acrid silver scent of a pureblood.

The cat lifted onto its forepaws, growling a warning.

"That woman has gone too far," the redhead declared in ringing tones. "Caging the fada is one thing. But my own bloody grandson?"

Words. But they might be important. The cat allowed its Marjani-part to surface enough to understand.

"I agree," said a silky voice. The fae king with the cold gray eyes followed him into the room. "My apologies, Roald."

Roald? From Marjani, the cat got a picture of a fierce redhead who captained the fae king's warriors. Another picture told the cat that the warrior could conjure fae balls, the fae version of grenades. Take a direct hit, and you were toast.

The Marjani-part blinked. Fane was Lord Roald's *grandson*?

The man—Fane—pushed up onto his knees and glared at both fae, his heart beating hard and fast. He was too hurt to be moving.

The cat rose, anxious to go to him. To make him better.

More talk from the two purebloods. Then the king snapped his fingers and Fane's cage opened. He half-crawled, half-fell out and then, with a pained grunt, drew himself up to his full height.

"The boy needs healing," snapped the redheaded fae.

The fae king inclined his head. A fog-message formed in his palm and then disappeared. Thirty seconds later, a tall blonde with the serene presence of a healer entered the tower. Clucking her tongue at Fane's injuries, she set a hand on his back and urged him to sit.

"I'll stand." Fane glanced at the cougar. It could *feel* him willing it to trust him. That he'd get it out of the cage.

The cat stilled, its gaze flicking between him and the cold-eyed king.

"As you wish." The blond healer kept her hand on the small of Fane's back. Magic hummed in the air.

Fane's eyes drifted half shut.

The king gave the cat a small, satisfied smile. He might not have ordered the cat's imprisonment, but he was happy to have it in his power.

The cat whipped its tail back and forth. *Come closer if you dare.*

But the iron sapped its strength. It rested its head on its paws and stared at the king, unblinking, knowing that made the fae nervous.

"She's got pride," Roald murmured to the king.

"Yes."

They examined the cat. It curled its lip, letting them see a sharp white fang. Roald just shook his head, and the blond king's mouth curved in amusement.

Fane murmured a thank you to the healer. The bruises on his face had faded and the egg-sized lump on his temple had gone down. The blonde must be a powerful healer.

Fane crossed the room to the cat. "Shift," he murmured. "Don't give them an excuse to treat you as an animal."

The cat shook its head. The animal was strong. A fighter.

"Jani," he said. "Shift. *Now*."

The cat resisted.

Not Jani—cat.

The fae king and his warrior moved closer.

"Please, love." Reaching through the iron bars, the blond man smoothed a hand down its head.

The cat nuzzled his palm and without meaning to, let down its guard. Instantly, Marjani elbowed her way into its consciousness, saying, *Shift. I need to talk to Sindre. Bargain with him.*

Too much talking, the cat shot back.

Now, Marjani insisted. *Unless you want to be stuck in this cage until we die.*

The cat grumbled but conceded the point.

The shift this time was long and hard. It was too soon after the last one, and the cat was still recovering from its injuries, its quartz almost depleted of energy. Its head started to pound again.

Marjani surfaced in time to understand. Her entire body iced.

She wasn't going to make it. She was going to die, stuck halfway between forms.

29

*N*o. Terror seared Marjani's spine.

She sucked the quartz dry, but there still wasn't enough energy. Black edged her vision.

The cat panicked and tried to stop the shift, but that only made things worse. She fought with the frightened cougar for control. They'd gone too far to stop now.

Fane crouched beside the cage. "Shift, my beautiful cat," he crooned. "You can do it."

Love poured from him. She *felt* it, like something she could touch, grab hold of. The cougar calmed, and Marjani saw her chance.

She lunged at that love like a lifeline to yank herself through the shift—and then she was crouched on the sheepskin as a woman. Her breath shuddered in.

Goddess, that had been close, and not just the shift, either. She scraped her hands down her face. For a while there, she thought she'd finally gone feral.

She stood up, Fane rising with her. Her knees wobbled. She locked them, hoping Sindre wouldn't notice.

On the plus side, shifting twice had gone a long way toward

healing her. Only the knot on her skull and the slash on her thigh still hurt.

The king's gaze traveled down to her bare toes and back up, taking in every detail. If she'd had any doubts about what he wanted, that look erased them.

She lifted her chin and stared back. The fingers of her free hand twitched, yearning for the security of one of her blades. It was her worst nightmare: to be trapped in her human form with no weapons.

Like the night she was kidnapped.

She swallowed over the crater in her throat.

"Get dressed." Fane gestured at her clothes.

Clothes. Right. She glanced down at the tangled pile. The sweater was a lost cause, but the T-shirt was only ripped in a few places. She picked it up and stood, unmoving. Sipping breaths.

The bars of the cage pressed in on her. Her skin prickled.

Lord Roald muttered something impatient, but Fane gave her an encouraging smile. "Go ahead."

Yes. You're alive and healing. You still have a chance if you keep your head.

She didn't bother with her bra, just put on the black briefs. The T-shirt was next. She palmed the quartz as she pulled the shirt on, and as she stepped into the cargo pants, slipped the precious chunk of rock into her front pocket. But without her blades, she might as well be naked.

Naked and defenseless.

A cold drop of sweat slid down her spine. Her heart slammed against her ribs so hard she was sure everyone in the room could hear it.

The blond healer crossed the room to Marjani, her gray eyes compassionate. "She could use healing, too," she told the king.

Fane faced Sindre. "Let her out, and allow Ilka to heal her. You promised her no cages."

"So I did. But she didn't agree to the bargain, did she?"

"Fane," said his grandfather. "Stay out of this. It's between the king and the fada."

Fane ignored him to glare at the king. "Let her out," he insisted. "Or I swear I'll make sure her brother hears about this."

The two men locked gazes.

Marjani caught her breath. Was Fane batshit crazy? If he wasn't careful, Sindre was going to do that fucking frozen thing on him again.

Lord Roald cleared his throat. "The boy has a point. The fada before her were outcasts from their clans, or else had willingly entered into a bargain with Blaer. This woman is the Baltimore second. If she dies, her brother will stop at nothing to avenge her. You'll be fighting off assassination attempts for years."

The king considered that. "Very well. Blaer took her without my permission anyway." He snapped his fingers again, and the door swung open.

Marjani leapt out, and then wavered woozily on her feet. Immediately, Fane was there, wrapping an arm around her, lending her his strength.

He was warm and solid, and even covered in blood, had that faint scent of the outdoors she liked so much. She wanted so badly to lean on him.

But she saw a muscle in Sindre's jaw flex. Better not give him an excuse to hurt Fane again. She slipped out of his grip and put some space between them.

Ilka made a small, concerned sound. "You've used a lot of energy, between healing and shifting. If you'll allow, I can give you a boost."

Marjani hesitated, but the healer's scent held nothing but compassion. "Thanks," she replied. "I'd appreciate that."

Ilka ran a hand down Marjani's back, and her skin warmed as life-giving energy spread throughout her. Her pounding heart calmed, and her breath sighed out.

"That's better." The healer rubbed her back. "I wish I could do more," she said in an undertone, "but…"

Their eyes met. "Thank you," Marjani whispered back.

Ilka gave her a last squeeze before moving away.

Meanwhile, Fane had turned back to Sindre. "We were on our way back," he said in a hard voice. "You didn't have to set the goblins on us."

"That was Lady Blaer," the king returned.

"So she did it without your permission?" Lord Roald's lip curled. "God's balls, the night-fae woman grows bolder every day."

"Yes." Sindre's face seemed carved from ice. "She does."

Ilka stepped forward. "If I may speak, your highness?" When the king nodded, she said, "The fada is better, but she needs rest." She looked at Fane. "Both of them."

Sindre cut her off with a curt thanks. "That will be all, Ilka."

She inclined her head and glided out of the room.

"My tower." The king's gaze swept over Marjani, Fane and Roald. "Seven o'clock. All three of you. Consider this your invitation to dinner."

"We'll be there," Roald said.

"And Fane?" Sindre added. "Bring Marjani to the north tower first, and then return at seven for dinner. That's an order."

Fane nodded tightly, but Sindre had already 'ported out.

Dinner? Marjani thought. But then, the fae liked to think they were so civilized—as they forced you into unwilling bondage.

"You fool." Fane's grandfather scowled at him. "What were you thinking, to get involved with a fada?"

"Her name is Marjani."

The fae warrior raked his fierce hawk's eyes over her. "She's an animal, boy. And worse, the king wants her."

"Damn it, she's *not* an animal. She's a person—just like you or me. And the king can bloody well keep his hands off her."

Roald's heavy cinnamon brows lowered. "By the gods, you don't deserve my help."

Fane glowered back. "When have you ever helped me?"

"Who do you think vouched for you with the king?"

"That wasn't you, it was my dad."

"Aye, Arne brought you to the king's attention, but it was I who asked him to give you a chance. And this couldn't come at a worse time." Roald shook his head. "I've requested that the king declare you a full member of the court."

"A full member?" Fane got a funny look on his face. "You'd do that for me?"

Marjani looked from him to his grandfather. A full member of the court? She wasn't sure exactly what it meant, but it was obviously a big deal.

"You're my grandson, after all. And I have some small influence with the king."

"But you never said anything..."

"Well, what did you expect? You're a mixed-blood, and on top of that, you're too much like your father. Wayfarers, not warriors." Roald's mouth turned down as if that said it all. "But as I said the other day, I've been keeping an eye on you. You've made me proud. In your own way, you have courage. And you've proven your loyalty to the king."

Fane gave a short nod. "Thank you."

The big redhead raised a hand. "Let me finish. But this, this is an embarrassment. The whole court knows you snatched this fada from under the king's protection and ran away with her. You want to have a woman like her, fine. But not a woman that Sindre wants. Where's your common sense, boy?"

"The king's *protection*?" Fane's voice was coldly furious. "He wants Marjani as his plaything. He offered her anything she wanted—wealth, power. And when she turned him down, he tried to use her love for her friend to force her into accepting his *geas*. I saved her from him, damn it."

The two men glared at each other. It was Roald who looked away first. "The king awaits," he ground out, and stalked from the room.

Fane watched him go, his body rigid, before turning to her. "I'm sorry you had to hear that. He's old and set in his ways."

"I know." She twined her arms around his neck and gave him a crooked smile. "Thanks for sticking up for me. Here I thought you were just another fae asshole."

He smoothed the backs of his fingers over her cheek. "Do me a favor."

"What?"

"Don't lump me with those arses."

"You got it."

They grinned at each other, but it was the kind of smile you give when everything is about to go to shit.

"I have something for you." He pulled her switchblade out of his pocket.

Her jaw dropped. "How in Hades did you get that?"

"Wayfarer, you know. Quick hands."

"But you were unconscious. I saw you myself."

"I came to while we were still on the ground. It was just a few feet away. I managed to grab it before the goblins saw it." His throat worked. "I have to take you to the king's tower, Jani. The *geas*—it's pulling on me."

"I know. But this. I—" She slid the blade in and out a few times. Despite a few dents, it worked as good as ever. She clenched her fingers on the handle. "Thank you. It's the best gift you could have given me."

"Better than diamonds or pretty clothes?" He set his hands on her hips.

She lifted her eyes to his. His eyes were so clear, like falling up into the sky.

"Way better," she husked. "Light-years better."

His grip tightened on her. "I won't let him have you. I swear on my mother's grave."

"Oh, Fane." She came up on her toes to kiss his scruffy jaw. "I love that you said that. But—" She halted, but they both knew what she was thinking.

What could Fane do against one of the most powerful fae in the world? And there was the *geas*, too.

"I'll think of something. Promise me you won't agree to his bloody bargain."

"You know I can't promise that."

"Damn it, Jani." He pulled her hard against him, her face pressed to the crook of his neck. She heard his heartbeat beneath her cheek and it came to her. Like lightning on a dark night or a crack of thunder that rocked her to her soul.

Her breath snagged. This was why the cat had called him *Mine*. Why she'd felt his love and had been able to draw on it to finish the shift.

Because the mate bond had budded, fragile as a just-born rose. Her mom had told Marjani she'd know it when she felt it, and oh, she did. It made her hot and yearning and needful— and sad to the depths of her soul.

Because she couldn't let that beautiful, delicate bud grow into anything. For so many reasons, they weren't right for each other. She was a fada soldier. He was the stupid-rich, classy-as-fuck envoy of the ice fae king. She could never fit into his world.

And as for Fane fitting into hers? Yeah, right. She could just picture him living in a den in Baltimore. And what would Adric say? He might be more tolerant than Leron, but if his sister—and second—came back mated with a part-fae, it would cause trouble.

"Jani?" He set a finger under her chin and tipped up her face. What he saw there made him furrow his brow.

Then his face changed. His eyes crinkled and his lips curved. For once, she didn't see a trace of wryness or irony in his expression.

Just wonder and heat.

He said her name again, low and rough. "*Jani.*"

Mate. That was the cougar.

Her heart lurched. "No," she rasped and turned away.

Fane grabbed her upper arm. She stilled, and he wrapped his arms around her from behind. "When this is over, we're going to talk."

"No."

"Yes," he returned, soft but firm. Warm lips traced the side of her neck. "Do you think I'll let you go just like that? No fucking way."

And here she'd thought he was laid-back. But it made her smile, deep inside, to know he wanted her so much. Even if it would never work.

She pushed at his arms and got her nape nipped in retaliation.

"I want your promise." A growled demand.

She blew out a breath and gave in. Because really, what was she afraid of? Give the man a few days, and he'd see for himself how impossible this thing between them was.

"Fine." She let her head rest against his shoulder. "I promise."

"Good." He kissed the spot he'd nipped. "And now, we'd better go before the king sends someone looking for us." He urged her toward the door with a hand on her back.

She halted. Corban had lifted his head to watch them. She slipped out of Fane's grip.

"Wait for me outside," she told him. "I'll be right there."

"Leave him." Fane's gaze followed hers. "We don't need any more trouble."

"I can't."

"Then I'm staying right here."

She recognized that tone. He wasn't going to budge. Still, she tried one more time. "I don't want you to see this."

"Jani," he said, very patiently. "I've seen a hundred turns of the sun. Where do you get the idea you have to protect me?"

She dragged a hand over her stubbled head. "Stay then," she gritted, and crossed to her cousin.

Corban pushed himself up to stand on trembling legs, chest working like a bellows. Tiny sparks of light spread over his black fur, dim but visible, and then he changed to man. Somehow, he'd found the strength to shift.

He crouched on the floor of the cage, lungs heaving. He'd always seemed larger than life: a dominant, compelling man like his father. Now he was emaciated, his brown skin covered with sores, deep lines of pain scored on his face.

She felt an unexpected wave of sorrow. If only she could call Adric—let him handle this. But her smartphone didn't work inside the castle, and besides, he was three thousand miles away in Maryland.

She set her jaw. "Tell me what happened to Luc. Why is he with that fae bitch?"

Corban lifted his head, and she braced herself for a sneering comment about how she'd managed to get herself captured not once, but twice.

When he said, "I'm ready," it took her a few beats to understand.

She drew a serrated breath. "Not 'til you tell me what happened to Luc."

Corban didn't seem to hear. "Use your fucking knife. Don't let me die like some animal in a cage."

Her fingers tightened around the switchblade handle. "Why should I show you any mercy?"

"Because it's Adric's fault I'm here."

She scowled. "Oh, no. You don't get to put this on Ric."

"He sent me after Lady B."

"So? You were supposed to turn her over to the king, not ally yourself with her."

"I'm not stupid, Jani. I knew Adric sent me to India to die."

"Because you gave me to those river fada, you bastard. We both knew you were behind it, even if we couldn't prove it."

His big hands clenched on the sheepskin rug. "Without any backup, I was an easy target for Lady B. So instead, I made a deal with her—she'd help me win alpha, and I'd protect her from Sindre. But the king kept sending people after her, and she gave up and came home. Somehow they worked out a truce —she has him wrapped around her little finger now. And I'm in here." His gold eyes burned into hers, filmy and tinged with madness. "So my loving cousin owes me."

"Like hell. You brought this mess on yourself. You worked against him from the day he took over as alpha."

"I should've been alpha, not him."

"No fucking way. It was a fair challenge. The stronger man won."

Corban growled.

"You just don't get it, do you? Ric is stronger than you in every way that counts. The clan has a chance now, under him."

Her cousin closed his eyes.

She rubbed her nape. Why was she fighting with him? He was going to pass out without her learning anything.

"Tell me what you know about Luc," she said, "and I'll do it."

Beside her, Fane tensed.

Her chest squeezed. She didn't want him to see this. He'd probably never killed a man in his life, while she'd killed so many, their faces ran together in her mind.

"Go," she hissed. "I promise, I'll be there in a minute."

He crossed his arms over his chest. "I'll wait."

"*Please*," she said, but all she got was a shake of his head.

Then Corban spoke, and she turned back to him. Maybe it was better if Fane saw her as she really was—a killer. Then she wouldn't be forced to reject the mate bond, because he would.

"He's...with her," Corban said. "The lady."

"He went with her willingly?"

"Yes. She...told him...only way...to help you."

"She lied to him?"

"Don't know."

"It might not be a lie," Fane inserted. "You're alive, aren't you? That may be due to the bargain he struck with her."

Oh, Luc. Marjani briefly closed her eyes.

"So he's bound to her?" she asked. "He accepted her *geas*?"

"Yeah. She has a thing for fada lovers. Luc's probably even enjoying himself." Corban's lips stretched in a death's-head grin. "Until he...pisses her off."

"Is that what you did? Pissed her off?"

A shrug. "I told you...what you asked. Now...do it."

"One more thing. What did you tell her about our quartz?"

Her cousin's eyes slid sideways. That was all the answer she needed. Her breath caught at his treachery.

"Damn it, Corban. What the fuck have you done?"

"Couldn't...help it. She'd heard something. Figured...some of it out herself. I tried to...bargain with her. But I lost."

"Jani." Fane touched the small of her back. "We have to go."

"I'll be right there." She crouched next to the cage. Corban's eyes met hers through the iron bars.

"You don't have to do this," Fane said. "I know it's why you came, but he'll be dead by tomorrow anyway."

She shook her head. It wasn't about her revenge anymore, but how could she explain that to Fane? She barely understood herself.

"Do it." Her cousin crawled forward until they were just inches apart. He stared at her, his body trembling from the effort to keep himself on all fours. "Or are you too weak?"

Anger spiked through her. Not because he'd called her weak—she knew he was simply trying to goad her into doing it—but because she was going to have to kill her own cousin. Yet another death to haunt her.

"Fuck you." She pressed the catch releasing the blade. "I hope you go straight to Hades."

"Count on it." His mouth twisted. "Wondered if...you had... it in you."

"Believe it. I learned from the best, remember?" She slid her arm through the bars, careful not to touch the iron.

Corban gave a weak chuckle, before turning his head at an angle so she could slice his artery. He closed his eyes.

She took a deep breath, and then did it, quick and clean. It took a minute for him to bleed out. She set a hand on his shoulder and waited. She needed to witness this, so she could report to Adric that he was really dead.

And because even a bastard like her cousin didn't deserve to die alone.

Corban's eyelids fluttered. "Tell Adric...not doing...so bad."

She swallowed over a boulder-sized lump. "I will."

Air rattled in his emaciated chest—and then he lay still. His heart gave a few rapid, erratic beats and then lurched to a stop.

"Peace," she whispered and stood up. She wiped her blade on her pants leg and then shoved it into her pocket.

Her eyes met Fane's. She lifted her chin. Just let him look down at her. She refused to be ashamed.

But he held out his arms. "Come here."

Her mouth worked. She stared at him miserably, and then

stumbled the three steps between them. His arms wrapped around her, strong and comforting.

"You did good," he said. "It was a kindness to put the poor man out of his misery."

Her breath rasped out. He was right. So why did her heart feel like a weight had been attached to it?

She'd hated Corban, but he'd still been her cousin. And a member of the clan.

She closed her eyes and breathed in Fane's clean scent. "I wish…"

He nodded against her hair. "Me, too."

"Why the hell did I have to meet you? I was doing just fine without you."

"I know you were."

"No, I wasn't," she contradicted. "I was going feral. I *am* going feral. It's just too fucking hard to be a human."

And then she was blubbering like a baby. Deep, wrenching sobs that felt like she was being turned inside out.

"Hush, now." Fane rubbed her back. "It's okay, love. It's okay."

She cried harder. Because it wasn't okay, and it hadn't been for a long time. The Darktime had taken her mom and dad, and good friends like Jace's sister Takira.

And although the Darktime was supposed to be over, bad things just kept happening.

"I'm…so tired," she said on a sob. "So fucking tired. Of all the killing. And I can barely control my animal anymore. It wants out, and I'm not sure why I shouldn't let it."

"Oh, love." Fane rocked her back and forth like she was a child. "I'm so sorry. Your cougar is beautiful, but so is the human part of you."

Her breath rasped in. "But it's so…hard to be human," she said to his chest.

The cat was so much less complicated. Straightforward.

Basic. Mess with it, and it would rip out your throat and not lose a moment's sleep.

"I know." Soft lips brushed over her temple. "But you're not an animal, you're a fada. And I'm pretty sure that means accepting every part of you. Woman. Cougar. Even that small part of you that's fae."

She took another rasping breath and nodded. He was right. She'd just been trying to forget it.

"And you know what?" He pressed a kiss to each of her eyes. "I want to learn every part of you. Everything. Because that's what makes you who you are."

His words were balm to her broken soul. For so long, rage had been a bitter black knot in her chest.

Now, the knot slowly unclenched. Her sobs slowed until she hung in Fane's arms, drained.

"I love you." Fane stroked a hand over her head. "Whatever happens, remember that, okay?" He waited until she nodded before saying, "Stars, I hate to say this—but we have to go. The *geas* is pulling on me. And if we stay here much longer, that bitch might come back."

"Okay. Okay." She took a deep breath and then pushed away from him. She scrubbed at her face, knowing she must look like shit. And why did she care? But she did. Fane made her care about things like that.

He took her by the arm. "You all right?"

"Yeah." She took a last look at Corban. The lines of pain bracketing his mouth had smoothed. He looked almost peaceful. That was something, anyway.

Her jaw tightened. "You know what? I hope it pisses off Lady B to find him dead. The woman's a monster."

His smile held absolutely no humor. "It will. That, I can guarantee."

He reached for her, but she shook her head. "Let me wash first." Crossing the room to the kitchenette, she turned on the faucet as hot as she could stand and scrubbed her hands and arms.

As she watched the blood-stained water swirl down the drain, the shadows in the tower thickened. Her fangs pricked her gums.

She washed the tears from her face and strode back to Fane. "Let's get the fuck out of here."

"Yeah." He twined his fingers through hers, and together, they headed down the stairs.

30

---

ates. As they exited the tower, Fane tightened his grip on Marjani's hand. He'd sensed the bond come to life, warming him from the inside out. Filling him with wonder—and hope, small but stubborn.

Through the bond, he'd *felt* her fear that he'd judge her for taking her cousin's life. But he'd known it was a mercy killing. He hurt for her, but he understood.

Gods, he'd hated seeing her cry. She might as well have reached into his chest and cracked open his heart. So much pain, his warrior woman had endured. Sometimes fate was one cruel son of a bitch.

When they got out of this—and they *would* get out of this—he'd spend the rest of his days showing her there was more to life than what she'd seen so far. Maybe that wolf fada would be better for her, but then again, maybe not.

A serious woman like Marjani needed someone to help her lighten up, make her smile. A man like Fane.

They set out for the north tower. Suddenly, the maze was nearly impossible to navigate, narrowing until they could barely squeeze through the tall walls, spiraling in on itself like a twisted skein of yarn and sending them down multiple dead-ends.

Marjani plodded alongside him, shoulders hunched a little. He hated to see her so subdued. He wracked his brains for a way to help her escape, even if it meant fighting Sindre's direct order. But the king knew she was here. How far would she get?

Anger churned in Fane's stomach. He felt so goddamned powerless.

"Cat's balls," Marjani muttered. "Does the man want us to get to his tower or not?"

"Oh, he wants us there." Fane glared at the towering white wall that had sprung up out of nowhere to block them. "He's just playing one of his fucking games." And messing with Fane's head. He was a wayfarer, a man always on the move. He hated small, enclosed spaces, and Sindre knew it.

At last, they came upon a familiar passageway filled with fae heading to dinner in the great hall. No one seemed surprised to see Fane and Marjani's fading bruises and tattered clothes. But then, gossip spread like wildfire through the court.

Most of the fae barely noticed them, uncaring what a mixed-blood and a fada were up to. Some shook their heads, their mouths in disapproving lines. A few smiled and nodded.

Fane kept a firm grip on Marjani's hand, proud to be seen with her. She was strong. Beautiful. Caring. And if she had a problem with you, she'd tell you straight out, instead of circling around the subject like these beautiful, two-faced creatures.

So he nodded back to the friendly fae, and ignored the rest.

"So." Marjani gave him the side-eye. "You're the famous Lord Roald's grandson. I had no idea."

"Trust me, he wants it that way. I'm a wayfarer, which means I'm a frivolous SOB who'd rather drink a beer with you than fight. Just like my dad. Roald blames it on my human grandmother—except humans don't have Gifts."

Her lips twitched. "If the shoe fits..."

He hooked an arm around her neck, glad she seemed to be feeling better. "We prefer to say we're well-rounded. What's wrong with enjoying life's pleasures?"

"Don't change, okay?" She reached up to squeeze his hand. "The world needs more people like you."

He nuzzled her ear. "I gave up trying to change a long time ago. Too much work. And I like me as I am."

She shook her head. "You're impossible."

"Now you sound like Roald." He released her to slip through a narrow opening.

"But you *would* like to be a full member of the court," she said when they were side by side again.

He lifted a shoulder and let it drop.

"Why? What would it mean, exactly?"

"The short answer? I'd be one of them. Right now, there are rituals I can't attend. Magic I can't access. And I have to smile and pretend not to see when one of them sneers at me."

"And that's important to you—to be accepted as one of them?"

He jerked his head in assent. "I'm one of Sindre's top envoys, but I'm so low in the hierarchy I might as well be dirt under their feet. If the king declared me a full member of the court, it would make me a pureblood in every way that counts. I could even mate with a pure—" He snapped his mouth shut. "Not that I'd want to. Not now."

Yeah, it had been his goal once. But not any longer.

She stopped and he did, too. The expression on her face made him reach for her, but she held up a hand. "Don't."

"Don't what?"

"Don't give up your dreams. Not for me."

"But I want to. Those dreams mean nothing if I don't have you."

"Fane." Lines formed between her brows. "This thing—it can't go anywhere. You know that, right? Nothing has changed."

Anger clogged his chest. Anger, and a touch of panic. "The hell it hasn't. You felt the bond, same as me. Don't try to tell me you didn't."

She looked at her bare toes.

"Go ahead," he growled. "Tell me we're not mates."

"I can't," she said in a barely audible voice.

"Then what's the problem?"

"You and me." She shook her head. "I'm my brother's second."

"So? What, you took a vow of celibacy?"

That almost got a smile out of her. "No, but I can't leave the clan. My brother needs me. The *clan* needs me. There are so few of us left after the Darktime."

"We'll figure it out." He reached for her, but she took a step back.

"You don't understand. Adric will never accept you. He can't."

He let his hands drop back to his sides. "Why the hell not? He accepted Evie, didn't he?"

"She's not under a *geas*. How could we trust you?" She shook her head. "I'm sorry, but it just wouldn't work."

"Okay." He dragged in a breath. Where was his so-called charm and negotiating ability when he needed it? But he couldn't seem to leave it be. "Maybe you're right. But after I serve out the *geas*?"

She stilled, her eyes searching his. "Are you asking me—?"

"To wait for me? Yeah." He stepped closer and framed her face. "Don't answer—not now. Just think about it, okay? I know it's a lot to ask, but you felt the bond, too. I know you did." He smoothed a thumb down the smooth butterscotch curve of her cheek.

She opened her mouth to speak, but he stopped her words with a finger. "Later. Somehow, I'll come to you in Baltimore—

or get word to you. I promise. Now come." He took her hand. "We must be almost there."

He was right. They turned a corner and there was the door to the north tower. It swung open and they stepped into the anteroom—and into a howling snowstorm that blew up out of nowhere, engulfing them in a blizzard of icy flakes.

"Bloody hell." He tightened his grip on her hand. "I'm not leaving you here," he shouted.

"You have to," she yelled back. "I'll be all right."

The wind whirled around them like a mini-tornado, jerking Marjani from his grip. The next thing he knew, what felt like a giant hand slammed into his chest, shoving him toward the outer door.

"*Jani*." He tried to reach her but for every step forward, he was forced two steps back. The door opened and he was thrust into the hall. He clung to the doorjamb, bellowing her name.

The dark-haired Irish fada appeared out of the swirling white ball. The wind died, leaving just a few stray flakes drifting down, and a sudden, unnerving silence.

"Welcome, Marjani." The Irishwoman gave a dignified little bow. "I'm Jewel. The king has directed me to see to your needs."

Fane tried to re-enter the tower, but couldn't step over the threshold. Fury shook him.

"Damn you, Sindre," he yelled. "Let me in, you bastard."

Jewel clucked her tongue at him. "Don't worry yourself, now. She'll be fine. I'm to get her ready for dinner, that's all." She held out a hand to Marjani. "Come, *alanna*. You look like you could use a nice hot bath and a change of clothes. And perhaps a cup of tea?"

Marjani nodded at Fane. He knew she sensed the truth in Jewel's words, same as him. "Go ahead. I'll see you at dinner."

He hesitated. Gods, he hated to leave her. Still, what choice did they have but to follow Sindre's orders? The king had made it clear he wanted both Fane and Marjani at the dinner. What-ever he intended, it involved them both.

"She'll be fine," Jewel repeated. Her gaze caught his. "I promise."

He gave a curt nod and headed back to his room, hating how helpless Sindre made him feel. It was like playing cards with a hand you weren't allowed to see. But what could Fane do but play out the hand?

In his apartment, he dragged off his ruined clothes and threw them into the garbage chute. Unlike Marjani, both his shoes had remained on and somehow made it through the attack with only a few scuff marks. He left them on the floor next to the closet and headed into the bathroom. He'd have liked a soak in the tub, but he contented himself with a hot shower and a shave.

He racked his brains for a way to save Marjani. Maybe if he signed on to serve Sindre for another ninety-nine years? But he was afraid there was nothing he could offer that the king wanted more than her.

With a muttered curse, he set down his razor and strode naked out of the bathroom.

His father was sprawled on the easy chair, long legs stretched out, a beer in his hand. It was like looking into a mirror—the two of them had the same blond hair, dark brows and narrow face. A poet's face, his mom had said.

Arne grinned up at him. "There's my boy."

That was his dad. Always sure of his welcome. Fane hadn't seen him in years, and he acted like they'd just met last week.

"Hi, Dad." Fane glanced at the door, which apparently he hadn't locked. "Just come in and make yourself at home, why don't you?"

"I have, thank you." Arne raised the beer bottle to Fane and then stood up, arms open wide. "Now give your old dad a hug and act like you're glad to see me."

"You know I am." Fane hugged him back. "Where the hell have you been, anyway?"

"Oh, here and there." Arne slapped him on the back. "I hear you're having dinner with the king."

"You've been talking to Roald."

Arne waved his bottle noncommittally and settled back into the easy chair. "Why don't you get dressed and we'll have ourselves a chat?"

"I'd like that." Fane headed into his closet, emerging a few minutes later in clothes fit for a dinner with the king: black leather pants and a collarless shirt in a fae material that changed from navy to light blue when he moved. Clasping a gold bracelet around his wrist, he turned the wood chair to face Arne and sat down.

"So. Let me guess." He leaned back in the chair, fingers interlaced behind his head. "Roald ordered you to bring me to my goddamned senses. Give up the fada female, and stop embarrassing the family."

His dad chuckled. "Something like that."

"Consider it done. And the answer is no."

The skin around Arne's blue eyes crinkled in amusement. "Fair enough. Roald is breathing fire, though. Something about how you owe him and the Morningstar name. Oh, and he threw in something about diluting a bloodline that can be traced back to the first fae warriors."

"Like hell. I've been at the court for sixty turns of the sun, and in all that time, he's spoken to me less than a dozen times. I don't owe the man a bloody thing."

Arne's good-looking face turned serious. "Forget Roald. He's always growling about something or other. And he's a fine one to be talking about diluting bloodlines—he mated with my mother, after all. No, it's the king you should be worrying about. He makes a powerful enemy."

"You think I don't know that?" Fane sat up and leaned forward, hands on his thighs. "I love her, Dad."

"Lovers come and go. Life's too short—"

"And time goes by," Fane finished for him. "Yeah, I know. But…" He stared unseeingly down at his bare feet. "I think she's my mate, Dad."

"I see." Arne took a thoughtful sip of beer. "That changes things."

"No kidding."

"You can't hide from the king. It might take a decade, but he'll hunt you down."

Fane dragged a hand over his wet hair. "So we'll bargain with him."

"What can you offer that he doesn't already have?"

Fane's stomach sank. "I don't know, but I'll think of something. I have to."

A knock sounded on the door. Fane opened it to find three tall, stern-faced warriors—a woman and two men. The woman informed Fane that they'd been sent to escort him to the north tower.

Fane nodded. It was unnecessary, and the king knew it. He'd sent the warriors as a warning. "I'll be right out." They tried to object but he repeated, "I'll be right out," and shut the door in their faces.

He sat on the chair and put on his shoes and socks.

Arne rose to his feet. "I'm coming, too."

"Yeah?" Fane glanced up, surprised. He'd expected his dad to make some excuse and then get the hell out of there. "You sure?"

Arne shrugged. "I've known the king a lot longer than you. Who knows? I might be able to help. And besides, he always sets a good table."

ewel led Marjani to a staircase of brushed steel and sparkling white granite that wound around the outside of Sindre's tower. When they reached the second floor, they crossed a glass skyway to a three-story wing and then continued up to the top floor.

"Here we are." Jewel ushered her into a large, airy apartment with sky-colored walls and long, narrow windows with a view of the windswept tundra.

The living room alone was three times the size of Fane's apartment. A couch and three chairs in an embroidered silver fabric were grouped around a glass-and-wood coffee table. Hanging from the ceiling were three ethereal silver chandeliers lit with flickering fae lights, and several thick, fleecy white rugs were scattered across the polished parquet floors.

Marjani's mouth slackened. She'd never been in a place half so gorgeous. "So this is how the other half lives."

Jewel gave a small smile and indicated a bedroom. "The bath's in here." She directed Marjani past a round pedestal bed into a bathroom with a pink marble bathtub the size of a small pool. Lush ferns, English ivy, and other green plants spilled from niches in the pink-and-beige tile, and the fixtures appeared to be solid gold.

Marjani's brows climbed. "I thought I was supposed to be the king's prisoner."

Their eyes met. "Oh, you are," the other woman said. "Don't mistake it for a moment. Would you like help with your clothes?"

It took Marjani a second to understand that the other woman was offering to help her undress. She gave a firm shake of her head. "No, thanks. I've got it."

"As you wish." Jewel crossed to the pink marble tub and turned on the faucets before sprinkling a sweet-smelling bath salt into the steaming water. "There are the towels." She indicated the thick white towels draped over a heated rack. "Help yourself to anything else you see. I'll be back in a few minutes with your tea."

"No tea for me. But I'd like a glass of water if you have it."

"As you wish." Going to a small cooling unit in the wall, Jewel removed a bottle of a fancy Icelandic water and poured it into a crystal glass before handing it to Marjani.

"Thank you." She took a sip and then inhaled slowly.

Even this close, the woman didn't have a scent. And there was that big, black-haired bodyguard who looked so familiar. Now that Marjani thought about it, he reminded her of Dion do Rio, the Rock Run River Fada alpha.

She narrowed her eyes. "Who are you, really?"

The other woman busied herself shutting the taps. "The fae call me Jewel."

"Which tells me nothing. You know I'm a fada, right?"

"I do." Jewel straightened. "From the Baltimore clan, I'm thinking."

Their eyes met. Marjani knew she should mind her own business, but something niggled at her. "You're a fada, too, aren't you?" And some kind of water fada, since she didn't wear a quartz.

Jewel tilted her head in assent.

"And that big bodyguard, he's your mate?"

The other woman's cobalt eyes flickered, telling Marjani she'd guessed correctly. But all Jewel said was, "Your bath is ready. Will you be wanting anything more?"

When Marjani said no, the other woman inclined her head. "I'll be in the living room. Call me if you need anything."

As soon as the door closed behind her, Marjani stripped off her ripped, bloody clothes. She hid the switchblade and her quartz beneath a towel on a ledge next to the tub where she could easily reach them, and then climbed into the bathtub.

The first thing she did was soap up a washcloth and scrub herself. Hard. When you shifted, the dirt and other stuff—like blood—got left behind. So she wasn't that dirty, but she still felt the need to clean herself.

It had been that kind of a day.

Maybe she *was* weak. She could just hear Leron sneering about her taking a mixed-blood lover. And mate with Fane? Her uncle would've run her out of the clan.

But it didn't feel weak, this thing she had with Fane. It felt like something that could make her stronger.

She finished scrubbing and reached for her quartz. Its song was barely audible, the crystals drained of energy. She closed her fingers around it and then sank beneath the hot water with a little sigh. The water was just the right temperature, and it smelled like a flower garden.

There was no hurry. Her internal clock told her she still had about a half an hour before she had to meet Sindre.

Above her, fae lights floated near the ceiling, their colors changing from pink to gold and back again. Her clenched muscles loosened. She set her quartz on her solar plexus, leaned back against the smooth marble and let her eyes drift shut.

She'd had time to come up with a plan while nursing Fane. She was starting to intuit the basic, underlying structure of the maze. She was pretty sure that with the help of her quartz, she could find her way to the portal Fane had taken her through the other day.

She couldn't open it herself, but a portal was like a fae ward, only instead of keeping people *out*, a portal allowed you to pass each way. And fae wards often had a fatal weakness—they couldn't detect the fada when they were in their animal forms. The wards simply didn't "see" the fada as people, but as animals.

So the plan had been to spring Luc, make their way to the portal, and then shift and go so deep into their animals that the portal allowed them to pass out of the castle—and back into the human world. It would have been a risk, since Marjani would've had to cede complete control to the cat. Still, for Luc, she would've done it.

But now Luc had accepted Blaer's *geas*. That fae bitch would make a pet of him, maybe even keep him in a cage.

Tears stung her eyes. *Damn wolf fada. Who asked you to sacrifice yourself for me?*

Luc tried to give her an out by removing himself from the equation so that Sindre couldn't use him to force his *geas* on her. But she was afraid the king would think of something else. The man was old and scary smart.

Her fingers tightened around her quartz. If only she could call Adric. Because she was fresh out of ideas.

Either she accepted Sindre's *geas*—or she got him alone and slit his throat. The tricky part would be escaping his body-guards afterward and finding her way back to the human world. The only possible way would be to shift to her cougar and slip through the portal, but she wasn't all that eager to tangle with the cougar again.

Her breath sucked in as she relived those terrifying moments when she'd been sure she wouldn't make it through the shift. The cougar had almost won. Without Fane's help, she'd be dead—or feral.

Life was fucking strange. She'd come to Iceland prepared to die, as long as she took Corban with her. At least she'd go out with some honor.

Now Corban was dead, but she'd changed. She very much wanted to live, see where this thing with Fane went.

It won't be hard to get Sindre alone. All you have to do is flirt with him. Let him touch you.

A tremor raced over her skin.

To shift afterward, though, she'd need her quartz. She smoothed a thumb over the triangular amethyst conglomerate at the top. The crystals would take hours to recharge. Right now, they were only at ten percent of their normal energy levels, but she'd shifted twice in just a few hours. For her to safely shift a third time, they had to reach at least fifty percent.

She'd have only one opportunity to escape. So she'd have to stall Sindre until the quartz had recharged. Hopefully, the dinner would last several hours.

The bathwater had cooled. Marjani pulled the plug and stood up. She was drying off when Jewel knocked on the door.

Marjani palmed the quartz before calling, "Come in."

Jewel entered with an aqua-green dress draped over one arm. "The king sends this to you with his compliments."

Marjani fingered the flirty little skirt. She'd never owned anything so beautiful. Clearly fae-made, the aqua fabric was tissue-fine and shot with gold thread.

Releasing the skirt, she resolutely shook her head. "Tell Sindre thank you, but I'll wear my own clothes. I left a backpack when I was here before."

"I have it. But he won't like it."

"Just get me the backpack, please. Unless he'll be angry at you."

"He will." Jewel shrugged. "But it won't be the first time."

"Fine." Marjani stuck out her hand. "I'll wear the damned thing."

"You'll need this, too." The other woman produced a bra-and-panty set of gossamer gold.

Marjani couldn't help a purr of pleasure as she put them on. The silky material felt so good against her skin.

Next came the dress. It was simple but elegant, with spaghetti straps and a scooped neck. As she dropped it over her head, it fit itself to her curves as if it had been sewn just for her.

"I'll be right back with the shoes," Jewel said.

While the other woman was out of the room, Marjani stashed the switchblade and quartz in her bra. It wasn't easy finding a place where they didn't show under the dress, but she managed.

Jewel returned with a pair of gold satin pumps with tiny crystals scattered across the toes and a big bow on each heel. Marjani eyed them skeptically.

"Do I look like a high-heels-and-bows kind of female?"

"You don't. But you *do* look like one who knows that camouflage can be a good thing. Do you want them to see you as you are—or as a high-heels-and-bows kind of female?"

Marjani sighed. "Hand them over." She stepped into the heels and turned to look at herself in the floor-length mirror.

A stranger stared back at her. A classy stranger with long, toned legs and surprise in her dark eyes. The aqua-green was a pretty contrast to her skin, and when she moved, the gold thread caught the light so that she seemed to shimmer.

Yeah, she still had a few bruises, but she barely recognized herself. "Damn," she whispered.

"Don't you look beautiful?" Jewel's eyes swam with tears.

Marjani bit her lip. "You okay?"

"Don't mind me. It's just that my daughter is around your age. It's been so long since I last saw her. She was a little girl when—" She pressed her lips into a line and shook her head.

"I'm so sorry. Is there something I could do—take her a message, maybe?"

Jewel clutched Marjani's hand. "Could you?"

At a rap on the door, they sprang apart. A golden-skinned elf with big green eyes stuck her head inside. "The king requests your presence at dinner."

"She'll be right there," Jewel replied, and the elf nodded and shut the door again.

"Here goes nothing," Marjani muttered.

Jewel squeezed her shoulder. Suddenly, her blue eyes deepened to a navy that was almost black, and her face went dead white, so it looked like those scary midnight eyes peered through a mask.

"Jewel?" Marjani gulped. "You all right?"

The other woman seemed not to hear. "Make the wrong choice," she replied in a toneless voice, "and you'll never get home."

Marjani's nape prickled. Jewel was a Seer. Suddenly, the pieces snapped into place.

This must be Ula Gallagan, and the black-haired guard her mate, Nisio do Rio. Nisio and Ula were Dion's parents, and Nisio had been alpha until the couple disappeared about fifteen turns of the sun ago.

"What is it?" she whispered. "What do you See?"

Jewel/Ula looked right through her. "The end of the game is the beginning," she said in that low, eerie voice, "and the heart wins over strategy every time."

Marjani's hand went to her chest and the quartz she'd stowed in her bra. "I don't understand."

The other woman's breath whooshed out, and her eyes returned to their normal blue.

"Please." Marjani grabbed her. "Tell me what you See. What do I need to do?"

The river fada's expression was troubled. "I didn't See anything else. That came to me as a prophecy—words, nothing more. Every Sight is different. All you can do is think on it, and perhaps it will help. Then again, it might not make sense until it's too late."

"But…"

"I'm sorry, love." Ula moved a shoulder in a small shrug. "You're on your own. If I could help you, I would. When we first got here, I tried a couple of times. But the king always finds out. And it's not me he punishes, but my mate."

Marjani's heart constricted. "I understand. And it's okay."

The river fada gripped Marjani's arms. "You're a warrior," she said in a voice pitched for her ears alone. "But that switchblade you have in your bra won't do you any good here. You'll have to find another way to fight him I can tell you one thing—he'll try to use your greatest weakness against you."

Marjani swallowed. "My greatest weakness?"

"A person. A thing. Even an idea. You may not even know what it is, but trust me, the king will find it."

"But how can I fight that?"

"With us, he used the fact that we're mates. He hurts one to bend the other to his will. But he also promised us that if we accepted his *geas*, the clan would prosper, and he made it happen."

Marjani nodded. Even though Rock Run's territory was just thirty-five miles from Baltimore, the two clans had bad blood between them, so she didn't know much about them. All she knew was that less than two decades ago, the Rock Run River Fada had been in trouble, and then Dion had somehow turned things around—after his parents had disappeared.

"That's the king's weakness," Ula added. "He's never broken a promise. I think he can't—his fae blood is too powerful."

Marjani's gut tingled. "So if I can get him to promise the right thing..." She trailed off. Because she had to get Sindre to promise—what? Hopelessness welled up in her.

You've got a plan, remember?

But her plan had been admittedly crude, a last-ditch attempt to save herself. If she could somehow use this information to craft a better strategy...

Another tap on the door.

"Be right there," Ula called. She pressed her cheek to Marjani's. "You know who I am?" she whispered.

"I think so. The Rock Run alpha's mom."

Ula dipped her chin in assent. "If you do escape, all I ask is that you inform my children that we're alive and well. That's the hardest thing, knowing they believe we're dead." Her throat worked. "And tell them not to come to Iceland again. They're just putting themselves in danger for no reason. We're serving out a *geas*. Even if we wanted to leave, we couldn't."

She released Marjani. "You mustn't keep the king waiting," she said in a normal tone.

Marjani nodded and followed Ula into the hall where the elf awaited.

As they walked back down the spiral staircase, it occurred to her that Ula's daughter must be Rosana do Rio. The young woman Adric couldn't seem to forget, even though he knew that as alpha, he had to mate with another earth fada. He couldn't mate with a river fada—especially the Rock Run alpha's sister—without creating a huge rift in the clan.

Marjani had warned Adric to stay away from Rosana. "She's not for you," she said.

Now she mentally cringed. Goddess, she'd been a self-righteous ass. If she got home—*when* she got home—she owed Ric an apology.

Because she understood now how you could want someone

all wrong for you. Logic didn't enter into it. What had Ula said? *The heart wins over strategy every time.*

On the tower's main floor, someone had swept the snow into white heaps against the walls. In the background, a high, otherworldly voice crooned a song in an ancient fae language, and magical fires that cast no heat had been lit in firepits scattered around the large, circular space.

In the center stood Sindre and Roald, deep in conversation. They made an imposing pair—the king with his long, almost feline body and coldly perfect face; and the fae warrior with his broad shoulders, wide chest and hawkish features.

The king had changed into a long-tailed, shimmering silver shirt and blue pants that fit like he'd been poured into them. His white-gold hair hung loose around his shoulders and hanging from his neck was a fiery diamond as big as Marjani's quartz. Other diamonds glittered on his fingers, and a heavy, diamond-studded platinum bracelet encircled his wrist.

Roald had secured his mane of copper hair with a leather tie. He wore a black tunic embroidered with sinuous red and green dragons, and three emerald-and-gold hoops ran up the outside of each pointed ear.

Ula squeezed Marjani's hand and dropped back. The perfect servant, when once she'd been an alpha's mate.

And she was the lucky one. What the king had in mind for Marjani was worse.

She squared her shoulders and headed toward the two ice fae.

---

he click of Marjani's heels against the white marbled granite sounded loud in her ears. Sindre and Roald turned to watch her.

"That will be all," the king said to Ula.

"Very well." With a nod, she left Marjani alone with the two purebloods.

Marjani quelled the cowardly urge to run after Ula and beg her to stay. Instead, she kept moving, stopping a few feet from the men and inclining her head like the alpha's second she was. "Good evening, my lords."

"Good evening, Marjani *mín.*" Sindre looked her over with unmistakable satisfaction. "You look lovely. I thought that dress would suit you."

She wanted to growl that she wasn't "his" Marjani, but she forced herself to thank him. "So do you," she added.

He lifted a brow in question.

She smiled sweetly. "Look lovely, I mean. The silver brings out your eyes."

Take that, you condescending prick.

A beat passed, and then Sindre broke into the most genuine

smile she'd yet seen from him. "Thank you," he returned, while beside him, Roald harrumphed.

Two elves bearing trays of appetizers emerged from one of the arched doorways. A third elf, a white-haired, dark-skinned man with a cheery smile on his round face, appeared at Marjani's elbow.

"Some nectar, Miss?" He offered her a sparkling gold liquid in a crystal goblet.

Marjani's eyes widened. She'd heard of fae nectar, of course. An army could travel for days on the sparkling drink, which magically provided both energy and necessary nutrients.

"Thank you." She accepted the goblet, no longer worried about eating and drinking Sindre's offerings. He wanted her to willingly accept his *geas*, which meant no tricks on his part.

Sindre touched his goblet to hers. "To a productive negotiation."

"I look forward to it, your highness." She let her lips curve.

His left brow quirked.

She'd surprised him. Good. That was the plan: Flirt with Sindre. Let him think she'd changed her mind so she could catch him off-guard—and then strike.

She brought the goblet to her mouth. The nectar smelled amazing, like ice wine and apricots, and tasted even better.

Fane arrived along with a man who looked so much like him that she blinked. Same lean good looks. Same blond hair, although the older man's reached halfway down his back. Same wry smile and gravelly voice.

"Arne," said the king. "I wasn't aware you were invited to dinner."

"My lord." The handsome blond fae inclined his head and then grinned. "I assumed it was an oversight, since both my father and my son were included."

Sindre's answering smile was indulgent. "I'll tell the elves to set another place."

Marjani barely heard as Fane gave her a slow, hot look that moved down the aqua dress to the silly satin heels and then back up.

"Hey, there." His deep voice was soft. Intimate. "You look like you're feeling better."

She couldn't control her body's reaction at that heated look and voice. Her nipples tightened and her stomach hollowed out. But her reply was cool because she had to convince Sindre she'd switched her interest to him. She couldn't even tell Fane why, because she knew he'd try and stop her.

"I am," she said. "And you?"

A small frown creased Fane's brow. "I'm good, thanks."

He edged closer, and she edged back. His frown increased. Just as he opened his mouth to say something, Arne turned to her.

"And you must be this Marjani I'm hearing so much about."

"Yeah?" She eyed him warily.

"Meet my dad," Fane said in a wry but affectionate tone. "Arne Morningstar, this is Marjani Savonett."

"Peace to you and yours," she said to Arne—and let out a squeak when he pulled her into a hug.

"Peace to you and yours." He kissed both her cheeks and murmured, "I'm here to help."

Their eyes met, and she nodded.

The five of them formed a circle. Roald was the only one not drinking nectar. Instead, he had his broad hand wrapped around a frosty mug of beer.

Lord Roald's grandson. She looked from Fane to the fae warrior.

She'd assumed Fane was basically a hanger-on at the ice fae court, but he had a powerful, high-ranking grandfather. It explained a few things—like why he was still alive. Sindre might punish Fane—she'd seen that up close and personal—

but even the king would think twice before killing the grandson of the captain of his guard.

And on top of that, his father, Arne, was clearly a favorite of the king.

The five of them made small talk. Arne managed to bring the tension down a few notches, joking and telling stories until even Roald unbent enough to chuckle. It was kind of surreal—she'd gone from a cage to a freaking cocktail party.

Except one of the men wanted to steal her freedom and another—Roald—barely managed to be polite to her.

Still, that left her two allies, if Arne could be trusted. She'd been in worse situations.

She sipped her nectar, enjoying the little charge the sparkling liquid gave her.

Sindre waved one of the ever-smiling elves over. "Try the salmon tartare," he said. "It was caught just this morning and prepared with lime sauce."

The tartare was mounded on a tiny cracker. The salmon's fresh, raw scent made her cat salivate. She practically inhaled the first one, and the king urged her to have another as more fae arrived, decked out in designer clothes and expensive jewelry. The men ran their eyes over Marjani as if she were a T-bone for sale, and the women glanced knowingly from her to the king.

Marjani tightened her fingers around the goblet's crystal stem, fighting the urge to bare her fangs at them.

A few feet away, Fane exchanged air kisses with a statuesque redhead in a tight black dress that barely covered her ass. "Viktorie. You're looking beautiful, as always."

"How kind of you to say so. And you, love?" The woman ran a possessive hand down his arm. "How have you been?"

Ha. And he says he doesn't fit in.

Marjani clenched her teeth so hard it hurt.

Mine, hissed the cat. *Mate.*

No, she snapped back.

A tall blonde with skin a shade darker than Marjani's ran practiced eyes over her dress. "I love that green. Is it a Favreau?"

She shrugged. "Hell if I know."

"She's a fae designer," the blonde explained, a little too helpfully. "French."

"It is." Sindre touched the small of Marjani's back. "Specially made for my guest."

Another round of knowing looks was exchanged. Marjani set her jaw, the small pleasure she'd taken in the dress evaporating.

The blonde's mouth curved. She smoothed a hand down her own outfit, a slinky gold number with cutout shoulders. "I knew it. I absolutely adored her spring collection."

"I prefer Adèle myself," a silver-haired woman interjected.

"Adèle?" The blonde waved her hand dismissively. "She's so last year." She glanced at Marjani. "Don't you agree?"

She shrugged. "Never heard of her."

The silver-haired fae's look was pitying. "She's a fada, you know. The animals don't bother with fashion like us frivolous fae."

Both women laughed.

Marjani flashed on Corban's wasted body, and Luc, forced to accept the *geas* of one of these snobby females. She raised her chin and showed her teeth in a grin that had both women stepping back.

"No. I have better things to do."

"Of course," the blonde said hurriedly. With a muttered excuse, she and her friend slunk off to join another group.

"My sweet," Sindre said in her ear, "I'd appreciate it if you wouldn't terrorize the other guests."

She gave him the same toothy smile. "It's your fault for inviting an animal to dinner."

The corner of his mouth quirked up. "We'd better keep you

fed, then. Here, try the caviar." He heaped a spoonful of shiny black eggs on a small round of bread and handed it to her.

She took a cautious bite. The briny flavor was unexpectedly good. "Not bad," she allowed. "Tastes kind of like the sea."

"Have another then."

The man was definitely going all out for her. If she didn't know he was a cold, scheming SOB, she might have even fallen for it. But she was hungry and she could travel a long way on a full belly, so she let him ply her with appetizers.

Fane had extricated himself from the redhead to chat with his father, but she sensed his growing tension—and hurt. It made her own shoulders tighten.

She sent him a pleading look and he shuttered his eyes. She let out a small sigh of relief until she realized the two of them were practically reading each other's minds. And they were definitely sensing each other's emotions...like mates did.

No. She deliberately gave him her back.

He didn't like that. She *felt* his disbelief and agitation.

This is so not good.

Lord Roald joined Arne and Fane and they started a low-voiced conversation that no one but a fada could've picked up. She sipped her nectar and unashamedly eavesdropped as Sindre greeted another guest.

"I've been in talks with Lord Hamar," Roald told Fane. "His daughter is interested in taking you as her consort."

Marjani's stomach constricted. From the corner of her eye, she saw Fane glance at the redhead in the black dress.

"Lady Viktorie?"

"That's the one. A lovely woman, and strong. She'll give you healthy children."

Claws pricked at Marjani's fingertips. *Like hell.*

"But what about the mate bond?" asked Arne.

Roald waved his hand. "Children will come as long as

neither of them is bonded elsewhere. Fane has proven himself in that regard. There are no guarantees, but it's likely."

"It's likely," Fane repeated flatly. "And I'd be her consort, not her mate."

"Of course," said Roald. "You can't expect a pureblood to offer you more."

"Of course."

"Naturally," Roald added, "the offer is contingent on your becoming a full member of the court."

Marjani gritted her teeth. She was happy for Fane, she was. This was it, the thing he'd spent six decades working toward—full acceptance in the ice fae court. He'd even be the consort of a fae lady.

And Marjani had told him herself that the two of them didn't have a future. So why did she want to scratch out Lady Viktorie's tip-tilted brown eyes?

"Please tell Lord Hamar that I'm honored," Fane told Roald. "Deeply so. But I'm not interested."

"You'd choose the fada female over a pureblood fae?"

"I would." Fane swallowed. "I do."

Oh, Fane.

"Try these." The king appeared at Marjani's elbow with a small plate of appetizers.

"Thank you." She forced herself to smile and accept the plate.

A female elf in a flowing green tunic and striped leggings came forward and bowed to Sindre. "Dinner is served, your highness."

He nodded and flicked his fingers. A long wooden table materialized in the center of the room, its gleaming surface set with heavy silver chargers topped with paper-fine ivory porcelain. Down the center snaked an ice sculpture of intricately carved flowers and vines lit by cut-glass votives. The finishing touch was the tiny fae lights that drifted down to arch over the table in a sparkling bower.

Marjani gaped. She'd bet there were only a few fae in the entire world who could teleport an object that large without even touching it. Good lord, the man was powerful.

"Well," she muttered, "that's handy."

The king's lean cheek creased. "The elves prepare the table in the kitchen. I just 'port it in."

They took their seats, Roald to Sindre's right and Marjani to his left. Arne took the chair on her other side with Fane across the table next to his grandfather.

She met Fane's eyes. He lowered one eyelid in a wink, and she dropped her gaze to her plate.

"Prosecco?" asked the elf in the green tunic, and when Marjani nodded, the elf removed her empty goblet and set a glass of sparkling wine in its place.

The first course arrived, delicate spring greens topped with walnuts and cranberries. She ate the salad and sipped her prosecco as the fae gossiped about people she didn't know. Cat's balls, she just wanted this to be over with.

But she knew the fae. She might as well enjoy her dinner, because Sindre would get to things in his own good time. And the more time her quartz had to recharge, the better.

Arne launched into a story about his travels that had everyone grinning and shaking their heads. Sindre leaned back in his chair, smiling with the rest, but his glittering gray eyes kept turning to her. She felt like a rabbit staked out for a wolf.

The second course arrived, a dish with cod and berries and some other ingredients she couldn't name, but it was delicious. More wine was served, but Marjani switched to water. She needed to keep her head clear.

Roald murmured something to the king about Blaer, and Sindre said, "She's no longer at the court."

Roald lifted a brow. "She got away?"

Sindre's mouth hardened. "Lady Blaer has been stripped of her position as my advisor and banished from the court for a year and a day."

All around the table, brows shot up.

Marjani exchanged a look with Fane. That was good news. She concentrated on buttering a roll. "And the man from my clan?"

Sindre moved a shoulder. "I don't keep track of Blaer's servants."

Her fingers clenched on the butter knife. "He's not her servant. He's her prisoner."

"Is he?" Sindre sipped his wine. "He accepted her *geas*. I can tell you this—he's not in the castle. I assume he left with her."

"I see." She set down her roll and stared at her half-eaten fish.

Further down the table, a man laughed, and her stomach turned over, the rich food threatening to come back up. That these fae could sit here in their expensive clothes and jewels, and eat and drink and laugh as if Luc meant nothing.

Her fangs pricked her gums. The cat wanted to taste some fae blood—and she was tempted to let it.

Fane set down his fork. She shot him a fierce *stay-where-you-are* glance.

A hand touched her back. Arne, in a quick gesture of comfort. "Did I tell you the story about the human and the pot of gold?" he asked the king.

"Yes," said Sindre, "but I don't think our guest has heard it."

Marjani released her breath. She only half-heard the story, a long, involved tale of a man who'd do anything to get rich, even trap an elf, but she silently blessed Fane's dad for giving her a chance to calm herself.

The elves cleared away the second course and served the next, a small steak surrounded by mushrooms in a wine sauce.

The meat was so tender it practically melted in Marjani's mouth, but she only managed to eat a few pieces.

A few more courses followed, interspersed with tiny glasses of sorbet to clear the palette, but Marjani couldn't even pretend to enjoy the food. It was funny, during the Darktime there'd been times when she'd been so hungry, she'd have done almost anything for a meal like this. Now, though, she just wanted this interminable dinner to be over.

She checked her quartz. The energy level had reached thirty-five percent, still too low.

At a nod from the king, the elves cleared the table. A cheeseboard was passed and after-dinner drinks served.

In an unguarded moment, she glanced at Fane. Their gazes snagged, and she *felt* his concern.

That's when it hit her. With Luc gone, Sindre had nothing to hold over her—except Fane. What if the king realized they were mates? Or at least, that the bond was a possibility.

He uses mates against each other. Hurts one to bend the other to his will. And it wouldn't be her that Sindre would hurt—it would be Fane.

She wrenched her gaze from Fane's, heart thundering in her ears. From somewhere far away, she heard Sindre say, "Are you finished?"

She nodded and they rose, followed by the rest of the company. They drifted to the couches and sat in small groups, but the king guided her to a more private spot near the leafless trees. The place between her shoulder blades itched—behind them, Fane was watching.

"Your dinner was satisfactory?" Sindre asked.

"Yes." She forced herself to focus on him.

"Good. Whatever you want, it's yours. Clothes. Jewelry. Just speak to Jewel or one of the elves. You'll find I'm a generous man."

"Are you?"

His gaze was on her mouth. She nervously moistened her lips, and he leaned close, his mouth a whisper from hers.

"Emeralds," he murmured. "Or rubies. They'd look stunning with your skin and eyes."

Arne and Fane approached from the side. Fane had that determined look on his face, the one that said he'd decided on a course of action and nothing would change his mind.

Her stomach lurched. She was running out of time.

She angled her body toward Sindre. "Emeralds?"

"Mm." He stroked a cold finger down her cheek.

She captured his wrist and made herself smile up at him. "Why don't we go somewhere less...crowded?"

Behind her, she heard Fane's sharp inhale.

Sindre's answering smile was smug. "You read my mind."

Fane pushed himself between her and the king. "Enough, Sindre. Let the woman go. She's done nothing to deserve this."

The room went silent, save for the hushed, otherworldly music. The temperature dropped. Goosebumps prickled Marjani's bare arms. "Fane."

His look seared her. "I'll be damned if I let you take his *geas.*"

The king's eyes narrowed at his envoy. "I see you've decided today is a good day to die."

Her entire spine tightened. "*No,*" she rasped.

Fane narrowed his eyes right back at Sindre. "She doesn't want you. She wants me."

"My lord." Arne slung an arm around Fane's shoulders and eased him backward. "I apologize for my son. He's still young."

Sindre's perfect features could've been carved from marble. "Not too young to know he shouldn't interfere with a negotiation."

Roald shoved his way into their little group. "By the Goddess, boy. Have you lost your mind?"

Fane shook off Arne's arm and glared back. "I'm. Not. A. Fucking. Boy."

"Enough." Sindre's nostrils flared. "On your knees. Apologize to me, and I may let you live."

Fane's knees bent. With an effort, he locked them. His mouth opened and shut as he fought the order to apologize.

"No," he gritted, tight-lipped. "I've done nothing to be sorry for. And I'll be damned if I ever go on my knees to you again. I, Fane Morningstar, am breaking the *geas*."

Roald's fair skin reddened. "Like hell."

"Fane!" Marjani said. "Stop this, damn it."

Neither he nor the king seemed to hear her.

"You'd break your sworn oath?" Sindre asked. The already cool room grew even colder. A light snow began to fall.

"I am. And Marjani Savonett goes with me." Fane grabbed her hand. "I'm claiming her. She's mine. My mate."

"And what does that leave me?" Sindre returned.

"You get everything I've earned since accepting the *geas*."

"But I'd get that anyway," he reminded Fane in silky tones. "Those are the terms you agreed to. No, I think I'll keep the fada."

Fane's chin lifted. "Then take my Gift as well."

---

33

*S*hock reverberated through the room.

Marjani slowly shook her head from side to side. She had to stop this. She tugged at her hand but Fane tightened his grip.

"Trust me," he mouthed.

"Be very certain," Sindre said. "You'll have nothing. You might as well be a human. And your name will be known far and wide as an oath breaker."

Fane swallowed audibly, but when he spoke, his voice was strong. "I'm certain."

"*No,*" Roald growled. "He takes it back. No grandson of mine breaks his word." He swung to Fane. "Have you no honor?"

"I can speak for myself," Fane retorted. "And I will *not* serve a man who would force my mate into his *service.*" He glared at the king. "There is no honor in that."

"Honor?" His grandfather spat the word out. "Where's the honor in breaking a vow made to the king himself?"

"Sometimes," Fane returned, "you have to choose the lesser of two evils. Yes, I'm breaking a *geas,* and I'm truly sorry if that reflects on you and Arne. But Marjani doesn't deserve to be kept here against her will. Her only crime was to enter the ice fae court without permission. If the king is merciful, he'll accept my bargain and let her go."

"It's a tempting offer." Sindre tilted his pale blond head. "But doesn't the woman have to agree? According to fada tradition, the female must accept the claim."

"She will," Fane said. He raised his voice so it rang out in the huge room. "I, Fane Morningstar, am mate-claiming Marjani Savonett now, before all of you and the God and Goddess." He glared at the king. "Try and touch a mated fada and she'll kill herself rather than let you have her."

Marjani's mouth fell open. The man was mate-claiming her *now*? But he was correct. If they mated, her animal wouldn't accept anyone's touch but his.

Mate, the cougar agreed with satisfaction.

"But it's not up to you, is it?" the king responded. "It's up to our guest."

Everyone looked at her. Fane's grip on her tightened. "Jani?"

Gods, she was tempted. Her whole body yearned toward him. A fada might go centuries without finding her or his mate, and some never did. When you were fortunate enough to find your mate, you accepted it as the gift from the gods it was.

"You bloody fool," Roald ground out. "You'll lose everything. Your money. Your honor. Your chance to have children with a pureblood."

"Not everything." Fane didn't take his gaze from her. "I'll have Marjani."

"You leave me no choice, then." Roald crossed his arms over his massive chest. "If you persist in this foolishness, I'll disown you."

Arne made a shocked sound. "Father. You don't mean that."

"I'll not claim an oath-breaker as my blood," the fae warrior returned.

Fane whitened. "That's your decision, of course."

Marjani's lungs squeezed. She couldn't let Fane give up everything for her. It was bad enough that he'd lose all his money, but she refused to let him throw away his chance to be accepted by not only his grandfather, but the ice fae court.

Make the wrong choice, and you'll never get home.

What else could it mean but that she must make the sensible choice? Not the one she might want, but the one that was best for them both.

She gently extricated her fingers from his. "You're right," she told Sindre. "I haven't accepted his claim."

"Then accept it." That was Fane.

"I can't," she answered, her gaze on the king.

"Why the fuck not?"

She turned to face him. "I don't owe you an explanation. This is between me and King Sindre."

Fane's head jerked back as if she'd slapped him.

Her throat closed. She swallowed thickly. "I propose a game," she told the king.

His eyes sharpened. "A game?"

"Yes. A competition."

The king was bored, a weakness she could use against him. Fane had told her that right at the start. Fane had wrecked her chance to quietly assassinate Sindre, but the tingle in her gut told her this was even better. She just had to tempt the king into making a promise.

Fane grabbed her arm. "Damn it, Jani. Don't you see this is exactly what he wants?"

"Be silent," Sindre snarled, "or be gone. The choice is hers."

Fane jerked her around to face him. "Jani?"

She gulped. Inside, the cat lashed its tail in agitation. She dug her nails into her palms and ruthlessly forced it down.

Fane reached for her through the bond, but she slammed her heart closed to him.

He uses mates against each other.

"You and me?" She shook her head. "It would never work. No, I think I'll strike my own bargain with the king."

Fane's mouth twisted. He looked from her to the king and released her. "I see."

No, you don't.

But she didn't say it. Instead, she raised her chin. "It's what I want."

Sindre turned a slow, *I've-got-you-now* smile on Marjani. The falling snow glittered on his hair and shoulders like magic dust. "A competition, you said?"

"Yes." And suddenly, she knew exactly what to do, her Gift settling on the perfect strategy. "A test of my skill against yours."

"Explain."

"Me against your maze. If I find my way through the maze and escape the castle, I go free—forever. No tricks, no loopholes. And you give me a half-dozen of those diamonds you showed me the other day." Even six diamonds would go a long way toward getting the clan back on its feet.

"If you escape the castle," Sindre repeated.

He didn't think she could do it. It was clear he controlled that odd maze, but what he didn't know was that she could use her quartz as a GPS. Of course, she'd still have to make it through a portal. She'd just have to hope that her plan to escape as her cat worked.

"Yes," she said.

"Very well. But I have a condition, too. You will only have until dawn tomorrow."

Her palms were sweating. When she'd come up with her plan of escape, she hadn't expected to do it under the king's very eyes. She rubbed her palms on her skirt and opened her mouth to agree, but Fane interrupted her.

"What if I offer my Gift for her freedom?"

Sindre didn't even look at him, just flicked his fingers. Fane jerked and grabbed his chest. He doubled over, his breath juddering in and out.

This time, the ice didn't start at his feet. Sindre had gone straight for his heart.

Arne swung to face Roald. "Stop him, damn it."

The burly redhead set his jaw. "The boy has chosen his path."

Arne cursed and turned to Sindre. "My lord, please."

Fane gave a strangled moan.

Arne continued pleading with Sindre, but she didn't hear them. Something dark and red filled her head. Fane was dying. She felt the clench in her heart.

Mate.

And just like that, something inside her broke open.

Fane was right, and so was the cougar. It was Marjani who was wrong. She and Fane were mates. They did this together, or they didn't do it all.

In one smooth movement, she pulled her switchblade from her bra and launched herself at Sindre. Grabbing him by his long blond hair, she jerked back his head and pressed the tip to his carotid.

"Stop it—*now*. Or you're dead."

The king hissed in pain as the iron seared into his flesh.

Inside, the cougar snarled to be let out. *Kill. Death.* The man had attacked their mate, and it wanted blood.

She pushed the sharp point in a little deeper. "I mean it."

"Fine." Sindre flicked his fingers.

Fane's breath sucked in and she felt his pain lessen. She eased off the pressure of the point against Sindre's throat.

Roald made a move toward them, and she whipped her head around, teeth bared. "Come any closer and I'll shove this blade into his fucking brain."

Gripping her wrist, Sindre forced the switchblade a little

away from his throat. At the same time, Fane staggered toward them.

Hell. He was going to just keep coming until he either died or got her away from Sindre. He was that determined to protect her.

She had to do something. Now.

"Change of terms," she gritted, her voice barely human. "Fane Morningstar goes with me. If we escape, then you free us both."

"And if you fail?"

"We'll both stay here and serve you. That is, if Fane agrees."

"I do," he managed to gasp out.

Behind her, she heard the hum of powerful magic. She glanced over her shoulder. A light glowed in Roald's palm as he conjured up a fae ball.

Arne stepped between her and his father. "Let them work this out."

"Get out of my way," the warrior ordered, "or I'll blast you, too."

"No," Arne drawled. "I don't think I will. She won't hurt the king. If she meant to kill him, he'd already be dead. This is her way of bargaining with him."

Sindre squeezed her wrist. Her fingers went numb and ice spread from her hand up her arm. Then as quickly as it had started, the ice melted, and she realized it had been a demonstration, a taste of what he could do if he really wanted.

She stared back, unblinking. She was fast, and almost as good with her left hand as her right. Maybe he'd win and maybe he wouldn't.

"Let me go," he said, "and we'll talk."

She jerked her head in assent and released him, switching her knife to her left hand. Her right hand prickled painfully as the feeling returned to it, but she ignored it, her gaze locked on the king.

"I accept your terms," he said. "But you both must escape the castle by dawn. If even one of you fails, you'll accept my *geas* for a fae year and a day, and Fane will serve out the rest of his term, plus an additional ninety-nine years."

She and Fane exchanged glances. Then Fane gave a firm nod. "Done."

"Done," she echoed.

"But Fane Morningstar still loses everything." The king turned an icy stare on his envoy. "His wealth—and his Gift."

"His Gift?"

"He offered, and I accept. It makes the game more interesting."

Her stomach sank to the soles of those stupid satin heels. "No! That's not part of the bargain."

"Then he stays with me."

Fane's body went stick straight. "Take it."

Sindre's lips pulled back in a smile that made it very clear he wasn't human. "I already have."

34

The loss of Fane's Gift shuddered through him. He felt like a fucking limb had been torn off. He set his jaw and tried not to throw up.

His magic was gone, and with it, a vital part of himself.

A cold sweat pricked his forehead. Without his Gift, he was defenseless—and worthless to Marjani.

His intrepid mate closed her fingers around his. "If we escape the castle by dawn," she told the king, "you'll also restore Fane's Gift. That's nonnegotiable."

His abused heart punched in his chest. It was a chance. Sindre wouldn't bargain with Fane, but Marjani was a different story.

The king regarded her as if she were an interesting species. Fane could count on the fingers of one hand the fae who'd dare openly thwart Sindre when he had his heart set on something. The man who could buy and sell whole nations hadn't been able to buy this one woman.

No wonder the king wanted her so badly.

"You're in no position to be adding conditions," Sindre told her. "The bargain is set."

"No." Her chin jutted. "It's not. I did *not* agree to Fane losing his Gift, and neither did he until *after* the bargain was set. You talk about dishonor? Where is the honor in tacking on a new condition after a bargain is made?"

The temperature in the room dropped below freezing. The snow came down harder.

Fane locked his knees and tried not to look as weak and lightheaded as he felt.

It was Arne who broke the deadlock. "What's the harm?" he murmured to Sindre. "It adds another dimension to the game."

Thank you, Dad.

A long silence during which Fane held his breath.

Sindre gave a curt nod. "Very well. If you both escape the castle by dawn, I'll return Fane's Gift. *If.*"

Hope surged in Fane.

Marjani inclined her head, regal as a queen. Goddess, he loved this woman.

"That's acceptable." She stuck out her hand. "We have a deal."

Sindre pressed her fingers. "The bargain is set."

He raised his voice, repeating the agreed-upon terms for all to hear. "Witness my words: If both Marjani Savonett and Fane Morningstar find their way through the maze and out of the castle by dawn, they will be free to leave Iceland with no retribution from me. You, Marjani Savonett, will receive six diamonds worth at least two hundred thousand dollars in the human world, and I'll release Fane Morningstar from the rest of the geas and return his Gift."

Beside him, Marjani gave an audible swallow. "Two hundred thousand dollars," she whispered.

"But," Sindre added, "if either of you is still in my castle at dawn, you, Marjani Savonett, will accept my *geas* for a fae year-and-a-day, and Fane Morningstar will serve out his *geas* plus another ninety-nine years. And his Gift will be mine."

Fane squared his shoulders. "Agreed."

"Agreed," echoed Marjani.

Around them, the room was buzzing. Roald gave Fane a last, contemptuous look and then deliberately gave him his back. One by one, everyone but his dad and Sindre turned their backs on him, too.

Fane kept his head high. Let them scorn him as an oath breaker. He knew it wasn't so black and white. Sometimes a man had to choose between two opposing points of honor, and he'd chosen to protect Marjani.

But that didn't mean it wasn't hard.

He waited, tight-lipped, for his father to join the others. The king would expect a show of loyalty. Arne was his longest-serving envoy, and one of the few half-bloods granted full status in the court.

But his dad didn't turn away. Instead, he put a hand on Fane and Marjani's backs and urged them toward the door. "I hope you know what you're doing," he muttered to Fane. "Even the fae get lost in that bloody maze."

"You think I don't know that? But I had to do something."

The two of them exchanged a look, and then his dad moved a shoulder. "Hell. If it was your mom, I'd have done the same thing."

"Don't worry, I have a plan," Marjani said.

His dad looked skeptical. "You'll need it."

Marjani's backpack had appeared next to the oak door. When Fane asked where it had come from, she just smiled. "A friend."

Arne squeezed Fane's shoulder. "I'll keep the king occupied as best as I can. Go with the Goddess. Both of you." He winked at Marjani and strode back to the center of the tower. "Who wants to bet on the fada?"

An excited ripple of voices responded. "Me!"

"I will."

"I'll put ten thousand on the king."

Diamonds, the court's preferred currency, exchanged hands, with Arne keeping the bank.

Marjani shook her head. "They really don't see us as people, do they? They're betting as if it were a fucking horse race."

"Their loss." Another wave of dizziness hit him. He reached for her arm. "Let's get out of here."

But Sindre 'ported in front of the door, blocking it. He raised a glass of wine to Marjani, ignoring Fane as if he was less than dirt. "Dawn is at 6:17 a.m. I'll see you then, love."

His nephews—the blond twins—strode up to flank them, their expressions avid. They loved a good bet, and Fane suspected they hoped that if Marjani were forced to serve Sindre, they'd get a chance at her. Bastards.

Marjani's eyes flashed turquoise. "I'm not your *love*, and I plan to be long gone by dawn."

She slipped out of those fuck-me heels that Fane knew must be from Sindre, and tossed them in the powdery snow at the king's feet—first one, then the other. They landed with a puff of white.

"We'll see," he said with a little smile and moved aside.

She slung her backpack over a shoulder and slid an arm around Fane's waist. "Ready?"

Lightness filled his chest. Even if they did escape, he was out of a job and stripped of everything he'd earned since accepting Sindre's *geas*. But hey, he'd be with Marjani, and he'd still have his Gift—and he'd never again have to kiss Sindre's cold white arse.

Things could be worse.

"Ready." He wrapped an arm around her shoulders and together, they walked past Sindre and the twins. The oak door swung open and then slammed shut behind them with an ominous thud.

The maze stretched in either direction, the path wide but with no openings to be seen in either direction. He waited until they went around a corner before pulling her to a halt.

"Jani? I meant it. I'm mate-claiming you."

"Now?"

"Now."

A shadow crossed her face. She set her palm to his heart. "Fane—think. If we lose, he'll use the bond against us."

"Is that why you didn't accept my claim?" He heard the anger in his voice, but damn it, if the woman was still trying to protect him, he was going to turn her over his knee when this was over.

"He'll hurt you to control me. Like he did just now." She rose up onto her toes to whisper in his ear. "You know those river fada he keeps as servants? The woman and I talked while I was getting ready. She told me he hurts her mate to punish her. Do you think I could stand by and watch him hurt you?"

"Fuck that. I can take anything that SOB dishes out. At least if you're my mate, he'll stop trying to seduce you." He gripped the back of her head and tilted it so that her face was angled up to him. "Accept the claim. We'll do this together. If we lose, at least let me have that much. I'll know he can't touch you."

Her throat worked. Her mouth opened. Rather than hear another no from her, he covered those soft, dusky-rose lips with his own. Spearing his tongue into her mouth.

Prepared for a fight.

But she didn't fight him. Instead, her breath released with a sigh and her taut little body melted against him. He forgot how shitty he felt as his dick went iron-hard.

He kept his one hand behind her head, holding her mouth where he wanted, while his other hand went to her round little ass. He molded her to his body, pressing his insistent erection into her belly. Against his chest, her nipples pebbled through that sexy scrap of a dress.

She undulated her hips against his, and said something that sounded like, "All right."

He dragged his mouth from hers. "That had better be a 'Yes, Fane. I accept your claim.'"

A smile trembled on her lips. "It was."

"Say it. I want the words."

"Yes, Fane. I accept your claim." Her smile broadened and then she was beaming up at him.

Inside his ribcage, something warm and luminous bloomed, like a piece of the sun trapped in his heart.

He gathered her closer. "Goddess, I love you."

Her eyes widened. "I feel it. It's humming inside me like my quartz does."

"The bond?"

She nodded. "Not that you're getting out of the mate ritual, but we're bonded."

"You see me arguing?" He gave her another kiss to seal the deal. When he released her, another wave of dizziness hit him. He dragged in a breath.

Her brow creased. "You're hurting."

He massaged his chest with the heel of his hand. "I need a little time to recover, is all."

"And I have zero healing ability." She placed a hand over his and eyed him worriedly. "First he stole your energy and then your Gift. I'm surprised you're still upright."

"It was worth it to get you away from the king." He rested his forehead against hers. "I'm some bargain as a mate, aren't I? No money, no job, and an oath breaker on top of it."

"Yeah." She caressed his shoulders, her tone so tender. "You know you're out of your freaking mind, right? Giving up everything for me?"

"No, I'm not. This is the sanest I've ever been. But I wanted to spoil you—buy you things, take you places. Now, even if we get out of this, I'll have nothing except my Gift. Oh, and a house in Newfoundland. I'm pretty sure he can't take that; it was mine before I accepted the *geas*."

"Fane." She gave him a little shake. "You're all I want. And when we get home, I'll show you just how happy I am to be your mate."

Home. He liked the sound of that.

He hadn't had a home—not a real one—since his mom died. His chest warmed even more, Marjani's love pouring through the mating bond. Melting Sindre's ice and healing the pain.

"All right, then." He took her hand. "Let's get the fuck out of here."

Instinct had him drawing on his Gift to spirit them out of there. But it was gone. He set his jaw and started walking. He'd just have to get used to it.

They turned a corner—and halted.

They were outside the castle. Above them, the first quarter moon peeped above the horizon on a chilly September night. His breath hitched. He and Marjani spun around, looking at the jagged black castle behind them.

She spoke first. "He let us go—just like that?"

Uneasiness prickled Fane's spine. "This isn't like him."

Her eyes met his. "Maybe he has something else planned. Anyway, let's get the hell out of here while we can. Just let me change first."

She was already dragging off her dress. She knelt on the tundra to rummage in her backpack, covered in only a couple of silky gold scraps.

His mouth dried. He could just make out the shadows of her nipples, and when she leaned forward to dig deeper in the pack, the gold material stretched taut over her round behind.

She stilled and glanced up. "You're looking. I feel it."

"Yeah. Does it bother you?"

She shook her head. "I like it. I never thought I'd be so comfortable with a man again. But with you, I am."

"Good. Because I intend to do a lot of looking." He waggled his brows at her. "Among other things."

Her lips twitched as she pulled on her jeans. "Don't distract me."

"Sorry," he said meekly.

She just snorted and finished putting on her clothes—a T-shirt and a gray hoodie. She shoved her feet into a pair of sneakers and slid the switchblade into her front pocket.

The dress she rolled up carefully.

He scowled. "Leave it."

She hesitated. "I know *he* gave it to me, but it's pretty—and it must have cost an arm and a leg."

"Leave it," he repeated. "I'll buy you another one. Even if I have to save up for a year to do it."

She gave the dress a last regretful look and then with a shrug, dropped it on the grass. "I don't have anywhere to wear it anyway."

Fane slung the pack over his shoulder. When she objected that he should take it easy until he felt better, he said, "When it gets to be too much, I'll let you know."

"Men," she muttered, but stopped arguing.

He pointed west. "That way. We'll find a portal to the human world. From there, we can hitch a ride to Reykjavik."

"What about your SUV?"

"It's Sindre's now."

"Oh. Right."

They started jogging across the tundra. At least this side of the castle wasn't as boggy as the south side. Still, without his Gift, Fane felt like he was running through molasses. He grimly slogged on.

They'd gone about a mile when he realized nothing had

changed in their surroundings. The moon was the exact same height in the sky, and the castle hadn't grown any smaller.

He muttered a curse and halted.

"What's wrong?" Marjani asked.

He knelt to finger a clump of weather-beaten grass. It felt real, but... "Sindre's Gift is chicanery. The man can create illusions so real you can touch them."

"You think we're still in the maze."

"Yeah. I do."

Her nostrils flared and then she let out a single pithy word. "You're right. I smell silver. Just a hint, but it's obvious now I'm aware of it."

"Damn it, I should have expected this." Fane rose to his feet. "I know what he's capable of, but I thought he'd use the maze itself to mess with us."

"He did. If we're still in the castle, then we're in the maze. We just don't know it."

He nodded grimly. "How in Hades can we get out of it when we can't see where it begins or ends?"

"Or when dawn comes."

They met each other's eyes.

And then the illusion faded, and they were in the maze, the pearly walls towering over them. Before them was a forked intersection with three options—left, center or right.

"Gotcha," Marjani murmured. "Or do you have us?"

Fane peered down each of the paths, looking for a landmark, but all three were blank as a sheet of paper. "I have no fucking idea where we are. The maze is impossible to navigate without Sindre's permission."

The adrenaline that had fueled his jog had dissipated. He leaned over, hands on his thighs, suddenly so weary he could barely keep on his feet. Beside him, Marjani slumped against a wall.

"Nothing is impossible," she said, but she didn't move.

Silence fell. A thick, watchful silence.

The walls on either side pressed closer, squeezing in, inch by slow inch. His nape tightened. He shook his head from side to side.

It's not real. It's an illusion.

Beside him, Marjani drew a jagged breath, and he knew Sindre was getting to her, too. A hot, cleansing fury swept through him. She'd been through so damn much, and now she had to survive Sindre's mind games as well.

Mind over matter, Fane.

He had to be strong for Marjani. He touched her hand, and damn if the encroaching walls didn't recede a little.

"We have to keep moving," he said. "Part of Sindre's Gift is that he can manipulate things to seem worse than they are. He tries to steal all your hope."

Her mouth tilted wryly. "He must not know what the Darktime was like. Okay." She let out a long breath. "Let's do this."

He nodded and straightened back up, and then reeled as the maze swooped around him.

"Take it easy." Marjani grabbed his arm, twin creases between her brows. "I wish I could help, but I have no healing Gift."

He swallowed dryly. "I'll manage. But now would be a good time to hear that plan of yours."

She touched his cheek, concerned, and then nodded. "Okay, here's what I think. An illusionist can only fool a living thing. He can't fool an inanimate object like my quartz. And I've been studying the maze every chance I got. I think I've figured out its underlying logic."

He shook his head. "I told you, that won't work."

"But north, south, east and west don't change. I can use my quartz as a compass to keep us on track."

He nodded slowly. "It's worth a try."

Setting her hand over where her quartz was concealed by

her hoodie, she focused for a few moments. When she opened them, she said, "We're a little east of the north tower. Where's the closest portal?"

He dropped his voice. "The one by the east tower—the one I took you out of the other day."

"Okay." She pointed toward the left fork. "East is that way."

"Lead on."

35

———

This time Marjani took the lead, since the maze had narrowed to where they had to walk single file. The path twisted and turned, but she simply consulted her quartz at each intersection. At first there were only a few openings, but then doors and forks in the path started appearing every few yards, forcing her to keep referring to her quartz.

Midnight came and went. Fane halted. "We should've reached the east tower by now. Hell, we've had time to walk around the whole damn castle."

She frowned down at her quartz. "As far as I can tell, we're basically where we started. It's like the entire structure has been twisted into a new form. It's not anything like it was last week." She scowled. "How the hell does he do that? Keep us walking but never going anywhere?"

"I don't know, but it's fucking brilliant. Even if someone breaks in, he can keep them wandering and confused for as long as he wants. Sometimes he doesn't bother to send the guards to get intruders, just waits until they collapse from hunger and exhaustion."

Her chest tightened. She raised her gaze to Fane's.

"It's almost one o'clock. We've spent close to three hours trying to get out already, and we haven't gone anywhere."

"Hey." Fane rubbed her arms. "He hasn't won yet."

"No? I feel like a fucking lab rat, running on a wheel as fast as I can without getting anywhere."

A low chuckle sounded from somewhere nearby. She whipped out her switchblade and turned in a slow circle, but there was no one to be seen.

Fane blew out a breath. "It's just Sindre, messing with your mind. You have to fight it."

Weak. You're weak.

"Sorry." She returned the switchblade to her pocket. "You're right."

Fane pointed left down yet another narrow passage. "I don't think we've tried this way yet."

Once again, they followed the path around what felt like the entire castle. She tried to key into the maze's underlying logic like she had before, but there didn't seem to *be* an underlying logic anymore.

Then things got worse. The tiled floor turned into a bog.

They slogged through it, feet sinking into slimy black muck, the icy water sloshing around their calves. Marjani frowned. Something seemed funny, and then she realized what it was. All she smelled was the faint scent of silver.

"Wait." She grabbed Fane's arm. "If it's really a bog, it should stink like a rotten egg. But it doesn't."

His nostrils flared. "You're right."

"It's not real," she said. "It's another illusion."

They continued walking, more confidently now. But the icy water rose higher until it was at their waists, then their chests. Fane shrugged out of the backpack and held it above his head.

"Just in case," he said.

When it reached her throat, Marjani had trouble

convincing herself that the bog wasn't real. The cold seeped into her bones and her feet felt like blocks of ice.

She stumbled and knew a moment of stark terror when the black water closed over her head. She came up, choking and coughing. Fane grabbed her, and she clung to him, shaking with cold.

"Get on my back," he said.

She shook her head. "I'm okay," she said between chattering teeth. "You're...the one...hurt."

"Get on my back," he repeated evenly. "The man's a genius at illusions. If he convinces you that you're drowning, you will. It won't matter that it's all in your head. Your lungs will seize and you'll die anyway."

She gave a hard shiver and sucked in another mouthful of water.

"*Now*, Jani."

"Okay, okay."

He shifted her to his back. Slinging the backpack over a shoulder, she twined her arms and legs around him and Fane continued slogging his way through the water. He was half-walking, half-swimming now.

Then Sindre took pity on them—or more likely, he didn't want to actually kill them, just scare the crap out of them. After all, he couldn't enforce a *geas* on a dead person.

Whatever the reason, the land sloped up. When the water reached Fane's waist, she slid off and walked alongside him until they stepped onto the dry blue tiles again.

Marjani instinctively started to scrape the greenish-black slime off her arms and hands—and then swore under her breath. "I'm clean." She held up her hands for Fane to see.

"Me, too." He showed her his own unsoiled hands.

"Holy mother, he's good."

Fane nodded grimly. "What time is it?"

"Two-thirty."

"Less than four hours."

Their eyes met. She knew his thoughts must be running along the same lines as hers. What did it matter if they had four hours or four minutes? They were no closer to escaping the castle than when they'd left the north tower.

Weak.

She dragged a weary hand over her face, her mouth gritty. "I'd kill for a glass of water."

"Yeah." He squared his shoulders, but his lean face was gaunt. The man was running on fumes.

Then they both froze as a door opened in the unending white wall, but it was only Ula, dressed for bed in a plain cotton nightgown, her hair in a long black braid. In her hand was a large glass of nectar.

"You didn't get this from me." She shoved it at Fane.

He took it and handed it to Marjani. "You first."

"No, you."

"Hurry," the river fada hissed. "Arne's distracting him, but I don't have much time."

"We'll split it." Marjani drained half the glass. It was just what she needed, quenching her thirst and spreading warmth through her tired and chilled body.

She handed the nectar to Fane, and he gulped down the rest before returning the empty glass to Ula. He touched her arm. "Thank you."

"Yes." Marjani gave her a quick hug.

The other woman jerked her head in acknowledgement, and then slipped back through the door. It closed behind her and the wall smoothed out as if nothing was there.

Fane rubbed his forehead. "Was she really here, or was that just another hallucination?"

"She was here." Marjani rose on her toes to whisper, "We have a deal, me and her. When I get home, I promised to give a message to her family, but I think she would've helped us anyway."

He nodded. "She's a good woman," he whispered back. "And thank the gods for that, because I feel much better."

They kissed, and for a few seconds, Marjani forgot all about Sindre and the maze as a warm, needful ache spread through her lower abdomen.

The quartz was outside her hoodie, nestled on her chest between them. Fane lifted his head and traced his fingers down her neck. A lazy turquoise light swirled inside the smoky gray and purple, and he lightly stroked a thumb over it.

Marjani tensed, but it didn't hurt—it felt good. She lifted her gaze to his. "No one can touch our quartzes but close friends or family—or a mate."

"Sorry." He lifted his thumb. "I didn't know."

"Don't be." She moved his thumb back to the quartz. "When it's you touching me, it feels good, like you're stroking me."

"Yeah?" His grin was wicked. "Like I'm stroking you where?"

She slanted him a look from beneath her lashes. "Where do you think?"

Against her belly, his cock jerked and lengthened. "You're a bad woman to tease me right now."

"Am I?" She extended a single claw and scraped it down his cheek, shadowed with his night beard. "I think I like being bad."

"Hold that thought, okay?" He put his mouth to her ear. "When we get out of here, I'm going to fuck you, so hard. But right now we have a maze to solve. And I have an idea. The illusions are designed to trick our senses, right?"

She pulled back to look up at him. "Yeah. Why?"

"The eyes are easier to trick than the sense of touch. So why don't we try closing our eyes? Then we can feel our way along the wall and—"

"We should be able to tell what's really there," she finished, hope springing up in her. "Let's try it."

They agreed that Fane would lead while she held onto him so they wouldn't lose each other. She looped the fingers of her left hand through his belt, setting the other hand on the wall.

"Ready," she said, closing her eyes, and he started walking. Within seconds, the wall changed and straightened out.

She caught her breath. "I think it's working."

"Me, too." He picked up the pace.

Another ten minutes had passed when they heard a high-pitched gibbering. Goblins, and from the sound of it, headed straight for them.

Her eyes flew open.

"This way." Fane jerked her into a tiny alcove with barely enough room for them to stand side by side.

The gibbering grew louder. A small pack of the short, wild-eyed creatures streamed around a curve, animal skins draped over their shoulders and tied around their thick waists as loin cloths, pointed teeth gleaming. Their stench hit her like a shovel to the gut.

She slapped a hand to her mouth and tried not to wretch. "No illusion."

"Yep. Pretty sure those fuckers are real." He took short, shallow breaths.

"Take this." She released the catch on her switchblade and shoved it at him. "I'll fight clawed."

"Have I mentioned I haven't a bloody idea how to use this thing?"

"It's iron. You don't have to know how to use it." She kept her gaze on the screeching goblins. "Just cut them anywhere and it will hurt. Even better, aim for their eyes—or balls."

"Remind me never to make you angry."

The pack was almost upon them—only five goblins. Sindre was giving them a sporting chance.

She bared her teeth and took a fighting stance, knees bent, claws out.

Beside her, Fane mirrored her stance, the switchblade up and ready, his other arm bent at the elbow to block blows. He gestured with one hand. "Come on, you bastards."

In spite of their danger, she let out a huff of amusement. The man was a fast learner—or a talented actor. If she didn't know better, she'd think he was a trained soldier.

With a howl, the goblins were upon them.

But this time, Marjani and Fane had the advantage. The two of them might be outnumbered, but they had their backs to the wall, so the goblins had to attack them head-on.

And she had cat-fast reflexes. Even Fane was slashing the knife through the air lightning-fast, parrying each attempt to jump him. So he hadn't lost that part of his Gift, maybe because it wasn't magical, just part of his genes.

A goblin aimed his sharp teeth at her leg, but she slammed the toe of her sneaker into his balls and he collapsed with a groan. She tore out its neck with her claws—and then spun to the left and took out another goblin's eye.

A third jumped at her—a female, this time. She caught her in mid-air and wrenched her head to one side. Her neck broke with an audible snap. Two more goblins came at Marjani—the one with the missing eye and a new one, and she quickly and efficiently took them down, too.

She turned to the last goblin just as Fane got in a lucky jab to the goblin's throat. Blood spurted from the goblin's artery, and he wavered and then crumpled to the tiles. They'd won, with only a few minor cuts to show for it.

Marjani dragged in a breath as Fane shot her an exuberant grin. "How'd I do?"

"Not bad." She smiled back, amused at his elation. But that was adrenaline from the fight. "I'll make a fighter out of you yet. And now, if I can have my switchblade back?"

He handed it over, and she methodically stabbed the long, thin blade into the heart of each of the five goblins. When she looked up again, Fane looked a little pale under his tan.

"Sorry," she muttered. "But they have magical blood, same as us. I have to make sure they're really dead." She wiped the blood on an animal skin and slipped the knife back into her pocket.

"No need to apologize. You're right." He let out a long breath. "We're close. That's why he sent the goblins."

"The end is also the beginning," she murmured. "Make the wrong choice and you'll never get home."

"What?"

"It's just something Jewel said." She rubbed her arm over her forehead. "Have you noticed that as soon as we recognize an illusion, it disappears?"

He nodded as they started walking again. "But those goblins were no illusion."

"No."

She stopped in her tracks as it hit her. Sindre's illusions were designed for humans. If she shifted, her cougar might see through them where her human mind couldn't.

"What is it?" Fane frowned down on her.

Her gut tingled. This could work. She *knew* it.

But would her cougar cooperate?

He'll use your greatest weakness against you.

She dug her nails into her palms. *I can't go feral. I have too much to live for.*

But Fane was here to help if she had any trouble, the mate bond strong and steady between them.

And maybe her greatest weakness wasn't her cougar, but her *fear* of it. That the cat would take over, that she'd become a feral.

You're not an animal. You're a fada. I'm pretty sure that means accepting every part of you.

Fane was right. She had to stop fighting the cougar. To trust it, which really meant trusting herself—because her cougar wasn't a weakness, it was a strength.

"I have an idea." She grabbed Fane's arm. "I think if I changed to cougar, I could see through the illusion. The maze might not even detect me. Fae spells have trouble recognizing fada in their animal forms."

"So you're going to shift?"

She nodded. "When I'm done, grab hold of my fur and don't let go, even if it looks like I'm walking through a wall."

"Okay." No argument, just a confident nod. "Don't worry, I trust you."

He meant it. Through the bond, she *felt* his unquestioning belief in her. It both shattered her heart and healed it at the same time.

She dragged off her clothes and stuffed them in the backpack, keeping nothing but her quartz.

Fane shrugged into the pack and then pulled her into a kiss. A deep, thorough kiss—his hard body against hers, his shirt silky against her bare nipples. Through his pants, his cock nudged against her mound, thick and insistent.

Need curled through her. Deep within, the cat rubbed up against her skin, purring.

He lifted his head, blue eyes dark with wanting. They stared at each other for a moment, and then Marjani gave a little shake of her head to clear it.

"What was that for?"

"I just want you to remember that I love you."

"Oh, I will." She pressed a kiss to the soft hollow at the base of his throat, and then stepped back, fingers wrapped around her quartz.

"You got this," he said with complete confidence.

"Yeah." Because she did. She believed in herself—and her cat.

And I am not *weak.*

Taking a deep breath, she let herself resonate with the tiny crystals, but before she could shift, Fane disappeared. *What the fuck?*

"Fane?" Heart thumping, she aborted the shift. "Where are you?" She turned in a circle.

No answer.

"Fane?" she called louder. And then she screamed his name. "*Fane!* Where are you?"

Somewhere nearby, Sindre breathed a soft laugh. She didn't know how she knew it was him, but she did.

Anger blazed through her. "You can't do this, you asshole. We're supposed to solve the maze together."

Cool fingers touched her bare shoulder. She whipped around to find the ice fae king looking down at her.

His mouth curved. "That wasn't part of the bargain."

36

"Jani?" Fane scrubbed his hands over his face and looked again, but she'd disappeared.

What felt like a giant fist squeezed his lungs.

"Jani!" he roared. "Where are you?"

But he was alone in a small room. No, make that an ice cave. No windows. No doors. And the icy blue walls reached twenty feet high.

"No," he rasped.

Because Sindre didn't want Fane—he wanted Marjani. In fact, the king might intend to let Fane rot in this small, confined space.

And Marjani would be forced to accept Sindre's *geas*, because the bargain said they *both* had to escape the castle by dawn.

Fane ran his hands over the icy walls, desperately searching for a hidden door or window, or even just a crack in the smooth surface. Anything that would get him out of here and back to his mate. But he worked his way around the entire room without any luck.

He eyed the wall. On a good day, he might be able to leap high enough to grab the top and then swing his legs up and over. But he was tired and Gift-less.

He *felt* Sindre smile.

His spine tingled. He glanced around, even though he knew he was alone in the room.

"You're a bloody prick, you know that?"

Silence, but snow began to fall.

He gave a savage grin. Damn, it felt good to finally tell Sindre what he thought of him.

Adrenaline surged through him. Backing up, he took a running leap at the opposite wall, but he only made it three quarters of the way up before he dropped back to the floor.

Hell.

Shrugging out of the backpack, he took a deep breath and tried again. The third try, he almost made it, his fingers just six inches from the top. He tried to scramble the last few inches, but the wall was too smooth. He slid back to the floor, losing a couple of buttons off his shirt in the process.

He tried again. And again, until he was bent over, hands on his thighs, sucking in oxygen.

Mind over matter.

He eyed the wall. Sindre had stolen his Gift, but as a former wayfarer who could make himself virtually invisible, Fane knew something about illusions himself.

As he'd told Marjani, they only worked if the viewer believed in them.

He heard the murmur of voices and stilled. Marjani and Sindre.

No fucking way.

She's mine, you bastard. My mate. My beautiful cat.

He took a deep breath to calm himself. Sindre was messing with his head.

Forget him. Think about Marjani instead. Focus on the mate bond—you can use it to get to her.

Warmth filled his chest, and he felt a strong but invisible thread connecting him to his mate. He straightened his spine and stared at the wall in the direction the thread seemed to be coming from. Was that an opening?

It disappeared.

Don't fight it. His strength was going with the flow. He needed to remember that.

He grabbed the backpack and let his gaze soften and relax. *Yes. There.*

Keeping that soft, hazy focus, he walked through the wall.

MARJANI GLARED at the ice fae king. "What do you mean, that wasn't part of the bargain?"

His chiseled lips curved. "The two of you solving the maze together. I don't recall promising that."

Marjani replayed the wording of the bargain in her mind. He was right. All he'd said was that both she and Fane had to escape the castle by dawn. Nothing in the bargain said they had to do it together.

Thrice-damned fucking fae.

Her growl actually had him backing up a step, but he recovered quickly.

"What would you give me for this, I wonder?" He raised a hand. Dangling from his fingers was the substitute quartz; the one Blaer had stolen from Marjani.

She swiped at it, just to throw him off.

"No, Marjani, *mín.*" He closed his fingers around the milky chunk of rock. "I think I'll hang onto it for now."

She shrugged. "You do that."

The fae king eyed her. "I thought you earth fada needed your quartz."

"We do. But I can get by without it." She looked at the quartz in his hand as she spoke, so it was perfectly true. She could get by without *that* quartz.

Her own quartz was hidden against her side, her fingers holding it loosely so her hand appeared empty. Thank the gods Fane had suggested the substitution.

"Where did you get it, anyway?" she asked. "I thought it was lost."

"This?" The king tossed the milky quartz lightly into the air by its leather thong, catching it on the way down. "Lady Blaer gave it to me in return for shortening the period of her banishment. She tells me I can use it to control you." He gave it a squeeze. "Is that true?"

She met his eyes. "No."

His gaze probed hers. "So one of you is...mistaken." He muttered an incantation.

Marjani froze. Blaer must have shared the secret with Sindre.

The North African fae who'd help create the original earth fada had gifted the quartz and its special energy to them alone. But like most fae gifts, it came with an edge—with the right incantation, an earth fada's quartz could be used to compel him or her to obey a fae.

And the king had the complicated phrase correct in every particular.

She forced herself to shrug. She was damned if she'd help Sindre puzzle this out. "I guess it's Lady Blaer, then."

With a shrug, he pocketed the quartz. "I don't need tricks like this anyway." He moved closer, his voice deepening. "Marjani. Are you sure you want to do this?"

She opened and closed her mouth like a beached fish. The

man was so beautiful, she couldn't tear her eyes away. His white-blond hair glimmered, his eyes a brilliant silver.

He smiled, and her knees went weak. Those chiseled lips promised so much pleasure. She could almost feel them tracing over her naked breasts, making their way down to her clit...

"Why do I want you so much?" he murmured, almost to himself. "I think it's because you're so serious. Life means something to you."

She somehow managed to find her voice. He might be beautiful, but he wasn't Fane. "And it doesn't to you?"

He moved a shoulder. "I prefer it to death."

She stared up at him. *This isn't real. You're not my mate.*

The bastard was using a glamour on her. She growled and the spell broke.

The wall across from them wavered. Fane stalked through, hair dusted with snow and deep smudges beneath his eyes. His shirt had lost a few buttons, and he was breathing hard. Dark stubble had sprung up on his jaw. He looked exhausted and primitive in a way that stole her breath—and not in the artificial way that Sindre had.

He hauled her up against him. "Get away from her, you bastard."

Sindre did a double take, then his brow flicked up. "You're more powerful than I realized. Perhaps I could still use you after all."

"Go to Hades. I'm leaving." He squeezed her shoulders. "With my mate."

The king's jaw loosened. His gaze swung to her. "You'd choose him over me?"

"I already have." She leaned into Fane. He was her man. Her *mate.*

Something cold whispered over her skin. Sindre was pissed off.

That told her more than anything that this was it, their final test. They had to pass it—or they were fucked.

"Get out of our way," Fane ground out. "Let the game play out—or forfeit."

Smart. Marjani could tell the king didn't want to appear a poor sport, especially since other fae had bet on the outcome.

Sindre inclined his head and then muttered a short incantation. The air around him warped in a dizzying way as he 'ported out of there.

"We're close." Fane nuzzled her cheek and then released her. "He wouldn't have interfered if we weren't. I think you're right—you need to shift."

With a nod, she brought her quartz to her heart. Fane winked at her, his confidence in her palpable.

Closing her eyes, she drew on the quartz's energy—and let the change take her.

It was a hard shift. She'd shifted too many times in too short of a period, but at least her quartz's energy level had reached seventy-five percent.

She determinedly maintained her focus. This wasn't just for her, it was for Fane. She couldn't stand the thought of him being in Sindre's power for another day, let alone another century plus however many years he still had to serve of the first *geas*.

Energy rippled over her, and then she landed on all fours. She stowed the quartz in the pocket of her cheek and looked around with her cat's keen vision. The maze was still there, but she could see a straight line to the outer edge, as if the maze were a patchy white mist overlaying the true path.

Gotcha.

Fane had donned the backpack while she shifted. He stroked a hand down her spine. "Did it work?"

She nodded—and then realized she was the old Marjani

again—the Marjani where the cat and human worked together and shared thoughts and emotions.

He threaded his fingers through the fur at the scruff of her neck. "Ready when you are, beautiful."

The cat liked being called beautiful. It purred and rubbed its head against Fane's hip in thanks—and marking him as hers, just in case that redheaded ice fae female hadn't gotten the message.

They set off, Fane's eyes shut, one hand gripping her fur. They came to the first dead end, and the cat walked right through it.

The next dead end actually was the end of a passage, but now she saw the opening to the right. She walked through, Fane right beside her.

Around her, the maze shifted. Grew dark.

Stupid man. Didn't Sindre know cougars had incredible night vision?

With a lash of her tail, she paced forward, following the line as it zigzagged toward a portal, increasingly confident.

An icy mix of sleet and snow began to fall. A wind whipped crystals into her eyes. The cat snarled and kept going. They were almost to the portal.

They reached the end of a passage, and the maze became the inner wall of the black lava castle.

"You did it, love." Fane's grin split his face as he touched the rough black wall. "I know where we are now. Come." He turned left, still holding onto her fur.

They came to a portal. Marjani couldn't see it, but she sensed an opening in the wards.

Fane flicked his fingers and said the incantation that would allow them through. But the portal remained closed. He scowled and tried again.

Nothing.

Fane said something low and ugly. "I'm not a member of the court anymore. The portal won't allow me through."

She nudged him aside. Time to test her theory and see if her cat could pass through. Then she halted. What good would it do if she left—but Fane remained trapped on the ice fae side?

They'd lost.

Ice balled in her stomach. She pressed against Fane.

He crouched down and enveloped her in a hard hug. "I love you, Jani. I swear, I'll figure out a way to get him to release you from the geas if it's the last thing I do."

Suddenly, the wind and snow stopped as if a switch had been thrown. Into the silence came the crunch of footsteps on the snow. She and Fane whipped around.

Sindre was back.

Marjani's lip peeled back in a snarl. Fane took a step toward him, hands fisted. "Let us out. We made it through the maze. We won."

Sindre's head tipped to one side, considering. "Actually, I'd say it was a draw. You made it through the maze—but you're still on this side of the portal."

"Because you changed the fucking rules."

The king ignored him to speak to Marjani. "It's a pity you met that mixed-blood first. We would've made quite a pair, you and me."

No way in Hades.

"My congratulations," Sindre said.

Both their jaws dropped.

The king chuckled. "It was a most entertaining game—and that tips the balance in your direction." He snapped his fingers, and a blue velvet bag settled between Marjani's front paws. "There are your diamonds. And you," he said to Fane, "have your Gift back. Now get out of Iceland—and if I were you, I wouldn't ever return."

Fane recovered enough to thank him. "Trust me, we won't."

The king said a phrase in fae and flicked his fingers. The air around Marjani and Fane warped. She just had time to snatch up the pouch of diamonds in her teeth before her stomach lurched and everything went dark.

The next thing she knew, she and Fane were alone on a cliff overlooking the ocean. To the east, the breaking dawn sent a gleaming gold trail over the dark waves crashing below.

37

Fane threw an arm around Marjani's neck. "We did it!" He planted a kiss on her furred cheek.

She rubbed her face against his, purring loudly.

"And damn." His eyes widened. "I have my Gift back."

She let out a happy yelp.

"Thanks to you, my hard-ass negotiator." He gave her another hug and then rose to his feet. "But I don't think we're in Iceland anymore."

They were on a narrow dirt path scattered with lichen-covered rocks. A chilly wind ruffled her fur and whipped Fane's hair back from his face. A half mile to the south, colorful boats bobbed in the harbor of a small fishing village.

"Well, hell." He squeezed his nape. "That's the village where I grew up. He sent me back to Newfoundland. And I still have a house just outside the village. It's even empty—the renters left a few months ago and I haven't gotten around to finding someone else. You up for a run?"

Of course.

She passed the blue velvet bag to him, keeping the quartz in her mouth, and waited as he secured the diamonds in one of the backpack's pockets before setting off down the trail, her loping behind.

The path wound along the cliff before sloping downward through a sweet-smelling pine forest. Halfway down, they came across a stream. Fane dropped to his knees to drink in great gulps, while she crouched beside him, lapping as fast as she could. It was delicious, clean and cold. She felt like she hadn't had a drink in days, other than that half-glass of nectar. How long had they been wandering in the maze, anyway?

After drinking their fill, they set off again. Ten minutes later, they reached a windswept headland on which was perched a little blue saltbox house with white trim. The wide front porch held a couple of weathered Adirondack chairs and a trio of empty flowerpots. Fane felt under one of the pots and emerged with a key.

"The water and electricity should still be on. A woman from the village comes in every couple of weeks to clean." He unlocked the door and ushered her in. "Welcome to my home, love."

They were in a small foyer with wide pine flooring and a timber-frame ceiling that opened into the kitchen. Fane set the backpack on a kitchen table the same bright blue as the house. To their left was a living room with a large fieldstone fireplace and rustic wood furniture.

Marjani liked it. A lot. She bumped her head against Fane's leg to tell him so.

"The bedroom is upstairs," he said. "And there's a bath up there, too."

The refrigerator was turned off, the door left open to air it. "There's no food in the house," Fane said as he closed the door and plugged the refrigerator in. "But we can get something in town." He pulled out his wallet and swore. "Bastard even took my cash."

Marjani decided it was time she shifted. As she rose to her

feet, naked, she removed the quartz from her mouth and set it on the table.

"Gods, you're beautiful." Fane's blue eyes took her in hungrily. A lean arm snaked around her waist, pulling her close for a kiss. When he let her up, he set his forehead against hers. "I'm sorry."

Her brow creased. "Why?"

He indicated the house. "This is all I have now. I owned it before I accepted the *geas*, so he can't take it from me. And I have a bank account in town—like the house, it's mine from before I worked for the king. I'm not sure how much is in it, but it's something."

"Fane." She framed his face. "I love it—and I don't even have this much. I share a den with my brother."

"But I wanted to give you—"

"Hey." She set a finger on his mouth. "This isn't the fae court. You don't have to buy my love."

He blinked and looked at her, arrested. "You're right."

"I know I am."

He sucked her finger into his mouth, and her inner thighs clenched. His mouth was so warm and wet, the eyes gazing into hers promising heated things. He released her finger and she swayed toward him.

He kissed her and then set her a little away. "Lord knows I want you, but I should feed you first. We can get something to eat in town."

"I *am* hungry." She slid her arms around his neck. "But I want this more."

Fane's hands moved down to grip her ass. He dragged her up against him so she could feel his erection through his leather pants. "I shouldn't. You..."

He trailed off as she rubbed her breasts against his shirt, the material rasping pleasurably against her nipples.

"Yeah," she said in husky whisper, "you should."

He lowered his mouth to hers again. It was a deep kiss, full of need and love. She took that love into herself and returned it, stroking her tongue over his, sucking it into her mouth.

He traced his lips down her throat. He was licking her nipple when her smartphone pinged from the kitchen table.

"Leave it," he murmured.

She drew a shaky inhale. "I can't. It's Adric. I should give him a call, let him know I'm okay."

"Right." He kissed his way across her breasts to her other nipple before releasing her. "Make it quick," he said as she reached for the quartz.

"I will." When she turned back, he was shrugging out of his shirt. The hand holding the quartz dropped to her side as she took him in: broad shoulders, an abdomen ridged with lean muscle. Curly hairs formed a dark T that arrowed into the waistband of the black leather pants encasing his long legs.

And he said *she* was beautiful... She swallowed, still not quite believing he belonged to her.

He dropped the shirt on a chair and rummaged in a cupboard for two glasses. She watched the play of his muscles across his back and shoulders as he ran the water and then filled the glasses.

That leather-clad ass was a woman's hot dream—firm, muscled. Perfect. She wanted to lean forward and take a bite.

He turned to hand her a glass of water and caught her staring. His mouth quirked, but all he said was, "You thirsty?"

"Thanks." She dragged in a breath and accepted the glass. "You know what? I'll just text Adric for now."

After taking a drink, she shot off a quick message to inform her brother she was safely out of Iceland and would call later. Then she sauntered the few feet to her sexy mate and stroked her fingers down the lean, hard muscles of his chest.

"Wanna show me the bedroom?"

His eyes glittered. "Fuck, yeah."

Setting a hand on the small of her back, he urged her toward the living room and the stairs leading to the second floor. She barely had time to snatch up her quartz on the way by the table.

Fane stopped at the foot of the narrow flight of stairs. "After you," he said with a gentlemanly nod.

She started up, and then realized his letting her go first had nothing to do with being a gentleman when he smoothed a hand down her ass. She laughed at him over her shoulder. "You're a bad man, Fane Morningstar."

He grinned back. "I like the view from back here."

Joy bubbled up in her. And that was so wonderful, to feel happy when she was naked with a man—happy, and turned on.

She swiveled to face him and just to tease him, moved up, one step at a time, her gaze locked on his.

The grin wiped from his face. He followed after, stalking her, slow and sexy, his face level with her breasts. His gaze went to her nipples, which had formed hard points of arousal, and then down to the nest of curly black hair at the apex of her thighs.

She walked up another two steps, but Fane remained where he was so that his head was now level with her navel. When she moved her foot to the next step, he reached out and snagged her by the hips, halting her. His mouth touched the soft skin beneath her navel, and then moved lower to brush over her curls.

She stilled, waiting. And then his mouth touched her clit.

Heat streaked up her spine.

He lapped at the swollen bud of flesh, his tongue warm and wet. Her thighs tensed. He nudged her legs apart so he could get deeper, swiping his tongue over her sex.

Her lungs jerked. With a moan, she grabbed the railing and locked her knees so she wouldn't fall down.

But he only took a few teasing licks before moving his

mouth up her body again. He gave a hard suck to each nipple, leaving them moist and aching, and then turned her around.

"Keep going." He caressed her bottom.

She forced herself to focus. She was only three steps from the top. She took them a little clumsily, but Fane was right there to steady her. He put an arm around her, his long fingers spreading over her belly, his lower body pressed against her ass, the leather cool in an exciting way.

The second floor was narrower than the main floor. A slatted wood bed with matching end tables was at one end, and across the front wall was a row of four windows overlooking the ocean. A ladder-back chair was set next to a bookcase spilling over with books, and a red door led to a bathroom with black-and-white tiles and a clawfoot tub.

Fane opened a couple windows to let in the air while she drew down a pretty red-and-white quilt. She set her quartz on an end table and then sat on the bed as he toed off his shoes and tried to peel off the leather pants. They got stuck partway down his thighs, and she smothered a laugh.

He grinned back. "Damn leather. But the ladies seem to like it."

"This lady sure does." She watched as he sat on the ladder-back chair and pulled the pants the rest of the way off along with his socks before rising to his feet, fully aroused.

Her eyes went to his cock, flushed and hard, the tip curving toward his stomach. She tensed, her amusement draining away. Her heart raced in a panicked little rhythm.

"Jani?" He took a step toward her and she had to force herself to remain seated. "What's wrong?"

"I'm sorry. It's not you. But—" She shook her head.

"Oh, sweetheart." Sitting on the bed beside her, he set his hand on the mattress between them, palm up.

She dug her nails into the sheets. "I thought—"

"What?" he prompted.

She made a low, unhappy sound. "That I was done with this. You're my *mate*. How can I be afraid of you? And I was having fun, damn it."

"Take my hand." A low, comforting rasp.

She looked at his open palm.

This is Fane, she reminded herself.

Mate, the cat added.

She let out a ragged exhale and uncurled her fingers from the sheet to place her hand on top of his. It felt good: cool, but firm.

"I don't think it works like that," he said. "You won't be all better in a day. Or a month. Or even a year."

"But I *want* this, damn it. I don't want to be afraid. I'm so fucking tired of being afraid."

"It's okay." He threaded his fingers through hers. "I want to be with you any way I can. The sex is just icing on the cake. We can take it as slow or fast as you want."

The tightness in her shoulders eased. She took a calming breath.

"This helps. Just sitting with you. Holding hands."

"You *will* get over this. I know it." He leaned toward her. "Can I kiss you?"

Tears pricked her eyes. He was being so damn careful with her.

"Yeah," she said in a barely audible voice. "I'd like that."

He set his free hand on the side of her face and brushed his lips over hers. "I love you." His mouth touched one cheek. "I will always be there for you." He traced his lips across to her other cheek. "I will never, ever hurt you."

What felt like a boa constrictor wrapped around her chest. Her throat worked. "I know you won't."

His eyes held hers. "I want you to promise something. That if I ever do anything to scare you, you'll tell me. Or just smack me upside the head and tell me to stop."

She worried her lower lip. "Oh, Fane."

He smoothed a thumb over her cheek. "Promise me, Jani."

She gave a jerky nod. "Okay. Yes. I promise."

"Good." Releasing her hand, he lay back on the mattress, his erection mostly deflated, and patted the sheet next to him. "Come here. Cuddle with me."

She knelt next to him. His cheeks and chin were shadowed with stubble. He folded one arm beneath his head, his bicep bulging, a tuft of dark hair in his armpit.

Desire twanged through her. Only a hint—but she welcomed it, focused on that warm tingle instead of her fear.

She ran a hand down the washboard ridges of his abdomen, just to see if she could. It felt good, the touch grounding her.

She did it again.

The cat purred. *Mine.*

"You could be a model," she told him. "If you're looking for a job."

He let out a startled laugh. "I don't think so."

"Oh, you could be. But you know something? Never mind. I want you all to myself."

His cock twitched and lengthened, and this time, it just fed the warm tingles.

His smile was slow and intimate. "I know you're the only woman *I* want. The only woman I'll *ever* want."

"Good. Because if that red-haired fae lady starts rubbing up against you again, I just might have to take her down."

"Just so you remember it goes both ways."

"Of course. We're mates. And I don't get off on making men jealous." She toyed with the wiry nest of hairs encircling his cock. "You're dark here. Like your beard."

He sipped a breath, and she knew he wanted her to stroke him. But she didn't. It was more fun to tease. Instead, she circled her index finger around the base as he watched, heavy-lidded.

"You like to play, do you?"

She tilted her head, considering that. "Maybe I do. When it's you."

"Have at me, then," he said in the tone of a man sacrificing himself.

She couldn't help smiling—and the boa constrictor released its grip on her chest. "All right. But you can't move."

Placing her hands on either side of his hips, she leaned forward to lick him. Slow, languorous licks. He stilled, his free hand clenching, but he kept it on the bed.

"Mm." She pressed a kiss to his hard stalk. "I like how you taste."

She drew her tongue up and down him, swirling it around the cap. Tonguing the sensitive underside.

He groaned. "Jani?"

She hummed against his flushed skin. "Yeah?"

"You're killing me here."

She wrapped her fingers around him, lapping at the salty pre-cum coating his head. "Should I stop?"

"Gods, no."

She gave a soft hum against his cock and then took him fully into her mouth. As she relaxed and began to enjoy herself, the mate bond heated in her chest.

She felt his excitement, and it fed her own, turning her insides hot and liquid.

She played with him for long minutes, learning the taste and feel of him. And when he reached for her, saying, "I have to be in you," she was as ready as him.

She crawled up his body, kissing each male nipple, smoothing her hands over the dark, gold-tipped hairs on his chest. But when she reached down to take him inside her, he gripped her hips and lifted her higher—and then scooted down the bed, muttering something about "returning the favor."

She knew the man had a talented mouth, but this time was even better than the first time. He positioned her so she straddled his face, and then opened her with his thumbs so he could swipe his tongue along her weeping slit.

"God's balls," he growled. "You're so wet." He went to work on her clit, sucking and swirling his tongue around it in slow, incredibly arousing circles.

She arched her back and set her hands on her calves, opening to him.

"That's it," he husked, low and rough. "It's your turn to stay still. All you have to do is enjoy it."

Shivers tripped up and down her body. Her skin heated. She gripped her thighs and moaned his name. Close...so close, but not quite there.

"Take it, love."

He gripped her thighs, his thumbs brushing the soft skin next to her sex. Meanwhile, his mouth kept up its magic. He swirled his tongue through her juices and thrust into her, while his thumbs toyed with her clit. She felt like he was touching her everywhere.

He pressed a kiss to the sensitive skin of her inner thigh.

"Fane..." She shook her head.

He rubbed his lips over her other thigh. "Tell me what you want," he coaxed.

She brought her hands to her breasts and pinched them. "Please," she said. "Touch me. Take me." And had the brief, sure realization that there was no shame in begging. Not when it was her and Fane. This wasn't meant to break her, just pleasure her.

Then her whole body went taut as a wire stretched to its limit.

"That's it," he murmured. "Come for me, love." He gave a hard suck to her clit.

Her sex clenched. Lightning shot up her spine, flashed behind her eyes.

She grabbed the headboard and held on as the climax rolled over her in endless, searing waves. When she opened her eyes again, she was surprised to find the room was still filled with sunlight. She could've sworn a storm had broken over the bed.

He gave her a last lick and then slid out from beneath her. She rolled onto her back and he came over top of her. Setting his forearms on either side of her head, he captured her gaze—and slid into her.

"Fane," she moaned, the thick glide almost too much against her sensitized flesh.

He halted in mid-thrust. "Too much?"

"No." She wrapped him in a hard hug and they shared a kiss. She could taste herself on him, a salty musk. "I like it. Just like that—nice and slow."

"Then that's what you'll get." He stroked out and then back in. Sweet, easy strokes, parting her a little more deeply each time, until he was all the way in.

She squeezed around him, enjoying his moan of pleasure.

"Fuck." He stopped moving. "No condoms. You want me to pull out?"

Her eyes widened. *A cub—her?* She'd never, ever thought she'd be a mother.

The idea warmed her to her toes—but not today, or even this year. She pressed her lips to his stubbled cheek.

"Yeah. For now, anyway—I want you all to myself for a year or two. But someday, yeah. I'd love to have a baby with you."

He met her eyes, his soft with affection. "Exactly what I was thinking."

He started to move faster, harder. Angling himself to stroke against the knot of pleasure on the upper wall of her pussy.

It seemed with every stroke, their bond grew stronger, so

that she was feeling his arousal along with her own. She closed her eyes and tightened around him, and came again in another hot, bright explosion.

"That's it, love," he said on a groan. He thrust in hard and then pulled out to spend himself on her stomach.

His head rested on the pillow beside hers for a minute. Then he rolled onto his back, tucking her into his side. She set a hand on his chest. He was warm and a little sweaty, his heart thumping as if he'd run a race.

For a time, they were silent in the sunshine-filled room. Then Fane kissed her forehead.

"I'll do my best to be a good dad. I know I could've done better with Evie, but I was always afraid the king would use her against me. And yeah, some of it was me being an arse. I didn't want the court to know I had a kid with a human mother." He swallowed. "Gods, that sounds so fucking shallow. But it's the truth."

She tangled her fingers in the fur on his chest. "She loves you. You must have done something right."

"Yeah?" He looked at her, pleased. "You think so?"

"I do. But it's not too late—I think she'd like to get to know you better."

"I'd like that, too." He let out a breath. "Guess I'm coming home with you. You think your brother can make a place for an unemployed, penniless fae envoy?"

"He won't like it," she said, "but he'll come around. He loves me."

It wasn't Adric she was worried about so much as the clan. Everyone had expected her to mate with Luc. They wouldn't be happy when she brought home Fane instead, a part-fae who had been part of the ice fae court for six decades. Especially when they found out Luc had accepted a *geas* to save her.

She tamped down the guilt that flared in her. Now was for

her and Fane. She'd worry about Luc and the clan when they got back to Baltimore.

"But what about you?" she asked, those doubts she'd had in Iceland returning. "You gave up everything for me. You'll never have a place in any fae court again. You sure you want to mate with a woman from a poor clan in Baltimore?"

He touched her face. "Forty, even twenty turns of the sun ago, that might have stopped me. But now, all I want is you. You're too good for me, Marjani. You think I don't know that?"

He meant it. She scented the truth in his words, saw it in his eyes.

"And besides," he added, "I didn't do it only for you. The last few years, I could barely stand returning to the court. I just didn't have anywhere else to go. But now I do."

He rolled on top of her and, capturing her wrists in his hands, pressed them to either side of her head. The hard ridge of his erection nudged against her stomach.

"We're mates, Jani. I'm not going anywhere. Get used to it."

She frowned. "I don't want you to go anywhere. I just want you to be happy."

"Then stop trying to convince me I'd be better off without you."

She gave a jerky nod, and then turned her head, offering her throat to him. Inviting him to mark her in a way her cat craved.

He might not be a fada, but he understood. He stilled, and then lowered his head and bit her. Just hard enough to leave a mark.

Her hips rocked up. Heat bloomed in her belly.

He laved the mark with his tongue, and while she was sucking in a breath, thrust inside her again.

Their loving this time was hard and fast. Marjani let her wild side out, and Fane met it with some wildness of his own.

They ended with her on her hands and knees, him thrusting into her from behind.

"Touch me," she begged, and his long fingers stroked over her body, pinching her nipples and rubbing her clit until she split apart in another earth-shattering orgasm. He pulled out and came right after her, breath sawing in and out, spilling hot against her lower back.

After that, all she wanted to do was sleep, but she made herself call Adric first. He wasn't overjoyed to learn she was bringing Fane Morningstar back to Baltimore, but she was pretty sure he'd guessed they'd mated. She didn't tell him though. That news could wait until she was home.

"I heard from Luc," he said. "He told me what happened."

She gripped her quartz. "He's okay?"

"As far as I could tell. The fae bitch allowed him one call, and then he's not allowed to contact me for the length of the *geas*. I had to banish him from the clan, Jani. I can't have a man under a *geas* connected to me and the clan that way. She could use Luc against us."

"Oh, Ric." She rubbed a hand over her face. "I'm sorry."

"He understood. Hell, he suggested it. And he knows he's welcome back as soon as he serves out the *geas*."

"I tried to save him."

"I know you did. It's okay, Jani. He did it for you."

"That doesn't make me feel any better."

Adric blew out a breath. "What about Corban?"

"Dead."

Something about her tone made him ask, "What is it? He *is* dead, isn't he?"

"Yeah. I made sure of it."

"Good."

She sighed. "It's just...he was our cousin, Ric."

"That didn't mean he wasn't trying to kill us both. Corban could have accepted me as alpha. Hell, I made him a sentry. He would've made lieutenant eventually, if he'd just given me a reason to trust him."

"I know. You did what you had to."

"And so did you. You're...all right?"

"Yeah." She glanced at Fane. "Better than all right."

"Then get your ass back to Baltimore. I need you here. But keep an eye out for the night fae. The prince has eased off the pressure for now, but he's not going to let this rest."

"We'll get a flight as soon as we can. And Ric? I miss you. So much."

"Miss you, too," was the gruff reply.

She ended the call and crawled back into bed with Fane. Strong arms hauled her close to him.

"You're tired. Go to sleep."

"Kay." She curled up against Fane and fell like a stone into a deep, dreamless sleep.

When they awoke, it was early afternoon. After a long, hot bath in the clawfoot tub—and another round of lovemaking, this time tender and drawn-out—they hiked into the village.

It turned out Fane had close to a hundred thousand dollars in his bank account.

"I never touched it," he said with a shrug. "Just used it to pay for the house's upkeep. The interest kept compounding."

She snorted. "Must be nice to be rich."

"Well, I'm not rich anymore. But at least I won't be totally dependent on you. That would be one more black mark against me as far as your brother is concerned."

He withdrew enough to pay for their flights back to Baltimore, plus some extra, including some American dollars for after they crossed the border. Then they ate a chunky fish chowder in a pub and bought groceries, including a box of condoms. In a gift shop, Marjani even found a new leather thong for her quartz. She fastened it around her neck as soon as they left the store; the connection worked best when the crystals could vibrate against her skin.

Their errands done, they headed back to the cozy saltbox house and stole another night and day just for themselves. Adric would just have to understand.

To her surprise, Fane had a down-to-earth side. He pitched in with the cooking, chopped wood, took her on long hikes along the cliffs. When she mentioned it, he shot her an affronted look from where he was lighting a fire in the big field-stone fireplace.

"I spent twenty years as a fisherman," he growled. "And working for the king wasn't all sunshine and rainbows."

She bit her lower lip. "I'm sorry—I didn't think. You had to be pretty fucking tough to survive as his envoy."

He wrapped a long arm around her waist and pulled her close. "I'm not weak, Jani. Don't make the same mistake that my grandfather makes about me and my dad. Just because we're easygoing doesn't mean you can push us around."

She slid her fingers into his hair and pulled him close. "I know," she said against his mouth. "I was there when you gave up your Gift for me, remember?"

"And I'd do it again in a heartbeat," he said—fiercely, as if she were arguing.

She traced the tip of her tongue over the seam of his lips. "I know."

"I love you." He didn't wait for her to reply, just wrapped his other arm around her and gave her a kiss that she felt clear to her toes. And after that, they stopped talking and just loved each other in front of the fire.

The second day, he rented a sailboat and took her out on the Atlantic, showing her a hidden cove. They made love on the deck, with the sun shining down on them and a cold breeze biting into their skin.

"This is fun?" She rubbed the goose pimples that had popped up on her naked body.

"You'll warm up," he assured her, and then proceeded to show her exactly how hot he could make her.

On the way back to the village, she couldn't stop smiling.

Fane would've liked to stay longer, but he understood that she needed to get home. And it turned out that during that night in the maze, another ten days had passed in the human world. It was nearly mid-September.

So two mornings after they arrived in Canada, they caught a flight to Toronto and then back to Baltimore.

38

Marjani's brother was bloody scary.

A few inches shorter than Fane and cat-lean, with Marjani's warm brown skin and black hair dyed blond at the tips, Adric Savonett was younger than Fane had expected and good-looking, with a cocky smile. But his eyes were an opaque bronze that sized Fane up, looking for a weakness, like he was prey and not his sister's mate.

They'd landed in Baltimore around dinnertime. Marjani had taken Fane straight to her brother's den.

"You're back!" Adric met them at the outside door and dragged Marjani into a hug. "You're okay?" He held her a little away and scrutinized her face.

"Yeah." She slanted a smile at Fane. "Better than okay."

"Good. That's good." Adric gave her another hug and then turned to Fane. "This is him?"

"Yep." Marjani slid an arm around Fane's waist. "Fane Morningstar."

"Evie's dad." Predatory bronze eyes narrowed on him.

Fane decided it was time to speak. The fada respected

strength. "Yes." He stuck out a hand. "Peace, and good to meet you."

"Peace." Adric gripped his hand firmly. His nostrils flared, and then his irises blazed a spooky blue like the flaring of a corona. "Fuck." He scowled at his sister. "Tell me you're not mated."

"Cut the crap," Marjani snapped back. "You know I am. *We are.*"

"oath breaker."

Fane's jaw tightened. "I'm not proud of that. But if you've heard that much, then you know I broke the *geas* to save your sister. And in the end, the king officially released me from my bargain with him anyway."

"That's right." Marjani's chin jutted. "And you know what? I don't need your permission to mate with him."

"But we would like your blessing," Fane added.

"The alpha crossed his arms, biceps bulging in his green T-shirt. "How do I know you're not going to put a cub in her and then disappear like you did with Evie's mom?"

Fane drew a slow breath through his teeth. The man might be an alpha, but Fane wasn't a member of his clan and so was outside the hierarchy. And frankly, it was fucking irritating to be scolded by a man so much younger than him.

But for Marjani's sake—and because the man had a point, damn him—Fane replied calmly. "Because we're mates. And I *promised* her that if and when we have a cub, things will be different this time. And I give you that promise now, too."

"I have your word?"

"Yes."

Adric sneered. "But then, what does your word mean?"

Fane ground his teeth. But he'd known breaking an oath would put a black mark against his name that he'd have a hard time shaking. He'd probably have to spend the next century living it down.

"For Goddess's sake," Marjani burst out. "Like you haven't slept with half of the women in the clan, Ric. What would you do if you got a cub on one of them? Evie's mom wasn't his mate."

"I know one thing," her brother snarled. "I wouldn't leave the mother of my cub alone for years at a time."

"She took another partner," Marjani shot back. "Remember Evie told us that her mom remarried? Kyler's her half-brother. And later, after Kyler's dad died, Fane helped out when he could. He wasn't a free man—he was under the ice fae king's *geas*, and he didn't want the fae to know about Evie. Hell, I might've done the same thing if she was my kid. Those ice fae are cold bastards."

Adric turned back to Fane. "Exactly what did you do for the king?"

"I was an envoy."

"A spy, then."

"I was a messenger—a negotiator. But yeah, at times I spied for him."

Marjani bristled. "Look, Ric. Either you accept him, or I'm resigning as your second."

Adric's mouth hardened. Then he expelled a breath. "You know I don't want that."

She folded her arms over her chest. "Then stop the inquisition."

"Jani?" Fane gave her nape a light squeeze. "Let me talk to your brother. Alone."

"What?" Her look would've fried a lesser man. "You're going to send me out of the room so the men can settle this?"

He shrugged. That was it exactly, but he wasn't stupid enough to admit it. Instead, he brushed his mouth over hers. "Please, love?"

"Fine. See if I care if you ream each other a new one. I'll be at Suha's." She stomped out of the den.

Adric shook his head. "Hell, I guess you are mates. She wouldn't have left for me."

Then the alpha had him by the throat. Fane blinked. Damn, the man moved fast.

"If you hurt her," Adric grated in a voice that raised fine hairs all over his body, "I'll rip off your fucking balls and stuff them down your throat. I can't kill you—that would hurt Jani, too. But I can make you wish you were dead."

"Hey." Fane held up his hands, palms out. "I love her. I'll rip off my own balls if I hurt her."

He used his Gift to slip out of Adric's grip, because the alpha needed to know Fane wasn't powerless. He reappeared on the other side of the room.

Adric was right there. "Why? What could a man like you want with Marjani?"

His scornful gaze took in Fane's expensive rayon shirt and close-fitting jeans. All his old clothes had been left behind in Iceland, of course, but he and Marjani had done some shopping in Toronto during the layover between flights.

Fane's jaw clenched. "That's an insult to your sister. The better question is, *Why not?* She's smart, loyal. Beautiful, inside and out. And so brave she makes me ashamed. The woman faced down the ice fae king for me." Fane shook his head. "She struck a bargain with him, do you believe it? The man could crush her with the magic in his little finger, but she made him agree to her terms. I'm a wayfarer, but when I broke the *geas*, he didn't just take everything I earned while I was an envoy. He took my Gift, too. But she made him agree to a bargain that officially released me from the *geas*—and returned my Gift."

"Cat's balls." Adric looked a little sick. "I told her not to go to Iceland. But you can't stop my sister when she gets an idea in her head."

"I noticed." They exchanged a very male look of commiseration.

The younger man dropped onto the couch. Resting his forearms on his thighs, he interlaced his fingers and stared down at them. "I scented the mate bond. I know it's real."

"Yeah." Fane took a chance and sat on the other end of the couch.

Adric shot him a glance but allowed him to remain. "I thought I'd lost her," he said lowly. "She was going feral on me."

"I know. But I saw her shift multiple times. She was always in control."

"Yeah? That's good. And her scent has changed. It's not just the mate bond. She's calmer, more in control." He shook his head. "If that's due to you, then I owe you one."

"You don't owe me a thing. Maybe I can take a little credit, but she did most of it on her own. She killed your cousin Corban, you know. A mercy killing. Poor bastard was half-dead and locked in an iron cage."

Adric nodded. "She told me he'd died, but not the details."

"He was going to die anyway. She didn't have to kill him— she could've let him suffer."

"The prick deserved whatever he got."

"Yeah. Anyway, he begged her to do it. And when it was done, she cried her heart out."

The alpha's throat worked. "Jani never cries."

"I think," Fane said softly, "that was when she began to find her human side again."

"Tell me."

And so Fane sketched out the story of what had happened in the ice fae court.

When he was done, Adric shook his head. "Holy mother. I had no fucking idea."

"I'll tell you one thing. The ice fae are going to think twice before messing with the earth fada again."

"Because of Jani."

"Yeah."

Adric's lips curved. "That's my sister." He was silent for a few seconds, and then he sighed. "This mating. It comes at a bad time. The clan—I'm trying to bring us into the current century, but we were raised not to trust outsiders. Told that earth fada should stick with earth fada. When Jace mated with your daughter, there was grumbling, but Evie is hard not to like. And on top of that, she has a Gift that's useful to our healers, and that makes her an asset. You, though." The alpha shook his head. "A male, and one of the ice fae king's envoys? You're going to be a hard sell."

"Former envoy," Fane corrected. "And I may have more to offer than you think. I know details about every fae court, and most of the fada clans. I can give you a run-down on the people, who has the power, what their pressure points are...that sort of thing."

"Yeah?" Adric pursed his lips. "You're right, maybe we could use you. But you'll have to lay low for a while. The clan knew Marjani was struggling to stay in control of her animal. This could help—or be the final straw."

"Say the word and we'll leave."

"But Jani will go with you." The younger man scraped his hands down his face. "Fuck. I don't want that."

"You'll have to ask her, but—" Fane moved a single shoulder.

"You're mated. I know."

"It would tear her up to leave the clan—and you. I can tell you that much."

Adric jerked his chin in acknowledgment. "Then they'll just have to accept you."

He rose to his feet, and suddenly, Fane saw why Adric had won alpha at such a young age. His face was steely, his body language that of a man used to command.

"Marjani isn't just my sister, she's my second. With Luc gone, I only have three lieutenants. I need her. And if that means we have to accept you, we will." Adric stuck out a hand. "Welcome to the clan."

It wasn't the warmest welcome, but it was honest. After six decades at the ice fae court, Fane appreciated that more than the other man could know.

He gripped Adric's hand. "Thank you."

The alpha brought his left hand up to lightly clasp Fane's throat. When he stiffened, Adric said, "I'm marking you with my scent. The clan will know you're one of us now."

"Okay," Fane managed to say, although instinct urged him to knock the other man's hand away from such a vulnerable place.

Claws pricked his throat. A delicate touch, not enough to break the skin. Fane held steady. Something like approval shone in the alpha's metallic eyes. He raked the claws across Fane's skin, leaving a thin mark, and then clapped him on the back.

"Let's go give Jani the good news."

39

"Your Marjani mated with Fane Morningstar." Blaer dropped her little bombshell at breakfast.

Luc continued chewing his toast, even though it suddenly tasted like sawdust.

Jani had gotten free, then.

"It's true," Blaer said when he didn't reply. "I heard it from a member of the ice fae court itself."

So she still had spies at the court. Not that Luc was surprised. The woman had her fingers in pies all around the world.

He chased the toast with a gulp of coffee and then smiled at the fae lady. "Good."

Surprise flared in her midnight eyes. "But you want her for yourself."

"I did. But here's the thing about love, my lady. I want her to be happy. And if he"—he couldn't bring himself to say Morningstar's name—"makes her happy, then I'm happy."

Blaer scowled. "I don't understand you fada."

"No," he agreed. "You don't."

It was mid-September, almost two weeks since Luc had

accepted her *geas*. He'd stubbornly refused her offers—power, money. She'd even tried to tempt him with sex.

"I'll stay in the cage," he'd told her coldly.

But that asshole Corban Savonett had told her too much. She knew the secret words that gave a fae power over an earth fada, as long as the fae was also touching the fada's quartz.

She'd let Luc out of his cage and told him if he made one wrong move, Marjani was dead. Then she'd ordered him to remain still—like a fucking dog—and watch as her goblin horde attacked Marjani.

Just having her cold fingers wrapped around his quartz was painful enough. But he'd believed Marjani was going to die right before his eyes.

"Accept my *geas*," Blaer had said. "And I'll call the goblins off."

Luc had dropped to his knees there on the mossy black rocks and agreed. He just hoped Marjani knew he'd done it for her, not for anything Blaer could give him.

Blaer had kept her word. She'd called the goblins off—and then thrown Marjani into a fucking cage.

Luc had cursed himself for being an ass. If a fae could twist things to their advantage, they would. Now he was bound to serve Blaer for a fae year-and-a-day.

Still, he'd endure that and more, as long as Marjani was safe.

And the cages were gone, destroyed at Sindre's order—and Blaer had been banished from the court.

Now they were in Paris, along with a few of Blaer's closest allies—Jon and Krysten, and a golden-haired male named Jagger—and several fada who, like Luc, had accepted Blaer's *geas*.

He knew from Blaer's scent that she was a mixed-blood— half night fae, half ice fae. According to one of the other fada, her mother was a night fae priestess. The others suspected Sindre was her lover.

But Luc had scented something interesting; there was a blood connection between Blaer and the ice fae king. He'd bet good money that Sindre was her father, not her lover. It explained why the king had given her so much rope, until she'd apparently gone too far even for him.

Not that Luc had minded leaving Iceland and the ice fae. If he had to serve Blaer for ten years, he'd as soon not spend it at that cold, isolated castle. Just being surrounded by that many fae made his skin itch.

Jon entered the breakfast room and murmured in Blaer's ear. She rose to her feet. "We're leaving."

"Where?" Luc refused to act submissive. He responded like the lieutenant he was.

"Ireland. I've had word of something interesting. A water fada with something I want."

And Luc would probably be forced to help her ensnare the poor fool. He shoved back his chair and stood up. "Why?" he demanded.

"Why what?"

"Why trap fada? Put them in cages?"

"Because." She stalked around the table to him.

He stilled, keeping his face expressionless.

A cool finger traced his jawline, slid down to the hollow at the base of his throat. He couldn't help a hard swallow.

"I get off on your energy." She touched her lips to the side of his neck. "It's so...raw."

And then she bit him, just hard enough. His cock jerked.

He fisted his hands at his sides. "Get. Away," he said between clenched teeth. "Nothing in the *geas* says I'm your fuck-toy."

"Agreed."

Dark tendrils slid over his skin. Sucking on his helpless anger and humiliation.

Her smile froze him to the marrow. "I'm a night fae, darling. Yes, I want to fuck you, but this is almost as good." She patted him on the ass. "Now get ready. We leave in an hour. And Luc? That's an order."

The *geas* bit into him. "I understand," he gritted.

She took a step back. Her gaze dropped to the erection straining against the zipper of his fatigue pants.

A slow smile spread across her face, but she didn't say anything, just turned and strolled out of the room, hips swaying.

Smile all you want, bitch. It doesn't mean anything.

He'd use this opportunity to study Blaer. Learn her weaknesses. And the instant the *geas* was met, he'd have his revenge.

40

The evening of Marjani and Fane's mate ritual dawned clear and cool. They'd chosen to have the ceremony on the first day of fall—the equinox, when night and day are in balance. That seemed perfect to Marjani. Balance was what she'd found in Iceland, the balance between her dark side and her light side.

She'd been so angry for so long. With Corban and the river fada. With her uncle Leron, who'd made a young girl feel like less than dirt. Even with her brother, who hadn't realized she'd been kidnapped until it was too late—and she knew that wasn't fair, but rage isn't always rational.

She'd aimed herself like an arrow at one goal—avenging herself upon Corban. Yes, she'd done it for Adric, but also for herself. To gain back some self-respect. But Corban was dead and she had to discover who she was today, this woman without that anger fueling her.

She was never going to be the same as before the kidnapping. She'd been broken and although she'd put the pieces back together, there'd always be cracks. But the cracks didn't have to make her weaker. Maybe they made her stronger, sturdier; like pottery pieces that had been cemented into place.

She and Fane had talked about it late one night. She'd cried a little, but they'd been good, cleansing tears. She'd finally been ready to share the darkest things with someone. Fane had listened without judgment—and then held her close as he crooned a sad song in his low rasp.

Fane's mate gift to her had been a gold heart with two jagged halves that fit together. When she'd opened the box, her throat seized up. He really did understand.

She wore one half of the heart next to her quartz, and he had the other on a leather cord around his neck.

"It's time," Suha murmured now. The two of them were alone in Adric's den, dressing for the ceremony.

Marjani examined herself in the bathroom mirror. For the ceremony, she'd chosen a fire-engine red dress with a form-fitting bodice and a skirt that flared around her legs. On her feet she wore caged heels the same red as her dress.

She ran a hand over her cropped hair and smiled at herself. It felt good to be wearing a bright color, like a flower that had been deep underground and had once again emerged into the sunlight.

"You look amazing." Suha gave Marjani's bare upper arms a squeeze. "That man of yours is going to swallow his tongue."

Their eyes met in the mirror. "So do you." She smiled at Suha, who wore a matching lime green dress.

"Thanks." Suha smoothed a hand down her skirt. "Beau likes me in this color." Beau was a big, laid-back bear whom Suha had been dating for the past few months.

Marjani turned to face her friend. "You really do like Fane, don't you?"

"Yeah. The man's a charmer."

Marjani chuckled. "He is, isn't he?"

"And he worships the ground you walk on, which gives him major points in my book. You're a lucky woman—but I think you already know that."

Marjani nodded. "I do." Her hand went to the gold half-heart next to her quartz.

Suha handed her a bouquet of bright, late-summer flowers, and together, they walked up the steps to the backyard.

Adric had closed off their street for the party and told the drug dealers to get lost for the evening. Evie and some of the other women had created a flowered arch of sunflowers, lavender, cosmos, zinnia and other flowers in the backyard.

As Suha and Marjani emerged from the den, the clan drummers beat out a slow, complicated rhythm. The small yard was full, the entire clan present.

Nerves jumped in her stomach. She knew some of them hadn't come willingly. The old prejudices weren't going to be swept aside that easily. But Adric had made it clear that she was going to remain his second, and they'd better support her and her mate—or else leave.

Dusk had fallen. A few fae lights wafted in air currents above the yard. All around her, earth fada eyes glowed in the fading light as an almost full moon rose above the rooftops. The five drummers sped up the rhythm.

Marjani bit her lower lip. If only her mom and dad could've been here—and Luc. But maybe her parents *were* here—in spirit, anyway—and she knew she had to let go of her guilt about Luc. He'd be okay. Adric would make sure of that.

The clan had formed a spiral for her to follow to the center of the yard where Fane waited along with Adric, who as clan alpha would perform the ritual, and Jace, who'd agreed to stand as Fane's best man.

With a last hug and a whispered, "You got this, girl," Suha started into the human labyrinth.

Stomach still tense, Marjani squared her shoulders and

followed. Because even though Adric had laid down the law, that didn't mean people had to do more than tolerate her mating. And this was the first time she'd seen most of them since leaving for Iceland six weeks ago. She felt like everyone was looking at her extra hard, wondering if she'd really recovered.

But nearly everyone was smiling—real, genuine smiles. Voices thanked her for all she'd done for the clan and murmured congratulations. "Blessings on you both."

Marjani's throat clogged. She hadn't expected this show of support.

Then an old woman named Lily fastened a gnarled hand on her arm. "We're proud of you, girl. And your mama and dad would've been, too. You beat that fae king at his own game."

"Thank you, Lily." Marjani kissed her papery cheek and moved on, smiling now, her nerves gone.

She was almost to the center when she saw Evie. The pretty blonde grinned and bounced a little on her toes, overjoyed that Marjani and her dad had mated. Nearby, Kyler stood with a couple of the younger soldiers, legs apart and skinny arms folded over his chest like the soldiers beside him.

The last person she passed was an impassive Zuri. She knew he was suspicious of Fane, unhappy to have a former ice fae envoy so close to both Marjani, and by extension, Adric. Fane would have to prove himself before Zuri accepted him. But he politely inclined his dark head to her.

And then she rounded the last curve and all she saw was Fane. Her tall, blond and gorgeous mate, his lower face covered with the trim beard he'd grown since leaving Iceland. He held out a hand, unsmiling—and yet inside, he was so happy she felt it warming her own chest.

She took his hand. He squeezed her fingers, and together, they faced her brother.

Adric gave her a formal nod as the drums fell silent. Suha took her place at Marjani's side, and Jace stood next to Fane.

"Welcome to my den," her brother said in a carrying voice. "Please join me in blessing the bond of my sister and second, Marjani Savonett, and her mate, Fane Morningstar."

She faced Fane, and they recited the simple, beautiful words they'd prepared. First Fane, who spoke of his love and admiration for her, and then it was her turn. Most people had heard at least part of their story, but she made it clear Fane had been willing to give up everything for her—his money, his job, even his Gift.

When she said, "You gave me back my cat," she heard some of the women sniffing. But it was only the truth.

Adric's mouth edged up. He'd guessed her strategy—sway the clan to Fane's side. It wouldn't happen overnight, but already, Fane was making friends. As Suha said, the man was a charmer.

When it was Fane's turn, he first presented her with a new iron dagger, saying, "Because this is what you need to feel safe."

She bit her lip. "Thank you." She wanted to say she didn't need it, but that would be a lie. Then she noticed the blade, inscribed "Badass M," and laughter bubbled up inside her.

She reached up and gave him a quick kiss. "I love you, Fane Morningstar."

His breath jerked in, and then he gave her a broad smile.

For a few seconds they stared at each other, and then she realized she was smiling too, a grin so wide it almost hurt her face.

"Jani?" Adric cleared his throat. "Do you accept Fane's claim?"

"I do," she said without taking her gaze from Fane's. "For the rest of my life, and beyond."

"Congratulations," Adric said, and called the blessings of the God and the Goddess down on them.

Fane framed her face with his hands. He didn't say anything, just brought his mouth to hers in an achingly sweet kiss. When she surfaced again, the drummers had launched into a cheerful reggae beat. Other musicians joined them, including a steel drummer, and bright, happy music filled the air, a song that her Jamaican mother had loved.

Her eyes met her brother's. "Thank you," she mouthed, knowing he must've asked for it to be played.

During the big party that followed, she danced with Fane first. He wrapped his long arms around her. "Say it again."

"Say what?"

"That you love me."

"But—." She stopped dancing, arrested. "Was that the first time I said it?"

"Yep." He gently urged her to continue dancing. "I've said it, more than once. But you never said it back."

So that was why his breath had jerked in; he wasn't sure she loved him. "But you're my mate."

"That doesn't mean you have to love me. I know I'm not exactly the man of your dreams."

She came up on her toes to murmur in his ear. "Only because you're so much better than anything I could have dreamed up."

His grip tightened on her. "I love you, Jani. You're the best thing that ever happened to me."

They danced in silence until the song ended, their steps in perfect harmony, her heart so full it felt like it might burst.

The music changed, and Adric claimed the next dance. "I like that dress," he told her. "It's about time you wore something besides gray and army green."

She wrinkled her nose at him. "I was pretty hard to live with, wasn't I?"

He shrugged. "I could've lived with that Marjani, as long as you were happy. But you weren't."

"No."

Just then, Fane danced past with Evie. He sent her a quick smile, eyes crinkling at the edges, and then dipped his head to listen to his daughter.

She looked back at Adric. "I didn't even really know what happiness was. Not until Fane."

"Then I'm glad you mated with him."

The party lasted well into the night, but at last everyone went home. Adric left his den to them for the night, sauntering off with Zuri and four women. It was clear the six of them had plans.

Marjani just rolled her eyes and headed back inside with Fane. In the living room, she turned the quartz fire on low. The flames flickered, amber and blue.

"Well." Fane framed her face with his palms. "It's official, mate."

"Yeah." She smiled up at him. "I love you."

"And I love you." His voice had that sexy rasp that never failed to turn her on. Heat curled through her belly.

His mouth went to the turn of her shoulder. A tiny nip and her knees turned to jelly.

His hands were busy, divesting her of her dress. "Have I told you how beautiful you look tonight? And that you're fucking hot in red?"

She hadn't worn a bra. He pressed a kiss to each of her nipples, then crouched down to slide her tiny scarlet panties down her legs. "Lift your foot."

She obediently lifted each foot in turn and he pulled the panties over the caged heels. He touched the red straps. Heated blue eyes met hers.

"I think we'll leave these on."

Pressing a kiss to her inner thigh, he came back to his feet and lifted her up against his body. He was still dressed. She wrapped her legs around him, his clothes excitingly rough against her bare skin.

Between them, her quartz warmed.

"I can feel it." He gave her a slow, wondering smile. "Your quartz."

"Because we're mated. I think in some way, the crystals bonded with you, too."

"Yeah? Good. That way, you'll never leave me."

She sunk her teeth into his earlobe, a little harder than necessary. "Try and get rid of me."

His whole body shook in a belly laugh. "Damn, I love you. My own personal badass."

"Go to Hades," she muttered and dug her pointed heels into his ass.

Fane walked with her until her back touched the wall. "*My* badass," he repeated tenderly. "My sweet, sexy badass. I'm going to turn you around and take you hard. You'd like that, wouldn't you?"

Her womb constricted. She did like it hard.

And his words made her so hot and wet. Her mouth was suddenly filled with saliva. She swallowed and nodded, unable to speak.

He kissed her, long and slow. Sparks skittered up and down her body.

When he broke the kiss, she tore at his shirt. "Get this off."

Together, they peeled it off his shoulders and it dropped to the floor, forgotten, while she lightly raked her nails down Fane's back. Marking him in a way only the two of them would see.

Fane muttered something hot and dark. "That's it," he growled. "Scratch me, sweetheart."

He rocked his hips against her, making them both moan in pleasure. His mouth came to her throat and he gave her a love-bite, sucking hard so she'd bear *his* mark, too.

Her insides went liquid. She tightened her arms and legs around him and with a small, surprised cry surrendered to the heat as she came in a mini-orgasm.

"Love you," Fane said against her skin.

"Love you, too."

Still holding her high against his body, he walked with her to the bedroom. Someone had placed the flowered arch from their ceremony over her headboard to frame the bed. Three fae lights floated above the sheets, coloring the room a warm, sunset pink-and-orange.

Marjani caught her breath. "It's beautiful."

"Mm-hmm," Fane said, his mind clearly elsewhere. He set her on the bed, turned her around, and pulled up her hips so she was on all fours. "Stay there."

She heard the rustle of clothes being removed and dropped on the floor, and then he knelt on the mattress behind her. Cool fingers stroked her bottom.

"You have the sexiest ass...nice and curvy. And those red high heels are so bad."

She smiled over her shoulder at him. "I thought you'd like them."

"Oh, I do. A lot." He slid a finger between her thighs. "Sweet Goddess, you're wet."

With a moan, she went down on her forearms. "Don't tease me."

"I'm not. I'm very serious."

She gave a muffled laugh. "*Now* you're serious."

"And you're loving it."

"Mm."

He toyed with her, stroking her clit until she came in a hot rush. He didn't give her time to catch her breath, just rolled on a condom and thrust into her. Slow and hard and perfect.

Her sex tightened around him and he groaned her name. "That's it, love. Come around me. It feels so damn good."

Her inner muscles convulsed. Pleasure rolled through her in hot, endless waves. He was right behind her, pushing deep inside until she felt him at her womb, and then stilling as she moaned his name into the sheets.

Celebrating their mating in the oldest and best way.

EPILOGUE

$\mathcal{A}$dric shoved his hands into his pockets and stared out at the Inner Harbor. It was almost midnight, a few days before the winter solstice. The docked boats were tricked out with holiday lights.

His lips twisted. The humans loved their Christmas celebrations. Even most of the clan had put up a little tree and a few strands of lights. Adric hadn't bothered, since he was living alone again. Marjani and Fane had moved into Evie and Jace's den, taking Luc's old room.

He rubbed a hand over his face. Gods, he'd hated to banish Luc. He wasn't just a lieutenant, he was an old friend. But Adric couldn't have a clan member under the control of a fae.

But Adric was left second-guessing himself. Could he have handled it differently? Sent more men to Iceland?

No regrets. When he made alpha, he'd told himself he'd do whatever it took to keep the clan together, and fuck regrets.

But holy mother, it had been some year. Two cousins dead. The night fae on the prowl in Baltimore again. And both Sindre and Lady Blaer in possession of the earth fada's secret incantation.

At least his sister was on the mend, and back at his side as his second. She'd even helped Evie decorate Jace's den for the holidays. Their mom had always made a big deal out of Christmas, too.

On top of that, the message that Marjani had carried from Ula to Dion had put the Rock Run alpha in Adric's debt. So count that as another win.

He smiled just as a burst of icy raindrops hit his face.

He cursed and wiped it away. If there was anything his cat hated more than a cold night, it was a cold, rainy night.

He should return to the Full Moon Saloon, or better yet, go home. But he was too jumpy to sleep. He'd just end up pacing restlessly around his den.

Letting his head fall back, he stared up at the dark sky. Gods, he needed to get laid. It had been months, and he was so horny it hurt. There were plenty of women in the clan who'd be happy to welcome the alpha into their bed for a night, no strings attached. And he could always find a human female in one of the bars behind him.

But his heart wasn't in it.

Heels tapped on the cobblestone street behind him. His whole body went alert. He turned to look at the woman strolling toward him in a red leather jacket and tight jeans and knew this was why he'd been drawn to the waterfront.

You.

The last time he'd seen Rosana do Rio, it had been early summer, and she'd been naked. But not, unfortunately, because he'd finally talked her out of her clothes.

No, it had been because Adric was on Rock Run territory. Rosana had been with another sentry, cruising the Susquehanna as her river dolphin, and she'd shifted to woman to confront him.

The sight of her naked body was burned on his brain: her breasts high and slick from the swim, her legs long and sleek.

She knew as well as him that this thing between the two of them could never go anywhere, but when he'd taken her mouth in a deep, soul-stealing kiss, she'd let him—and then ordered him off her clan's land.

So what was she doing in Baltimore? And alone, when usually her brother Dion guarded her like a wolf with one pup.

His breath snagged. He covered it with a scowl. "Aren't you a little far from Rock Run?"

"I came to see you." Her long black hair hung in damp corkscrews around her heart-shaped face, and her big blue eyes were deep pools in the dim light, like a siren who'd emerged from the harbor to lure him to his doom.

"Yeah?" His heart gave a hard thump. He scraped his gaze insolently down her body—and tried to ignore his rapidly hardening cock. "Finally decide you can't live without me?"

"Screw you." She spun on her heel.

"Oh, no." He grabbed her arm. "You don't get to run away. Not this time. You're in my territory now."

She halted, lungs jerking. Too hard. She was pissed off, yeah, but beneath the anger he scented desire.

And because he wanted her so bad, his fingers bit into her arm. "Talk, damn it."

She whirled to face him. "Dion's right. You're an ass."

His smile was sardonic. "I love him right back."

Her hands balled, and he half expected her to take a swing at him. The gods knew, he deserved it.

But she blew out a breath and then with a visible effort, relaxed. "I'm here about Merry Jones."

So she wasn't here for him. Disappointment made his voice harsh. "She's okay?"

"Yeah. Except for the night fae prince demanding to know why Rock Run didn't inform him she'd died."

"What did Dion say?"

"That what happens at our base is none of the prince's

fucking business. Of course, he put it more politely. The prince still hasn't responded."

Adric nodded. He might not like the other alpha, but the man was smart. "So what's up?" he asked, releasing her.

Rosana immediately put a little space between them. He had to force himself not to grab her and keep her close. Inside, the cat was damn near drooling, it was so thrilled to be near her after six long months.

She shoved her wet black curls behind her ears. "You know me and Merry are friends, right? I mean, I'm eight years older than her, but she's like the little sister I never had."

He nodded. "Jace told me."

"Well, Merry's scared." She lowered her voice to subvocal level. "We all know that someday the prince will learn the truth and come for her. She's terrified he'll force her to go back with him to Virginia. Dion and Cleia told her there's no way they'll let that happen, but she's still worried. After all, she *is* his granddaughter."

His eyes narrowed. *What did Rosana know?*

But she simply waited for his answer, an anxious crease between her brows.

"Tell her not to relax," he said, affronted at a primal level that a cub should have any worry other than the usual ones of adolescence. "If that S.O.B. tries anything, he's dead."

She scrutinized him. "You mean that, don't you? Even though she's part night fae herself."

He scowled, angry and a little hurt that she harbored even a tiny doubt. "She's Jace's niece, which makes her clan, even if she lives with your people for now. And her mom was a good friend. I'll make sure Jace tells her."

"That's how Dion feels—that she's clan. But Merry's still worried. Look what happened to your clan when the night fae went after them."

He stiffened. "That was different."

"How?"

He hesitated, and then figured, why keep it a secret? "My uncle invited them in. The night fae didn't cause the infighting—they just fed on it, did what they could to encourage it."

"Oh. Is that why you—?" Her mouth snapped shut.

"Go ahead, ask." His lips peeled in a toothy smile. "Is that why I killed him?"

She shook her head. "Sorry. Not my business."

"That's right. It's not." He blew out a breath. "Look, you said what you came to say. I appreciate it. I promise, Merry's safe. If the night fae come for her, it won't be because of anything my clan did. And if her grandfather dares to steal her, I'll hunt him down myself."

She nodded her thanks. "If it comes down to that, Rui would go into Hades itself for her."

Which was only the truth. He studied her. "So why are you here?"

Even white teeth worried her lush lower lip. "Don't take this the wrong way, but I know you're planning something against the night fae—and I want to help."

He stilled. "And you know this—how?"

She moved a shoulder. "I get...hunches, that's all. And besides, everyone knows there's bad blood between you and the night fae. It doesn't take a genius to guess you might be planning something."

He prowled forward, erasing the space between them.

"Adric?" Her eyes widened, but she didn't step back.

He inhaled slowly, filling his lungs with her scent—rain and fresh spring flowers. Without his volition, his hand shot out, closing around her fingers.

Her breath hitched. As he brought her hand toward his mouth, her eyes came up to meet his. Holding her gaze, he traced his lips down the soft underside of her wrist.

Heat arced between them. Electric. Fiery. Speeding up his

heart, making his whole being contract with longing. It had always been like this, from the moment he'd first seen her six years ago at Dion and Cleia's mate-bonding celebration.

She moistened plump red lips and he stifled a groan.

"One night," he said, low and rough. "We'll go somewhere out of town. No one has to know."

Her jaw set. "Answer the question. Will you let me help?"

He leaned closer so their mouths were almost touching. "No. Fucking. Way."

She growled and tried to wrench her hand from his. Then suddenly, she froze, her fingers gripping his as her eyes went black.

"No," she rasped.

His scalp prickled. "Rosana?"

"The Darktime isn't over," she said in an eerie toneless voice. "The prince will destroy your clan from the inside out."

A chill ran over his skin. *She was a Seer.*

He hadn't known, and there wasn't much he didn't know about the do Rio family. They must keep her Gift a secret from everyone, even the rest of the clan.

"What do you See?" He gave her a little shake. "Tell me."

She didn't seem to hear him. There was a fraught silence, and then with a shudder, she came back to herself. She snatched her hand from his and pressed it to her chest, face closed. Tiny tremors shook her slim body.

"Goddess," she whispered. "That's insane. You can't kill him. You'll set off something you can't stop."

"Yeah?" He raised a brow.

Tell her she's the one who's insane. That you have no fucking idea what she's talking about.

But he couldn't bring himself to prevaricate—not to Rosana. The woman his cat had decided was his mate, even if the man refused to accept it.

She grabbed his arm. He tensed, but this time, nothing happened.

"Promise me you won't do it."

He showed her his teeth. "I don't have to promise you anything, love. We're nothing to each other, right? Because that's the way we both want it."

She flinched and let him go.

"Go home to your big brother. It's not safe for you to be alone down here at night." He leered at her, hating himself, but he had to get her out of here—and out of his life. "A big, bad cat might snatch you and carry you back to his lair."

She shoved her hands into her pockets, her pretty mouth set. "You don't scare me, Lord Adric."

He just stared back at her until she turned and stalked back the way she came.

He gave it a minute and then followed her. She headed around the harbor and he waited for her to shift to her dolphin, but she leaned against a scrubby little street tree and stared out at the black water.

He waited downwind until with a muttered curse, she walked the few feet to where a sleek purple sportbike waited. Slinging a leg over the seat, she flung him an unreadable look over her shoulder and then zoomed off, leaving him standing there, scowling and clenching his fists...and hollow inside.

Pre-order **Adric's Heart** *(Adric & Rosana's story) at your favorite bookstore! Out March 2020.*

Sign up for Rebecca Rivard's newsletter to stay informed: https://www.subscribepage.com/i6x3j1
As a thank you, Rebecca will gift you with "Lir's Lady," a steamy short story!

ALSO BY REBECCA RIVARD

THE FADA SHAPESHIFTERS

Stealing Ula: A Fada Shapeshifter Prequel (Nisio & Ula, set in Ireland)

The Rock Run River Fada

Seducing the Sun Fae (Dion & Cleia)

Claiming Valeria (Rui & Valeria)

Tempting the Dryad (Tiago & Alesia)

Sea Dragon's Hunger (Cassidy & Nic)

The Baltimore Earth Fada (The Darktime Trilogy)

Saving Jace (Jace & Evie)

Charming Marjani (Marjani & Fane)

Adric's Heart (Adric & Rosana)

Fada Shapeshifter Short Reads

Lir's Lady (#3.5—Lir & Isleen)

Shifter's Valentine (#3.6—Jenny & Chico)

Find out more and read exclusive excerpts: https://rebeccarivard.com/shapeshifters/

The Vampire Syndicate Romances

Pursued (Gabriel)

Craved (Rafael)

Taken (Zaquiel)

The Vampire Blood Courtesans

Ensnared: Star

Compelled: Cerise

Find out more: https://rebeccarivard.com/vampires/

Join *Rebecca Rivard's newsletter* to stay informed and be eligible for giveaways and sneak peeks. As a thank you, Rebecca will gift you with "Lir's Lady," a steamy short story!

Sign up at rebeccarivard.com or go to this link: Rebecca's newsletter

ABOUT THE AUTHOR

USA Today bestselling author Rebecca Rivard read way too many romances as a teenager, little realizing she was actually preparing for a career. She now spends her days with dark shifters, sexy fae and other magical creatures—which has to be the best job ever. When she's not writing, she walks, bikes and kayaks in the Chesapeake Bay area with her guitar-playing, storytelling husband.

Five of her novels have been awarded the coveted Crowned Heart Review from *InD'Tale Magazine* and the FADA SHAPESHIFTER SERIES was voted Best Shifter Series in the Paranormal Romance Guild Reviewer's Choice Awards.

Her books have also won the prestigious PRISM Award (*Charming Marjani*) and the PRG Reviewer's Choice Award (*Saving Jace*), and have finaled in both the RONE and the HOLT Medallion.

facebook.com/RebeccaRivardRomance

instagram.com/rebecca.rivard

goodreads.com/rebecca_rivard

bookbub.com/authors/rebecca-rivard

amazon.com/author/Rebecca-Rivard